ENCHANTED
BY HIS TOUCH

"Ah, Laurie . . ." He traced her cool jaw with his knuckle and twined his fingers through her silky hair, combing it back from her face. With her head resting on his hand, he tipped it back and trailed kisses along her cheeks, her slender throat, then he took her mouth.

"I want you, Laurie. God, how I want you. Have I moved too fast? Frightened you?"

She knew that if she didn't step away from him then, she wouldn't be able to later. His voice was deep, mesmerizing, and passionate. "I've never felt this way before."

"Never?"

She shook her head.

His chest expanded.

His lips touched hers. It was sweet torture beyond her imaginings. She melted into him, knowing if she withdrew, she would surely regret it the rest of her life . . .

Gentle Hearts

DEBORAH WOOD

DIAMOND BOOKS, NEW YORK

This book is a Diamond original edition,
and has never been previously published.

GENTLE HEARTS

A Diamond Book / published by arrangement with
the author

PRINTING HISTORY
Diamond edition / April 1993

ISBN: 1-55773-882-3

Diamond Books are published by The Berkley Publishing Group,
200 Madison Avenue, New York, NY 10016.
The name "DIAMOND" and its logo
are trademarks belonging to Charter Communications, Inc.

PRINTED IN THE UNITED STATES OF AMERICA

10 9 8 7 6 5 4 3 2 1

My heartfelt love and gratitude is with the memory of my husband, Larry, who believed in my ability to draft a story before I did, understood my obsession with writing, and overlooked my forgetting to make all of those dinners. "This one's for you."

ACKNOWLEDGMENTS

I wish to express my gratitude to Kent Muller, a cattle rancher and the authenticator for my ranching research. Without his generous and tolerant assistance, and without the use of Willard Muller's personal library, Gabe's ranching skills would have been negligible.

My very special thanks to Carol Harbison, Assistant Librarian with the Southern Oregon Historical Society, for all of her help. And Billie Conner, Los Angeles Public Library, Research Department, for her diligence and sensitivity to odd requests from writers.

May 1869

Laurie Preston looked out the open window just as the Sacramento–Portland stagecoach rumbled to a stop in a cloud of dust. There was no turning back now. Now she would have to make a new life for herself.

The driver climbed down and opened the door. "This here's Ashly Mills, Oree-gon." He extended his rough hand to Laurie. "Your stop, ain't it, ma'am?"

Laurie stepped out of the dirt-encrusted stage, shook the fawn skirt of her traveling dress, and momentarily relished the breeze that cleared away the dust. She watched the driver climb back up and reach for a small trunk.

He looked down at her. "This one yers?"

She nodded before anxiously glancing up and down the short street. No one appeared to pay any particular attention to her arrival. Laurie nervously smoothed one glove, then the other. She had expected to be met by a Mr. West. But the street was empty.

After the driver put her trunk down, she stood in the shade of the general store. She mentally listed various reasons why Mr. West wasn't there and evidently hadn't

1

sent anyone for her: his daughter was sick, the cattle had stampeded—a lot she knew about that—or a wheel had come off his buggy. Several minutes later she began pacing back and forth.

The stagecoach driver roared an unintelligible command and snapped a whip over the horses' heads. Laurie hurried into the general store, barely escaping the rising cloud of dust left in the stage's wake.

The welcome aromas of leather goods, brine from the pickle barrel, and coffee beans the clerk scooped out helped to soothe her irritation. Three women stood chatting near the yard goods. She nodded to them in passing and went over to the counter. Their anxious whispers carried to where she stood.

"He'll never get anyone to stay out at his place to care for that child, the poor mite. She'll spend the next few years on a leading string and grow up wild, mark my words," said one.

"Unless she's sent to a foster home," added another.

"No decent woman'd live out on that ranch, anyway. There's no one there but the child, and his poor missus in the ground barely six months. Why I . . ." The voice faded as the women moved farther away.

Laurie struggled with her confusion about Mr. West. Surely he had been told of the date of her arrival. The clerk finished with his customer and shuffled over.

"Sir, do you know Mr. West?"

The clerk's almost colorless, blue-gray eyes roved slowly over her figure. "Yep, do fer a fact."

She took one step back and raised her chin. "Has he been here yet? He was to meet the stage." She remained poised, despite her discomfort at the man's smirk.

The clerk hitched up his trousers before answering. "You jist missed him." He glanced at the three women. "He's likely halfway back to his ranch by now."

Laurie sighed and asked, "Can you give me directions to Mr. West's ranch?"

"Yep. Jist foller the road east till you git to a fork with a stand of black oak trees straight 'n front of you. You kin see the house a few miles up the north fork." The man shot a stream of brown tobacco juice from between his stained teeth. It landed on the planked floor behind the counter. Then he leered at Laurie. "I could take you if you don't wanna drive yerse'f."

No way would she subject herself to a ride alone *anywhere* with this man. "That won't be necessary. Thank you."

The clipped sound of Laurie's low-heeled shoes echoed in the hushed store as she passed the same three women on her way out, grateful to escape. Before she latched the door, she heard the women begin chattering all at once. Thus far, she was not favorably impressed with Ashly Mills.

She stood on the boardwalk outside the general store, clutching her reticule. The sign overhead creaked. She glanced around and noticed a man walking in her direction, his dusty hat pulled down, shading his eyes. The man continued ambling her way.

She waited, trying not to appear anxious. Had Mr. West returned for her? As he advanced Laurie smiled, ready to greet him. The man, however, merely tugged on the front of his hat and passed on by.

She should have known better. After all, the clerk had told her that Mr. West was probably home by now. The only way she would get to the ranch was to rent a buggy and drive out there on her own.

She hurried down the street toward the livery, rallying her frayed enthusiasm for her new life. The large wooden barn sat just off the main street and across from a stream, bordered by lush cottonwood and willow trees. She approached a tall burly man pounding a horseshoe and inquired if he had a buggy for rent.

The man set his work aside and rubbed his hands on his homespun pants. "Sure enough, miss. You want it now?"

"Yes, please."

"It'll be fifty cents," he said, wiping a dusty sleeve across his sweaty brow.

Laurie nodded and handed the coins to him. "My trunk is by the general store. Could I impose on you to lift it into the buggy for me?"

Fifteen minutes later Laurie followed the rutted tracks leading out of town on the Stage Road. Holding the reins in a death grip, she felt her stomach flutter like the beating wings of a hundred butterflies. This isn't working out at all like I had planned, she thought.

Several miles ahead, she made the last turn leading to the ranch. The trail wound up a low grassy knoll. The hills just ahead were thick with pine trees. At the rise she passed a wooden sign with a large rounded *W* carved deep into the weathered surface. A little farther on she came to the ranch house, a wide two-story rectangle of sturdy logs. It was well cared for, she noted with relief. A family home.

Laurie's resolve was a little shaky as she slowed the horse to a walk. She hadn't met Mr. West, but his aunt, who engaged her, had assured her that the situation would be ideal. Laurie certainly hoped his aunt was right.

Laurie brought the horse to a stop by the hitching rail in front of the house. After again brushing the dust from her clothes, and with her stride more confident than she felt, she stepped up the worn split-log stairs onto the porch and rapped on the heavy door.

Suddenly a man with coal-black hair filled the tall doorway, his hand on the frame. Her pulse raced beneath her collar. "Mr. West?" She stared at his hand, the width of one of the logs siding the cabin, while he pinned her in place with his frigid gray gaze. His aunt Penelope had also told her, "My dear, trust me. You will be perfect for the job." His aunt obviously had a peculiar sense of humor.

"Who wants to know?" Gabe West barred the doorway and perused the woman standing before him. With appealing curves in her Sunday go-to-meeting dress and gloves, she sure was a sight easier on the eyes than most.

"I am Mrs. Preston. The stagecoach must have been overdue. I believe I arrived shortly after you left town." When the lines between his full, jet brows deepened, Laurie stepped back. During the interview for this position, she had formed an image of Mr. West: a little stocky, of medium height, and good-natured. This man certainly did not fit any of her notions.

"Who sent you out here? No," he said, waving his right hand, "never mind. Just leave." Was she some holier-than-thou missionary from Portland come to save a motherless child?

Gabe moved to close the door. Sending her out here may have been someone's idea of a joke, but he wasn't playing along.

Her clothes were definitely of better quality than he'd seen in Ashly Mills, and her pale creamy face showed that she spent little time outside of her parlor. Would the women around here never leave him be? He didn't want to deal with another woman pestering him with accusations, especially not in his own home.

Laurie reached out but stopped just short of touching the man's arm. "Wait . . . please. You *are* Mr. West?" He couldn't dismiss her so easily. She just wouldn't allow it.

"I'm Gabe West."

"Thank goodness." She sighed. "For a moment I thought I didn't follow the directions correctly."

Laurie used to dream about having her own little girl. Now she watched an adorable, tiny blond child with large blue eyes run to the doorway. "I was hired to care for your daughter. Is this Ammie?" She must take after her mother, Laurie thought; the child is as fair as the father is dark.

Gabe lifted the child and settled her against his chest before he glanced back at Mrs. Preston and nodded. The woman stood there looking so innocent, with eyes the shade of good sippin' whiskey and that proper little bonnet. Yet he'd faced other "innocent" faces that had turned accusing and mean. Now it seemed the women weren't content to harass him in town; here was one on his doorstep.

"She's *Aimée*. Now that you've seen her, you can go." Gabe had hoped his daughter wouldn't come to investigate. At least she was too young to understand the barely disguised charges that were sure to be hurled at him at any moment.

Ammie popped her sticky thumb into her mouth and stared at the newcomer.

Laurie reached out to touch the child, but Mr. West blocked her. "Hello, Ammie." She longed to take the little girl in her arms. "I'm Laurie. Was that lemon candy?" she asked, ignoring the child's rude father.

"You've satisfied your curiosity. Good day." Gabe stepped back and started to close the door. Of course, whoever had put the woman up to this had told her his daughter's name.

Laurie took a deep breath and clasped her hands in front of her. "Mr. West, although I have been through an interview with Mrs. West, I understand your wanting to hear my qualifications. I like children, feel capable of caring for your daughter, and I need to earn an income. What more would you like to know?"

The earlier meeting with his aunt had been much more comfortable. Now Laurie's stomach felt as if a rock had settled in it. Surely he wouldn't reject her after she had traveled so far.

Gabe gritted his teeth and glared at the woman. "My wife died last December. Who put you up to this?"

Laurie stared at him. "Mrs. Penelope West." Mrs. West hadn't warned her to expect resistance, but caring for a darling little girl like Ammie would be wonderful, she realized, almost like having a daughter of her own. And she desperately *needed* this position.

"Penelope? You know her?"

"Yes . . . no. I mean—" She tried again. "Mr. West, *do* you need someone to take care of your daughter? Or has

someone played a vicious prank at my expense?'' she asked
in a soft voice.

She watched his facial muscles tense as he raked his
coal-black hair from his eyes. The movement defined his
lean cheeks and strong jaw even more clearly. Laurie began
to doubt the wisdom of taking this position, *if* there was one.
Gabe West radiated the type of virile strength she had
always shied away from. But she lacked the funds to return
to Sacramento, and besides, there was nothing there for her
now.

She had felt comfortable with her husband, Sherman,
though she had married to please her father. Sherman was
slightly taller than her own five feet four inches and portly.
He had also been quiet and retiring, something that obviously could not be said of Mr. West.

Ammie squirmed and Gabe tried to settle her before he
glanced back at Mrs. Preston. Not one woman in town, fat,
thin, young, or old, would come out to tend his daughter
while he worked. Now this woman with her velvety eyes
and rustling skirts arrives at his door and announces that she
has the job. She didn't look strong enough even to lift a pail
of water, let alone Ammie. Why, he could span half her
waist with one hand.

Ammie lunged for Laurie, who caught the child and
nearly fell to her knees in the process. The little blond girl
clung to her with surprising strength. Laurie stood up and
straightened the little girl's dress.

Gabe pushed the door back farther. ''Hell, you might as
well come in.''

Laurie entered the main room and looked around at the
solid plank furniture, an assortment of whatnots, and the
odd amethyst velvet drapes with brassy-colored tasseled
ties. She sat down on an aged, rod-back rocking chair by the
wide stone hearth and felt completely at home. Ammie was
still attached to her chest like a baby opossum to its mother.

''Mrs. Penelope West interviewed me, then employed me
for this position. She said she was your aunt.''

❧2❧

Gabe stared at her a full minute before he groaned and sat
down heavily. His aunt had written a couple months ago,
urging him to remarry and give his daughter a mother. "She
is my aunt."

Looking into his eyes, the gray of aged pewter, Laurie
sensed that his expression boded ill. She averted her gaze,
embarrassed to be caught gawking at him.

Laurie withdrew the letter from her reticule. "Your aunt
gave me this introduction." She handed it to him. "I
assumed you had asked her to interview women for the
position." She settled back slightly and spoke as if to
herself. "She said she had advertised in several cities
besides Sacramento."

Gabe's attention snapped from the letter to Laurie at the
last softly spoken remark. "She what?" he roared.

"She said she had—"

"Good God! The woman needs a keeper. I'm surprised
she didn't marry me off by proxy."

Laurie's arms tightened around the child. "Just one
moment, Mr. West. You can't possibly think I came out

9

here expecting to . . . looking for . . . for a husband!''
Her breath came in short gasps. She felt heat rising on her
cheeks.

The little girl squirmed. Laurie loosened her hold and
smiled down at the child, who settled contentedly within the
circle of her arms.

Gabe watched them. ''No. But if it were true, you'd be
wasting your time here.'' The soft curve of her mouth when
she smiled at his daughter was certainly an improvement
over the snarling lips that usually greeted him. But her eyes
were now just as angry as the others. ''I'd better read this.''

Leaning back, Gabe held the envelope a moment before
he ripped the end off. His aunt Penelope was a lovable but
scatterbrained busybody.

> . . . Since you refused to be sensible, I took matters
> in hand. Laurie Preston has a good character, loves
> children, and like you, appears bent on enjoying
> widowhood.
>
> As you can see, I've taken your needs to heart. You
> are now free to ride the range.
>
> Fondly . . .

Damn! Penelope had really done it this time. Gabe
glanced at Mrs. Preston. ''How far have you come?''

''From Sacramento, California.''

''Why did you agree to work for a total stranger?''

Bolstering her flagging resolve, Laurie stared back at
him. ''I need the position, Mr. West. Your aunt said I was
qualified and could start work as soon as I arrived.'' She
noticed she had been smoothing Ammie's skirt and stopped.

''What makes you think you can care for Ammie?''

''I spent several years helping our neighbor Dr. Ray-
don,'' she responded, ''and I believe I'm capable of
handling any minor bruises, cuts, or scrapes.''

Gabe watched Ammie tugging at Mrs. Preston's bonnet
strings and the woman's warm smile. Could he actually

consider hiring her? Deciding he must be a few bales short, he aimed to put a stop to this right now.

"My aunt can be meddlesome sometimes. I'm sorry you came such a distance." He stood up. "You can put her down now." The woman was so soft she wouldn't last more than a few days, even if he did hire her. What a pity, he found himself thinking. Ammie needs loving care, especially a woman's.

Though Gabe's deep voice sounded pleasant, his expression wasn't. Laurie couldn't believe what he was saying. "Mr. West, I've been traveling on a stagecoach for almost four days. Are you telling me that your aunt did not employ me in your stead?"

Gabe paced the length of the room. "She did not. I never would've permitted it."

Laurie sagged back against the chair. The stage fare and her time were lost. A ruse. "The position sounded too good to be true." She sighed. "And the stagecoach has already left."

She hadn't heard the vicious accusations against him, he realized in amazement. And she didn't appear to be aware that the women in the area believed that he killed his wife. He slowed his pacing and studied her. He needed to be free—to work and get away from the house. After spending six months with a child who he claimed was his, he sometimes wondered when the nightmare would end.

If she meant what she said, the woman might be an answer to his prayers.

Laurie nervously looked around the room and noticed a small wood-framed mirror near the front door. To the left of the mirror was a four-peg hat rack. A holster complete with gun hung from one peg. She shuddered. When she glanced back at Mr. West, his mouth had softened. Hoping to catch him during a vulnerable moment, she quickly asked, "What other duties would I have?"

"Caring for Ammie would be enough," Gabe said absently. He paused by the window, wondering what he'd gotten himself into. Ammie should have been his most precious treasure. Instead she was a constant reminder of his deceased wife's infidelity.

Could he trust Mrs. Preston with Ammie? He glanced back at Laurie Preston. She appeared to be caring, and Ammie was taken with her. Penelope had not only recommended the woman, she had hired her, and he desperately needed to get away from the child so he could sort out his feelings for her. Besides, this was what he wanted, even though he had trouble admitting it, wasn't it? "You can stay, Mrs. Preston."

As relief spread through Laurie she exhaled a drawn-out sigh. "Thank you, Mr. West." She kissed Ammie's pale brow.

The woman was almost glowing. Was she that desperate for a job? "Did you leave your baggage in town?"

"My trunk is outside, but I have to return the buggy to the livery."

"I'll bring the trunk in and follow you back to town." He managed to pick up his daughter, who was vigorously resisting him. "I'll catch up with you," he added, feeling Ammie's wet linens.

Laurie nodded and returned to the buggy, feeling self-reliant for the first time in her life. She wouldn't have to remarry, as her family and friends had urged, to be protected and cared for like a porcelain figurine, or condemned to live as an unpaid housekeeper/wife. Moreover she had the distinct feeling that the little girl really did need her.

It took all of Laurie's strength to control the horse, which strained to run all the way back to town. The return trip to the livery sped by while she envisioned her future in the lush green valley.

She forced the horse to a walk before entering the town and soon pulled up in front of the livery. The burly man came out to meet her.

"You're back early. Will you need it tomorrow?" he asked, waving to the carriage.

"No, I won't." Laurie climbed down and flexed her fingers. "Thank you very much. Mr. West is coming for me." The smell of horses, manure, and sweat radiated from the man and the warm interior of the barn. She stepped back and gazed over at the nearby willow trees, hoping for a fresh breeze.

"Sure 'nough," the man said, his eyes suddenly coming to life as he took a closer look at her before trudging away, shaking his shaggy head.

The air felt cooler as Laurie heard the rattle of a harness and looked up. Mr. West's wagon rounded the corner and moved toward her. He seemed even larger, even more physically intimidating outdoors. The brim of his battered, high-crowned hat shaded his eyes, but there was no concealing the set of his strong jaw, even at a distance.

"Are you ready, Mrs. Preston?" Gabe felt sure he was making a mistake. The woman was dressed in costly clothes and surely had more in her trunk. But even if she only stayed a week or two, he decided with silent cynicism, he would be able to check on the herd, his men, and come to terms with his situation. That would be something.

"When you are, Mr. West." Laurie stepped to the side of the wagon and spoke to Ammie while he climbed down from his seat. The little girl was secured with ropes to prevent her from falling out.

"We haven't time to dawdle. I want to get back before sunset." He stood beside Mrs. Preston, waiting to hand her up to the wagon seat.

She placed her gloved hand in his, and then she faced him. The dark felt hat that shaded his eyes nearly matched his coal-black hair. Captured by the intensity of his gaze, she barely realized he had lifted her to his wagon with those two capable hands until he released her.

Laurie twisted around on the wooden seat and glanced down at Ammie. She sat forlornly like a sack of forgotten potatoes. The poor little dear, Laurie thought.

"Can she sit on my lap? She can't like being tied up back

there.'' Laurie wanted to hold the little girl and needed something to do with her hands so they wouldn't reveal how unsettled this man made her feel. And the bench seat on the wagon now appeared far too intimate.

Gabe shrugged. ''Sure.'' He reached over and untied the rope around his daughter's waist. ''Come on, you're going to ride up front with Mrs. Preston.''

As Gabe set her down on Mrs. Preston's legs Ammie stuck her thumb in her mouth. He watched her stare with wonder at Mrs. Preston. For the flicker of a moment he felt jealous. ''Damn,'' he mumbled as he walked around the rear of the wagon.

He decided that as long as Ammie took to her, he'd tolerate the woman because it suited *his* purposes. He headed the team of horses back toward his ranch, reluctantly curious about the woman his aunt had chosen to care for his daughter.

He settled back, his foot up on the boot, his attention on the rutted road. Ammie appeared content with Mrs. Preston, but he still wondered about that flash of extreme happiness that had lit up the woman's face. ''Is your family in Sacramento?''

''Yes . . . no.''

''Which is it?''

''They are buried there.'' Laurie smoothed Ammie's tangled hair from her face and purposely changed the subject. ''This is a beautiful valley. Have you lived here long, Mr. West?''

''Close to fifteen years.'' He glanced over at her and pursued his own thoughts. ''There aren't many unattached women here about, and few travel alone. I'm surprised you did.''

''My husband passed away over a year ago.'' Laurie glanced beyond Gabe, her gaze on the blue-green hills. ''My funds were low, and I need the position to support myself. That's why I answered your aunt's advertisement. When she explained that I would be living on a ranch in

Oregon, I was not put off by the idea of moving." She righted her bonnet and pointed out a circling hawk to Ammie.

"Ashly Mills certainly isn't Sacramento."

"No. I don't expect it to be."

Gabe drove the last miles in silence, going over his duties for the next day in his mind, but every time he turned his head in Mrs. Preston's direction, a sweet scent wafted his way.

For the first time in days Gabe thought of Ruth, his deceased wife. As soon as they were married and she was away from her harsh, fanatically religious father, she had changed drastically. She exchanged her staid, practical dresses for more daring costumes and a strong, almost offensive fragrance more suited to a brothel. He quickly learned that she had harbored other desires she felt she could satisfy once free of her family.

He regarded Mrs. Preston and wondered how she would change now that she was away from her family. At least the woman appeared biddable. He tightened his grip on the reins as the horses picked up speed, knowing their feed wasn't far away. "Do you have any idea what life's like on a ranch?"

Laurie's hand stilled on the little girl's arm. "No, but raising a child on a ranch couldn't differ much from raising one in the city."

He glanced at her. "You *have* taken care of children, then. In the city."

Laurie shook her head. "Mr. Preston and I were not blessed with children."

"But why did you compare the city to the ranch?" Lord, he'd forgotten how women talked in circles and never said a damn thing straight.

"I merely meant that children are children wherever they grow up, and I've never heard of classes being taught on the finer points of motherhood. I'll manage, Mr. West, as I imagine our mothers did."

God help Ammie . . . and me, he thought. What on earth was Penelope thinking when she hired this woman? Was she punishing me because I refused to marry again?

Ammie was such a sweet, affectionate child; Laurie felt sure she was going to love her new position. And Mr. West? She would spend her time with Ammie and keep her distance from the man. He was obviously distracted and, Laurie believed, still grieving for his wife.

Laurie followed Mr. West into his daughter's room. With Ammie in her arms she wandered around the sunlit, airy room, stopping at the foot of a small bed set in the corner. "Will I be staying in here?"

"That won't be necessary. There are two bedrooms upstairs. Choose whichever one you want. I'll bring your trunk up after I see to the horses." Gabe paused at the connecting door to the kitchen. "There's a cast-iron cook stove in here to cook on." He considered her a moment and left.

Laurie smiled inwardly at his boasting while she watched him square his shoulders and walk with long, determined strides through the kitchen.

"Shall we go upstairs, Ammie? You can help me decide which room will be mine." Laurie took the little girl's hand and chattered while they made their way back to the main room.

The staircase was blocked by a gate, which took some effort to unlatch. Not wanting to chance Ammie falling, Laurie lifted the child to her hip before climbing up the smooth split-log stairs.

The curtains were drawn closed in the first room, but Laurie could make out a dark, floral-print bedspread lying haphazardly over the bed and a matching covered chair. A basket of faded, dried flowers, perched on a bureau, looked older than the house. Ammie buried her nose against Laurie's neck. The room felt airless, but Laurie noticed the faint odor of cheap perfume.

Ammie pushed against Laurie, struggling to get down. "No, no, me . . . go."

Laurie quickly stepped back and closed the door. Once they had left the room, Ammie calmed down. "Is this better?" Ammie nodded, so Laurie opened the door to the second room and stepped inside.

She glanced about and smiled. Though the square-post bedstead and unadorned chest of drawers were plainly crafted oak, the workmanship and years of polishing showed in the straight lines and deep luster of the wood. The curtains were homespun and held open with matching ties. This room, like the others, had a braided rag rug covering most of the floor. Though dusty and stuffy, the room didn't feel oppressive like the other.

The front door closed, and Laurie heard Gabe's approaching footsteps on the stairs. She returned to the hallway and stood between the two rooms.

He lowered the trunk to the floor. "Which one did you decide on?"

The rooms were so different, but she would comply if he suggested the darker one. After all, she had spent her life fitting into situations not of her making. That was a woman's lot. Laurie's gaze went to the open door before she faced Mr. West.

"Either one will do nicely."

He had seen her wistful glance and went into the open room. "This one's uncluttered." He lowered the trunk and placed it at the foot of the bed. "I'll move the wardrobe from the other room in here." This had been his room. Why had she chosen it? he wondered.

He'd felt sure Mrs. Preston would prefer the room his wife had decorated and occupied within months of their marriage. "This is what *women* like, not the plain rooms you insist on keeping throughout the house," Ruth had ranted while she moved her belongings upstairs.

"Thank you."

"Come on, Ammie, let's go dig up some grub for

supper.'' Gabe reached to extricate his reluctant daughter from Mrs. Preston's arms. Ammie turned away from him as his hand slipped between her stomach and Mrs. Preston's breasts.

Laurie sucked in her breath at the touch of his large hand. She stood perfectly still, unable to move, and certainly unwilling to look up into his gray eyes.

He muttered an apology, yet his gaze lingered.

Laurie felt her cheeks burn. He finally lifted his daughter from her arms. The door closed. She was alone in the bedroom, but she could still feel his warm touch on her breast.

Gabe West was her employer, Ammie's father, and nothing more, she reminded herself, aware of the heat and color still staining her cheeks. He had only been trying to take hold of Ammie. Laurie kept reciting those words as she quickly unpacked her trunk.

❧3❧

Ammie sat in the chair her daddy had made for her, watching the lady with interest.

Laurie finished setting three places at one end of the table and knelt by Ammie's chair. "Would you like to help me?"

Ammie peered at her daddy before she nodded shyly.

"Thank you, Ammie. We'll fold the napkins." Laurie went to the sideboard and began searching.

"They're in the top, left-hand drawer." Gabe continued stirring the stew and started humming. It suddenly occurred to him that the house didn't seem so lonely anymore.

Laurie found an apron wadded up in one corner. She shook it out and hung it over the back of her chair before she picked out three rumpled napkins. She went over to the little girl. "You hold this side," she said, placing Ammie's little hands on the edge. Laurie made a game of bringing their hands together while they folded the large square piece of material.

Once Ammie sat with a flat rectangle in front of her, Laurie showed the little girl how to smooth it out with her hands. "There. That looks much better."

"Daddy," Ammie said, pointing to the place at the head of the table.

Gabe glanced over in time to appreciate the sight of Laurie bending over the table. A man could get used to this. His mind elsewhere, he grabbed for the kettle with his bare hand. "Da . . . gumm't!"

"Here, let me serve. You should dunk that hand in water to cool it off." Laurie took the pot to the table and dished out the stew.

Gabe did what she suggested. However, after he dried his hand, he looked up to find Mrs. Preston at his side. She took his rough hand in her soft one and gently smeared some grease on the burn. He didn't feel any pain, only a strange tenderness when her fingers skimmed his hand.

"You aren't left-handed, are you, Mr. West?"

"No." He lowered his hand. She wasn't there to fuss over him, just Ammie, and his voice reflected his frustration. "The food's getting cold. We'd better eat." He turned away from her and joined his daughter at the table. "Hungry?" He reached over and tucked the napkin into the neck of Ammie's dress, then carefully cut the meat into tiny bites before setting the plate in front of her.

Meanwhile Laurie took her place at the table, noting that she would see to the child's plate in the future. As she watched she could still feel his large, rough hand in hers. They were nothing like her husband's hands. Sherman's pale skin, and his touch, had been soft, so unlike that of Mr. West's callused palms.

Ammie picked up a bite of meat and began nibbling on it. Then she pointed to the bread at the other end of the table. "Want some."

Tearing a slice in half, Gabe glanced at Mrs. Preston, who appeared to be staring blankly at Ammie's plate. "She likes bread soaked in gravy. Sometimes that's all she'll eat." He placed the bread on Ammie's plate and smothered it in the gravy before cutting it into bites.

"I would appreciate anything you can tell me about her habits and preferences. Is she always so quiet?"

"Mm-hmm." Gabe ate quickly, keeping an eye on Ammie. He was used to doing double duty and still had the evening chores ahead.

During supper Laurie watched Mr. West and Ammie eat in silence, remembering that when she was a little girl, her parents talked during the evening meal. She was relieved when the somber experience ended.

Gabe stacked the dishes and grabbed a wooden bucket. "I'll do them when I'm finished outside." He got to the kitchen door and paused to glance back at Mrs. Preston. She sat there looking as confused as Ammie. "You want to get her ready for bed?"

"Yes, of course." Laurie felt chastised for not knowing their routine and exactly what he expected of her.

Laurie found a clean cloth and wet it in the bucket. "Let's wash your face." She wiped Ammie's mouth and chin. Then she looked around and found another empty bucket, with a wider mouth than the one Mr. West had taken.

"You can help me get more water for your bath." She unfastened the leather belt holding the child in the chair.

With the little girl's hand secure in her own Laurie went outside. "Where is the water pump, Ammie?"

The child pointed to one end of the log ranch house, then gestured toward the barn. "Daddy."

"He's working in there, isn't he?"

Ammie nodded.

"Let's see if we can finish your bath before your daddy comes back."

Laurie's respect for mothers grew a hundredfold when she set the bucket in front of the spout, then jostled the little girl while trying to work the pump handle. Each time she bent sideways, her waist-length corset dug into her tender skin, so she put Ammie down.

Laurie soon learned that walking in a slightly bent-over

position, in order to hold the little girl's hand, and carrying a full bucket of water was no easy task either.

Once in the kitchen, she released the child's hand and put the water on to heat. Ammie sat down, content to watch while Laurie searched through the kitchen, then Ammie's room, for soap, towels, and the child's nightclothes.

Laurie felt like the outsider she was, looking in cupboards and through drawers. She gathered the necessary items and lighted a lamp in the darkening room. When the water was hot, she filled the wooden tub half-full.

"I've never done this before, but you have. Let's see how we do together, shall we, Ammie?"

Once Ammie's dirty clothes lay in a heap on the floor, and Laurie started to lower the child into the water, she learned another lesson. Roll your sleeves up before starting the bath. However, it was too late for that. Ammie felt like a slippery bar of soap and just as difficult to hold on to.

The door to the house opened and closed. Concentrating on her young charge, Laurie dismissed the shuffling noises coming from upstairs. She was rinsing the little girl's soapy body when she heard Mr. West return downstairs.

Gabe entered the kitchen and watched as Laurie taught his daughter anatomy.

"Tilt your chin up," Laurie said, nudging Ammie to show her what she had said. Laurie held one of the little girl's arms in her hand.

Then Ammie saw her daddy. She squealed and slipped.

When the child lost her balance, Laurie's breath caught in her throat. Water sloshed over the rim of the tub. As she struggled to settle the little girl Laurie became aware of Gabe West's presence.

He leaped forward and braced Ammie. When she started giggling, he relaxed. "Laurie Preston, have you ever bathed a child before?" The woman's face was pale, and she was breathing hard.

Laurie kept her attention on the little girl. "Not recently,

but we'll be fine. She moved so quickly, she startled me."
She sat back on her heels and waited for his reprimand.

Gabe eyed his daughter. "You mind Mrs. Preston." He
stood and went over to the bucket of fresh water. After he
drank a dipperful of the cool liquid, he sat down at the table.

Laurie nervously continued, trying to make a game out of
bathing. By the time she lifted the little girl from the tub, she
and the floor were both soaked, but Ammie was smiling.

After Laurie finished dressing her, she spoke to Gabe.
"I'll clean up the mess. When do you usually put her to
bed?"

"Around this time. She'll slow down now that the
excitement's over."

"She's probably never had a bath quite like the one
tonight." Laurie felt her damp clothes, suddenly aware of
how the fabric clung to her, and tried to shake out her skirt.
"Her hair needs washing, but I'll have to do that tomorrow." Feeling self-conscious under his close scrutiny, she
asked, "Is there something I can do for you?"

He didn't look away for a long moment, then shook his
head. He hadn't been this close to a woman in months, at
least a year, he quickly calculated, not even Ruth. Ignoring
her question, he glanced down at Ammie. "Looks like she's
ready for bed."

Laurie went into the small bedroom and turned down the
bed. When Mr. West did not follow her, she returned to the
kitchen and found him in the same position while Ammie
played with a puddle of water. Laurie took Ammie's hand
and paused for Mr. West to bid his daughter good night.

Gabe ruffled the child's hair and waited for Mrs. Preston
in the kitchen. She returned a few minutes later. "I'll be
riding out early in the morning. Can you manage by
yourself?"

"Ammie and I will be fine. Is there anyone else here?"
Laurie bent to pick up the wet towels.

"You'll be alone for the day. I only have three regular
hands now, and they're with the stock. The milk's kept in

the springhouse.'' He noticed the armful of towels then. ''Let me have those. The line's out back. I'd better show you around.''

When he reached for the towels, she pulled back, instinctively hugging the bundle to her midsection, hoping he would not notice the tremor of her hands. ''I'll hang them up.''

Her reaction brought a shockingly vivid image of Ruth recoiling from him. Grabbing the lantern, Gabe led Mrs. Preston to the clothesline. He'd tried to forget what a hell Ruth had made of his life. In fact, it wasn't until after her death that he had realized just how bad it had become. He wasn't about to let Mrs. Preston or anyone else do that to him again.

Laurie followed in his wake. His sudden animosity was frightening. Surely her carrying the wet laundry was not all that important.

Watching her drape the towels over the clothesline, he forced himself to calm down before he spoke. ''I'll milk the cow before I leave. The springhouse is over there.'' He held the lantern out toward a small roof showing below a knoll. ''The bunkhouse is beyond the barn. You'll see the hen-house in the morning. I'd appreciate your gathering the eggs.''

She nodded, wishing she had some experience with that chore. The nearly full rising moon cast strange shadows. The air felt especially cool against her damp clothes. She shivered and wrapped her arms across her chest.

He noticed her shivering and grabbed her slender arm. ''You're almost as white as that towel. Why didn't you tell me you were cold?'' he demanded, rushing her back to the house. ''You'd better change or you'll come down with a fever.''

Gabe hadn't meant to sound so gruff, but he couldn't help himself. His mother had succumbed to a lung inflammation more than ten years earlier, and he still lived with a fear of chills and fevers.

Laurie felt like a child and resolved to give him no cause to treat her so again. Once inside the house, she freed her arm and faced him. "I think I can manage from here, Mr. West." She started for the stairs.

"I'm turning in now. You better change in front of the fire." He set the bar in place across the heavy front door and went to his room opposite the kitchen end of the log house.

Halfway up the stairs, and before she heard his bedroom door close, she said, "Have a good trip," and continued up to her room. She appreciated his suggestion, but she wasn't about to chance doing so.

Closing the window she had left open to air out the room, she realized she had forgotten to bring a light up with her, but she could make out the dark shape of the wardrobe and smiled. She found her way around the room by the moon's dim light, hastening to strip off her soggy clothing and donning a soft nightgown.

Too late she remembered she had also forgotten to make the bed. In her exhausted state, she didn't care. She rolled herself up in the cover and was asleep within a few moments.

Downstairs in his large, warm bed, Gabe lay listening for the unfamiliar sounds of a stranger in his home. Once Mrs. Preston had closed the bedroom door, he could only hear an occasional squeak from a floorboard. It felt odd having a woman he really didn't know living in his home—sleeping in his old room.

Laurie rolled over and stretched. It was light outside. She jerked upright in bed. "Ammie," she whispered. She quickly padded over to the washstand to find that she had not filled the pitcher the night before. After slipping into her wrapper, she grabbed the empty container and dashed downstairs in her bare feet.

The plank floor was frigid. She darted to the kitchen and through to peek in on the little girl. Ammie lay sound asleep, her thumb resting in her slack mouth. Laurie quietly closed the door and went to the water bucket.

Holding the full pitcher with both hands, she made her way slowly to the main room. As she neared the hat rack she heard another door open and jumped. The water in the pitcher sloshed, some spilling onto her toes.

Gabe stood in his bedroom doorway. He had overslept and was anxious to leave before Laurie Preston came down. But there she stood, barefoot, dressed in her nightclothes with her long auburn hair swinging above her waist. She reminded him of a startled doe. No, he thought, don't call her Laurie. Mrs. Preston was definitely safer, considering how inviting she appeared just now.

He cleared his throat. "Mornin'."

Laurie felt herself begin to tremble. "Mr. West." She knew she should keep walking, yet she couldn't help looking at him, couldn't help feeling the strength he radiated. "I must have overslept." He was dressed and his coal-black hair combed.

"No, you didn't. It's early."

"I'll dress and start breakfast." She felt uncomfortable. She had never thought how awkward it would be to live in another man's house.

"I don't have time." He started for the door and paused. "I might be late getting back tonight."

Laurie watched him leave and groaned aloud. If one could begin a new position doing everything wrong, she surely had. At least he would be gone all day, giving her a chance to accustom herself to the house and her responsibilities.

She completed her toilet, selected her most serviceable muslin dress, and went down to start breakfast. Soon she heard her new charge begin to stir.

"Good morning, Ammie," Laurie greeted the little girl from the doorway.

Ammie stuck her thumb in her mouth and used her other hand to rub her eye.

"Come on, sweetie, you must be hungry."

"Dadthee?" Ammie asked, her thumb still secure in her mouth.

"He'll be back later." Laurie picked up the little girl, then felt her wet linens and laid her down. So much to learn, she found herself thinking.

It was midmorning before Laurie remembered she had to gather the eggs and wash the little girl's hair. She put water on to heat.

"How would you like to go outside, Ammie?" Laurie fitted the child on her hip, which was becoming a habit, and went out.

"We can have a picnic dinner." At the mention of food, Laurie realized that she had not fed the chickens.

While Laurie tossed handfuls of feed, Ammie giggled at the picking birds. The last of the feed having been handed out, Laurie searched for a basket and went into the henhouse to gather the eggs. All but two of the hens were out pecking at the feed.

"Oh, Lord, give me strength," she muttered, reaching out toward the first hen. The bird started pecking at her hand but didn't move. "Well, get up," Laurie said, nudging the side of the bird. It still didn't move, only glared at her speculatively.

"Ammie, I wish you could help. Your father said all I had to do was care for you."

Ammie leaned forward and slipped her small hand beneath the hen and withdrew an egg. She held it up to Laurie's face.

"Thank you, sugar." Laurie held up the basket and Ammie carefully placed the egg on the bottom. "Now, it's my turn." Laurie observed the second hen, took a deep breath, and reached under the bird. She sighed when she found the egg.

After they had collected the other eggs from the empty nests, Laurie carried them over to the springhouse. She found the milk, a crock of butter, and other stored foods when she explored the cool building. She felt like a child herself, having never lived on a farm.

The day passed in a flurry of unfamiliar activities. While the little girl napped Laurie sat down and made a list of daily chores she must remember. She was starting a new life. She had not understood the enormity of her position yesterday, when she had so anxiously arrived, ready to begin work.

That night, after she had put Ammie down to sleep with a story, Laurie lay in her own freshly made bed looking out through the partially open window. A light current of mountain air cooled the room. The night sounds were different from those in Sacramento—an occasional distant howl instead of boisterous voices, rustling branches and animal sounds instead of rattling horse harnesses and wagons creaking. Bygone memories of her husband intruded into her reverie.

Sherman, twenty years her senior, had quickly grown complacent during their first year of marriage. He had been content with her presence and required little else than her obedience and an efficiently run home. Long after she had fallen into a fretful sleep, the sound of an approaching horse was familiar and brought a smile to her lips.

Laurie stretched, feeling the stiff, sore muscles she had never given a thought to before. The sun was just rising on her second day at the ranch. At least she knew what to expect this morning.

She hummed while she considered her dresses, two muslin and three calico. She had brought only her most serviceable clothes, garments she felt she could work in.

One item she was decidedly going to dispense with, for a while anyway, was her corset. Her waist still felt bruised and raw from the previous day's gouging. She chose a loose-fitting dress and wore only one petticoat. After brushing her long hair over her shoulders, she quickly twisted it up into a bun and left her room to begin her duties.

Laurie put the kindling in the iron stove and started the fire, brought in a fresh bucket of water, then went to the springhouse for milk. She felt very proud of herself as she checked the list she'd put in her pocket. She was right on schedule.

Laurie poked her head into Ammie's room and was rewarded with a shy smile.

"You look happy this morning." Laurie grabbed clean linens, then returned to the kitchen to dampen one before changing Ammie. "Can you say Laurie? That's my name." She pointed to herself. "Laurie. Now you say it."

Ammie lay there looking up.

"I know you can say Daddy. Won't you try to say Laurie?" She tied the linens and picked Ammie up for a hug.

Ammie pointed at the window. "Daddy."

"Yes, sugar, your daddy works out there, but not today. We'll have to make do on our own." Laurie finished dressing the little girl, then brushed her silky blond curls. "Now you're ready." Ammie slipped from Laurie's reach and darted into the kitchen. "Good. You want to help me make breakfast."

Laurie secured Ammie in her chair and started cooking. She heard the front door open and close quietly. A floorboard groaned. She was alone, miles from town. She listened, but only heard the pounding of her heart.

She slid her hand across the table and gripped the large knife she'd used to slice bread. She crept lightly, with far more confidence than she felt, toward the living area. Suddenly Gabe appeared in front of her.

"Damn." The sight of Laurie Preston coming at him with that knife nearly scared the pants off of him. "What the hell are you doing, woman?" Gabe felt his fingers digging deep into the wrapped meat in his hand.

"Oh," she cried. "I'm so sorry. I didn't know you were home." She quickly hid the knife in the folds of her skirt and tried to calm her racing pulse. "I thought we were alone."

"Put that away before you hurt someone." He followed her back to the kitchen, set the meat on the table, and glanced at his daughter.

Ammie timidly looked up at Gabe. "Orie," she said, pointing to Laurie.

"Orie, is it? I'm glad you two are making friends." He gazed at Mrs. Preston.

Her long auburn hair was pulled back in a bun, and her calico dress was neat but plain. It sure wasn't going to look that nice a few days from now. If she stayed, he reminded himself.

"Have you eaten, Mr. West?"

"I came in to fry up some ham 'n eggs." He reached for the frying pan on the stove.

Laurie filled the coffeepot and set it over the fire. "I'll get the eggs."

She dashed out to the springhouse. Laurie gathered the front of her skirt up with one hand and carefully placed a half-dozen large eggs into this temporary nest.

She returned to the kitchen and had put the eggs on the table before she noticed that Mr. West was cooking two large slices of ham in a skillet. "Are you expecting company?" His deep and melodic laughter startled her.

Gabe saw her dismayed expression and gained control of himself. "You said you'd been married. Didn't your husband eat?"

"Well, of course but . . ." Laurie felt herself blushing, which only increased her embarrassment. "What can I do to help?"

"Make some soda biscuits. I'll take a few with me." Gabe poured a little milk into Ammie's cup and handed it to her. "It won't take long."

Laurie searched around and found a bowl and ingredients. If he had not personally agreed to hire her, she would swear she was unwelcome. At times he even appeared to resent his own daughter. At least he was leaving shortly. The man surely knew how to unnerve her.

Gabe sat at the table, eating. Laurie coaxed Ammie into eating small pieces of biscuit dipped in a coddled egg. Laurie's gaze briefly met Mr. West's. In the moment before he looked away, she thought she saw a surge of loneliness in the depths of his gray eyes.

Ammie chewed the bite in her mouth and pointed to her daddy's plate. "Me want, me want."

Quickly cutting a tiny bit of her own ham, Laurie offered it to Ammie. "It will take me a few days to get used to her tastes." She talked to the little girl while she cut more bites for her.

For a split second Gabe expected to see his mother when he glanced across the table. Like Laurie, she used to chatter at mealtime. "Ammie usually doesn't want meat." Gabe gave his daughter a piece of biscuit, marveling at her newfound appetite.

"Do you usually feed her only what she wants?" Laurie held the spoon out to the child.

"She'll eat sugared oatmeal mush, and pudding when we have it." Gabe mopped his plate with a biscuit and moved his chair back.

"Would you like to play while I clean up in here? Then we can go outside."

Ammie sat on the floor and watched. It didn't take Laurie long to clean up, all the while chattering to Ammie.

Since she'd had no children of her own, Laurie didn't know at what age Ammie could be expected to say more than a few words. She decided to work on Ammie's vocabulary. From what Laurie had witnessed, Ammie wouldn't learn much from her father.

Laurie shook out the dishtowel, hung it over the handle on the stove, and noticed Ammie. She was standing in the doorway brushing at her hair.

Laurie went over and knelt by her. "Good girl." She took

Ammie's hands and clapped them together. "Your hair looks pretty."

Ammie beamed. She reached out and touched Laurie's hair.

Laurie picked up Ammie and hugged the child to her breast. She's such a dear, Laurie thought, kissing the top of her head. She felt an ache, deep within her, and realized that this was the closest she would come to being a mother.

❧4❧

Gabe walked in in time to see Mrs. Preston cuddling his daughter. It stopped him cold. He couldn't remember the last time he'd seen Ruth hold their daughter that close.

Ammie's sudden giggle broke the spell.

Laurie stood with the laughing child clinging to the front of her dress when she saw Gabe in the doorway. "Is there something you wanted, Mr. West?"

Mrs. Preston's light, creamy complexion had become decidedly pink. He motioned to the table. "I forgot the biscuits."

Laurie went over and wrapped the remaining biscuits in a napkin. "Will you return by suppertime?"

"I should. But you two go ahead and eat without me. I'll probably have something with Old Ben." Gabe focused his attention on his daughter's now somber expression. "See you later."

Gabe rode north to check on his gamble. Before trailing the herd up to the spring pasture, he had sold off all but forty-five of his long-horned cayuse cattle, those of Spanish

33

origin, and laid off most of his cowhands. He then purchased twenty red poll cows.

He was taking a big chance starting a new herd, but he felt sure his investment would pay off. In a few years he would be selling beef superior to the cayuse, so prevalent in Oregon. And if his luck held, he would be making another addition to his small drove in a few days.

Gabe rode through the bunchgrass, summer feed that grew so abundantly. He approached one of his remaining three cowhands and called out, "Howdy, Ben."

The old man glanced up and returned Gabe's greeting. "What ya doin' up here?"

"Wanted to see how the polls are doing."

"They's jist fine." Ben removed his battered, wide-brimmed hat and wiped the sleeve of his shirt across his lined brow.

"Yesterday I checked on Nate. He should have the cayuse here in a couple days." Gabe looked up the narrow valley to where his cattle were grazing.

"Yep."

"I have to make a trip north. I want you to stay at the ranch and keep an eye on things for me."

Ben gaped at his boss. "I cain't sit no young'un!"

Seeing the horror on the old man's face made Gabe chuckle. "I hired a lady, Mrs. Preston, to take care of Ammie. I need you to take care of the chores."

"What kind of a woman cain't milk a cow 'n feed the lil critters?" Ben made some unintelligible sounds of male outrage. "When ya want me there?"

"You can pack up now and have supper at the house."

"I kin fix my own grub."

The two men rode in companionable silence. Gabe would've liked to have talked with Old Ben, but he was true to his breed by being as miserly with his words as he was generous with his grub.

When they arrived at the summer camp, Ben quickly set to putting his bedroll together with all his worldly possessions and tied it on his second horse along with his soogan, scraps of material sewn together to form a thin mattress.

"I'll ride back with you after I see Danny." Gabe kept his mount at a walk as he rode by the cattle.

He had to admire their beauty. They had filled out, were healthier looking than the bonier cayuse. These cows were the beginning of his dream.

Gabe didn't greet Danny Whitefeather until he was well beyond spooking the small herd. "How're you doing?" Gabe and Danny had been friends for nearly fifteen years. Danny's father was white, his mother Modoc and Klamath Indian. He took after his father except for his dark eyes and straight hair.

"Trying to stay awake. Where's Old Ben going?"

"Back to the ranch. I've got to see about the Durhams." Gabe tipped his hat back and dismounted.

"How's Ammie doing? And where is she?"

"She's fine. I hired a woman, Mrs. Preston, to care for her." Gabe looked at the cattle, but he was remembering Mrs. Preston. Laurie. She'd taken to his daughter quick enough, but she sure was strange around him.

Danny sat watching Gabe's expression. "What about *Mister* Preston? You hire a new hand?" He struck a sulfur match and lit a cigarette.

"She's Widow Preston." But she sure didn't fit the image the title implied.

Frowning, Gabe wondered why she hadn't remarried. She certainly appeared to be all a man could want, but then looks were like the shell of an egg. How had that lesson slipped his mind so quickly?

"Ah, that's good. An older woman is wise with the young ones." Danny exhaled and watched the smoke drift away.

"She's not dotty yet. Far from it." Gabe removed his hat, knocked the dust off, and plopped it back on his head. "I want to get back before the milk cow puts a new hole in the barn wall. I'll bring more supplies tomorrow."

Danny nodded, a wry grin turning up the corners of his mouth as Gabe wheeled around and rode away.

Laurie was sitting at the table feeding Ammie when she heard horses enter the yard.

"Daddy."

"I'll see, but you still have to finish your apple sauce." Laurie peered out through the window. "You're right, and he's brought someone with him." She went back and sat by Ammie. "Two more bites now."

Ammie swallowed and twisted around in the chair. "Daddy?"

"Okay, sweetie. We'll go meet him after I clean your face." Laurie took the end of the towel, dampened it, and washed the wiggling child's face.

Halfway across the yard, Laurie saw an elderly man leave the barn and amble toward one of the outbuildings. She stopped in the wide doorway of the barn. The aroma of hay and leather blended with other, less pleasant odors. Gabe's large lean body dwarfed the little stool he sat on while he milked the cow.

"Orie!" Ammie squawked, her blond curls bouncing like little springs as she strained against Laurie's grasp.

The cow kicked out with her back leg. The milk pail spilled and Gabe was knocked backward, off the stool. "What the blazes! Don't you know enough to keep her quiet while I'm milking?"

Gabe stood and slammed the stool back in place. After righting the pail, he quieted the wide-eyed cow. Then he faced Mrs. Preston. "I suppose you took her to the chicken coop and let her stir them up, too." Damn, but he knew this arrangement wasn't going to work. Running his hand along the cow's side, he asked, "What did you want?"

Everything had happened so fast, Laurie could do no more than pick up Ammie and step back. "Your daughter wanted to see you." She glanced at his back, adding in a whisper, "Though I don't know why," as she spun around and fled.

Gabe followed her out. "Wait up!"

Laurie stopped; her heart pounded wildly. Ammie burrowed her head into her neck.

Gabe smoothed his daughter's hair and spoke softly. "Come here . . . punkin." Calling Ammie "punkin" was difficult and made him feel no closer to her, but he hoped it sounded friendlier.

Ammie peeked up at her daddy, a curious, almost wary look on her face. She stuck her thumb into her mouth and stared at him.

"It's okay." Gabe patted Ammie's back awkwardly. "I wasn't mad at you."

He glanced at Mrs. Preston. She stood there with her shoulders slumped and a withdrawn expression on her pale face. He suddenly felt as if he had beaten her.

"Look, you have to teach her not to scream around the stock. Surely you know that much."

"I do now, Mr. West. I'll take her in."

Laurie could feel her whole body quaking. She would have to guard her errant tongue, for he must have heard her spiteful comment. Surely he would dismiss her, and she had been trying so very hard to please him and not give him a reason to exercise his temper. She must avoid irritating him, or she would certainly be searching for a new position.

"You can take her down by the creek. She likes to play there."

He turned away from Mrs. Preston, who held Ammie with such tenderness, and returned to the barn. Had his show of temper frightened her so? Well, she'd get used to it, he thought, and wondered what it would take to get *her* in an uproar. He realized he wanted to see her eyes light up and color come to her cheeks.

Dangerous, he thought, but an intriguing idea nonetheless.

* * *

Laurie took Gabe's advice. She went to the house for a towel, then took Ammie to the creek. He had not fired her. That should have been a great relief, but it only caused her to worry about the next time she angered him.

Finding a sunny spot, she sat down by the edge of the winding stream with Ammie on her lap. "I'd wager you would like to play in the creek."

Ammie leaned forward and began slapping at the water. One flat-handed smack sent up a spray of large drops that wet herself and Laurie. Ammie giggled and started hitting the water with both hands.

"I should have brought soap and towels. You're a water bug." Laurie was soon giggling with the little girl.

While watching Ammie play, Laurie considered Gabe West's attitude toward his daughter. Something his aunt Penelope had said came to mind. "Gabe adores his daughter, of course, but he's rather like a ram trying to nurse a calf." Maybe that was all it was. He simply felt ill at ease, especially in front of her.

An hour later they returned to the house. Ammie had worn herself out and was drowsy. Laurie wondered where Mr. West was, but her first concern was to get Ammie settled for the night.

A few minutes later the child was asleep and tucked in her bed. Laurie tidied the kitchen before lighting the lamp in the main room. She rearranged a few whatnots, setting apart two daguerreotypes—one a woman with kind eyes, the other a man who resembled Gabe West, in carved wooden frames. Despite the vivid purple drapes and gold-tasseled ties, the room felt warm, loving, a place that had once known laughter and happiness.

Deciding to take advantage of Gabe West's absence, she went upstairs and gathered her things. If she hurried, she could bathe in the creek and return before he did.

Moonlight filtered through the willow trees. Laurie enjoyed the tranquillity and the opportunity to bathe herself.

Attending the young child gave her little time to herself, which she had come to value in the last year. She needed those few solitary minutes.

It didn't take long, though, before she was shivering and quickly finished her bath. She wrapped the towel around her wet head and made her way back to the house.

After Gabe had finished up in the barn, he went to the bunkhouse and shared supper with Old Ben in the cook-shack attached to the ranch hand's sleeping quarters. Old Ben offered camaraderie rather than conversation, and Gabe preferred that tonight to being with Mrs. Preston. She had a way of making him feel restless, always aware of her presence.

"Well, I'd better turn in. I'll introduce you to Mrs. Preston in the morning." Gabe left without waiting for a response.

He was walking across the wide hard-packed yard to the ranch house when he saw Laurie Preston standing, or rather, bending over by the pump. As she rubbed her head with a towel, her body twitched rather enticingly, and her skirts swung around her ankles. He found himself chuckling aloud at the sight, the first good laugh he'd had all year.

Laurie snapped to attention, her damp hair falling over her face and down her back. "I didn't know you were out here!" She tossed her hair back from her eyes.

"And I thought you were upstairs." There she was, once again, standing before him with the bodice of her dress plastered to her body.

Laurie shook the towel, making a cracking sound, and hung it over the pump handle, then picked up the soap and her toothbrush. "Good night, Mr. West."

Gabe watched her scurry into the house and waited to see a light in her room before going inside. He didn't want to run into her again. Minutes ticked by. No light appeared from her window. Tired of standing out in his own yard while he had a very comfortable bed inside, he gave one last glance at the second-story window before he entered the house.

With a few swift movements he lay abed, trying to think about the cattle he wanted to purchase on his next trip. But he kept thinking of Laurie Preston drying her hair in the moonlight.

He flopped over onto his stomach determined to ignore his feelings about Laurie and remember what his life was like when Ruth died. The memory of that horrifying day was enough to cool his ardor and keep him awake well into the night.

He had ridden into the yard and had been met by Sheriff Jenkins. With little preamble the sheriff had told him, "Mrs. Tuttle found your wife's body. Says she saw you leavin' when she arrived." Jenkins stared Gabe in the eye. "How was your wife when you left this mornin'?"

Gabe blanched and his mind reeled. "I didn't see her." Ruth couldn't be dead! "We'd had words. I just rode out." He started across the main room, then spun back around. "Where's my daughter?"

The next morning Laurie went down early to prepare breakfast. She started the cook fire before going out in the predawn twilight to the springhouse. The air was cool, and two fading stars were still visible. She strolled with a lively step, humming while she thought about the day ahead.

After putting the coffeepot on the stove, Laurie checked on Ammie. She was sitting up in bed, pulling the covers up into a pile around her.

Laurie pretended she didn't see the little girl. "Ammie, are you hiding?" She made a game of searching each corner of the room. Lastly she got down on her knees and peered under the bed.

Ammie pulled the blankets over her head and giggled.

Waiting until she slowly counted to ten, Laurie sat back on her heels. "I know you're here somewhere." She picked up a corner of the blanket. "Not there."

The large mound of covers moved and Laurie laughed. "Are you under there." She lifted the blankets up. "Peek-a-boo."

Ammie giggled and tried to scoot away before Laurie captured her. "You're starting the day early, I see. Well, let's get you dressed."

Each day it became a little easier to change Ammie. Laurie buttoned up the small, full-length, sacklike gown and noted that the little girl was outgrowing it. She was not much of a seamstress, but making Ammie a dress would be fun.

Soon Ammie was belted in her chair, and Laurie was adding slices of ham to the hot skillet. She set the table, taking time to tell Ammie the name of each utensil.

"Before long you'll be tall enough to set the table." Laurie smoothed the child's blond hair.

Ammie heard familiar footsteps and jerked around. "Daddy, c'mere."

Gabe ruffled Ammie's hair in passing. "Mornin', Mrs. Preston." He went over, picked up his cup, and filled it with fresh, hot coffee. After taking a sip, he glanced at the skillet. "Having company, Mrs. Preston? There's a lot of ham there." His lips quivered with only the barest hint of a smile.

Noting the rare sparkle in the depths of his pewter eyes saved Laurie from making a foolish retort. "You said you would introduce me to Old Ben. I assumed he would be joining us this morning." He should smile more often, she thought, returning his kindness before she moved the ham aside and added the eggs to the pan, as she had seen him do.

"He won't come up to the house. You can meet him after we eat." Gabe took his seat at the table. "I'll be leaving in a little while. Going up to Eugene City to see about buying some Durham stock. I'll be gone a couple weeks. Is there anything you need?"

Laurie dished out his food and set the plate in front of him. "You seem to have everything." Then she glanced at

Ammie. "I would like a couple lengths of material. Your daughter is outgrowing her present wardrobe."

"We'll go into town after I get back." He quickly mopped up his plate. "You should do fine while I'm gone."

"Are you expecting anyone to pay a call?"

"No."

"What about Mrs. West's family? Do they come to visit Ammie?" His jaw tensed, and she realized she had made a mistake by mentioning his in-laws.

"Never have." He scooted his chair back. "When you're finished, come out and meet Ben."

He stopped near Ammie's chair. "Clean your plate so you can come out too and say good-bye." He squared his shoulders and left.

Laurie contemplated having two whole weeks of peace as she finished feeding Ammie and nibbled at the food on her own plate.

"Wan see Daddy." Ammie began struggling to get out of the chair.

"Hold still, sweetie. He won't leave without saying good-bye."

Soon she was carrying Ammie across the yard to the barn. She was not about to let the child run screaming to her father. Laurie stopped in the wide doorway and waited for Mr. West to see them.

Gabe noticed her shadow before he saw Mrs. Preston standing in the early-morning sunlight. "Ben, come on over here."

Laurie watched the old man she had seen the evening before amble toward Gabe.

"Mrs. Preston, this is Ben. He'll be taking care of things while I'm gone. If you need anything, I'm sure he can help." He nodded to Ben. "Mrs. Preston. You remember Ammie."

The old man removed his hat and glanced at Ammie. "Yep, sure do." Nodding, he said, "Missus."

Gabe watched as Ben returned to work. "He doesn't say

much, but he'll help any way he can. If you need him, you'll have to call or search him out. He won't come to the house.''

"He doesn't seem very friendly."

"He's used to keeping to himself. He can't wrestle a bear anymore, but he's a good hand." Gabe finished tying down his roll on the back of his saddle and led his horse out into the yard before he faced Mrs. Preston and his daughter.

"You be a good girl and mind Mrs. . . . Orie."

Ammie puckered her brows and cocked her head.

He chuckled at her impish expression. She seemed to change a little every day. "You mind Laurie. Okay? If you're good, I'll bring you back a surprise." He leaned over, kissed her, and mussed her hair again. As he stood up he met Laurie Preston's soft gaze.

"Orie, too, Daddy," Ammie said, pointing to Laurie's mouth.

Gabe cleared his throat. He didn't want to think about kissing her, how her lips would feel on his.

Laurie felt his breath on her neck and trembled. Thank goodness he hadn't taken his daughter's innocent suggestion. She refused even to contemplate the possibility of their relationship being more than that of employer to employee.

"I don't think so." He stepped back, his gaze on Laurie, so much friendlier than Mrs. Preston—so much more dangerous, too. "See you in a couple weeks."

Laurie waved and encouraged Ammie to do the same. When he paused at the rise in the road, glanced back, and tipped his hat, she lowered her arm.

The smile lighting his eyes was for his daughter, as was only proper, and softened the usually harsh lines of his face. Laurie had been looking forward to his departure, but now she knew the log ranch house would feel much emptier without him.

Could she spend the rest of her days extracting happiness

from other people's lives? Yet there was no other choice, she realized. To have a child of her own, she would have to marry again. That meant giving up her freedom, being subject to her husband's demands.

The price was too high.

Laurie kissed Ammie's pink cheek. "We'll do some sewing while your daddy's away. You can help me find some material and make you some play clothes."

⋇5⋇

Gabe turned west on the main road, the image of Mrs. Preston's flushed face still vivid in his mind. The idea of kissing her was intriguing. How could he explain to an eighteen-month-old child that Mrs. Preston was being paid to care for her? That she was wasn't a member of the family.

Ammie would soon learn. After all, it wasn't as if he and Ruth had been affectionate, or even friendly, since Ammie's birth. He kept his mount at a steady pace. The sun felt warm on his back as he rode through Ashly Mills. He nodded to Sam Carter, the owner of the general store.

Sam's friendly greeting didn't fool Gabe. He knew the man had hoped he would stop and pass the time of day. Sam was as bad as Mrs. Merkle, who spread tales faster than the telegraph, and his store was the perfect wellhead for both. The news of Mrs. Preston's living on his ranch, in his home, had most likely become common knowledge.

She hadn't asked to go to church or to the store yet, but she would. Ruth had begged him to teach her how to drive the wagon so she could get to town at least two or three times a week. Even his ma, who had dearly loved the ranch she'd helped his father build, had looked forward to going to town and having a chance to visit with a friend or two. But Ruth's interests had been different from his ma's.

The stagecoach road wound ahead of him like a forgotten rope in a pasture. If Laurie Preston left, could he compensate for her absence with the little blond girl he called his daughter? The image of Laurie cuddling Ammie was as sharp as the pines alongside of the road. His grip tightened on the reins.

Mr. West had been gone for one week. Laurie kept busy by cleaning, playing with Ammie, and taking walks with her. She had to keep busy, keep from thinking about Gabe. Mr. West, she corrected herself as she decided to get started on Ammie's play clothes. "Where shall we start, Ammie? There must be some yard goods or old clothes stored someplace." Laurie started in the little girl's bedroom, searching through the bottom drawer of the small chest, an old trunk set in the corner of the room, and under the bed. She smiled and sat back on her heels. "There's no box under there. Want to go look upstairs with me?"

Ammie shook her head and backed away.

"There's nothing to be afraid of. You can sit by the door." The most likely place to look was the bedroom across from the kitchen, but she couldn't enter that sanctum.

She had to admit she was curious, though. Had Ruth decorated it like her room upstairs? Was Mr. West trying to keep her memory alive? After all, he had suggested that Laurie take the other room. As she took Ammie upstairs Laurie hoped Gabe West wouldn't mind her looking there for scrap material.

Laurie opened the door next to hers and went directly to the window. She pushed and strained against the barrier. At last the window gave, allowing a flow of fresh, cooler air into the dusty, stifling room. After tying the heavy drapes back, Laurie noticed that Ammie had stopped in the doorway.

The furniture in this room was unlike the rest of the house. Every piece had carved scrolls and flowers, even the dainty chair. The wardrobe, now in her room, was no different. Laurie gazed around the room and felt a shiver race down her spine. It wasn't the colors of the drapes, though dark and heavy; it was the atmosphere. This had been Ruth's room.

Taking Ammie's hand in her own, Laurie knelt down. "Come on in, sweetie, I won't take too long. After I finish, we can have dinner outside."

Ammie shuffled in and sat cross-legged on the floor just inside the doorway.

Laurie didn't want to invade the deceased woman's room or snoop through the clothes; she only wanted to find some discarded material. Deciding the top drawers of the bureau most likely held the smallclothes and items the woman used most frequently, she stooped down and tugged open the bottom drawer.

Inside were several reticules, a crumpled cotton bonnet, and a generous length of crimson velvet wrapped in tissue. With her hands still on the knobs, she slid the drawer closed. "No, red velvet is definitely not practical. Let's see what's on the bed."

Laurie found herself facing an assortment of feathers grotesquely sticking out from dresses as dark and oppressing as the room. All of the gowns were in vivid purple, magenta, or a myrtle color, and most immodestly cut with gaudy spangles.

She touched a particularly garish dress. When Mr. West hired her, he'd said his wife had died last December. That's why her clothes had been in the wardrobe as if she had just left. He was still suffering the loss.

Riffling beneath the skirts, Laurie hoped to find some plainer clothes. She felt some soft material buried deep in the pile and pulled it forward. It was a faded green skirt.

"Yes, this might do." She shook it out and held it up.

"What do you think, Ammie? Would you like a green dress?"

Ammie reached for the old skirt. She wrinkled her nose, then let her hand drop to the floor and scooted back.

"I think we'd better wash it before we start cutting." Laurie reached for Ammie's hand when she heard a wagon rumble up to the house. Looking down from the open window, she saw a thin woman climb down to the ground.

She picked up the little girl and went down to see who was calling. She opened the door and was facing a woman of medium height with a thin face, dark eyes, and a sour expression that reminded Laurie of someone who had been sucking on a pickle. "May I help you?" At that moment she noticed the wagon was leaving.

The woman looked Laurie up and down before fixing her with a piercing stare. "I am Bernice Newton, and I am here to see my sister's grave."

After two days of dawn to dusk riding, Gabe skirted Eugene City, anxious to meet with Jameson Randolph. As much as he had tried to avoid thinking about his conflicting feelings about Ammie, he knew he had to face them.

Since Mrs. Preston's arrival, seeing Ammie had become a painful reminder of Ruth's infidelity. Even now it was hard to believe the modest, thoughtful, and trusting girl he'd married had rapidly changed into a brazen, self-centered, quarrelsome stranger. He still remembered the day she moved her belongings from their bedroom.

He had returned from checking on the herd to see Ruth carrying an armload of clothes upstairs.

"Why are you back so soon? I thought you wanted to spend more time with your precious cows," she said.

"Those *cows* provide your clothes, food, and the money you spend, madam. What are you doing? We can't afford another new wardrobe for you right now."

Ruth had laughed so hard she nearly lost her balance on

the stairs. "I'm moving up to my own room—out of your pawing reach."

He should have known. From the first Ruth had avoided his sexual advances. In fact, in retrospect, they were intimate only a few times. But what was he to do? They were married, and he had taken his vows seriously, so he'd put his energy into the ranch.

Unfortunately she had not honored her pledge. She had never actually admitted that she carried another man's child—except when she'd called to the man while she was in labor. He had to concede she appeared relieved when he hadn't denied the child was his. His thoughts had come full circle, and he still had not resolved his dilemma.

Ammie was innocent, sweet, and deserved a father's love. He had taken care of her daily needs since Ruth's death, but he couldn't bring himself to love her like his own. Mrs. Preston appeared to take to the child right away. Maybe it was easier for a woman, he reasoned.

He knew how it felt to live with a child and *know* without a doubt that the child wasn't his while he proclaimed to the world that she was. When he returned home, he promised himself that he would try harder. It wasn't the little girl's fault, and he shouldn't treat her like it was.

"I'm sorry, Mrs. Newton, but as I said, Mr. West is away on business and not expected back for another week." Laurie stood in the main room with Ammie clinging to her skirts.

"That is *Miss* Newton." The woman clamped her lips together and glanced around the room. "I did not come calling. Are you the new Mrs. West?"

Laurie's mouth dropped open for a moment. "No! I'm Laurie Preston . . . Mrs. Preston. I look after Mr. West's daughter, Ammie." She attempted to move the child into view but was not successful.

Bernice looked down her nose at Laurie's skirt. "It seems the child needs a firm hand. Spare the rod and spoil the child." Her attention went to the amethyst drapes, and she frowned. "However, if you would tell me where I can find Ruth's grave, I will not bother you further."

"I am sorry, but I don't know where it is." Laurie took a step into the room. "Please, have a seat. I'm sure Mr. West would want me to extend his hospitality." She caught Ammie's arm and untangled her from the skirt. Laurie wasn't exactly sure how Mr. West felt about his sister-in-law, but she couldn't imagine him refusing her a room.

Bernice Newton adjusted her grip on the valise. Her gaze skimmed over the room. "I had not planned on staying."

"At least spend the night. You can have Mrs. West's room. Please, follow me." Laurie led the way upstairs, musing. The wagon driver had left; Bernice carried a valise, and yet she hadn't planned on staying. Laurie didn't know what to think as she opened Ruth's bedroom door and allowed Bernice to enter. "I'll pack up the clothes directly."

Bernice came to a sudden halt just inside the doorway. "You must be mistaken. This could not have been Ruth's room." She whirled around and faced Laurie. "My sister was a quiet, God-fearing woman. She could never have . . ."

"I only know what Mr. West has told me." Laurie shifted Ammie from one hip to the other. "Excuse me a moment, I'll be right back."

She took Ammie back downstairs, speaking as they went. "Miss Newton is your aunt, and I need to help her." Laurie continued on through the house to the little girl's room, picked up a shirt, and began to retrace her steps. "I want you to sit down here and practice buttoning a shirt." She showed the child how to accomplish the task and watched her a minute before going back up to Ruth's room.

Ammie sat on the floor near the gate at the foot of the stairs, her face screwed up in concentration. In one hand she held the button on the front of her shirt, while a finger of the other hand poked through the buttonhole.

Trying to hide her amusement, Laurie went back upstairs. Bernice hadn't moved an inch during her absence, though the plain bonnet covering her brown hair appeared slightly cockeyed. Laurie stepped around her. "I'll take those clothes and put fresh linens on the bed."

"Is there . . . I mean . . ." Bernice's voice faded at the sight of the low-cut, magenta dress decorated with sequins that Laurie had just lifted from the pile. She stumbled over to the chair and dropped down. She mumbled, "God's retribution," and began praying.

Working as quickly as she could, Laurie moved the mound of clothes into her own room and made the bed for Bernice. "I'll leave you to settle in now." She hurried back to check on Ammie.

Ammie picked up the button and tried to push it into the opening. After a few tries she shoved the material away from her. "No!"

An idea had come to Laurie while she shared Ammie's frustration. "Later I'll try to find some larger buttons for you to work with." Ammie's expression was not what Laurie would have called enthusiastic.

Gabe rode alongside a large fenced pasture that appeared to reach the coastal mountain range bordering the Willamette Valley west of Eugene City. He pulled up at the hitching post and recognized Jameson Randolph, the man he'd come to see.

"Good morning, Mr. Randolph. I don't know if—"

"Gabe West! I'd about given up on you." Jameson lifted a struggling little boy up out of a barrel before turning back to Gabe. "It's amazing how those young'uns can clamber all over. Well, since you're here, I guess you've made up your mind. I'll saddle a horse and show you around."

Randolph joined Gabe and led him through north pasture until they came to a fenced-off section. Beyond stood a Durham bull. The short-horned bull had straight legs and a short head and neck with a wide chest. His rich coat gleamed dark red.

"He's magnificent."

"That he is. How many head do you have?"

"Forty-five cayuse and twenty red poll. I'd like to get another hundred purebred cows next summer." One day he would have a herd many times that size, he reminded himself. It would just take time.

"Where'd you find red polls?"

Gabe laughed. He'd thought they might gain Randolph's attention. "From a young man who drove them west in hopes of starting a ranch. He'd started out with fifty. By the time I met up with him, all he'd wanted was to sell the few head that'd survived the trip."

Randolph nodded. "His dreams were grander than his experience proved to be. I've seen it before." He surveyed the pastured stock. "My present herd is so large I'm running into grazing problems."

"I wouldn't mind dealing with that problem. Have you considered grazing them east of the Cascades? I hear the bunchgrass is plentiful there."

"I've thought about it. It doesn't seem practical. At least for now."

As they rode along Gabe carefully observed the lowing cattle, their throaty sounds music to his ears.

Randolph sat back in the saddle. "How many head did you have in mind?"

"A hundred cows. Eight bulls."

"Would you be interested in buying say, three hundred head, if the price's right?" Randolph tugged at his battered hat with seeming nonchalance.

"How good a price?"

"What do you say to two thousand dollars for double that number of cows and heifers, ten bulls, and a hundred yearlings, ready to breed next summer?"

Gabe whistled softly.

"I need to cut back. Want to start planting that northernmost part of the pasture. I've been thinking this valley's too fertile just to graze cattle. Guess I'm getting too old to keep all my coins in one pocket, so to say.''

''That's about twice what I planned on spending. As much as I'd like to, I can't go any higher than sixteen hundred. For now anyway.'' And he shouldn't even spend that much right now, but how could he pass up this opportunity?

''I can let you have three tried and five untried bulls, the yearlings, and say forty cows and sixty heifers.'' Randolph halted his mount.

Gabe held out his hand. ''Done. I'd better see about finding a couple trail men.''

''That shouldn't be too hard. There're usually cowhands in town looking for work.'' Randolph led the way back to the house at an easy pace. ''We should be in time for dinner. You'll stay, of course.''

Having made the best purchase he had ever heard of, Gabe enjoyed the meal and conversation. As soon as was politely possible, he took his leave and returned to Eugene City. The most likely place to start was the saloon. No matter how thin a man's purse, he always had coin for drink.

Laurie stood facing the front door, covering her eyes while Ammie darted around looking for a place to hide. Laurie had initiated the game when the weather turned cold. ''Are you hiding, Ammie?''

''Me hide.''

When Laurie could no longer hear the little girl moving around, she uncovered her eyes. ''Here I come.'' She had peeked under a small table and behind one heavy drape when she heard high-pitched giggles.

Ammie jumped out from behind the rocking chair and squealed, ''Boo!''

Laurie spun around and smiled. ''What a good hider you are! Now it's my turn. You can find me.''

Ammie went and waited in the kitchen until Laurie called, "Ready."

The little girl first looked where she had hidden, then around the table when Bernice's distant footfalls on the stairs froze her.

Bernice eyed Ammie. "What are you doing, young lady?"

Ammie frantically looked around the room. "Orie!"

Laurie stepped out from behind the drapes. Ammie ran over and hugged Laurie's legs.

Clearing her throat, Bernice approached them. "Do you feel it useful to encourage the child's wilder instincts?"

"Children need to play, Miss Newton. It provides mental and physical exercise." Laurie picked the little girl up and swung her around. And, she thought, children need to have fun, laugh, and feel loved. "Ammie, would you help me collect the eggs?"

"Me hep, Orie," Ammie said in all seriousness and vigorously nodded her head.

Laurie hugged the small child a moment longer before she set her free. She found it hard to consider caring for such a dear little girl as work. Indeed, she felt more satisfied than she had a right to be. "Is there something I can do for you, Miss Newton?"

Bernice stiffened her back. "I have never had a servant and do not need one now." She marched toward the kitchen.

Laurie was determined not to allow Bernice to spoil the rest of the day. She had become accustomed to collecting eggs, but she enjoyed making a game of it for her charge, rather like reenacting that first time she faced the hens. She glanced back at the house on the way to the springhouse, but someone moving across the yard caught her attention.

Gabe West had been gone two weeks. Even though Laurie knew he had not returned, she prayed he would soon. Just the glimpse of trousers and boots was enough to send her heart racing. She couldn't possibly miss him, she decided, although an inner voice chided her for such a blatant lie. In moments, Laurie realized the figure was Ben ambling from the barn.

Ammie saw him and started waving as she called out, "Be-en, Be-en, Be-en. C'mere."

Laurie walked over to him. "Good morning."

Ben snatched the weathered hat from his head. "Missus." As he gave what might pass as a smile to Ammie, his leathery face broke into an expanse of lines. "Hi there, young'un."

"You've been here over two weeks, and we've hardly seen you. Are you all right?"

"Yep, jist fine."

"Would you join us for supper?"

"Thanky, missus. I got vittles in the shack. You got 'nough mouths to feed, I reckon."

"Maybe another time." He's seen Bernice, Laurie thought, and glanced down at Ammie. "Tell Ben good-bye."

"Bye, Be-en."

The cool air inside the springhouse smelled of damp earth and stored beef and pork. Laurie left the door open and used the shaft of light to guide her way. Looking at the amount of eggs that were adding up, she wondered if she could sell them in town. But first she had better make something for dinner.

It was a plain but nourishing meal, and Bernice did not complain. In fact, she said very little. Laurie put Ammie down for her nap afterward and when she returned to the kitchen, she found Bernice washing the dishes. "Thank you, Miss Newton."

Bernice did not look up. "Idle hands are the devil's delight." She snatched up the dishtowel and a plate.

Laurie didn't know quite how to respond to that so she changed the subject. "Would you like to ride into town with Ammie and me after her nap? It's a lovely day."

Bernice's hand worked vigorously on the clean plate.

"I'll bide my time here. You are expecting Mr. West soon?"

Laurie nodded. No matter what she suggested, Bernice never wanted to join in. "Yes, any day."

Laurie went in search of Ben, suddenly anxious to sell the eggs. He offered to hitch the horses to the wagon for her. By the time Ammie woke up, Laurie had bathed in the creek, laced the boned corset with displeasure, and dressed. Ammie was readied in the same orderly manner.

Bernice was just pouring a dipper of water into a glass when Laurie paused in the kitchen. "It's not too late to change your mind and go with us."

"Mrs. Preston, I told you why I am here. I do not want to be entertained and will leave as soon as I see my sister's grave." Bernice straightened the chair in front of her. "Please do not think of me as a guest. I am sure you have your hands full with that child."

"We won't be long. Let's go, sugar."

Ammie, held in place with Gabe's belt, sat next to Laurie on the bench. She was taking it upon herself to sell the eggs, but she planned on either crediting Mr. West's account or giving him the money. The ride into town did not take as long as Laurie had anticipated. She noticed a few people looking her way as she pulled up in front of the general store. She smiled but concentrated on unfastening Ammie.

Laurie entered the store and went straight to the counter. The same clerk she had spoken to before stood staring at her.

"Good day. Do you buy eggs?" She put the basket on the counter and uncovered them.

The man glanced down. "Sometimes. How many you got?"

"Nineteen. They're all good."

Ammie curled into Laurie's chest, her hands tightly clutching Laurie's shirtwaist while her face burrowed into Laurie's neck.

The man lifted the eggs out of the basket one at a time,

placing them precariously near the counter edge. "Some ain't as fresh as might be. I'll give ya fourteen cents."

Laurie rubbed Ammie's back, trying to comfort her. "Is that all? I was sure they were worth at least two cents apiece." She glanced at the shelves behind the counter. Spices, crackers, and tea filled a few boards. There was also a glass jar of candy sticks.

"Not ta me." He ambled down to the far end of the counter, where another woman stood looking at some ribbons.

Oh, she wanted to scream. It wasn't fair. If Mr. West had brought the eggs in, he would have received the higher price, she was sure. But she was a newcomer, and she wasn't used to haggling over prices.

The man sauntered back over to her. "Make up yer mind?"

"Does Mr. West have an account here?" She kissed Ammie's soft cheek, then added, "Never mind. I'll take the money."

The man's leering smirk widened as he pressed the coins into her hand.

She felt a blush heat her cheeks. "How much is the stick candy?"

"Two for a penny."

She placed a penny on the counter. "Lemon, please."

Laurie pocketed the balance of the egg money rather than bother with her reticule, took the candy, and left the store without browsing as she had planned. Before the door latched, she heard three unrestrained voices.

"She settled in fast enough."

"Well, I never . . ."

"Brazen hussy . . ."

The Durhams plodded along, grazing as they traveled east. Gabe rode point while the two men he'd hired in Eugene City took turns riding swing and drag. As they neared the summer pasture Gabe rode to the off side of the herd. Their progress was easily controlled. The cows naturally moved more slowly going up the gradually sloping terrain.

Danny Whitefeather emerged from the trees on the far side of the herd. Gabe waved and Danny rode forward to ride point on the off side. They stopped at the boundary to the pasture and watched the Durhams join Gabe's much smaller, established herd.

"What do you think?" Gabe sat back in the saddle.

Danny shook his head. He couldn't miss Gabe's idiotic grin, even in the near dark. "Take up rustling, or can't the man count."

"Randolph's cutting back. I got a hell of a buy." The tail end of the herd joined the others and Gabe followed.

"Nate's here. Arrived last week."

"Good. The two of you should be able to handle the herd. I'll send Ben back tomorrow."

Gabe was anxious to return to the ranch and see Laurie, but he felt bone weary after the last two weeks. Besides, he had to pay off Curly and Red in the morning. While Gabe bedded down under the protection of a stand of firs, Danny took the first turn at "singin' to 'em," also known as night herding.

6

Laurie added a log to the fire and warmed her hands. The clouds were clearing to the west, but it was still cold. They had settled in the main room, Ammie on a wooden footstool, Laurie in the rocking chair, and Bernice on the hearth mending a stocking.

Laurie rummaged through her sewing box for thread to match the old sleeve she decided to use for the button sampler and stacked several spools of thread on the floor for Ammie to play with. The fire crackled. Laurie glanced down at the little girl and watched her examining the spools for a moment before she threaded the needle.

She heard the sound of a horse's hooves in the mud outside but assumed it was Ben.

"Daddy!" Ammie screeched, and ran to the door.

Before Laurie could put aside her sewing, Bernice dropped her mending and followed Ammie. Laurie stared in horror as Bernice tripped over the stack of spools.

Laurie made a grab for Bernice, but she had already landed in an undignified position on the floor. "Here, take my arm."

"Orie!" Ammie tugged on the door latch, rattling the door. "See Daddy. . . ."

"Wait, Ammie. Your aunt Bernice fell down." Laurie put her arm under Bernice's. "Put your weight on me."

Bernice grudgingly obeyed. She was almost up when she winced and grasped onto Laurie. "My leg . . ." With Laurie's help she made it over to the settee. "I warned you about that child," she hissed.

Ammie ran over and tugged on Laurie's skirt. "See Daddy."

Laurie picked up Ammie and regarded Bernice. "I'd better see who's here."

"Oh, of course. Spoil the child . . ."

With her teeth clamped together to keep her silence, Laurie hurried to the door. Was it *him*? He'd been gone twenty-two days. Holding Ammie against her wildly beating heart, Laurie jerked the front door open.

"This is ridiculous," she murmured, dashing out to the porch. She stopped near the edge. It was Gabe West. Ammie called to her father. While Laurie tried in vain to quiet the child she stared unabashedly at her employer.

Gabe West moved with a subtle strength. His clothes looked like they had been worn the entire time he was away. He dismounted and waved his hat. His steady gaze seemed to penetrate her cool facade. She knew she was being foolish, but she felt a thrill of anticipation.

Gabe plopped his hat back on and automatically removed the saddlebags as he watched Laurie Preston. Her skirt swung softly around her ankles. He turned away when he couldn't resist smiling. Does absence make the heart grow fonder?

Anyway, he was glad he'd ridden in this morning instead of during the night. He wouldn't have been greeted with such an unexpectedly pleasant homecoming. Ben came out and took the reins.

Gabe sauntered to the house, appreciating the welcoming smiles. "Easy, Ammie. You'll bruise Mrs. Preston." He reached out and mussed the child's hair. "We wouldn't want that, would we?"

His gaze fixed on Laurie Preston. "Ammie looks healthy. In fact, the country air seems to agree with you, too."

"We're fine, Mr. West." Laurie hesitated, but he made no move to take his daughter.

Ammie stuck her thumb in her mouth and reached out with her free hand, trying to touch her daddy's chin.

He grinned at her and rubbed his bristly jaw. "I need to wash up and shave, don't I?"

Ammie nodded, her thumb still secure in her mouth.

Gabe stepped to the side of the door. "Let's go in. I think I have something to keep you busy while I go to the creek." He entered the main room and set his saddlebags on the floor before he realized they weren't alone.

Laurie followed his gaze. "Miss Newton is anxious to speak with you." She put Ammie down and began picking up the spools of thread. "Unfortunately she tripped over these when we started for the door."

Gabe stared at the sour-faced woman glaring at him. There was something strangely familiar about her and yet . . . "How may I help you, Miss *Newton* . . . ?" He moved forward one pace.

"Ruth's older sister, Bernice." She moved her injured ankle back under her skirt. "You have not changed, I see."

"Bernice? I'm sorry. I just spent over two weeks on the trail and still have dust in my eyes." He glanced at Laurie Preston.

Laurie went over to Bernice. "Would you like a cold compress for your ankle?"

Bernice nodded without taking her attention from Gabe. "I came to see my sister's grave. Mrs. Preston evidently doesn't take the child to visit her mother."

You took your time paying your respects, he thought. He glanced around, almost fearing who else might be lurking in the shadows. "You came by yourself?"

Bernice clasped her hands as if in prayer. "Father went to

his reward this spring. I—'' The knuckles of her clasped hands turned white. ''I was not able to come before now.''

Gabe understood. After their wedding Ruth had said her father would remove her name from the family Bible. ''If you'll excuse me, I'll wash up. I can take you to visit Ruth's grave then, if you're up to it.'' He went to his room and called Ammie.

Laurie turned her toward her father's room. ''Go on, sugar.''

Ammie peeked around at Bernice and quickly joined her father.

Gabe withdrew the present he had promised Ammie and placed it in front of her. ''I didn't forget. Go on. Open it . . . punkin.'' He'd gotten the gift as a peace offering, of sorts. He couldn't keep treating the child like a stranger.

Ammie stared at the brown paper wrapping, listening to her father's encouragement. She reached out and turned the package over.

Gabe slid his hand over, trapping the loose end of the paper, and watched Ammie's curious expression as the cloth body of the doll appeared. When she didn't move to pick it up, he did.

''It's a store-bought doll.'' He held it out to her. ''She's yours . . . to play with.'' He felt so damn awkward.

Ammie backed away from it.

''Here, it's all right.'' Gabe picked up his daughter and sat on the edge of the bed. He settled her on his lap before reaching for the doll. ''It's your baby. See.'' He held up the doll. ''Don't you want to hold her?'' He put the new toy into his daughter's hand.

Ammie pushed the doll away. ''No.''

Gabe put the doll on her lap. She shrieked and knocked it off of her legs. ''It's okay,'' he said, patting her awkwardly. But it wasn't. She was reacting to the doll the way her mother had responded to Ammie, and it angered him. This would probably confirm Bernice's feelings about him. It was much easier to deal with his herd and ranch hands than with a woman or this small, crying child.

Excusing herself from Bernice, Laurie went to the doorway of Gabe West's bedroom. "What's wrong?"

"She's frightened." Gabe bounced Ammie in an attempt to soothe her, but she continued crying.

"Come here, Ammie." Laurie held her arms out to the child.

Ammie hiccuped, slid to the floor, and ran into Laurie's embrace.

Laurie dropped to her knees and took the little girl in her arms. "What happened, Mr. West?" He appeared as agitated as his daughter and thought they both needed comforting.

He held up the doll he'd thought would bring smiles to Ammie's guileless face, now a face with her mother's pouting mouth. "I gave her this. I thought she'd like a store-bought doll." Damn, but Laurie Preston had the prettiest eyes, and they were staring at him with pity. At least she didn't pout.

"Would you please give me the doll." The poor child. Laurie hadn't even thought about little-girl toys, but she should have. She sat down on the floor Indian fashion and took Ammie onto her lap.

"Look, Ammie. Your daddy picked out this pretty dolly just for you. She has blue eyes, like yours. Doesn't she have a nice dress?" She kept rocking slowly and held the doll just within Ammie's reach.

Gabe watched his daughter peek at the toy while her whimpers slowly subsided. "I think I'll wash up now."

"Ammie will be fine. She can help me with Bernice."

After one last look, Gabe nodded and gathered a change of clothes. He'd forgotten. There were times when Laurie Preston and Ammie behaved so naturally together that he almost felt like an intruder.

After cutting Ammie's meat into small bites, Laurie noticed Gabe watching her. An unsettling warmth spread through her. "May I get you something?" She wasn't sure when he'd become Gabe in her mind, but it was all right as long as she addressed him formally. Especially now that Bernice was staying with them, she thought.

"Everything's fine. Did you have any problems while I was away?" His mother had called the kitchen the heart of the house, and it would be that now if Bernice weren't seated across from his daughter with an unpleasant expression on her plain face. He smiled at Ammie.

"None." He had calmed down and so had Ammie. Laurie glanced at the child, pleased to see her eating the meat and green beans, and then at Bernice. "Can I get you anything?"

Bernice placed her fork on the plate, dabbed her mouth with the napkin, and shook her head.

Laurie watched her finish the last bite and polish her plate with a slice of bread. The woman still ate like she hadn't seen food in a month. Laurie glanced over Gabe's shoulder at the cup holding the egg money.

"I hope you don't mind. We went into town one day." She got up to refill his coffee cup. Bernice didn't partake of coffee.

Gabe wanted to groan. He had hoped Laurie would remain safe from the town gossip. "Did you run low on supplies?"

"No. The hens were busy. I hope you don't mind my selling the extra eggs." She poured the coffee, put the pot on the stove, and scooped the coins from the cup. "I only got fourteen cents." She held out her hand. "I did spend a penny on candy."

Gabe accepted the money. Her slender fingers felt cold against his palm. "One cent, huh. Did you charge your other purchases to my account?"

Laurie resumed her seat across the table from him. "I didn't buy anything else." She handed Ammie her glass of milk. "It was a nice ride."

"Oh? Did you meet anyone?" He broke off a piece of

bread and moved it aimlessly around his plate. Maybe he should have warned her. But what could he have said that wouldn't have frightened her off?

Laurie shook her head. "Do you mind if I take Ammie into town?" She fed the child another bite and tried not to think about those damning words she had overheard. Thank goodness Bernice hadn't gone with them. Those women. They didn't understand that it was the only position available to her, or that Ammie needed her.

He watched a few wisps of her shiny hair flutter when she moved her head. "Of course not. Why would I mind?"

"When I arrived, you seemed rather suspicious of me." She shrugged her shoulders. "I thought I should ask." A fleeting look of pain crossed his rugged features. Had she inadvertently reminded him of a bitter, past experience? She hadn't meant to hurt him.

He couldn't talk to her about that now, in front of his daughter and sister-in-law, so he let the subject go. "I couldn't see hauling the supplies all the way from Eugene City. I'll go in town later and pick them up."

Bernice sat with her hands clasped on her lap. "Mr. West, would you be kind enough to take me to my sister's grave this afternoon? Afterward I will be on my way and out of yours."

"I can manage, but you're not going anywhere with that leg. You can't even walk on it." He pushed his chair back and stood. "I'll see about making some crutches for you."

Eager for an excuse to leave, he went out to the barn. As he rummaged around for suitable wood he tried to fit the image he had of Bernice, the few times he'd seen her when he was courting Ruth, with the woman in the house. She had been a retiring woman, even then.

"Are you comfortable?" Gabe managed to lift Bernice up to the wagon's bench seat. She wasn't heavy, just board stiff, as if she expected him to ravish her.

"Thank you." Bernice straightened her skirt and folded her hands on her lap.

Gabe held the horses to a walk. They didn't have far to go. When he'd had to bury his parents, he fenced off a small area beyond the barn. They were nearby but not within sight as he went about his daily chores. Those first weeks were so difficult he couldn't stand a reminder of their passing within sight. Last winter Ruth had joined his parents.

He brought the wagon to a halt within a few feet of the split-rail fence. "Do you want to get down, Bernice?"

"Yes." Her attention was focused on the carved grave marker.

Gabe went around the wagon and lowered her to the ground. "Lean on my arm. The ground's a little rocky beneath the grass." He understood her reluctance. Her father must have convinced her that he was the devil incarnate.

Bernice made her way to her sister's grave. "I would like a few minutes alone with her, Mr. West."

He nodded and walked away. At least, with her father dead, she was now free to lead her own life. He glanced back at her. She stood with her back stiff as a post, head bowed. The breeze rustled her drab gray skirt. He shook his head and wondered how long it would take her ankle to mend.

As Laurie bent to check the flour Gabe watched her slender back. "I'm sure we'll need more. Sugar, too. I didn't do much baking, but we must be running low. And unless you churned some butter, I'd better buy more."

"I've never used a churn." *All you have to do is take care of my daughter,* he had said. She didn't really include churning butter part of that agreement. "The arrowroot is nearly gone; you should probably get salt and coffee, too."

Laurie watched the list grow longer as Gabe added more items to it than she had mentioned. The pencil was dwarfed in his large, sun-browned hand. She went to see if they were out of cinnamon, anything to change the course of her unsettling thoughts.

"Is there something *you* want, Mrs. Preston?" It occurred to him that she hadn't asked for a thing for herself. That small trunk she arrived with couldn't have held much, but she was neat and clean each day. And, he thought with a desire to smile, she wore plain dresses.

"Nothing I can think of."

"I'll bring your wages back with me." He folded the list and tucked it into his trouser pocket. Before he changed his mind and invited Laurie Preston to go with him, he said, "See you later," and departed.

Gabe watched Sheriff Jenkins approach the general store. "I haven't seen you for a while. Learn anything new?"

Jenkins shook his head. "Still working on it." He tipped his hat back. "Heard you got a woman out at your place, takin' care of your young'un. That true?"

"You weren't this concerned about my daughter five months ago." Gabe felt his muscles tense.

"There's been talk. Thought you'd want to know." He cleared his throat. "Look, it ain't none of my business. Some of the ladies have said the woman—"

"Mrs. Preston," Gabe cut in.

"Yeah, well they said this Mrs. Preston hasn't been seen at church. . . ." He waited for West to respond.

Gabe glanced at the general-store window and met Mrs. Merkle's piercing stare, her nose pressed against the glass. "Mrs. Preston may attend church anytime she wishes. I'll be glad to tell her she's been missed. My sister-in-law's also at the house. I assume she's included in the invitation."

Jenkins coughed and cleared his throat. "I don't suppose you have any new ideas as to who might have wanted to do in your wife?"

"None at all." Gabe had nearly gone crazy trying to figure out who had killed Ruth and why. None of it made any sense. He had left solving the murder to the sheriff.

"Good day, West." Jenkins meandered down Stage Road.

Gabe shook his head and went into the store. Mrs. Merkle harrumphed as he passed, but he continued on to the counter. "Sam." Gabe handed the man his list of supplies.

Sam reached for the boxes of spices on the list and placed them on the counter. "You know that widow lady sold me some of your eggs?" He went over and picked up some of the other items.

"She gave me the money, though it was hardly worth her time." Gabe nodded to two women who passed by him with eyes fixed on some distant point as he wandered down the counter where the ribbons were displayed.

They were soft, sliding over his rough fingers. One caught on the edge of his fingernail. It would look pretty holding back Laurie's long, thick auburn hair. "Sam, add a length of pink and one of yellow to that order."

"Sure. Want any lace to go with that?"

"Have something on your mind, Sam?" Gabe stared at the little man and watched him squirm. "Spit it out."

"I ain't got nothin' to say." He quickly filled the order. "Comes to six-forty-five. Want it on your bill?"

"No. I'm paid up. Think I'll keep it that way."

Gabe entered the main room and paused. The last log on the grate in the fireplace burned brightly. Bernice was seated on the settee, a large open Bible on her lap. Ammie sat on the floor holding the doll he had given her. Nearby, Laurie Preston was sewing, her foot barely keeping the old rocking chair in motion. He joined them, taking his usual seat, opposite Laurie's.

"Warm enough? I could build the fire up."

Laurie glanced at Bernice, then leaned forward to feel Ammie's hands. "She's all right. I'll put her to bed in a little while." She sat back and finished attaching the last of the large buttons she had found to the piece of cloth.

Gabe stared at the flickering flames, listening to Bernice's finger slide along the edge of the paper before she turned the page. When he found himself counting the pages, he broke the silence. "Ammie," he said, pulling a ribbon from his pocket, "I got this for your hair." He handed the pink ribbon to his daughter.

Ammie grinned and reached for it. "Douwee." She started wrapping the shiny ribbon around the doll.

"Here, let me help you. I think your daddy thought it would look pretty on your hair. Let's see." Laurie smoothed the little girl's blond hair back and tied the ribbon around the tiny pigtail. "Very nice. We could make you a dress to wear with it. Would you like that?"

Ammie nodded. "Me hep."

"I'm counting on you." Laurie sat back and reached for the scissors.

Gabe watched Laurie Preston's able fingers ply the needle to the cloth. The fire hardly cast enough light for her to sew by, but her cheeks took on a pleasing glow. "Is that Ammie's? It looks too old to be worth your effort."

"It is a project for her. She's having trouble putting buttons through their holes, so I thought these large buttons might be easier for her."

Bernice looked up from her reading. "She does not need frivolous entertainment. You should read to that child from the Bible *every* night."

Gabe ground his teeth. Was that holier-than-thou tone of voice a family trait? "*That child* is your sister's daughter. Your niece, and her name is Ammie. I would appreciate your using it."

Bernice stared at Ammie. "She does not resemble you." Her attention went from father to daughter and back again.

"No. She doesn't." Gabe met Bernice's cold stare. She and her sister had more in common than he had at first realized.

"We have no blondes in our family."

Gabe raised one dark brow. "Your hair's much lighter

than Ruth's was.'' He went over and added another log to
the fire.

Bernice clapped the Bible closed. She raised herself up
and balanced on her good foot. She held the large volume
against her chest and secured the crutch Gabe had made
under her other arm. ''Good night.''

Laurie watched Bernice take one tentative step and
rushed to help her. ''I'll carry the Bible for you.'' She took
the book and held her arm out to steady the other woman.

Laurie returned to the main room a few minutes later.
Gabe watched her, adding to her discomfort. She glanced up
toward Ruth's old room. ''Are you upset because I offered
her your hospitality?''

He shook his head. ''I guess I'm just surprised she came
after so long. I wrote Ruth's family about her death but
never heard back from them. Didn't expect to.''

Laurie sat in the rocker. The peace was a balm. It's hard
to believe, she thought, that one person could radiate such
bitterness.

A pop from the burning log sounded like a rifle shot in
the quiet room. Gabe reached into his pocket again. Buying
the ribbon for her had been a stupid idea. He watched her as
he withdrew the second ribbon. ''This might go with one of
your dresses.'' His hand shook a little when he held the
yellow ribbon out to her.

Laurie looked up, amazed. She reached out hesitantly.
The silky length felt warm where he had held it. She
dropped the sewing to her lap. ''Thank you, Mr. West.''

Without thinking about her actions, she draped the ribbon
across her lap and released her long hair from its knot at the
back of her head.

Gabe watched in fascination as her hair tumbled down
her back, the rich reds and golds shimmering in the firelight.
Too soon the ribbon bound her glossy mane at the base of
her neck.

''I haven't worn my hair down in years. It feels good.''
She swung her hair around so it fell over one shoulder, and

glanced up. Gabe was watching her with an odd expression. What was she doing? Making a fool of herself, she realized. For a moment she had felt carefree and very young. Laurie glanced down at the child on the floor between them.

Ammie yawned.

"I think it's your bedtime, young lady." Laurie picked up Ammie and stepped over to Gabe. "Thank your daddy and tell him good night."

"Tank you." Ammie held the doll in her arms. "Nigh, nigh, Daddy."

"Sweet dreams, punkin." He watched as Ammie rested her head on Mrs. Preston's shoulder. This was what he had wanted, someone to mother his child and free him to work. It had never occurred to him that he might miss what he had resented.

Laurie hummed and spoke softly as she changed and dressed Ammie for the night. When she was tucked in and droopy-eyed, Laurie told her "Hey Diddle Diddle" and kissed her before turning the lamp out.

She stopped in the kitchen for a glass of water. It was too early to go to bed, and she didn't feel sleepy. This is ridiculous, she thought, forcing her feet to move. She returned to the main room and found it empty.

The fire had been built up, so Laurie took her seat nearby and plied her needle to the remaining buttonholes. She was starting on the last one when Gabe came in the front door. The needle slipped. She gritted her teeth and worked to undo the errant stitch.

Gabe went over to a small table and picked up his pipe. "Do you mind if I smoke?" He watched her, waiting for her to look over at him. He felt disappointed when she kept her attention on the button sampler.

"Not at all." Her husband had smoked foul-smelling cigars. If she could put up with them, surely a pipe would be no worse. Besides, it was his home.

Gabe filled the bowl of his father's pipe and tamped the tobacco down before striking the sulfur match to it. He exhaled a puff of hazy blue-gray smoke. The familiar ritual was relaxing. He didn't smoke often. Ruth used to order him outside, preferably to the yard, at least to the porch. He sat down across from Laurie Preston. For the first time in many months, he was at peace just staring at the fire.

Laurie breathed in the aroma of the tobacco. It smelled good, but she couldn't place the fragrance. She glanced at him through her lashes. He sat with his long legs stretched out in front of him and a serene expression on his tanned, rather rugged face. She completed three more stitches, snipped, and tied off the end of the thread.

She fastened all the buttons through their matching holes and set the sampler aside. The easy motion of the rocking chair seemed to drain the tension from her. Gabe appeared to have accepted her as part of the family. She reached up and slid her finger along a length of the yellow ribbon.

He glanced over and saw her finger the ribbon. It was as pretty on her luxurious hair as he had envisioned. His gaze focused on her hands, rougher, not as well manicured as they had been when she arrived. She had worked hard and was apparently adjusting to life on a ranch. Would she be there for the fall roundup? He realized he wanted her to be, then directed his attention to the burning log and watched as one end of it fell, sending up a shower of sparks.

Laurie started at the noise. She sat up and gathered her sewing things. "Can I get you anything before I retire?"

"Nothing for me." He reached into his pocket. "Here's your pay. I'll settle with you like the men, once a month, if that's okay with you." He placed the money on her open hand and felt her tremble.

She inhaled abruptly when she saw the amount. "Is this correct?" She had counted forty dollars. That couldn't be right.

"That's your pay through June. Are you planning on running out on me before the end of the month?"

"Oh, no! I adore Ammie, and . . . I wouldn't do that to you." She noted his grin. He was teasing, she realized, closing her fingers over the money. She tucked it into her skirt pocket. "Thank you."

"You earned it. Ammie's happy and well cared for." Better than he had hoped.

Not knowing what else to say, Laurie went out to the necessary. When she returned, she picked up her sewing items and paused on the way to the stairs. "Good night, Mr. West. Thank you, again," she said, touching the yellow ribbon.

"My pleasure." He listened to her soft steps as she climbed the stairs and entered her room. What the hell was he doing? His life was finally his own. He didn't need or want a woman to get under his skin again.

He tapped the cold pipe on the rock siding in the fireplace and set it back on its stand. He surveyed the odd assortment of whatnots Ruth had placed around the room. He refused to look at those awful purple drapes, one of Ruth's little surprises. They'd be the first to go. He had an urge to pitch all the clutter into the fireplace, but most of it wouldn't burn. One day soon, though, he would rid the room of her tender touches. Maybe he should consult Laurie about new drapes.

Gabe whistled softly on his way outside.

7

Laurie sat on her bed, staring at the money she had earned since her arrival at Gabe West's ranch. In just over five weeks she had earned almost as much as she had found hidden in Sherman's bureau drawer after his death. She felt a sense of achievement as well as a profound pleasure in her independence.

She folded an embroidered hankie around the money and placed it in one of the pillowcases for safekeeping. After changing into her nightgown, she doused the lamp and fell asleep.

The next morning she entered the kitchen and saw Gabe starting breakfast. "Good morning." Tiptoeing across the room, she peeked in on Ammie and then closed the door. "She's still asleep."

"Bernice hasn't come down." Gabe nodded at her and motioned to the stove. "Have some coffee. Breakfast'll be ready before long." He sliced thick pieces of bacon and put them in the frying pan.

Laurie poured herself a cup of coffee and blew on it before taking a sip. "Did you start the biscuits?"

He shook his head. "I was hoping you'd volunteer."

She set to work and had the soda biscuits in the oven before he was ready to add the eggs to the frying pan. "Ammie must be awake by now. She couldn't sleep with the smell of bacon cooking."

When Laurie checked this time, she was rewarded with Ammie's giggles as she ducked beneath the covers. "Now where did you go?" Laurie said, playing along with the child.

"Ammie . . . where are you?" She peered under the bed and around the room, all the while calling to the little girl.

Ammie shrieked with delight and threw the covers away from her. "Orie, me here."

"You little scamp." Laurie grabbed clean linens and a change of clothes. "Are you hungry?" She untied the little girl's linens and stared. Then she grinned. "You're dry! Good girl." She quickly glanced around. "I'll be right back," she promised.

Laurie dashed into the kitchen, skidding to a stop by the table. "Where's a chamber pot?"

Gabe stared at Laurie and started to laugh when she ran out of the room. You'd think a grown woman wouldn't be in that much of a hurry, he thought.

She fumbled with the gate at the bottom of the stairs and raced up with her skirt held high. With the empty pot from her room in hand, Laurie ran downstairs and through the kitchen to the small bedroom.

Ammie stood by the bed in a puddle, tugging at the bed covers.

Laurie set the chamber pot on the floor and knelt by the little girl. "Oh, sweetie. You tried!" She lifted Ammie out of the puddle and grabbed at the stack of dry linens.

Gabe followed Laurie into his daughter's room and quickly understood Laurie's urgency. "There should be a smaller pot in here. Need some water?"

"Thank you," Laurie replied, hoping Ammie wouldn't

be upset about her accident. She quickly bathed the little girl and dressed her.

Ammie ran into the kitchen and stopped by her chair.

Gabe turned and smiled. "Mornin', punkin." He lifted her up onto her chair and fastened the belt. "Ugh, you're getting heavy. You must like Mrs. Preston's cooking."

Laurie watched father and daughter. The trip must have been good for him, she thought. He seemed more at ease with Ammie since his return. The smile lingered on his rugged face when he broke the eggs in the frying pan. Laurie had just set the table when she heard Bernice coming downstairs.

"Good morning, Miss Newton." Laurie pulled out the chair and poured a dipperful of cold water into a glass for her. "How does your ankle feel this morning?"

Bernice sat down and settled her limb into a comfortable position. "It will be fine. Are those biscuits burning?"

Gabe opened the oven door. Laurie grabbed two handfuls of her skirt and yanked the tin baking pan onto the door. "Just golden brown."

"They're perfect, and the eggs are ready." Gabe filled the plates and set them on the table, aware of the soft rustle of Laurie's skirt as she moved around him.

She passed out the biscuits, buttered one for Ammie, and cut the child's food.

He took his seat at the same time as Laurie. "Dig in. Looks like you need a good meal." He bit off half a slice of bacon. The thought hadn't really formed before he had spoken, but once the words had been said, he knew it was true.

Laurie glanced over at him. The waist of her dress was loose, but what woman would complain about that? "We haven't missed a meal."

"We have plenty of food. There's no need for you to go without." He eyed Laurie. Women had to be hardy to survive in the country. Life wasn't easy here, not like in

Sacramento, where he felt sure she had never worked as hard as she had at his ranch.

She had no reply to his terse comment, so she spoke to Bernice. Before Gabe returned, she hardly said a word, but she couldn't be ignored. "Do you have any special plans for today?"

"Yes." Bernice dabbed the napkin on her mouth. "I want to make arrangements to return home." She returned her attention to Gabe. "I regret having to impose on you, Mr. West, but I have no other means to get to town."

"Bernice, I'll be happy to take you into town . . . just as soon as you are able to walk on both legs. Until then please make yourself comfortable." If he could put her on that stage with a clear conscience, he would.

She pressed her lips together. "I will not be beholden to you. I had a right to see Ruth's grave, but you cannot keep me here."

Gabe finished chewing and swallowed. "It's a long, uncomfortable ride back to Portland, not a Sunday drive."

Laurie watched the vein in Gabe's neck throb, a clear blue line, and shifted the conversation to his interests. "Did you accomplish what you wanted on your trip?" she asked, reaching over to help Ammie.

"More." Gabe wiped his mouth and felt the tension ease at the sound of Laurie's husky voice. "I'd hoped to buy a hundred head of Durhams. But I was able to get two hundred and forty head."

His expression became wistful, and Laurie understood how much he loved his ranch. "Your ranch must be very large."

"We'll go up to the north pasture one day. The Durhams are a sight to see."

Gabe finished his breakfast in a few quick gulps. "Ben's going back with me. I'm taking supplies up to the men today."

Laurie returned Gabe's nod as he left the table. "Would

you like to practice with your button sampler while I wash dishes?'' she asked Ammie.

Ammie followed Laurie when she went after the sampler, then sat down on the floor in the kitchen. Ammie grasped a button with her left hand and poked a finger of her right hand through one hole.

''I'll be right back, Bernice.'' Laurie went to Ammie's room and located the small chamber pot beneath several infant wrappers. Pink pansies trailed along the rim with a garden in bloom on the bowl. She placed it on the floor by the bed and returned to the kitchen.

''Miss Newton, do you have any needlework I can get for you?'' As she was putting away the frying pan Ammie sidled over and tugged on her skirt.

''Orie, hep me.'' Ammie looked down at the tangled buttons on her shirt.

''Of course I will, in just a moment. Miss Newton?''

''I do not waste my time on useless pursuits, Mrs. Preston.''

Laurie rebuttoned Ammie's top and forced a lighthearted tone to her voice. ''We'll keep busy.'' She grinned at Ammie, lifted her up in the air, and swung her around.

As her legs swung outward, Ammie giggled and wrapped her arms around Laurie's neck. ''Moe, moe, moe, Orie.''

After twirling around a couple of times, Laurie set the child down and steadied her before reaching for the old basket. ''We're going to gather eggs.''

On their way back across the yard after collecting the eggs, Laurie glanced at the barn. The doors were open, and the wagon was gone. She paused and gazed toward Ashly Mills, realizing how isolated she was at the ranch. She didn't even know where the nearest house was located.

As she crossed a hard-packed barren yard to the house, Laurie contemplated the idea of buying a used buggy. Sherman had nearly had apoplexy when she'd asked him to purchase one for her.

''Spend a hundred and thirty dollars on a new buggy!

You have two strong legs. Exercise them." She could still hear his outraged voice. Of course, he never walked anywhere. But common sense told her that even if an old buggy was not completely beyond her means, a horse, feed, and Lord only knew what else probably would be. No, it wasn't practical, not now anyway.

As he neared the herd Gabe slowed the team of horses. He paused to watch the cattle meander and graze in apparent contentment. Ben rode on to the other side of camp.

"So you finally remembered us." Danny nodded to Old Ben and started toward the back of the wagon as Gabe climbed down. "Ammie okay?"

"She's fine." Gabe hefted a large sack of flour over his shoulder. "You're unusually interested. Any reason?"

Danny carried an assortment of tools and followed Gabe, his expression bland. "You seemed anxious to get back to her." He glanced at Gabe. "What are these for?"

Gabe chose to ignore the subject of his daughter and especially Laurie Preston, whom he believed Danny was most curious about. "You need a storehouse. We can start felling the trees and stripping the logs today. Nate and Ben should be able to ride the line for a couple days."

"It's been quiet."

Danny and Gabe soon had the supplies stacked on the ground. By midday they had ridden farther up into the foothills and had cut down three trees.

"I'll take that one over there," Danny said, pointing beyond the nearby trees.

Gabe nodded and hiked in a different direction. He swung his ax, notching the tree. He worked with a smooth rhythm as his thoughts drifted to Laurie. She sure had taken good care of his daughter. The house didn't look bad either.

He had spent nearly six months at home with Ammie and knew how long and tedious the days could be. What was Laurie doing now? As he made the last two swings of the ax, the rustling branches reminded him of the soft whisper of her skirt.

He called to Danny, though the tree would not fall near him. Gabe heard the deep cracking sound and flinched as he watched it topple. The first time he had seen his father cut a tree down, he had accused him of killing it. Gabe realized he hadn't changed all that much.

Two hours later Gabe called a halt for the day. "We'd better start stripping these." They still had to get the logs back to camp.

Danny surveyed the felled trees. "Tomorrow we can cut west of here. That old stand's pretty dense."

"Good idea. It shouldn't take too many more logs."

Danny grinned. "Ah, boss, don't we get cabins?"

"Let's see how many logs we can get before you start designing your summerhouse." Gabe exchanged his ax for the handsaw. "We still have to strip the last logs."

Danny fetched another saw. "We can leave this till tomorrow—if you want to get back to the house." He peered at Gabe.

"Why wait? What are you really asking? Out with it."

Danny started cutting a branch. "Okay. How's your Mrs. Preston? You haven't mentioned her."

Gabe sank the teeth of the saw into a large branch. "Mrs. Preston appears to be doing just fine." Damn, he thought, wait till Danny sees her. If she had a face like a cow or even a beak nose, Danny wouldn't think twice about the woman.

"Ammie's taken to the woman, then. That's good. At least you can come and go without worrying." Danny spoke as he worked, once in a while glancing over to his friend and boss.

Gabe glowered. "Ruth's sister's at the house." He finished stripping one log.

"She came for a visit?"

Gabe shook his head. "Wanted to see Ruth's grave." He moved to the next log. "Unfortunately she sprained her

ankle and can't leave for a while. I don't envy Mrs.
Preston's spending her days with the woman.''

''That bad?''

'' She doesn't carry on a normal conversation, just spouts
proverbs and cold remarks.''

''How is Mrs. Preston taking the addition to your
family?''

''She seems better with Bernice than I am. But I'll have
to talk to Mrs. Preston about it.'' He cleared his mind of
everything except for the work at hand. Distractions could
be dangerous. Nonetheless Laurie Preston was a damn
pretty annoyance.

He attacked the next tree with a vengeance.

Laurie stirred the pot of stew. The kitchen was hot, but
Bernice sat at the table as composed as if it were a winter
day. ''Would you like more water, Miss Newton? I can't
seem to quench my thirst today.''

''Too much salt in the stew will do that.''

Laurie finished the glass of water and sat down at the
table. ''Miss Newton, I know you're not happy about
staying here, but I would like to call a truce.'' She shrugged.
''I don't know why you seem to resent us.''

Bernice stared at Laurie as if evaluating a piece of flimsy
merchandise. ''I have nothing against you, Mrs. Preston,
unless it is the fact that you work for *him*.''

''I needed employment. Mr. West wasn't able to work the
ranch and take care of Ammie at the same time, and he has
been most considerate.'' Laurie glanced at Ammie's door.
She was still playing in her room, thank goodness.

Bernice made a clucking sound. ''Just you beware. You
saw Ruth's room.'' She shuddered. ''Ruth was a good
Christian woman. It was *him*. He is the one who led her
astray.'' Tears began filling her eyes, and she dashed them
away with a jerky motion.

In all fairness Laurie tried to understand the other
woman's resentment, but she just could not imagine Gabe

leading anyone down the road to perdition. However, now that Bernice was talking to her, she didn't want to destroy their fragile truce.

"What pastimes do you enjoy?"

"I always tended the vegetable garden. Ruth hated getting her hands dirty." Bernice glanced at her fingers.

"That's why I haven't seen a garden here." Laurie heard Ammie and smiled at her. "Is your dolly sleeping?"

Ammie nodded, glanced at Laurie, and climbed onto her lap.

"Do you have any favorite recipes?" Laurie chuckled. "I never claimed to be a good cook. If there is something I can make or that you would like to make, I wouldn't be offended." Bernice's face actually became slightly flushed.

"I do like beef pie." Bernice avoided looking at the stove. "We could use the leftover stew."

Laurie bounced Ammie and grinned. "That sounds good, but I'm not sure my crust would be."

"Oh, I can do that—if you do not mind."

Laurie shook her head. "I'd appreciate your help."

She wasn't sure how much the child understood, but Ammie sagged against her breast. Laurie almost felt giddy with the release of tension.

Later, after Ammie's bath, she served supper. During the meal she coached Ammie on the names of the vegetables and Bernice even joined in. Before leaving the kitchen, Laurie stirred the stew and moved the pot to the back of the stove. Ammie brought out her new doll and followed Laurie into the main room.

The evening passed quickly while Ammie played with her doll, Bernice read her Bible, and Laurie attended to some mending. Before long Ammie yawned, and Laurie wondered if she should try to keep the little girl up to see her father.

Laurie glanced down after patching the second tear in one of Ammie's dresses. "I think it's about time for bed, sweetie.'' She kissed Ammie's soft brow and started for her room.

"No, Orie,'' the child said, yawning. "Me see Daddy.''

"Yes, you can see him as soon as he comes home. We'll just change your clothes now.''

Bernice looked up from her reading. "Is he always so late?''

"Mr. West said he had a lot of work to catch up on.''

A few minutes later Ammie was dressed for bed. Laurie carried the little girl into the main room and sat down in the rocking chair with her. Ammie snuggled into Laurie's lap as Laurie started a story about a little girl who lived in the city.

Laurie's voice trailed off when she felt the child's head slipping. "Oh, little one, you tried to stay awake. I just wish your daddy had returned to tuck you in,'' she whispered.

She continued the slow rhythm of the chair awhile longer. The room became cool. She should start a fire, but that would be a waste of wood, she thought, stifling a yawn.

Bernice set her Bible aside and rose. "Good night, Mrs. Preston.''

"Sleep well.''

A few minutes later there still was no sign of Gabe. "I'm sorry, sweetie,'' Laurie whispered to the sleeping child.

Laurie smoothed the soft curls away from the little girl's blond lashes and quietly left the room. After putting Ammie to bed, she paused and lowered the lamp wick before making a trip outside. On her way back to the house she heard the distant rattle of the wagon. It wouldn't do for Gabe to find her out there waiting for him, she thought, and dashed into the house.

As Gabe approached the house he kept the horses to a walk. He hadn't intended to return so late, but it had taken longer than he'd expected to strip the trees. He unharnessed and rubbed down both horses before turning them out in the small corral behind the barn. He stretched and rotated his tired shoulders. The idea of a hot bath was very appealing but impractical at such a late hour. But the hollowness in his stomach gnawed at him, and he could take care of that. He stopped at the pump and doused his head.

The house was quiet except for the muted scuffling coming from Ruth's old room. A dim light glowed from the kitchen. The aroma of warm stew drew him into the kitchen. Had Laurie intentionally left supper warming for him? He glanced at the table and saw one place setting. He smiled. He'd have to remember to thank her.

The next morning Laurie awoke to the sound of the front door closing. She jumped out of bed and rushed to the window to see if Gabe was leaving. After a few moments she stepped back.

Laurie grabbed blindly for a dress. She had little patience to do more than pull the brush through her long hair before dashing downstairs. She rushed into Ammie's room.

"Ammie . . . wake up. Your daddy's home." As Laurie spoke she lightly rubbed the little girl's back.

"Daddy?" Ammie curled into Laurie's arms.

Laurie had seen to Ammie's morning ablutions by the time she heard Gabe return to the house.

Ammie called to him in a loud clear voice.

When he entered the kitchen, Gabe heard his daughter's voice. "Shh, Ammie," he called, advancing in her direction. "Don't wake—" He stopped in the doorway a pace in front of Laurie and watched a swath of her auburn hair lightly flutter over her breast with each breath. "You're up early."

Oh, Lord, Laurie thought, staring at Gabe West. He was dressed only in work pants that defined his flat stomach, and his shirt was hanging open as if he had just shrugged into it. The only sound she heard was the thundering of her heart.

He leaned against the doorjamb. "Good mornin'."

Laurie nodded, not trusting her voice.

Ammie scrambled to the end of her bed. "Daddy!" she cried, and jumped.

Ammie flew up into the air. Gabe caught her and lowered her to the floor. "Hi, punkin."

Laurie took advantage of the distraction. "I'll start the coffee." If Gabe played with his daughter, she thought, he and Ammie would both be happier.

She went out to get the eggs, meat, and milk needed for breakfast. Gabe had a way of filling a room, she realized, and she hadn't been prepared for the intensity he was capable of exuding. The morning air calmed her nerves as she hurried barefoot over the cold ground.

She shivered and blamed it on her forgetting to put her shoes on, though in all honesty, that was only part of the reason. She couldn't help but be envious of Gabe's former wife. Surely marriage to him had been better than her own. No woman would feel indifferent to Gabe West.

Laurie entered the kitchen with her skirt drawn up with one hand, cradling the meat and eggs, while she carried a pitcher of milk with the other hand. Gabe was waiting for the coffee.

"Me hided, Daddy. Fine me."

Laurie smiled and set the milk down. "You'd better look for her. She likes to play hide-and-seek," she whispered.

Laurie seemed perfectly at home bunching her skirt up as a carrier and walking barefoot. This was more than he'd expected or wanted from her. He turned away and followed his daughter's voice.

As Laurie put the meat on the table and carefully set the eggs nearby, she heard Gabe call Ammie and the little girl's answering giggle. She stooped down and reached for a bowl and baking sheet. When she stood up, she noticed Gabe leaving Ammie's room. "The game over so soon?"

"There aren't many hiding places in there."

Ammie ran up to Laurie and pulled on her skirt. "Hide, Orie."

Laurie smiled and squatted down to Ammie's level. "I have to cook now. Why don't you play with your dolly until we eat?" She watched the little girl stick her thumb into her mouth and walk away. Didn't Gabe know how to play with his daughter?

"Here," Gabe said, reaching for the meat. "Let me help."

"Thank you." Laurie started the soda biscuits. "Ammie missed you last night."

He laid a slice of smoked ham in the frying pan. "I warned you I might be late."

Laurie finished the dough and moved to the table.

Gabe turned around and was brought up short as she stepped into him. He braced his hands on her forearms, almost circling them.

The tips of her toes were still touching his boots. She stepped back, but Gabe still held on to her arms. "I'm just clumsy this morning." She glanced at the bowl in her hand before she stared up into his dark eyes and blinked. His grip loosened, becoming a warm caress. "I'd better get the biscuits in the oven."

Gabe watched her lips—soft, pink, and oh so kissable. When he drew her forward, he felt her flinch and released her like the glowing end of a branding iron. What the hell was the matter with him? He slammed the second slice of ham on the pan and rewrapped the rest. Returning it to the springhouse would get him out of the house for a few minutes, enough time to cool off. Hell, even though Laurie gazed at him as if she might care, she shied from his touch just as Ruth had done.

When he returned a few minutes later, Laurie had placed the plates steaming with breakfast on the table. He lifted his daughter up to her chair and belted her in without saying a word.

"I'd better pour Ammie's milk. She must be thirsty. Oh, here's your coffee." She was babbling, but she couldn't seem to stop. Between his large hands holding her arms and the intense warmth in his eyes, so very close to her own, then his sudden retreat, she couldn't think.

Gabe didn't respond. He sat eating as if he were alone a the table.

Laurie had no appetite and thought the tense silence of the meal would never end. When Gabe scraped his chair back, she winced and stared up at him.

He should say "Thank you for saving the stew for me last night and for caring," but the words wouldn't come. Besides, he had to remember to keep their relationship on an employer-employee basis. If he didn't stare into Laurie's soft eyes, didn't listen for the rustle of her skirt, and didn't touch her, he decided his life would be much easier.

As he passed her chair, Ammie said, "Bye, Daddy."

Gabe lifted his hand in response but kept on walking.

Astounded by his thoughtlessness, Laurie rushed to distract the child. "Shall we go up and see if your aunt Bernice needs any help? Later maybe we'll make a cake."

8

"Of course, you'll have to taste the icing for me, too. And eat a slice after dinner."

Ammie nodded her small, blond head vigorously.

Bernice was hobbling into the kitchen when she suddenly screamed.

Laurie rushed to her side and steadied her. "What happened?"

Gritting her teeth and breathing heavily, the older woman managed only to point to her ankle.

Laurie pulled a chair over for her. "Rest here. It'll probably be cooler in the doorway with the oven going." The other woman's face was pale, but she was breathing easier.

Laurie went back to what she was doing and handed Ammie a spoon, asking her to put it on the table. Then she gathered the bowl and ingredients she needed. Under her guidance Ammie broke the eggs in the bowl and sat on top of the table, watching while Laurie added the sugar, flour, and soda. Ammie steadied the pan while Laurie poured the mix.

Bernice looked on. "Is it her birthday?" She nodded at Ammie.

"No. I think she was born in December." Laurie kissed Ammie's nose. "I'll have to ask Mr. West."

Bernice offered to check on the cake while Laurie, with Ammie's help, gathered the eggs and stored them, made their beds, and tidied up the child's room. When the cake was a perfect shade of golden brown, Bernice called Laurie. After the cake cooled, she creamed butter and sugar for the icing.

Laurie had whipped the mixture until her wrist felt it might be at the breaking point. She smiled at Ammie, dipped her finger into the icing, and held it out to the little girl. "Do you like this?"

Ammie stuck out her finger. "Moe."

Laurie showed Ammie how to scoop her finger in the icing. "After I frost the cake, would you like to have a picnic in the yard, Miss Newton?"

Bernice shifted on the chair. "I'll stay here."

"No, you won't. We'll go right out by the side of the house under the trees. It's a lovely day."

Laurie spread the icing on the cake before she asked Ammie to hand her the three leftover biscuits from breakfast and added meat slices to the basket. She set three small pieces of cake in a deep dish and carefully added it to the basket. She tried to tie a bonnet on Ammie's head and realized the child had outgrown it.

"We do need to see to your wardrobe." Laurie spoke more to herself than Ammie. "Now we're ready." She smiled at Bernice. "Would you like your bonnet?"

"No, thank you, Mrs. Preston." Bernice rose, balancing on her good foot. She looked out the window. "I'm fine."

The wistful note in Bernice's voice caught Laurie off guard. She grinned. "I'll spread an old blanket and help you out."

She placed an old blanket she'd found over the basket and left Ammie with Bernice. Today was her twenty-sixth birthday. She was finally independent, self-supporting, under no man's thumb—except her employer's. She spread the blanket in the shade of an oak tree before helping Bernice outside.

Ammie took hold of Laurie's hand. "C'mon, Orie. See."

"I will unpack the basket. She wants to play with you, Mrs. Preston. Maybe it will wear her out." Bernice shooed them away.

Ammie and Laurie picked wildflowers and played hide-and-seek around the bushes. When they came to several bees, Laurie quieted Ammie and explained that bees gather nectar to make honey and that she must never bother them. After dinner Ammie napped on the blanket while Laurie spoke quietly with Bernice.

Yes, Laurie thought, this is a wonderful way to celebrate her birthday.

Gabe crossed the yard from the barn and glanced up at the cloudy sky. He'd rather the rain would hold off a few days. He entered the house and caught a whiff of mouth-watering supper.

After plopping his hat on a peg near the door, he followed the sound of his daughter's giggling voice. Ammie sat in her chair at the kitchen table making designs in her food with her spoon.

"Hello. Supper smells good."

Bernice stared at him. "Wash up, Mr. West. Your pie is still warm."

Laurie blinked. Gabe stood in the doorway, a smile curving his sensuous mouth, his teeth looking uncommonly white against his tanned face. This man would surely remarry within the year, and she would have to look for another position. She didn't want to see him showering his affection on another woman, she realized.

"Daddy!" Ammie's shriek pierced the tense silence that reigned between the adults like cold water on a fever-racked man. She reached out and tried to lunge for him.

Gabe jumped to catch his daughter as she threatened to topple her chair. "Here, punkin," he said, steadying the chair, "you don't want to fall."

Taking advantage of this diversion, Laurie got up to serve his meal. She set it down at his place and resumed her seat. He had touched his daughter so gently with his work-roughened hands, and Laurie wondered what it would feel like to have him touch her as tenderly.

Gabe took a bite of meat and encouraged his daughter to do the same. After cleaning his plate, he sat back and looked at Laurie. "It must have been warm today."

She wiped her mouth with her napkin and reached over to do the same to Ammie's. "Yes, it was." She glanced to her left and back to Gabe. "Miss Newton made the crust for the beef pies. Isn't it delicious?"

"Mm, good." Odd, he thought, was she blushing? "You look like you've been out in the sun all day without your bonnet. Even Ammie's pink. What did you do?"

"We had a picnic." She gathered their plates. "I baked a cake this morning. Would you like a piece?"

Ammie pointed at the cake. "Me too."

Gabe glanced to where his daughter's attention was concentrated, then to Bernice. "Were you able to go with them?"

Bernice nodded.

Laurie sliced four pieces and served them, not meeting Gabe's scrutiny.

He gulped down a bite of the yellow cake. "This's good. Where did you go?"

"Just in the yard, near the oak tree. The kitchen was hot." Laurie pushed cake crumbs around on the plate with her fork. "It's my . . . I just wanted to do something different. Ammie wore her bonnet, though she has outgrown it. She was in the shade during her nap."

He scraped his chair back and stood glaring at Laurie. Bernice could have fallen, gotten hurt, had to prolong her stay. Damn, he couldn't handle that woman much longer.

Laurie drew herself to her full five feet four inches, her back ramrod straight. "We were fine. We didn't even leave the yard. Do you think I wouldn't take care with Miss Newton or your daughter?"

He leaned forward, his hands splayed on the table. "We don't want any more mishaps, do we, Mrs. Preston?" He knew he was being unreasonable, but he was mad. Damn mad. Mostly at Bernice's invasion. She was a constant reminder of Ruth, and Ruth's usually unpleasant nature.

"Does that mean I'm to get your permission before I do *anything*? Or would you rather I leave? If you're not satisfied with me, I'll—" Oh, no. She didn't want to leave, never see him again. Why were they having a stupid argument over a simple picnic? she wondered.

"Of course not! I just don't see any reason for you to take chances with Bernice's condition. Why, for God's sake?"

"Mr. West, it was perfectly harmless. I am fine," Bernice interjected.

"I just wanted to do something for my birthday," Laurie nearly shouted. Glaring at him, she belatedly heard her tone of voice and realized what she had said. She dropped down on the chair like a stone.

"Daddy, no!" Ammie screamed to be heard. "Orie nice."

Gabe glanced at his daughter and sighed. "I know," he stated gently. He looked back to Laurie. "Why didn't you tell me?" he asked softly.

Laurie shrugged. "It isn't something you announce." She stood up and started to clear the table.

Bernice interrupted. "Happy birthday, Mrs. Preston."

"Thank you," Laurie whispered.

Gabe reached for another bite of cake, his gaze still resting on Laurie. "Your birthday cake?" I wish I'd known, he thought.

Laurie nodded. The cake had lost its appeal. She started to clear the table.

He finished his dessert and began collecting the dishes.

"I'll take care of these and put Ammie down for the night."

Laurie gazed up at him, so close that she could feel his warm breath on her cheek. She stared at the sweep of his long jet lashes before she caught herself and looked away. "Why don't you play with Ammie? I'll clean up here." She put her words into action.

He reached out his hands and stopped her in midstride. "Not tonight. You haven't had a day off in . . . my God, over six weeks," he said in embarrassment. "That's my fault. Starting this Sunday, you'll have that day off each and every week. And you can go to church if you want."

He felt the tension in her shoulders where his hands rested. She seemed trusting, vulnerable. It would be so very easy to enfold her with his arms—if Bernice were not in the room. For the first time he was grateful for her presence. He dropped his hands, freeing her. "Go on. You deserve a rest."

Nonplussed, Laurie glanced over at Ammie, who sat watching them, confusion evident in her blue eyes. "Well . . . if you don't need me . . ." She turned and left the kitchen—and the house.

Bernice scraped her chair back. "I can wash up the dishes."

"It feels like rain. Don't go too far," Gabe called out as he watched Laurie leave before he turned to Bernice.

Laurie wandered in the direction of the creek, feeling strangely adrift. What had Gabe been so angry about? Was he afraid Bernice wouldn't leave? Then he admitted she should have time off. She hadn't even noticed or complained about that.

As quickly as his anger had flared, it had died. She didn't know what to make of him. Then she smiled, thinking about Gabe volunteering to spend time with his daughter. He seemed to have been avoiding her for the past several weeks.

Remember, Laurie told herself, you're only the hired

help. Ammie and Gabe were a family. If she kept her perspective and her distance from it, it might be easier when the time came to find a new position.

Gabe returned home early. He hadn't seen Laurie since her walk the previous evening, although he'd been sorely tempted to check on her that morning. He hadn't, but only after convincing himself that Laurie was a healthy and usually happy woman, unlike Ruth. If he'd checked on Ruth that last morning, would he have been able to save her? He'd never know.

He unharnessed the two horses and put them in the corral. As he entered the house he heard Laurie talking to his daughter in the kitchen.

"We'll have to see if we can get some lemons."

Gabe went in for a dipper of water. "Lemonade sounds good. I think Ed Larkin has some lemon trees." He gulped down some water. "I'll ride over and see if they have a few to spare."

Ammie ran over to Gabe and tugged on his trousers. "Me go, Daddy."

Gabe tousled his daughter's hair. "Sure. How about Laurie?"

"Orie, too."

Laurie took the empty glass from Ammie. "It would be nice to have a few lemons." She glanced over at Gabe. His sweat-stained shirt defined his muscular chest and forearms, and his coal-black hair lay plastered to his head where his hat had rested. She took a deep, calming breath before she spoke.

"Ammie's outgrowing her clothes. Even her bonnet is too small. Did your wife have any yard goods put away for her?"

"I doubt it. I'll take you by the general store before we see Ed. We can leave soon as I hitch up the team."

"I'll see if Bernice wants to join us." Laurie wiped

Ammie's face, straightened her dress, and picked her up, saying, "We haven't much time," as she dashed upstairs.

As Gabe brought the wagon to a stop by the hitching post, she was walking out of the house with Ammie at her side.

"Is Bernice coming?"

Laurie shook her head. "She said she was tired."

Gabe's hands encircled Laurie's waist and lingered there a moment before he recalled his decision not to touch her. Her faint citrus scent drifted his way. He handed her up to the wagon seat, grateful for that common courtesy he couldn't possibly ignore. After passing his daughter to Laurie, he took his place beside her on the bench.

With Ammie settled on her lap, Laurie steadied the child and let her thoughts drift back to her heated discussion with Gabe on her birthday. Tomorrow would be her first Sunday off, but there was nowhere to go close by, except for Sunday services. Had he mentioned or suggested she go to church? Whichever, he hadn't invited her to attend with him. She glanced at Gabe's easy posture against the backdrop of full, deep green pines.

"Mr. West, why did you bring up the subject of my going to church the other day? Do you feel I've been remiss?"

He studied Laurie from beneath his wide-brimmed hat. She held on to his daughter like a barrier, and her normally light peach complexion was pink. "I heard some of the ladies had expected to meet you at church." He returned his attention to the dirt roadway. "I just didn't want you to think you couldn't go if you had a mind to." He found himself hoping she wouldn't go, wouldn't put herself up to ridicule, wouldn't be embarrassed by rude comments he feared might be directed at her.

"I don't know how I'd get there. I haven't ridden horseback in years." Laurie noticed a rider approaching. "Do you know how much a used buggy would cost?"

His brows arched. "You want to buy a rig?"

"I've thought about it."

"You could probably find an old one for forty to fifty

dollars. But if you're worried about getting to church, I'll drive you, or you can take the wagon. I had the impression you were saving your wages.''

Laurie ran a finger around inside her shirtwaist collar. ''I am, but I thought if I could afford it, it might be practical to have my own transportation.''

Gabe snapped the reins, impatient to reach town. ''The wagon was good enough for my mother and . . . Ruth. And you'll just have to make do with it.''

Ammie pointed up to a tree. ''Birdy.''

''That's right, sugar. See if you can find another one.'' Laurie knew that buying a buggy was a foolish idea, given her finances. However, the more she thought about her need for transportation and Gabe's disapproving attitude, the more she wanted it. Later she would consider the minor inconveniences, like the expense of a horse.

''I'll accept your offer of a ride. Thank you. Bernice will probably want to go with me.'' It may even cheer her up, Laurie realized.

Gabe pulled up near the general store. He lifted Ammie down and held out his hand for Laurie. ''I'll walk you in.''

Taking Ammie's small hand in her own, Laurie entered the store. A quick glance confirmed that the clerk and four customers had noted their entrance. Laurie smiled and went directly to the table displaying the yard goods.

Gabe closed the door and watched the curious expressions following Laurie's movements. The click of her heels on the bare wooden floor was the only sound in the store. When the inquisitive onlookers turned their attention to him, he nodded and wandered over to the corner where the tools were stacked. He picked up an ax and held it with one hand, checking the balance. As he ran his thumb along the edge of the blade, he glanced over at Laurie.

She slipped her hand between the bolts of yard goods and lifted out a yellow calico. She held it up to Ammie.

Ammie looked at the cloth. ''Douwee, too.''

''Yes, of course we'll make one for your doll.'' Laurie set

aside the calico and added light blue chambray before deciding on a small rosebud print. "This should do. Come with me, Ammie."

Gabe met Laurie at the counter. "Will that be enough? What about nightgowns and . . ." He cleared his throat and stared at the material. "I guess all her clothes need to be replaced, don't they? I mean, she must be growing out of everything."

Laurie covered her smile. "If you'll watch Ammie, I'll pick out something suitable." She looked through the bolts until she found a pale pink, soft cotton and another of plain white.

Gabe nodded. He signaled Sam and felt the tension build. If the little bastard said just one uncalled-for word, he decided, he'd knock his teeth down to his stomach.

Sam acknowledged Gabe and addressed Mrs. Preston when she set down two more bolts of cloth. "Ma'am."

"A child's dress length of these, please." She indicated the dress fabrics. "And twice that of these two bolts."

Gabe laid his hand on top of the material. "Double that amount of each, Sam. I wouldn't want Mrs. Preston to run short."

Laurie looked up at Gabe and noticed a rare light sparkling in his pewter eyes. "Thank you, Mr. West."

Gabe frowned at the bolts. "Will there be enough for a bonnet?"

"More than enough. Blue for everyday, I think. And a matching bonnet for the rosebud dress." Odd, Laurie thought. He'd never shown this much interest in Ammie's clothes before. She glanced around as if looking for some item she had forgotten. The other customers were still staring at her, just as she had feared.

"Never mind them, Mrs. Preston," Gabe said softly. "Add three lengths of ribbon to match those red flowers, Sam. And some sharp needles."

"I'll need buttons and thread also." As Laurie chose the

buttons she wondered if her limited sewing abilities were up to the pretty dresses she would like to see Ammie wearing.

Ammie tugged on Laurie's skirt. "Orie, candy? Pease . . ."

Laurie straightened Ammie's bonnet ties and smiled. "Maybe next time. I think we've purchased quite enough today."

Gabe settled with Sam and had him add four pieces of cherry candy to their package. "Shall we go, Mrs. Preston?"

"Certainly, Mr. West." He seemed to be playing out some sort of act for the benefit of their observers, Laurie realized, and didn't mind doing her part. She had expected that Gabe would receive a warmer reception from his neighbors, but apparently their aloof attitude toward her now included him. She hoped attending church might help.

Once Laurie and Ammie were settled, Gabe headed the team back toward the ranch. "You still want the lemons?" He wondered what Laurie was thinking. He surely couldn't tell by her easy manner with Ammie. She was acting as if nothing unusual had happened at the store.

"If you don't mind."

Gabe turned the horses onto a side road and brought the wagon to a stop in front of a weathered, single-story wood-frame house. "I'll see if I can find Ed."

Laurie glanced at the house. In that moment she noticed the curtains move and felt sure someone was watching. Finally she heard Gabe talking to another man as they approached the wagon.

"Mrs. Preston, this is Ed Larkin."

Ed snatched the hat from his head. "Ma'am. I got a bushel of lemons in the barn and a couple more on the trees. You pick out as many as you want."

Laurie smiled at the wiry man with a sheepish expression. "That's very generous, Mr. Larkin." She followed him to the barn and avoided looking at the house. Mrs. Larkin must be as curious about her as the other residents of Ashly Mills.

Gabe took the burlap bag from the back of the wagon and caught up with Laurie inside the barn. He watched her pick out a handful of lemons. "You can put them in here."

"Fill the bag, ma'am. We got plenty." Ed smiled down at Ammie and spoke to Gabe. "We also got a passel of kittens." He motioned to the other side of the wide barn door. "Let her play with them awhile." He led the way, calling to the young cats.

Gabe took Ammie's hand. "You want to see some kitties?"

Laurie glanced around to Ammie. "Go on, sugar."

Ammie smiled at her daddy and went over to where several kittens were batting at bits of straw. She sat down on the hay strewn dirt and reached for a gray kitten with orange markings.

Gabe scratched the kitten's neck, then stroked its back with one finger. "Pet it like this, Ammie. It's just a baby."

Ed cornered a couple more kittens and set them near the little girl. "It's gittin' so when I milk the cow, it's hard to hit the pail for all the open mouths. Their mama's a good mouser, too."

"You've got quite a brood," Gabe agreed.

"Yep, too many. Your little girl 'pears to like that one. Why don't you let her take a couple home? By fall you'll not have a mouse in your barn." Ed stooped down and swished a piece of straw for one of the kittens to swipe at. "What do you think, Ammie? You want a little cat?"

When the bag was half-full with lemons, more than enough for their needs, Laurie decided, she walked over to where Ammie sat playing with the kittens.

Ammie looked up, grinning. "Pease, Daddy . . . Orie?"

Laurie scooped up a black kitten with a white chest and paws. She rubbed its neck and glanced up at Gabe. "She doesn't have any other children to play with, and she could learn to care for it."

Laurie, Gabe reluctantly admitted, had a point. Ammie didn't have anyone besides Laurie. And if she didn't mind, why should he? After all, it would stay in the barn. "Pick the one you want, punkin."

Ammie lifted the wriggling orange-and-gray kitten up with two hands and looked at Laurie.

"It is pretty. And look at its gold eyes." Laurie took the kitten before it scratched Ammie. "I guess it's this one, Mr. Larkin."

"Good choice. That one's a bit tamer than the others."

Gabe picked up the burlap bag on his way out of the barn. "Thanks, Ed. What do I owe you?"

Ed scratched his jaw. "Should be free considerin' you're takin' a cat. But my missus'd have a fit. Two bits and we'll call it even."

Gabe handed Ed twenty-five cents. "Thanks. Give Mrs. Larkin my best."

After setting Ammie in the back of the wagon and handing her the kitten, Laurie climbed up to the bench seat while Gabe paid for the lemons. What a day, she reflected. Gabe was not only generous with the purchases, he had also allowed Ammie to keep the kitten. It was a special day, indeed.

As they rode back to the ranch Laurie sat sideways to keep watch over Ammie. It also gave her the opportunity to observe Gabe. He sat back with a boot on the footboard, a serene expression on his rugged face. This man was becoming very dear to her. He treated her like a person, not a servant. Oh, Lord, she was doing it again, letting her imagination run wild.

Ammie screeched, "Orie!"

Laurie glanced over the seat to Ammie. "Oops!" As the kitten prepared to jump to the edge of the wagon, Laurie scrambled over the seat and grabbed it. "No you don't." She crawled over and sat down by Ammie. "I'll hold your kitten until we get home."

Gabe slowed the team and made sure everyone was safe before continuing. "You're sure you won't mind having that cat around?"

"Not at all. I had one when I was little." Laurie nuzzled the kitten. "Did you have a favorite pet when you were a boy?"

"A dog."

Laurie watched Gabe. "What kind?"

He chuckled. "A purebred American mutt, just like the family, my father used to say." He pulled up in front of the house to let off Ammie and Laurie before going on to the barn.

Laurie carried the kitten into the house and set it down in the kitchen. "Just watch the kitty. We can't hold it all of the time."

Ammie eagerly followed the kitten on her hands and knees as it explored the kitchen. After a few minutes she picked it up and stared at its twitching whiskers in total fascination. "Me kitty, Orie?"

Laurie set her reticule on the table and knelt by the little girl. "Yes, sugar, it's your kitty. Say, *my* kitty."

"My kitty."

"Good girl!" Laurie freed the kitten from Ammie's firm hold so it could resume its exploration. "You can help me make a bed for the kitty here in the kitchen."

❦9❧

Laurie found some rags, folded them, and made a bed for the cat by the stove. "We should pick a name for your kitty." The ball of fur darted under her skirt. Laurie scooped up the kitten and set it on the bed.

"What is all the . . ."—Bernice stopped in the doorway—"about?"

Ammie peeked from beneath the table.

Laurie smiled. "Mr. West allowed Ammie to bring a kitten home."

"Surely it will not live *in the house*?"

Laurie spoke to Ammie. "The kitty can play outside while we get the milk." She caught the cat and handed it to the little girl. "Be gentle. It's just a baby." Ammie held the kitten as carefully as an egg. "For now, Miss Newton."

Laurie opened the front door and followed Ammie out onto the porch. "Put her down here, sugar. She needs to run around for a while."

When they returned to the house with the milk, Ammie wanted to stay in the yard and play with the cat. Knowing

103

she couldn't leave the little girl outside on her own, Laurie let her bring the cat back in the house.

She was just about ready to serve supper when she heard Gabe close the front door. "Here, sugar, wash your hands."

Laurie heard Ammie's piercing scream and rushed over to her as Gabe ran into the kitchen. Laurie picked up Ammie and let the cornered kitten escape.

"What's that cat doing in here?"

After kissing the scratch on Ammie's hand, Laurie rubbed her back. Ignoring Bernice's I-told-you-so expression, she answered: "Ammie wanted to play with it, and I couldn't leave her outside by herself." She set a calmer Ammie down on the floor. "Just sit and watch your kitty. Don't pick it up, sugar."

"That cat's staying in the barn, not the kitchen. It's going now." Gabe reached for the cringing cat, but it scampered out of the room.

Laurie quickly turned her back to him. The sight of a tiny kitten eluding a large man *was* funny. "The cat's too young to stay out there by itself."

Bernice chimed in with, "Animals are not clean. They should not live in a house."

"Three months is half-grown and plenty old enough to start earning its keep. It can scare the mice off until it learns to eat them."

Gabe's voice made Ammie frown, though she didn't understand the words. "No, Daddy! *My* kitty." She ran after the cat.

Gabe stared after his little daughter in openmouthed astonishment. "What was that? She's *never* acted like that before! Aren't you teaching her any manners?"

Laurie pressed her lips together and composed herself. She couldn't remember ever seeing him so incensed, so shocked that his eyes became dark pools.

"That, I think, was a very young lady voicing her opinion." When Gabe continued staring, she added, "She didn't understand what you were saying, only that you were angry. Haven't you noticed how very attuned she is to your moods?'' He hasn't, she realized.

"Mad or not, I won't put up with a screeching, belligerent child. Do you hear me? I'm paying you to take proper care of her. That includes teaching her *good* manners. You can start this minute." He grabbed the back of his chair, jerked it out, and dropped down onto it. "She can eat after your talk."

Laurie marched out of the kitchen but slowed her pace as she approached the little girl. She wasn't about to extinguish Ammie's first spark of strength. She stooped down and took the child's hand. "It isn't nice to scream at your daddy, Ammie."

"Me mad at Daddy."

"Oh, Ammie, don't be mad. He still thinks of you as a speechless babe." She said the latter more to herself than the child.

As Laurie smoothed back Ammie's blond curls the child started squirming. "Do you have to go potty?" When Ammie nodded, Laurie took her hand and started for the door. She didn't have to change many wet linens any longer and was very pleased with the little girl's progress.

The trip outside would also give Gabe more time to calm down, Laurie hoped. Oddly enough his anger hadn't frightened her. She had found the whole scene rather amusing. The sight of one very small girl standing up to a man well over six feet tall, with his eyes flashing silver sparks, was funny.

Laurie led Ammie back into the kitchen and fastened her in her chair. Gabe didn't acknowledge their presence, so Laurie served Ammie. Bending close to the child's ear, she whispered, "Say, 'I am sorry Daddy,'" and motioned for her to speak.

Ammie waited until he looked up from his plate. "I sorry, Daddy." She quickly filled her mouth with a bite of bread.

Laurie smiled at Ammie and glanced at Gabe. He nodded and Laurie thought he appeared a little less edgy.

"Apology accepted, Ammie." Her quizzical expression did what her words hadn't, and he smiled. "It's okay. I'm not mad anymore."

Laurie sighed. "Good. That's over with. I think we still have some cake left over."

"You are spoiling that child, and you will rue the day."

Gabe didn't respond to Bernice. He was tired of arguing. He waited until Ammie had been tucked in for the night before bringing up the subject. "Did you put the cat out in the barn?"

Laurie glanced up from the drawing she was making of a dress for Ammie. Bernice was also watching her. "I think she's in the kitchen."

"I told you it stays in the barn. Ed said it would be a good mouser. It grew up in a barn. So it stays where it can hunt."

"I thought she—the kitten is a girl, I believe—was supposed to be a pet, a companion for Ammie." Laurie watched the light and shadows play over Gabe's obstinately firm jaw and shiny black hair. He's capable of being as nice as he can be considerate, she thought. Unfortunately at the moment he was neither, and she didn't understand why.

"Ammie can play with it in the yard." He knitted his brows and glared at her. "You'd better get it out of the house before it messes."

"Cats are very clean." Laurie stood up and took a few steps. "I'll take care of her." *Especially since you keep your door closed at night,* she mused on her way to the kitchen.

Sunday morning began earlier than usual for Laurie. She woke as it was just getting light outside. Slipping into her wrapper, she dashed downstairs and took the sleepy kitten out on her way to the necessary. She stopped by the springhouse for the milk, and the kitten followed her back into the house.

Laurie poured a little milk in a small bowl and set it on the floor. "Good girl. I'm glad you're a smart little cat."

She scratched its silky back and started for her room when she saw Gabe watching her.

"Good morning. I was just going up to dress." She snatched her lapels together with one hand and smoothed back her loose hair with the other.

Taking in Laurie's delightful state of undress, he forced himself to remain annoyed. "What's that doing in here?"

"She followed me into the house." Laurie glanced at Ammie's door. "If you'll excuse me . . . I don't want to be late for the service."

"You've plenty of time. It isn't even six yet." He picked up the bucket. "I'll get the water and start the coffee." When she didn't make a move, he added, "It *is* your day off, isn't it?"

He felt something brush his leg and glanced down. The cat was walking figure eights around his feet, rubbing against his ankles every few steps. He glared down at the animal, who didn't appear affected, then at Laurie.

She silently admired the way the cat held its tail straight up in the air as if it owned the house and dared Gabe to remove it. Laurie returned to her room and dressed with care. Although she had already met many of the townspeople, she wanted to look her best for the church service.

Gabe started the coffee, milked the cow, and left the cat in the barn cleaning its whiskers. He had breakfast ready by the time Ammie woke up. He felt as if nothing had changed in the last six weeks, until she told him she had to pee, and he had to deal with that situation. He had her belted in her chair when Bernice and Laurie entered the kitchen.

"Orie, want my kitty." Ammie strained the belt, trying to get out of the chair.

Bernice paused near Laurie's chair and glanced at her with one brow raised before moving to her own seat.

"Not now, sugar." Laurie moved the cup of milk within the child's reach. "Your daddy's made breakfast. You can play with the kitty later." She took her seat across from Gabe and stirred Ammie's oatmeal mush.

Gabe was relieved when the meal was finally over. He quickly harnessed the horses and brought the wagon to the front of the house. Soon everyone was seated, and he started for the church. Bernice sat like a pillar between him and Laurie, who sat stiffly with Ammie wiggling on her lap. Maybe he should have dressed, he thought, and accompanied her to the service. But as he stopped the wagon he knew his appearance wouldn't ease the way for her.

Laurie climbed down from the wagon and stepped aside so Gabe could help Bernice down. After Laurie straightened the fawn poplin skirt of her traveling dress, she smiled at Ammie. "Be a good girl. I'll see you soon, sugar."

Gabe watched Laurie, wondering what she had anchored her little bonnet down with. The feather waved about, but that scrap of material stayed secure. She looked as prim and proper as the day she arrived, and he silently wished her the best of luck.

"We'll be waiting here for you."

"Surely you don't mean to sit here during the service. Ammie—"

Gabe interrupted her. "Not the whole time. We'll be back." He noticed several people looking their way. "You'd better go."

Laurie nodded and glanced around. People were openly staring in their direction, and probably regarding her like they would a strange animal in a cage. She was the outsider, she knew, and must be a curiosity in Ashly Mills, where she guessed no more than fifty men, women, and children lived.

Laurie tried to assure herself that she was doing the right thing, told herself that she had nothing to fear from Gabe's friends and neighbors, and held out her arm to Bernice. They approached the small whitewashed, clapboard church. Laurie smiled and nodded to the men and women gathered there. A gaunt man of medium height with sandy-colored hair stood by the open single door and greeted the only two couples who entered ahead of Laurie.

"Good morning, ladies. I'm Preacher Inworth. Welcome

to our humble church, Miss . . . ?'' He extended his hand to Bernice.

"Newton.'' Bernice gave his hand a hearty shake.

Laurie accepted his limp hand and released it. "Mrs. Preston."

He squared his shoulders and looked around. "Well, Miss Newton, Mrs. Preston,'' he said formally. "I'm happy you were able to attend on this glorious morning."

Laurie nodded and followed Bernice midway up the aisle and over to the far end of the unadorned pew. Laurie sat with her feet together, her back erect, and her hands folded over her reticule on her lap. She acknowledged several people with a smile and nod when they glanced her way, but no one returned her gesture. It seemed their preferred seats were a few rows ahead of hers.

Bernice propped her crutch at her left, leaned over to Laurie, and whispered, "These people act as if they do not know you."

"They don't, not really," Laurie answered in a soft voice.

One woman, with quivering jowls and hawk-like eyes, paused at the far end of Laurie's pew and blatantly glared at her a long moment before sneering. "Two peas in a pod—that's what it is," she said, and stomped off to the first row with a wiry man at her heels.

Laurie was dumbfounded and more humiliated than she thought possible. She tried to ignore the people watching her, but it was impossible for her not to overhear their whispers.

"What is *she* doing here?"

"She certainly has a nerve!"

"She's not fooling anybody with her holier-than-thou attitude."

Bowing her head, for the first time in over a year, Laurie prayed for the strength to understand the narrow-mindedness of people. Years earlier the hypocrisy of several pious acquaintances had made her sick, though it hadn't been directed at her. Now it was. At the jarring sound of the front door snapping closed, she raised her chin and stared straight ahead.

"Are you all right, Mrs. Preston?" Bernice glanced around, then watched Laurie.

Laurie nodded. She didn't trust her voice.

Preacher Inworth did not waste time getting to the sermon. As soon as he stood with his hands braced on the pulpit, he began. "Fornication is a sin against God! And the devil's ever vigilant in his search for fornicators. The wages of sin are eternal damnation, sayeth the Lord!"

Laurie returned Preacher Inworth's grim stare. If this was the man's usual subject, no wonder Gabe hadn't offered to accompany them. The preacher scolded, raged, and threatened to bring down the wrath of God with his raised, twitching frail fists. To Laurie's dismay the congregation appeared to hang on every vile word of his inflammatory discourse. With stubborn determination she refused to allow her unshed tears to spill onto her cheeks.

The assemblage began to stir. Laurie wanted to escape outside to the fresh air, but knew Bernice couldn't walk fast enough. For once she was grateful for Bernice's silence. They were the last ones out of the church. Laurie was tugging at her gloves, trying to overcome her distress when she heard Gabe.

"Bernice, Mrs. Preston, over here." Good God, he thought without reverence, what have they done to her? Laurie's usual peach coloring had faded to ash gray, and he could see the agitated way she was jerking her gloves tighter. She'll pull her fingers through the tips if she doesn't stop. Even Bernice looked uncomfortable.

Ammie waved and bounced up and down on the bench seat. "Orie! C'mere."

"Coming."

Laurie quickly helped Bernice over to the wagon. She waited for Gabe to hand Bernice up and climbed up to her seat before he could help her.

Gabe snapped the reins and guided the team toward home with only a passing glare at Inworth. "What happened in there? You both look like sacrificial lambs." He glanced at Laurie again. He knew he shouldn't have let her go. But he had, and he'd have to think of some way to make it up to her.

She gave him what she hoped would pass for a smile. "Does Mr. Inworth usually preach fire and brimstone?"

He studied her pitiful imitation of her normally pleasant expression and longed to comfort her. But he had never been very good at that sort of thing. "I wouldn't know. He's been preaching here for a year now. I quit going long ago."

His gaze was so intense, Laurie felt as if he had reached out and embraced her. This time his close scrutiny warmed and comforted her. In spite of the contentment, his attention also served as a reminder. She had failed in her endeavor to create a rapport with his neighbors. In fact, she feared she had only done much more damage to Gabe West's good name.

Bernice stared ahead. "He was zealous. Reminded me of . . . Father." She pressed her fingers over her quivering lips.

That afternoon while Ammie napped and Laurie was outside, Gabe was stopped in the main room by Bernice. "Can I get you anything?"

"I would like to talk." Bernice closed the large Bible on her lap and folded her hands on top of it. When Gabe sat down, she did not mince words. "What is going on here?"

"*Going on?* What exactly do you want to know, Bernice?"

"The whole congregation treated Mrs. Preston like a pariah. She seems like a Christian woman. Have you compromised her like you did Ruth?"

Her self-righteous expression hit a nerve. "Mrs. Preston *is* a good, kind woman, and she adores Ammie. As to my conduct, do you honestly believe that I ravish anyone wearing a skirt?'' The flush of scarlet on her pale cheeks was a partial reward.

''I did not . . .'' She watched her hands as if they were someone else's. ''Tell me what happened to Ruth. Mama said she died in childbirth.''

It was his turn to be surprised. ''No . . . Ruth was found dead one morning. The doctor said it looked like poison.'' He shook his head and rose. It was easier to talk about Ruth while he paced. ''I just don't know. She'd changed, Bernice. Ruth wasn't the same.''

''Mrs. Preston said I could use Ruth's room. Was it really hers?''

He nodded without missing a step.

Bernice shuddered. ''Those were her clothes on the bed?''

Again he nodded.

Bernice covered her eyes and sobbed. A few minutes later she regained her composure. ''Is there more?''

He stopped and stared at the cold hearth. ''There's been a rumor about my having killed your sister.'' He turned and met her gaze. ''I didn't do it, Bernice. No matter our differences, I never could have harmed her.''

She stared at him. ''No . . . I . . . don't believe you did.''

The next day was July 4, a day of celebration, and Gabe was determined to bring a smile to Laurie's downcast expression. He awoke early and greeted her with a cup of steaming coffee.

''Mornin'.'' As he pressed the warm cup into her hand and felt the touch of her cool fingers, he was relieved to see a flush darken her cheeks. Her long auburn hair fell over her shoulders and down her back; somehow it lent an intimacy to their encounter.

''Hello.'' Laurie took a sip of the hot brew. There was something different about him this morning, she realized, a most intriguing sparkle in his eyes. She set her cup down. "I'd better check on Ammie."

"Let her sleep awhile longer. She'll come out when she wakes." He refilled his cup and sat down at the table, motioning her to join him. "I thought we'd ride over to Jacksonville today for the Fourth of July festivities. Would you like that?"

His question was voiced in an even deeper timbre than his usual baritone, with an added richness that sent a warm tingly feeling down Laurie's spine. But she knew she dared not pursue that frivolous notion. "Ammie would enjoy that."

He watched her intently. "But what about *you*?" She avoided his gaze, and he wondered why the hell he felt determined to have her look at him as if she cared about him.

"Me?"

"Wouldn't you like to see Jacksonville?"

She met his gaze. "I confess I would. Is it far?"

"A couple hours' ride. We can fill a basket or two and leave after breakfast." He stood. "I'd better start cooking." He set the frying pan on the stove. "Don't forget to bring some extra blankets. Ammie can bed down in back of the wagon on the way home."

"Of course. I'd better wake Bernice. You did mean to include her, didn't you?"

"Yes, of course."

Gabe insisted on making breakfast, so Laurie went up to Bernice's room. After knocking twice, she unlatched the door. "Good morning, Miss Newton."

"Is something wrong, Mrs. Preston?"

"Oh, no. Mr. West offered to take us to Jacksonville for the Fourth of July celebration. You will come with us, won't you?" Laurie stood in the hall, hoping Bernice would agree to join them.

Bernice limped over to the door and opened it. "I don't

think my presence would add to your festivities. I will be fine here.''

She started closing the door, but Laurie put her hand out and stopped her. ''If you're worried about slowing us down, don't. Ammie can't walk very fast, and it would be nice to get to town, hear people laughing, see them smiling. Please reconsider.''

Bernice nodded. ''If you are sure Mr. West will not mind . . .'' She watched Laurie.

''Wonderful. Would you like me to help you with anything? Mr. West is making breakfast, and we're going to pack a couple baskets for dinner.'' Bernice looked relieved and possibly a little excited.

''I will be down directly. Thank you, Mrs. Preston.''

Laurie smiled. ''Won't you call me Laurie?''

''And I am Bernice.'' She, too, smiled.

''Call if you need me.''

Laurie dashed downstairs. She really had to hurry. She located two baskets and began packing them. The air seemed alive with anticipation as she bustled around, gathering what they would need for the outing. When she finally made a trip outside, the kitten followed her into the house, demanding her morning meal.

She quietly poured some milk and placed scraps of meat on a dish for the cat, then helped Gabe pack food into the baskets. Ammie woke up, and Bernice came down to breakfast. While they ate, Gabe entertained them with nonsensical stories about their short trip, for Ammie's benefit.

Once they were on their way, Gabe settled back with his boot on the footboard and glanced at Laurie. ''I've been thinking on your idea about getting a buggy. I'll ask around. It would've made this trip a bit more comfortable.''

''I didn't mean to suggest you purchase one. After all, you need the wagon.'' She noticed a flatbed wagon approaching and hoped it wouldn't be the woman with the heavy jowls and predatory eyes.

Gabe called to Will as they passed. "His ranch's a mile down the road from mine."

Bernice glanced around as if just noticing where they were. "Are there many cattle ranches around here?"

"I've the only one now. Will raises sheep. Most of our neighbors farm."

Gabe's attention was captured by a small brown hawk. It glided lazily over the wheat field, suddenly swooped down, and flew off with a mouse in its hooked beak. He realized he hadn't paid much heed to the simple sights that he used to enjoy, not since last winter.

West of Ashly Mills, he pointed out the grist mill, the hot springs, and various houses. When they passed the small town of Phoenix, he declared that they were more than halfway to their destination. By the time they reached Jacksonville, Ammie was dozing in Laurie's arms.

Gabe slowed the team. "Looks like a lot of people had the same idea. I'll try to find a shady spot near the creek."

Laurie watched the sights in amazement. Many wagons and carts crowded into the town, slowing their progress. A young man stood on another's shoulders, waving a flag. She roused Ammie so the little girl wouldn't miss the sights. Laurie smiled to a woman and felt wonderful when the woman returned the greeting.

Gabe glanced at Laurie. "Happy?"

"Oh, yes. I didn't expect anything like this." She smiled at him and quickly averted her gaze to Bernice. "You must be used to these celebrations in Portland. I always enjoyed them at home."

Men and women and children milled around the streets. Laurie grinned at Gabe and realized for the first time that she, Gabe, and Ammie might look like a family. Feeling as if her stomach were swarming with butterflies, she clasped Ammie to her breast.

✤10✤

Bernice helped Laurie repack the basket after dinner while Gabe held Ammie up to watch the children's sack race. As a gangly young boy made it across the finish line, Bernice and Laurie joined them in time to cheer and hear the next men's event announced.

Laurie straightened Ammie's skirt and glanced at Gabe. "Do you shoot?"

"Most men here do. I'm no different."

"Did you bring your rifle?"

When he nodded, Laurie started walking over to where the shooting contest was being held. "Go on. We'll watch, won't we, Ammie?"

"Go, Daddy." Ammie tugged on Laurie's hand, trying to pull her forward.

Gabe gave in with a very masculine shrug, Laurie thought. Holding Ammie's hand securely in her own, she led the way from the growing crowd of spectators to a stump where Bernice could rest, and waited Gabe's turn. The first contestants shot at the row of bottles amid shouts,

117

whistles, and applause. When Gabe raised his rifle, she picked up Ammie and watched.

Bernice frowned. "That may not be a good idea, letting the child see those men firing guns."

"If it frightens her, we can take a walk. Are you comfortable?"

"I am fine, Laurie."

Gabe nested the brass butt end of his Winchester '66 against his shoulder, inhaled, took aim, and hit each of the five bottles on the distant plank. He heard the cheers but stared at Laurie to see her reaction.

She released the breath she had been holding and grinned. She held Ammie up higher. "Wave to your daddy, sugar." She couldn't believe how rapidly Gabe had shattered his targets.

He smiled and wiped his sweaty brow. There were enough cartridges to last him through two more elimination rounds, if he made it that far. He felt the surge of an odd desire to prove himself. He wanted *her* to be proud of him.

Laurie watched Ammie put her hands over her ears as she had showed her. A woman glanced at Ammie and nodded to Laurie. As she waited impatiently all but two contestants were eliminated. The final round was announced, and she watched the plank while the targets were moved even farther back. Gabe and one other man stood at the firing line. Laurie picked up Ammie and silently wished him good luck.

Standing back, Gabe allowed his opponent to shoot first. The man picked off four out of five bottles. Gabe stepped to the line and took aim at the first target, two hundred feet in front of him. He fired off five shots, and each of the five bottles shattered in turn.

"Daddy!"

As Laurie quieted Ammie the crowd erupted. Laurie was still awed by Gabe's skill with the rifle when she was swept aside by the wave of spectators offering their congratulations.

Gabe accepted the marksmanship award, a twenty-dollar gold piece, as well as backslapping and handshakes in the spirit in which they were offered. As soon as the opportunity arose, he slipped away and joined Laurie. "I'm ready for some lemonade. How about you, Bernice?"

"That would be nice." Bernice dabbed her forehead with her handkerchief and rose.

Laurie nodded. "Congratulations!" She put Ammie down and fell into step with him. "I had no idea you were so experienced with a rifle."

Gabe smirked. "Oh, you wanted to see me lose?"

"No! I didn't mean . . . it's just that . . . well, I just thought you might like to join in the festivities."

When they reached the wagon, she climbed up in the back before he could stop her. When she felt foolish, keeping her hands busy put her at ease. She filled a cup with lemonade and handed it to Gabe before she poured one for Ammie, Bernice, and herself.

Taking his daughter's hand, Gabe wandered under a nearby tree and sat down. He watched Laurie while she fussed over Bernice, then with the baskets in the back of the wagon. When it seemed she had done everything but scrub the wagon bed, she came over to where he sat.

"How would you like to join in the festivities?"

He was leaning back against the trunk of a willow tree, looking very self-satisfied. "I thought I was." Just as Ammie made a start for a butterfly Laurie grabbed for the cup dangling from Ammie's fingers.

"How about entering the sack race?" Gabe asked.

Laurie glanced at Bernice uneasily. "I don't think so. Surely that's for the children."

While Laurie squirmed, almost visibly, he watched the pink flush spread upward from her neck to her cheeks and thought it most becoming. "Then the three-legged race? I'll carry Ammie." Seeing the hesitation, he added, "*She'd* enjoy it."

Ammie came running up and held out her fist. "See,

Orie.'' When she lifted her fingers, there was nothing more than a brown smudge and a little dust. ''Where my bug?''

Laurie wiped off the little girl's hand. ''I'm afraid you squashed it, sugar.'' She returned the cups to the basket and tucked the napkin over the top.

''Ammie,'' Gabe called, hoping to distract her. ''Would you like to run in a race with Laurie and me?'' He smiled encouragingly at her.

''I can watch the child, Mr. West,'' Bernice offered.

Ammie looked at him in confusion.

Gabe nodded at Bernice but continued to address his daughter. ''Everyone runs. Do you want to run?''

''Orie, please?'' Ammie grabbed Laurie's hand. ''Go now.''

Laurie grinned. Ammie was becoming more like her father. Laurie's gaze went to Gabe. How could she say no to him?

He glanced at Laurie before looking back at his daughter. ''In a minute.'' When he looked up at Laurie again, she seemed to be stifling a grin. Good, he thought. She'll have fun in spite of herself.

Laurie dropped down by Ammie. ''All right. We'll race.'' Her gaze went to Gabe, and she shrugged. He'd won. He had a smug grin on his handsomely rugged face, but the jet lashes couldn't shield the depth of pleasure she saw in his gray eyes.

''Good. Bernice, you can cheer us on to victory.'' He stood and took Ammie's hand in his. He started to raise his other arm to Laurie and remembered Bernice. ''Shall we go?''

He registered them for the race and was given a length of rope. ''We have just enough time to tie our legs together and practice walking over to the starting line.''

Laurie stood holding Ammie's hand while Gabe knelt down next to her. She could see his shiny coal-black hair but not his hands. Then she felt his hand skim her ankle as he passed the rope around it. She glanced at Bernice and shrugged. The woman surely disapproved.

"Would you lift your skirt just a bit so I can make a knot?" The hem of her skirt raised to the top of her button shoe. After tying the ends of the rope, Gabe slipped his finger under the rope to make sure it wasn't too tight.

"We'd better practice. I don't want to break your ankle."

Laurie placed her left hand on his arm, and they took a tentative step. She leaned away from him and found herself struggling to keep her balance, until she felt Gabe's strong arm encircle her waist and steady her. His strength was warm and reassuring, and she felt very secure.

Gabe pressed his hand into her narrow waist and pulled her closer to him. "Let's try again." They took one cautious step, then another, moving along in a limping gait. "Come here, Ammie." He lifted her to his chest, and they started off again. As they plodded along his hand inched upward from Laurie's waist.

Laurie felt the rope pull against her ankle, but she was more concerned about their falling on Ammie than about the discomfort. "Are you sure you want to try this?" She did feel good with his arm around her, she admitted only to herself, though his hand was more above her waist than on it.

"Mm-hm." Holding Laurie at his side, he knew his decision not to touch her was impossible, unrealistic, and altogether unreasonable. Then he realized his fingers were pressing into her firm breast and moved his hand to her upper arm.

A few paces from the starting line, Laurie's left foot slid over a protruding root. She swayed forward before regaining her balance. She started to try again, but Gabe held her back.

He halted their progress. "This isn't going to work unless you put your arm around my waist for balance."

Laurie glanced around at the other pairs of contestants moving toward the starting point. Gabe was watching her with a smug grin, and she felt sure he was challenging her to comply. Although she'd never been that familiar with Sherman in public, or very often in private, she put her left arm around Gabe. But there was nothing to hold on to but his hard-muscled side.

He felt her light feathery touch at his waist and tensed. "Hook your thumb under my belt and grab onto it with your fingers."

She slid her thumb between his belt and the waistband of his trousers and hooked her fingers beneath his leather belt. This seemed even worse than trying to hold on to his side, or at least it probably appeared stranger, she thought.

"Come on, folks," the man with a megaphone called out to the paired contestants. "Everyone up to this here line. No jump-startin' either."

Gabe glanced down at Laurie. "Ready?"

"Just hold on to Ammie. I'll be fine." She locked her fingers onto Gabe's trousers, waved to Bernice, and they stepped up to join the end of the starting line.

The man with the megaphone called out again. "Get ready, set . . . go!" he shouted.

As Laurie lead with her right foot Gabe firmly guided her forward. Each time their bound foot stepped down, their bodies came together, and she found herself leaning into him. Brushing up against him caused a peculiar throbbing sensation in her chest. After a few steps she began anticipating the thrill tightening within her breast.

Ammie clung to his neck and bounced along as Gabe tried to keep his pace to Laurie's stride. They made fair time, considering their handicap. They struggled across the uneven grass field toward the finish line—three, four, five steps, and they neared the halfway point.

Laurie forgot propriety and lifted her skirts above her ankles. She knew she was slowing them down, so she lengthened her stride. A rock flew back from the pair just ahead of them. Laurie tried to avoid it, but her foot missed, and she stumbled.

Gabe felt her trip. When he tightened his hold, his hand slid over her breast. He was in midstride, and his attempt only made her efforts to right herself hopeless. As he pitched forward he jerked his left arm holding Ammie out to his side and shot his right hand down in front of Laurie to break their fall.

Everything happened so fast that Laurie only had time to put her free hand out in front of her. In moments she lay facedown on the ground, the back of her skirts up past her calves, with Gabe sprawled on top of her. Ammie screamed. She was pinned under his arm, inches in front of Laurie's face. Laurie could see that the little girl was frightened but safe.

Gabe relaxed his grip on Ammie, and she crawled forward, still crying. "Stay here, punkin." He pushed himself to his hands and knees. "Laurie, are you okay?"

The deep sound of her name brought a smile to her lips. He had called her by her given name for the first time, and it sounded lovelier than it ever had before. "I'm fine." She sighed. She rose to a kneeling position and reached for Ammie.

Ammie cried, "Orie," and squirmed over to her.

Looking up from Ammie, Laurie smiled at Gabe. "I think we lost the race."

He chuckled. "I think you're right." As he worked to unfasten their hobble he remembered how firm and warm she had felt to his touch. "Are you sure you're not hurt? I landed square on top of you."

What a way to find out how it would feel to be held in his arms. And more, she realized, feeling her cheeks grow warm, much more. She set Ammie down on her feet, brushed off their clothes, and set their bonnets aright.

"Good as new." Better, she thought, and resisted the impulse to grin. "What other activities did you have in mind for this afternoon?"

Bernice moved as fast as possible with her crutch and

called out when she neared them. "Mrs. Pres—Laurie, are you injured?" She came to a teetering halt.

"Only embarrassed."

"Is she all right?" Bernice indicated Ammie. "Her scream was quite terrifying."

Laurie checked Ammie's knees and kissed her. "I think she was just frightened."

Gabe waited until Bernice had calmed down a bit and Laurie was finished fussing with Ammie. "Feel like wandering around? The horse race's due to start soon."

They strolled down California Street. He put Ammie on his shoulders so she could see the sights. Laurie paused in front of the dry-goods store.

"That woolen cape's pretty, isn't it, Bernice?" It was wine-colored, and Laurie could imagine wearing it on a cold winter day.

Bernice shrugged her shoulders. "A little fancy for my taste."

A tall, lean gentleman walking in the opposite direction came up to them and doffed his stovepipe hat—red-and-white stripes around the sides with a dark blue starred brim and crown. He straightened up and handed Ammie a little flag and continued down the street.

Laurie served supper late in the afternoon after the horse race. While she repacked the baskets Bernice dozed under a tree. Ammie started yawning and curled up against her daddy. It had been a long day, Laurie reflected, but a wonderful day. She had seen a whole new side of Gabe West, a warmer, teasing, and happy Gabe. A much more dangerous Gabe.

He gently lifted Ammie and spoke softly to Laurie. "I think we'd better start back."

"I'll make up her bed before I rouse Bernice." Laurie laid the blankets out and put the little girl down. She smoothed back the child's soft golden hair, and Ammie went back to sleep.

Before Laurie could jump down from the back of the

wagon, Gabe took her by the waist and slowly lowered her. He paused when his eyes were level with hers and her soft coral mouth was just a sigh away from his. Her breath grazed his mouth, and his arms shook with the tension of wanting to touch his lips to hers.

Suspended in Gabe's large hands, Laurie braced her own on his shoulders and stared into luminous gray pools. His breathing sounded labored, raspy. Why was he doing this? she wondered, and almost wished he'd get angry with her. It was so much easier to deal with. He was her employer, and he would never be anything more than that.

"Please . . ."

"Please what?"

His resonant voice trailed down her spine, creating delicious havoc with her senses. "Put me down. Shouldn't we leave?" Oh *please,* she prayed, before I weaken and lean forward—see if his mouth is as powerful as it looks.

Gabe watched her eyes turn soft, yearning, then confused. Relaxing his arms, he eased her down to the ground. "You're right."

On the way back to the ranch, Laurie kept fidgeting with her hands. She didn't know what to do with them, and in her stomach was an odd hollow feeling. Bernice was resting beside Ammie. Laurie was alone on the seat with Gabe. He hadn't said a word after releasing her, and that was rather reassuring. He was usually quiet.

Laurie straightened the material and cut the last of the pieces needed for Ammie's new yellow calico dress. She set them aside and folded the remainder of the material. "After I've finished making Ammie's new clothes, I may have enough scraps to make her a comforter."

Bernice reached over and touched the calico. "That's how mother came by the yard goods to make ours, and old clothes."

Ammie went over to the kitchen table and stood by Laurie. "Dress for douwee, too?"

"I think we can make her a dress from a couple scraps." Laurie gathered a few oddly shaped pieces. "Let me see your doll."

Bernice shook her head. "When she is old enough to sew, she should make her own doll clothes. You should not encourage her."

Ammie handed Laurie the doll and reached for one of the scraps.

"I don't mind, Bernice. Besides, it won't take long." Deciding on a very plain sack dress for the doll, Laurie cut out the simple pieces. "When I was little, Ammie, I had a special doll named Elsie. What do you want to name your doll?"

Ammie watched Laurie a minute before she crawled under the table after the kitten.

Laurie sat down at the table and started laying the pieces out for the doll dress. "What about Betsy?"

Ammie stopped chasing the kitten and picked up her doll. "Can you say Betsy?"

Ammie smacked her lips together. "B-Bsty."

Keeping a sober expression, Laurie worked with Ammie until she could pronounce her doll's new name. We'll work on the cat's name later, Laurie decided. While she stitched on the doll's dress Ammie scampered around with the kitten.

Bernice jumped with an, "Oh" and looked under the table. "That animal should be outside. It is not healthy having it in the house, especially the kitchen."

"The cat probably would like to go out." Recalling a visit to a friend's house years earlier, and the way her friend's maid had distracted her friend's little girl, Laurie got out an old pan and a large spoon. "Ammie, why don't you make dinner for Betsy?" She put the cat out while Ammie was distracted.

Ammie took to the pretend game with little coaxing. Imitating Laurie, she mixed and poured imaginary ingredients and tried to feed it to the doll.

Later, after a modest cold dinner, Laurie put Ammie down for her afternoon rest and started sewing the dress while talking with Bernice in the main room. She was looking at the whatnots. "Would you like to talk about Ruth? She must have been pretty."

"She was. Nothing like me or Mama or Papa." Bernice spoke softly, as if to herself. "She had the most beautiful blond hair until she grew older. I used to wind it around my finger."

Laurie glanced down at her small, overlapping stitches. She hoped the dress would stand up to the abuse of an energetic child. "You must have been very close."

Bernice shook her head. "When Ruth noticed the boys eyeing her, she resented my 'hanging around,' as she put it."

"She had lots of beaux?"

"Papa would not allow that." Bernice stared at the daguerreotypes of Gabe's parents and dabbed at her eyes. "Papa was very strict."

"Mine was also, but somehow we survive, don't we?"

Bernice shrugged. "She should not have sneaked out that night. She never would have met Mr. West or . . . died." She bit her lips, struggling to keep her composure.

"Sometimes young women can be headstrong." Laurie put her sewing down. "I'll be right back." To give Bernice a few minutes alone, she made a trip outside.

She returned to the house and went in to check on Ammie. The bed covers were in a heap, so Laurie called out and went through the routine of looking around the room, under the bed, and finally beneath the blanket. Ammie wasn't there! The window was raised only three or four inches, in the same position Laurie had left it. She rushed back to the kitchen.

Laurie peered under the kitchen table and called the child in earnest. She ran into the main room. "Bernice, have you seen Ammie?" She looked behind every piece of furniture.

"No." Bernice frowned. "What's wrong?"

"She's gone!" The door to Gabe's room was still closed. Laurie opened it and thoroughly explored his room and closed the door after her.

Her heart was racing. Where could Ammie be hiding? Even though the gate still barred the stairs, Laurie didn't hesitate to look through the two upstairs bedrooms. Nothing. By the time she returned downstairs, she was on the verge of total panic.

"I checked her room again and the kitchen. She must be out in the yard, Laurie." Bernice worked her crutch with more dexterity than she had shown in the past.

Laurie led the way. She'd only gone out to the necessary for a couple of minutes. The thought of Ammie getting out of the house on her own was terrifying. Laurie headed for the barn. Ammie had never left the house alone, but Laurie didn't trust her own instincts.

"I'll look in the yard."

Laurie climbed over and around every barrel, tool, and object in sight. As she stared up the ladder to the loft, which she felt sure would be impossible for a tiny girl to do, she heard Gabe ride into the barn. Oh, Lord, what could she tell him? *I lost your daughter.* Give me strength, she prayed, and went to meet him.

Gabe dismounted and immediately noticed Laurie's ashen face and fidgeting hands. "What's the matter?"

She glanced around wildly. Fragmented explanations flitted through her mind before she finally answered. "I'm looking for Ammie." She held her breath.

"Why would you be playing with her in there?" The longer he stared at her, the worse she looked. "Was she out here *alone*?"

"No! Oh, I'm not sure. She must have awakened while I was out and decided to hide. Or maybe she—"

"Why the hell did you go off and leave her alone? Where was Bernice?"

"I didn't. Not that way. Bernice and I were in the main room while Ammie took her nap." Laurie heard a rustling sound above her. "I've got to find her." She ran to the ladder.

Gabe watched her trying to keep her skirts from hindering her as she cautiously started climbing the ladder to the loft. "She couldn't get up there!" Not waiting for her response, he ran to check the yard, starting with the livestock.

After searching around, Laurie decided he must be right and quickly descended the ladder, which was much easier than the reverse. She ran out into the yard and saw Gabe inspecting the corral. She dashed to the necessary and met Bernice just leaving it.

"You didn't find her?" Bernice asked.

"You didn't either." Laurie groaned.

When Gabe returned to the house, he found Laurie in the main room whipping the drapes out of her way in a frenzy. "I'll look in my room."

The only thing he saw under his bed was a year's worth of dust. The wardrobe was only a jumble of shoes and clothes, no Ammie. How the hell could Laurie lose his daughter? Most likely the only child he'd ever have. He charged toward his daughter's bedroom.

Bernice went into the kitchen.

Laurie crawled around the main room trying to discover if Ammie could see an unusual hiding place from that vantage point. Nothing but a dirty floor. She thought about going upstairs again but ruled that out. Behind the staircase. As Laurie scrambled to her feet she called Ammie and hurried over there, but that space was also vacant.

She had to retrace her steps, she decided, and went to look in Ammie's room again. She came to a sliding halt, face-to-face with Gabe. "You didn't find her." She slumped onto her chair, the sewing in a heap on the table. The house was eerily quiet to her alert senses.

"I put the kettle on, Laurie. Do you have any tea?" Bernice asked.

"Check those tins, Bernice." Gabe motioned to one of the shelves before addressing Laurie. "Tell me again, Mrs.

Preston. How could you misplace my daughter?'' He flexed his fingers while he waited for her answer.

Laurie trembled at his formal address. ''She was still asleep in her room when I stepped out for a minute, I'm sure. I don't understand how she could have left without my seeing her.'' She deserved his anger and more, she thought. Somehow she had to find Ammie.

''Mr. West, both of us were in the other room. I did not hear or see Ammie. You cannot blame Laurie.''

Ignoring his sister-in-law, Gabe directed his total attention on Laurie. ''I hired you to *take care* of my daughter! Nothing more. Just tend one small child.'' He pounded his fist on the table, punctuating his statement.

''Nooo, Daddy.''

Ammie's scream rent the air.

Bernice stumbled backward.

Laurie and Gabe both sprang for the lower cupboard at the same moment. He knocked her hand aside and snatched the door open. Laurie dropped to her knees and was rewarded with Ammie's innocent face looking out at her.

''Oh, sugar. Come here.'' Pots and pans tumbled out and rattled on the floor as Laurie dragged the smiling child out. Holding Ammie to her breast, Laurie mutely cried.

''Me hided, Orie.'' Ammie looked back to the cupboard. ''Kitty, too.''

''My God, that cat again!'' He began pacing around the kitchen then suddenly stopped short. ''Didn't you look in here?''

''Of course I did, everywhere. But I didn't see her.'' With her heart pounding in her ears, Laurie stood Ammie on the floor. ''You are a very good hider.''

''Yes, you certainly are, young lady.'' Bernice was fanning her face.

''If all of you are finished, I'd like to get a word in.''

Laurie stood and faced her glowering employer. ''Yes, Mr. West.'' Ammie was safe, thank God, and that was all that mattered. She felt at peace, even though she fully expected to be fired.

As Gabe stared at Laurie, conflicting emotions warred within him. On one hand, he wanted to grab her by the shoulders and shake some sense into her. On the other hand, his desire to wipe the fearful resignation from her lovely face was nearly overwhelming.

"Ammie, go to your room." Gabe noticed his daughter's lip quiver before she shuffled into her room, but he would not be deterred. He'd talk with her later. "Please excuse us, Bernice."

He waited for her to leave before speaking. "Now, Mrs. Preston." He was determined to keep his distance. "Can you explain how she could hide in that cupboard without your seeing her when you looked in?"

Laurie sat down at the table. As her fingers restlessly pleated her soft calico skirt she shook her head silently. Part of her wanted to rail at him that it was impossible to watch Ammie twenty-four hours a day, but Laurie felt so guilty that wasn't possible.

She raised her hands in a helpless gesture. "I have no idea how I could have missed her." With a heartfelt sigh she stilled her hands on her lap and gazed up at Gabe. "What happened is unforgivable, and I am very sorry."

He slumped down on the opposite chair, feeling more rational. "It is understandable, though." Shaking his head, he continued. "Children play games and are forever trying to outwit their elders." He focused on nothing in particular and thought aloud. "She's always been so quiet. It never occurred to me she'd think of really hiding—at least for any length of time."

Laurie spoke softly. "Quiet children aren't always happy." She recalled her own youth and the firm restriction against noise.

"I'd better check on the stock." He stood and started to leave.

"What about Ammie? Don't you want to talk to her?

Since you sent her to her room, I think you should be the one to let her out.''

Laurie went into the main room, giving him privacy. She was greatly relieved and satisfied with the outcome. At times she had worried about his casual, almost cavalier treatment of his daughter. However, she thought, his quick anger revealed his true affection for Ammie.

Laurie peeked under the table. ''How would you like to play outside?'' She untied the apron and laid it over the back of her chair.

Ammie crawled out from under the table. ''Kitty . . .''

''Come on. She'll follow us. Your kitty needs a name, Ammie.'' The cat ran out between Laurie's legs and paused at the edge of the porch, sniffing the air. ''She looks like she's wearing orange mittens, doesn't she?''

Ammie stared at her new pet. ''Mitzens?''

Ammie's puckered brows and cocked head brought a smile to Laurie's face. ''*Mitt-ens* are like my gloves. They keep your hands warm in the winter.''

''Mitt . . . ens. Mittens, c'mere.''

''All right, Mittens it is.''

Laurie went out into the yard with Ammie, and the cat scampered ahead. Seeing Gabe in the barn and knowing the henhouse should be avoided, Laurie wandered in the direction of the one-room cabin where Ben had stayed. As Ammie darted after Mittens, Laurie's gaze went to the horses in the corral.

She hadn't ridden in years. In fact, the only opportunity she had ever had to ride was when her parents visited friends. They had horses *and* a son. She had enjoyed those visits.

Gabe came out of the barn and saw Laurie looking at the corral with an innocent, dreamy expression. Ambling over to her, he took in the relaxed domestic scene. Ammie was wearing a yellow dress Laurie had just finished. She played with her pet, happy and carefree. Laurie had accomplished that, he thought. She had brought a warmth into his home he hadn't known since childhood.

He stopped near her. "Beautiful, aren't they?"

She jumped, his resonant voice both startling and arousing her. "They are."

"Would you like to try out the chestnut mare? Her name's Carly. She's gentle."

Laurie glanced over at him. "I haven't been on a horse since I was twelve." Her attention was drawn to the mare. "What about Ammie?"

"I'll watch her." A few minutes later Gabe led the mare over to Laurie. "I'll adjust the stirrups after you're mounted. You'll have to raise—" He forgot what he was saying and stared in amazement.

Laurie bent over, pulled the back hem of her skirt forward, and tucked it into her waistband. Standing on her toes, she put her left foot in the stirrup, grabbed the pommel, and sprang up—not high enough, though. "I told you it's been a long time."

"Who taught you to do that . . . with your skirt?" The image of her wearing her proper little bonnet and gloves was contrary to the woman standing before him with her skirts hiked up.

"Jimmy. He taught me how to ride."

"How old were you and Jimmy? Here." Gabe put his hands on Laurie's slender waist and lifted her up.

She swung her leg over the rump of the mare. "I was ten. I think he was fourteen."

He adjusted the stirrups and passed the reins to her. "Just stay at a walk." He went over and stood near Ammie while he observed Laurie. "Keep your heels down and in more."

Laurie patted the horse's neck. "Be patient with me, Carly." Holding the reins in her left hand, Laurie tried to relax and move with the mare. She circled the yard once and waved to Ammie as she rode by. As she continued around the yard she felt a new sense of freedom.

"Straighten your back—like when you're vexed with

me.'' He grinned at her and made sure Ammie stayed out of the way.

Sitting erect with your heels in and toes out is not natural, she decided. Her muscles felt tight, as if they might cramp, but she forced herself to follow Gabe's instructions. One minute she was at a walk, the next she was astride a sidestepping, prancing mount.

Gabe didn't see the cat until it veered off from the horse's sharp hooves. He ran over and grabbed the mare's halter. The horse calmed at his familiar command. ''You all right, Laurie?'' Her cheeks were flushed, and her eyes bright. And he thought she was beautiful.

''Fine. Just startled.'' She reached down and patted Carly's neck. ''Is the cat okay?''

''Don't worry about the damn cat. Had enough for today?''

''Not yet,'' she replied softly. ''I'd like to ride awhile longer.''

He released the halter. ''I'll put the cat in the house.''

Laurie nudged Carly and proceeded with her ride. While Gabe was occupied, she increased the circle, riding up to the rise beyond the house and back again. She pulled up when he came running out toward her. ''What's wrong?''

''You! I told you where to ride.'' This was a new side to Laurie. One that might be a pack of trouble and interesting, he had to admit.

''I am perfectly safe. I just want to walk her up to that other rise.'' She pointed to the west. ''What could happen? The cat's in the house, isn't she?''

''What about squirrels? Or snakes?'' He reached for the halter, but she jerked the mare's head away. ''Laurie . . .''

''Walk up there with me, then. You can bring Ammie.'' She didn't know what had possessed her, but she wanted more of her newfound freedom.

''No! You learn to handle that horse right here in the yard. Now walk in a figure eight from the barn to the house.'' If she wanted to ride, he'd put her through the paces—damned if he'd just let her take off like some green kid.

She patted the mare's neck. Laurie made three figure eights as he had instructed. "Not too bad, Carly." She knew she sounded cocky, but oh, it did feel good to do something well.

"Now I want you to circle the yard and increase the mare's speed. Merely *touch* your heel to her side. Don't kick her!" He went over and sat down by Ammie.

Laurie did as Gabe instructed, and Carly performed beautifully. Laurie made several turns and then touched only her right heel to the mare's side. The horse led with her left foot. That trick had just come back to her. She had forgotten that Jimmy had taught her how to lope.

"Good girl!"

Gabe stared in amazement. "Where did you learn that?"

"From Jimmy. Surprised?" He answered by raising one dark brow and frowning.

"You'd better stop for today or you won't be able to walk tomorrow." The mare wasn't the only one feeling her oats, he thought.

"Not yet," Laurie called.

She nudged the mare's side to increase her speed and guided her out of the yard toward the western rise.

❧11❧

Laurie led Carly back to the barn, where she unsaddled the mare and practiced grooming the horse. When Laurie was almost finished, she heard Gabe enter the barn.

"I'll do that." He reached for the brush.

Laurie pushed his hand away. "I don't mind." She glanced past him. "Where's Ammie?"

"Sleeping." He picked up a comb and began working on the mare's dark mane. "You're getting better. But you'll have to wear a decent riding outfit." He stood opposite her and watched her eyes sparkle before laughter erupted from her smiling mouth. God, he thought, she's beautiful.

Laurie bent over and brushed Carly's chest. "What would you suggest? A pair of your old trousers?"

"No!" He stared over the horse's neck, "*Definitely* not pants."

"I guess I could make a split skirt."

"As long as it covers your ankles." Those thin delicate ankles, he amended silently.

"Boots would do that." Laurie went over and scooped a portion of oats into the bucket and held it out to the mare.

Teasing him is fun, she decided, and started planning her riding outfit as she walked back to the house with a definite stiffness in her step.

She entered the kitchen and observed Bernice walking with a limp but without her crutch. "I'm so glad to see your ankle is getting better." Laurie went over to the bucket of fresh water.

Bernice came close to smiling. "Do you really like riding?"

Grinning, Laurie stretched her back. "Oh, yes. I hope after another day riding around the yard, Mr. West will allow me to venture farther afield." She massaged the small of her back.

Bernice eyed her skeptically. "Maybe you should ask him for some liniment."

"I'd rather have a hot scented bath, but I'll settle for a dip in the stream." She filled a glass with water and sipped on it. "Would you like to join me?"

"Oh, no. I . . . I have never . . . the basin and a clean cloth will suffice."

After looking through her meager wardrobe, Laurie decided to purchase material for her split skirt. Gabe was adamant about her not being seen with her skirt "hiked up," as he put it. Well, if a riding skirt would allow her more freedom, she would make one.

When she entered the kitchen, she noticed that Ammie's bedroom door was ajar and heard her talking. Thinking the little girl was talking in her sleep, Laurie quietly opened the door. Ammie was holding the kitten over her chamber pot.

"Mittens, go."

Laurie clamped her lips together to hide her amusement and went over to Ammie. "Mittens doesn't look very happy." The cat wiggled in the child's firm grasp, and Laurie was amazed it didn't try to scratch her.

"Make her go, Orie."

Laurie took the cat from the little girl's hands and set it free. "She'll go outside. Kitties don't use chamber pots."

Ammie stared at the pot a moment. "Me and Mittens go out?" She dashed off.

Laurie glanced at Bernice, shrugged, and followed the child. "Do you have to use the potty?"

Ammie stopped, shook her head, and continued on to the door.

Taking a firm hold of Ammie's hand, Laurie let the cat out and closed the door. "Let's get you dressed."

Ammie pouted and shook her head. "Want to go out."

"We will, as soon as you're dressed." Laurie led the little girl back to her room. "If I can hitch the team up, we're going to town."

Laurie paused on her way through the kitchen. "Bernice, would you ride in to the general store with us?"

Bernice looked up in surprise. "Why . . . yes."

A few minutes later, while Ammie scampered around the yard after the cat, Laurie went into the barn, wondering if she could manage the heavy harnesses. She was trying to lift one of them when she heard Gabe ride into the yard.

He dismounted near the barn, carried his saddle in, and put it over the rail. "Can I help?" He stood several feet away from her, the full force of his imposing personality trained on her.

"I was going to try harnessing the team." She dropped her hands to her sides.

"Were you bored?" He felt himself tensing up. Damn Ruth! She had thoroughly trained him. He knew better than to believe Laurie wanted to escape from the ranch.

"No. I wanted to ride into Ashly Mills for a piece of yard goods." A scowl marred his features for a moment, and she feared she had taken too much for granted. "I didn't think you'd mind." When he appeared to relax, she sighed.

"I'll get the wagon ready." He held her gaze.

He spoke softly, intimately. "Thank you." She responded in the same manner and quickly glanced away to call to Ammie. "Let's get our bonnets."

Laurie went out and looked around the yard. She finally saw Ammie squatting near a bush. With a brief look at the barn to make sure Gabe was still inside, she ran over to her.

"You said you didn't have to use the chamber pot." Laurie picked up Ammie and hurried to the house. "Don't ever do that again. Animals go outside. We do not." She quickly washed and changed Ammie before getting their bonnets. They met Bernice at the door and went out.

Gabe had the wagon ready when Laurie came out of the house. She looks more like Ammie's mother, he thought, than I do her father. That jolted him. When he'd first seen Ammie, he had hoped her hair would darken. But he realized now that her hair would never be anywhere near his dark shade.

He secured Ammie to the bench seat and handed Bernice up beside her. Then he put his hands on Laurie's narrow waist, and she rested hers on his shoulders. He stared down at her upturned face.

"Be careful."

The deep resonance of his voice brought gooseflesh down the back of her neck and arms, and Laurie felt heat rise in her cheeks. "I always am." She started the horses moving while she was still trying to slow her breathing.

"Bye-bye, Daddy," Ammie called out.

"Bye, punkin. Be a good girl."

Bernice and Laurie entered the general store. She saw two women from church and nodded to them. It'll take time, she reminded herself. She went directly to the yard goods.

Bernice stopped to look at a ready-made dress.

"Hold on to my skirt, Ammie. I won't be long." Laurie concentrated on the stack of dark, heavier fabric.

Wool was too warm for her purposes, so she set those bolts aside. After a few more minutes she had narrowed the

choice to hunter-green poplin or a brown twill a shade
darker than the mare.

She decided on the green poplin and picked it up. On her
way to the counter she noticed the woman with the
quivering jowls, the one who had scorned her before the
church service had begun.

The woman's dark, birdlike eyes fixed on Ammie and
scrutinized her for a moment, even though Laurie tried to
shield her. Once she had paid for the length of poplin and
had the parcel in hand, she started over to Bernice. Halfway
up the aisle, Laurie's path was blocked.

The woman jutted out her jaw and drew her brows
together. "You better start lookin' for another post 'cause
you won't be needed here much longer." She pursed her
thin lips and eyed Ammie before addressing Laurie again.
"You're not foolin' anyone." Then she stepped aside and
pulled her skirt back.

Laurie stared at the woman; her hand squeezed the parcel
while her stomach roiled. "Excuse me." The woman didn't
budge.

Bernice came up to Laurie, ignoring the other woman.
"Are you finished here?"

"Yes. And you?"

"I see no reason to stay." Bernice marched with a halting
step to the door and flung it wide.

Laurie ushered Ammie out of the store before the woman
could reply.

During the ride back to the ranch Laurie kept thinking
that nothing the woman said made any sense—not in church
or the store. Maybe the woman's a local character. That
must be it, she reasoned.

She stopped the wagon in front of the house and helped
Bernice down. She also lifted Ammie to the ground and
opened the front door before leaving the wagon in front of
the barn. When she entered the house, the aroma of dinner
greeted her. She paused in the doorway to the kitchen and
watched Gabe talking with his daughter.

"Don't like bad lady." Ammie looked over at Laurie.

Gabe watched Laurie with raised brows. "What's she talking about?"

"Just a woman who came up to us as we were leaving the store. I'll be right back." Laurie turned and went up to her room. Should I tell him about the woman? He had been so protective with her at the store, she wasn't sure if telling him would serve any purpose, except possibly to anger him, which she did not want to do.

Later that evening after Laurie had put Ammie to bed, Gabe relaxed across from her smoking his pipe. She sat in the rocker, putting the finishing stitches on the small bonnet. Bernice sat reading her Bible.

"Who was the woman at the store? What did she say?"

Laurie stopped the rocker. "I haven't any idea who she is, and what she said didn't make any sense." She shrugged and started the chair in motion.

Bernice glanced up. "It was the vile woman we saw at church."

"You didn't mention that, Mrs. Preston. What did she look like?" He looked from Bernice to Laurie.

"Taller than I am, graying hair, dark eyes." Laurie's attention returned to her sewing.

He removed the pipe from his mouth and leaned forward. "A heavy woman with little eyes and double chins?"

Laurie stared at him and nodded.

"That's the one, Mr. West. You know the woman?"

"Damn. Hannah Tuttle." He should have known. She had found Ruth's body and had accused him of murdering her. There was more, but he refused to acknowledge it. "What exactly did she say?"

Laurie didn't look up from her stitching. "In church or in the store?"

"Tell me everything she's said to you."

"On her way to her pew I think she said, 'Two peas in a pod,' or some such thing. This afternoon she warned me to find another 'post,' that soon I wouldn't be needed here."

She met his intense gaze. "It's nonsense. Does she go around muttering like that to everyone?"

Gabe shook his head. "The Tuttles own a large spread west of town." He swatted at a fly buzzing near his ear. "Hannah wanted the town named Tuttleville," he said absently.

"You mean she's not dotty?"

"Stay clear of her." He drew on the pipe and exhaled. "There's going to be a barn raising in a couple weeks. Gus Neilson said you'd be welcome. But the Tuttles will probably be there."

Laurie glanced out through the kitchen window. Bernice was watching Gabe leave. Her pained expression bothered Laurie. Bernice walked beyond the corral and picked a flower, then moved out of Laurie's sight.

Something wasn't right. "Ammie . . ." Laurie quickly cut and buttered a slice of bread. "Come here, sugar."

She picked up the little girl and wandered in the direction Bernice had taken. By the time Laurie caught up with her, Bernice was placing the flower on Ruth's grave. Laurie sat down on the grass with Ammie. "We'll wait here. Want a piece of bread?"

Ammie took the slice and searched for bugs in the grass.

Bernice's sobbing drifted on the breeze. Laurie waited until she stood on shaky legs before going to her. "Take my arm."

Bernice pulled a hankie from her pocket and blew her nose. "I did not mean to worry you. It is just . . ." She started crying again.

"You need a cup of tea. I wonder if we have any left?"

"A . . . little." Bernice hiccuped.

Ammie ran ahead as Bernice and Laurie went back to the house. Inside, Laurie busied Ammie with the sampler and made tea.

"I am sorry, Laurie. I just could not believe Mr. West forgot—" Bernice clamped her lips together and closed her eyes a moment before she continued. "Ruth's birthday." She covered her face with her hands.

Laurie put her arms around Bernice. "No wonder you're so upset."

"I wanted to leave, but I thought I should stay until after . . ." Bernice sat up straight, like a puppet whose strings had just been pulled. "How could he forget? Birthdays were always special to Ruth. She loved pretty packages and ribbons, and the only time Papa allowed us a present was on our birthdays."

Laurie smiled. "I always like birthdays and Christmas."

"Oh, Papa forbid exchanging gifts on the Lord's birthday. When Ruth was twelve, she made an awful scene one Christmas. She wanted a red coat. Papa called her a heathen."

"It must've been difficult for you and your sister."

Bernice stared at the tea left in her cup. "It was for Ruth." She shrugged. "I never questioned Papa's ways."

Laurie stopped in the kitchen to fill two glasses with water before joining Gabe. She had waited for the opportunity to speak with him alone, but now she hesitated. He might dismiss her, but she had to have her say. As a child, she had learned when best to approach her father with a request—after an especially appetizing meal, when he was in a lighthearted mood, which was rare, or when he was departing on a business trip. She had followed her mother's example with Sherman and found she had felt like a scheming child. Taking a deep breath, she left the kitchen.

Gabe listened for her soft steps and smiled when she approached, handing him a glass of water. "Thanks. Ammie settled for the night?"

"I think so." Laurie sipped her water. Lord, his smile made her stomach all fluttery. She sat down, wondering how to begin.

"Did Bernice tell you why she was upset?"

Gabe drew on his pipe before he spoke, and his gaze met

hers. "No. Now that her leg's better, I suppose she's anxious to get home."

Laurie shook her head. "Today was Ruth's birthday." A cricket rhythmically chirped outside of the window while Laurie's heart pounded in her ears.

It was July . . . 25? "God, I didn't even think about the date." He got up and wandered over to the window, gazing out into the dark night.

"Would you tell me about Mrs. West? I must admit, I'm confused. There's such a strong feeling about her death, but no one's mentioned missing her."

He continued looking into the darkness. "I'd be surprised if anyone did. You haven't heard the remarks."

"Tell me . . . please." She sat back and gave him what she hoped was an encouraging smile.

Gabe nodded and wearily rubbed his eyes. "It seemed so long ago—until now. Hannah Tuttle found Ruth that morning. She claimed to have seen me riding away from the house when she arrived." He shrugged. "She may have. I don't know."

Now Hannah Tuttle's behavior made more sense, but it didn't explain why she was so vindictive. "Where was Ruth when you left the house?"

"I didn't see her. She must have been up in her room."

"Wasn't that odd? Or was she a late riser?"

"She got up when she had to tend Ammie," he answered in a level tone.

Laurie wanted to comfort him, but she wasn't sure how or if it was her place to do so. He needed to talk about his wife's death, and she meant to help him. "Was Ruth ill?"

He shook his had.

"Please . . ." She waited until his gaze met hers. "Tell me about Ruth. Only Bernice has mentioned her. It seems odd."

"She didn't make many friends. She hated it here." Where do I start? he wondered.

"That must have been hard for both of you."

He nodded. He had been taken with Ruth from the first moment they met. She had gentle brown eyes that reminded him of a fawn, hair the color of dark honey, and a soft almost breathless kind of voice.

Laurie recalled snatches of comments made about Ruth. "From what Bernice has said, Ruth wasn't close to her father."

"He was a preacher . . . of sorts."

His voice was harsh, the words clipped. Laurie could feel his anguish but pressed on. "Did her father marry you?"

"No. He was crazy, wouldn't let Bernice, Ruth, or their mother dress in anything but gray dresses that covered them from chin to shoe tops. She ran away. We got married in Salem, on our way here. I wrote to her parents, but we never saw them again." He drew on the pipe and watched the bluish-gray smoke. "*That* was a blessing." He sighed.

Feeling this information wasn't what she needed, Laurie decided to ask a more direct question. "How did Ruth die?"

"How?" Gabe glanced at Laurie. There were fine lines between her brows, and she appeared not just curious but genuinely concerned. She would be, he thought. She'd immediately taken to Ammie, the cat, and even Bernice. Laurie had a right to know, though he was surprised she hadn't already heard.

"Poison."

Laurie covered her mouth and swallowed hard. It was a moment before she could speak. "You said you didn't see her that morning. Where was Ammie?"

He shook his head. "Asleep. It was still early." Gabe got up and strolled over to the window. "Ruth moved upstairs soon after she realized she was carrying a child. Said she wanted to be alone." He knew he was rambling, but so much of Ruth's behavior was disjointed—and so were his thoughts.

"Anyway, we didn't talk much." He paused and smiled at Laurie. "Like we are now. She screamed, sulked, or whined."

Laurie's hands gripped the smooth arms of the old rocker. "And the day before her death? Had you argued?"

"I've gone over that night a thousand times. She was quiet. Didn't even seem to mind Ammie's fussing. Then just before she retired, she started in. Something about a new wardrobe for a trip." He smoothed his hair back. "Anyway, I just left the next morning. I didn't want to see her."

"Did you ever find any poison?"

"Hannah Tuttle said there was a half cup of an odd-colored drink by the bed. Said it smelled funny. Sheriff Jenkins figured someone put something in Ruth's coffee."

"Did anyone think Ruth might have poisoned herself?"

"That's the only answer I came up with. But why?" He really needed to do something about the windows. Maybe Laurie would make new drapes. Hell, what would happen to Laurie and Ammie if he ended up in jail?

Laurie waited, allowing him time to think. "Was Ruth close to Ammie?" Harsh laughter erupted from him, startling her.

"She treated the child like any other chore that needed doing." Gabe stared at Laurie, willing her to understand.

"Our marriage wasn't right from the beginning. Within a month she began wearing clothes she said were more fashionable." He glanced at the table. He reached for a particularly ugly figurine of a young girl. It crushed easily in his grasp before he pitched it through the open window.

The tension he felt knotting his shoulders eased somewhat. "Before she moved upstairs, she started complaining about not feeling well, excuses. I caught her sneaking out at night. It wasn't long before I realized she was going to have a child.

"Thank God it was snowing when her time came, and I couldn't leave to get help. I delivered Ammie."

Gabe's hands balled into white-knuckled fists. "When she was giving birth, she called for the child's father."

* * *

"Today, Bernice? You're just getting to know Ammie." Laurie brushed Ammie's fine blond hair back from her face. "Don't wiggle so, and you can play with Mittens in a minute."

"I had not planned on staying here at all. Mama has not been well since Papa passed away. Besides, my ankle is fine."

Laurie had noticed Bernice watching Ammie with such love and longing, she couldn't understand why the woman remained so rigid. "There. Now your hair looks pretty. You can play."

Ammie peeked at her aunt, smiled, and darted out of the room.

"Have you told Mr. West you're leaving?"

"He said he would take me into town." Bernice rose. "I had better make sure everything is packed."

"I wish you'd told me sooner."

Bernice came close to smiling. "You will do fine, Laurie. Anyone with eyes can see the child loves you. That is more than many women ever have."

Laurie puzzled over that as Bernice went up to finish packing. Well, she thought, the least I can do is make a hot dinner and pack her a basket. She quickly built up the fire in the stove, put the kettle of soup on to heat, and made biscuits. She kept the meal simple, which suited her culinary skills as well as Bernice's preference.

By the time Gabe returned, Laurie had dinner ready. It was a quiet meal, and she was relieved when he actually talked with Bernice in a friendly manner. All too soon it was time to leave.

"Mr. West." Laurie took Ammie's hand and looked up into his face. "We are coming with you."

"Good." He ruffled his daughter's hair. Laurie's husky voice had the strangest effect on him.

Gabe half listened to the women's small talk. He now pitied Bernice more than he disliked her. Too bad she hadn't come to visit her sister, he thought. But would it have changed Ruth? He doubted it. He pulled around the corner by the general store and helped Bernice and Laurie down before going in to buy Bernice's ticket. That was the least he could do.

Laurie held on to Ammie with one hand, the basket with the other, and glanced at the store. "Would you like to wait in there?"

"I . . . no." Bernice checked her bonnet strings.

Gabe returned to the boardwalk and handed Bernice the ticket.

Ammie squirmed around. "Daddy . . . 'old me."

"Sure, punkin." He heard the stage and sheltered Ammie as it arrived in a whirl of dust. Bernice anchored her bonnet, as stoic as always.

The stage driver tossed a satchel to the ground, climbed down, and helped one woman out. "Jacksonville and north to Portland!"

Gabe handed the man Bernice's valise and held out his hand.

She looked at Ammie and removed a small bundle from inside her jacket. "You look just like your mama. May God be kind to you." She held out a tiny dress. "I hope this fits your doll." She kissed her niece and quickly stepped aboard the stage.

Ammie hugged the dress to her and smiled at her aunt.

Laurie wiped her damp eyes and pushed passed the driver to hand Bernice the basket of food. "Take care. And come back."

Gabe hauled Laurie back as the driver shoved the door closed. He nodded to his sister-in-law. "Thanks, Bernice."

Bernice leaned to the window and called, "Take good care of them, Laurie," as the stagecoach pulled out.

❧12❧

Laurie approached Gabe while he harnessed the team of horses. "Ammie's ready. She wanted to bring Mittens to see the cattle, too, but I explained why she couldn't." She found herself missing Bernice's company and was looking forward to the outing as much as Ammie.

"Mittens in this weather?"

"The cat." Laurie went over to one of the horses and patted its neck. "I'd rather ride Carly than in the wagon. I could follow you."

Gabe glanced up and shook his head. "Not with your skirts hiked up." He cinched the last strap. "Let's get a move on. The men need these supplies."

He wasn't sure how he'd gotten roped into bringing Laurie and his daughter along. Sure, he'd said something about bringing them up to see his herd—not the men. Old Ben would probably be the only one in camp, Gabe figured, so he could unload the supplies and leave.

Laurie held Ammie on her lap as they rode north. The rutted track led through high, swaying summer grass. She was reminded of smooth ocean waves until one wagon wheel hit a rock and jarred her back to reality.

She braced her feet and one hand to steady herself before glancing at Gabe. "I thought cattle grazed on the flatland." He was settled back, his hat pulled down, shading his eyes, and his dusty, worn boot was up on the footboard. He wouldn't look at home in a proper parlor, she thought, and smiled.

"They're up on the plateau. We'll graze them down closer to the house come winter."

"Does it snow here?"

"Not much down in the valley. But we get enough to cover the ground north of the house." He veered the team around a small boulder. "We can take Ammie up to the foothills this winter. She'll be old enough to enjoy the snow."

Laurie stared ahead, his last statement echoing in her mind. He sounded as if there were no question of her remaining in his employ. She hugged Ammie to her breast and pointed out a ground squirrel.

Gabe neared the grazing herd and pulled up. "There they are." He gazed out at one of the short-horned bulls.

Laurie studied the herd. "What kind are they?"

"Durham, sturdy healthy stock."

Ammie stared at the animals. "Cows."

"They are big, aren't they?" As Laurie spoke one particularly large beast lifted its head and appeared to look at them. She watched the dark red hair on the animal's wide chest ripple when it took a few lumbering steps forward.

"Will it attack?" Laurie locked her arms around Ammie.

"I think we're safe. A lone bull can be dangerous, but he's got plenty of heifers to keep him occupied." Gabe started the horses walking toward the camp.

Feeling the sudden rise of heat on her cheeks, Laurie quickly averted her gaze. Gabe said the most outlandish things, she thought, and wondered if he did it on purpose. At least Ammie was too young to understand.

He noticed the bright flush on Laurie's cheeks. He was a plain-talking man, he reasoned. He didn't know how to sugarcoat the truth and didn't care to learn.

Laurie saw a rider some distance away, but he didn't approach. Soon they came to a small log building with bedrolls neatly placed nearby. When Ben came out to greet them, Laurie waved.

Ammie spotted Ben and started calling to him in her usual, high-pitched cry.

"Shush. Remember what your daddy said, we must be quiet around the animals."

Ammie covered her mouth and nodded.

Gabe took Ammie and offered Laurie his hand. "Don't let her go near the herd."

Ben snatched his battered hat from his head. "Missus Preston."

"Nice to see you again, Ben." Laurie took Ammie's hand and wandered away from the men.

Gabe turned to Old Ben. "How're the Durhams behaving?"

"Them critters're fine. Not many strayin' off." Ben ambled to the back of the wagon. "Let's quit jawin' and git this in the shack."

Gabe hefted a fifty-pound bag of flour onto his shoulder and took it inside. A few more trips and they had the supplies stored. He was about to look for Laurie when Danny rode up.

"Hi, boss." Danny dismounted. "Bring anything besides bacon and beans?"

"Flour." Gabe couldn't help smiling at the sight of his growing herd.

Danny followed Gabe's gaze. "They're a hot-blooded bunch." His attention wandered. "Where's your company? I could swear you weren't alone in the wagon."

Gabe slapped his hat against his leg, knocking the dust off. "She's around with Ammie." Danny's eyes sparkled with mischief that Gabe was all too familiar with.

"Good. I haven't seen that little one of yours in months."

After putting his hat back on, Gabe went in the direction Laurie had taken earlier. Ammie's giggles made it easy to find them playing among the trees.

Ammie saw her daddy and ran to him. "Me hided from Orie."

"I'm sure you did. Do you remember Danny? He wants to see how big you've gotten." Gabe kept a straight face as he nodded to Danny.

Ammie peered up at the man. "Danny?"

"Hi, Ammie." Danny squatted down and whispered to her. "Did you lose Mrs. Preston?"

Ammie giggled and shook her head. "Orie," she called. "C'mere! See Danny."

Laurie had stayed behind, watching Gabe's expression. He hadn't looked very happy before he had called Ammie. She smoothed back her hair, straightened her clothes, and answered Ammie's call. "Here I am."

As Laurie approached, Gabe avoided looking at Danny. "Mrs. Preston, this is Danny Whitefeather, my range boss. Danny, Mrs. Preston."

Danny yanked his hat off and rubbed his hand on his rough pants before he extended it to Mrs. Preston. "A real pleasure, ma'am." He smiled and nodded at Gabe.

Laurie couldn't resist his dark, gleaming eyes and returned his smile. "Mr. Whitefeather." He was of medium height. His black hair was held back with a leather thong.

"Danny, please, ma'am. I hear you and Ammie are getting along just fine."

What else had Gabe said about her? Laurie wondered. "She's such a dear." She reached for Ammie, but the child ducked away.

Ammie ran behind Danny and dashed off to hide behind a distant tree.

"No, Ammie." Laurie gave chase.

Danny watched Mrs. Preston go after Ammie and glanced at Gabe. "So that's the Widow Preston."

Gabe stared after Laurie's scampering figure. "What?"

"Now that I've met her, I can see why you haven't been up here much lately." Danny looked at Gabe and laughed. "I never asked how you found her. I thought you were off limits with the fair ladies of Ashly Mills?"

Gabe scowled at Danny. "Aunt Penelope's responsible." As he watched Laurie raise her skirts and run, Ammie veered toward a grazing cow. "Damn it!" He bolted to head off his daughter.

Soundlessly Danny hastened after Gabe.

"Ammie, please." Laurie slowed down, fearing she was urging the child on. "Sugar, we can't play down here."

"See cows," Ammie called, racing off.

Gabe approached the critter slowly. Ammie wasn't paying any attention to where she was going, so he waited until she was several yards in front of him before he moved to grab her. He snatched her up and kept going until he was near Laurie.

He knelt down and stood his daughter on the ground facing him, his hands on her shoulders. "Don't you *ever* run away from Laurie like that again!" He shook her, wondering how else to get through to a small child.

Laurie covered her mouth to keep from screaming at him. He had only shaken Ammie once, but it was enough to jostle her head like a sock doll's. Forcing herself to stand back and allow him his right to punish his own daughter was almost impossible for Laurie. The seconds seemed like minutes, but Gabe waved her forward a moment later and released Ammie.

Laurie lifted her skirt and raced forward.

Gabe stepped back from his daughter. "She's fine. Don't let her get away again. If she'd gone much further or screamed, she'd have spooked the herd. She could've been trampled!" He stood there, fear for his daughter still pulsing through his muscles.

Laurie nodded. "Come on, sweetie." She spoke in a soft, lulling voice while drying the little girl's tear-dampened face. "You must stay by me." She took Ammie's hand and returned to the wagon.

Gabe ambled behind Laurie and was joined by Danny.

Danny glanced at his friend. "What're you so riled about?"

"You saw what happened. Ammie could have been killed."

Danny shook his head and eyed Gabe with a smile. "I don't recall our being overly concerned about danger when we ran through the stock pens or woods."

"That was different and you know it." Gabe swerved away from the wagon. "Nothing's the same since that woman came."

"You mean Mrs. Preston?" After Gabe frowned at him, Danny continued. "Well, I should hope not. You wanted a woman to take over Ammie's care."

Gabe grunted. Of course, it was easy for Danny to be so free with advice. He wasn't even married.

"Do you expect your daughter to sit all day and watch her fingernails grow?"

"She didn't used to be so rowdy. Damn it, I don't know." He suddenly started laughing.

Danny glanced over at Mrs. Preston. "She seems to have a good influence over Ammie."

"She's a woman." Why the hell did he feel like hitting something? It wasn't like him to fight or take out his restlessness on others. But damn it all, that woman tied him in knots! "So why can't she control one small child?"

"You or your daughter?" Danny dusted off his hat. "I'm going to see what Old Ben's done with those supplies."

Gabe calmed down after a short walk and wandered over to the wagon. Laurie was sitting on the grass with Ammie and they appeared to be looking for something. He was absently checking the harnesses when Old Ben came out of the shack.

"Vittles's on, ma'am, fellers." Ben gazed around at no one in particular.

Laurie glanced over at Gabe. He moved with fits and starts instead of with his usual fluid grace, and he still looked upset. "Go over to your daddy."

Ammie looked down at the grass and shook her head. "He's mad."

"He was very worried. He didn't want that big cow to step on you." Laurie tipped Ammie's chin up. "If you go over to him, I think he'll smile."

Ammie gave her daddy a sideways glance and stared at her shoes.

"Go on, sugar. Your daddy isn't mad." Laurie stood and placed her hand on the little girl's back, urging her forward.

She watched Ammie sidle up to Gabe. Before she said anything, Ben came out of the shack carrying another large kettle.

"Git it now or I'll feed it to the critters! Last chance."

When Gabe saw Ammie, he grinned and picked her up. "Hungry?" In a few strides he joined Laurie. "We'll stop to eat down the slope."

"Come on, boss," Danny called. "Ben won't serve it up till Mrs. Preston's been helped."

Gabe mentally shrugged and extended his arm in the direction of the rough table near the shack. "Seems Old Ben has made dinner for you."

Laurie smiled. "Be right there."

Ben handed Laurie a battered old tin plate and ladled a generous portion on to it. "Son-of-a-gun stew, ma'am."

"Thank you, Ben. It smells delicious." She turned to Gabe. "I'll take Ammie. She can share my plate."

Gabe peered into the kettle. "I hope those things are teeth." He winked at Laurie.

"Yeah. You want one?"

"Nope, I'll leave'm for you, Ben. Thanks anyway." Gabe took his plate and sat across from Laurie.

Danny stepped up to Ben. "I'll try one, but I don't want any ears."

Laurie stared down at the lumpy mass on her plate.

Everything was brown and nothing was distinguishable. One lump cut quite easily with the side of her fork. She knew they were teasing her. Nonetheless it was difficult to force a bite into her mouth. Her teeth came together as through butter. It was a tender piece of beef.

After tasting the bite, she fed Ammie one. "This is very good, Ben. Much better than my stew."

Ben grinned. "Thanky, ma'am."

Danny swallowed his mouthful. "Ain't bad. You should come up here more often, Mrs. Preston. Ben's partial to gopher pies on Thursdays."

Laurie rode Carly around the yard, wearing her newly finished hunter-green split skirt. Her thoughts strayed between the need to cut the rosebud print so Ammie would appear presentable at the barn raising, and the social itself.

If she simply went about her business of tending Ammie, she pondered, surely no one would think badly of her. After all, Ammie and Gabe were a part of the community, and he had spent his adult years in Ashly Mills.

She finished her Sunday ride and returned to the barn. After brushing down the mare, she returned to the house. She was inclined to resume her normal chores, but Gabe remained determined she have her day off, so she went up to her room.

When the material was laid out on her bed, Laurie studied her drawing. She wanted to duplicate a child's dress she had seen last spring, but ended up improvising. The dress would have a pleated, square bodice with a high waist and gathered skirt. Thanks to Gabe's generosity, she had enough ribbon for trim and bonnet ties.

Late in the afternoon she heard Gabe and Ammie outside. She gazed out of the window and enjoyed watching Ammie trying to teach her father how to play. Taking advantage of their absence, Laurie went downstairs and found one of Ammie's old dresses. By suppertime she had the bodice loosely stitched together and was ready to try it on the little girl.

Ammie ran to greet Laurie. "Why you not play with Mittens and me?"

Laurie went down on one knee. "I've been working on your new dress. If you hold still, I'll see if it fits."

Ammie didn't move, but her voice rang out. "Daddy, c'mere. See Orie."

Gabe stood in the kitchen doorway and watched Laurie fit three small pieces of cloth around his daughter's neck. Her hair was escaping from the confines of the tight bun. As she leaned forward auburn tendrils framed her face. With a little luck her hair would fall free of that infernal knot, spread out over her shoulders and down her back. He cleared his throat.

"Ready for dinner?"

Laurie glanced up. Viewing Gabe from Ammie's perspective was interesting. He resembled a giant—tall, dark, and . . . Her fingers were quivering, and she wouldn't allow herself to finish the thought.

Ammie tugged on Laurie's sleeve. "Why you look funny?"

Laurie quickly focused on Ammie. Ignoring the child's question, she said, "Be still, sugar. I'm almost done."

Ammie persisted. "Why, Orie?"

Laurie concentrated on her hands and shrugged.

"But you didn't say nothing, Orie."

Gabe stooped down and ruffled his daughter's blond hair, his attention never varying from Laurie. "Give her a chance, punkin."

On entering Plymale and Manning's Livery, Gabe saw a trim black buggy with three cream lines across the side. It was lightweight and would be easy for Laurie to handle. He was running his hand along the back of the drab maroon trimmings when he heard someone approach.

He turned and nodded. "Manning. Nice little rig."

Mr. Manning smiled and patted the dash. "The Goddard's a great little buggy.'' He glanced to the front of the livery. ''Want to trade your wagon?''

''No. Considering a secondhand buggy. What else do you have?''

''I've got a couple other's out back.'' Manning led the way. ''There's a Stanhope in good shape. And a couple buckboards.''

Gabe went over and took a closer look at the better of the two buckboards. ''Not bad. How much do you want for it?''

Manning tweaked the end of his full mustache. ''Say, fifty. I'll throw in the harness.''

Gabe nodded and ambled over to the Stanhope. It was dark green. The red striping had once been bright. The cloth upholstery still had years of wear, if no longer as handsome as it had been, and the top was fixed. The boot had been patched, but the wheels were in good condition.

''This's had a lotta wear.''

Manning shrugged. ''Owner claimed to be a traveling salesman, needed to carry more samples. Said he came all the way from Los Angel-ese, down in California.''

Gabe checked the window shades and found them in fair shape. ''What'll you take for this?''

''There's a lotta wear still in this buggy. Ain't that old, you know.'' Manning walked around it. ''Eighty-five.''

''I could get a new one for one-thirty.'' Gabe shook his head. ''Maybe I'll wait. That's too steep for me, considering the wear and all.'' He started slowly toward the hitching post.

''Wait up, West. Let's talk. What's your offer?''

Without turning, Gabe responded, ''Sixty-five, with the trappings.''

''Deal. You want to drive it home or pick it up later?''

''I'll hitch my horse to the back and take it now.'' He nudged the wheel with his boot. ''Now, about a horse.''

The ride back to the ranch seemed to Gabe to take forever. He leaned back against the seat and decided it was comfortable and the carriage well sprung. Buying the buggy was right. After all, Laurie was at the house all day with Ammie and had no means of getting help if she needed it. He hadn't gotten it as a gift, he thought. No, it was a necessity.

Laurie had just fastened the last button on Ammie's dress before the child darted after the cat. "Ammie, please come here. I have to fit your bonnet."

Ammie picked up the cat and stood in front of Laurie. "Put on Mittens."

"You first, sugar." Laurie sighed when the rosebud print bonnet fit with a little room to spare. "Perfect. Now for Mittens." She quickly placed the bonnet over the cat's head and off again.

"Ow!" Ammie dropped the cat. "Bad Mittens."

"Let her go. Kitties don't like dressing up." She handed the bonnet to Ammie. "You can try it on your doll."

Laurie heard what sounded like a buggy and glanced at Ammie. With nimble hands she smoothed her hair and skirt before going to the door. When she saw Gabe stepping down from the rig, she didn't move.

Ammie pushed Laurie's skirt aside and ran forward. "Daddy home?"

Gabe secured the reins over the brake and watched Laurie. "Do you like it?" Motionless except for her eyes, she just stared.

Ammie yanked on Laurie's skirt. "C'mon."

Laurie didn't trust her hearing.

The wagon was good enough for my mother and Ruth. And you'll just have to make do with it.

Slowly Laurie stepped over to the rig. The body of the buggy was dark green, the tufted seat also dark green, and it had a standing top with curtains. Plus the boot was more than large enough for her purposes. She tentatively touched the dashboard and stared at Gabe.

He saw the passion in her eyes. "Well . . ." He'd

thought she would run out, ooh and ah over his surprise. But she just stood there, staring longingly.

"It's beautiful. But I don't believe I can afford it. How—"

Gabe raised his hand and interrupted her. "I bought it."

"But you don't need it. You even said—"

"I thought it'd be easier for you to handle. I seem to use the wagon when you need it." Please, just smile at me, he thought.

"Oh." Not even Sherman had been so considerate. She walked around the buggy, touching the carriage and wheels in awe until she stood near Gabe. "Thank you."

She was glowing. Her voice was soft and her eyes appeared to be filling with tears.

"It's for your use. All I ask is that you be careful. I don't want you landing in a ditch." He patted the horse's neck, grabbed the cheek piece, and started for the barn. "Come with me. You can practice harnessing the horse."

❧13❧

Gabe pushed his chair back and stood up. "You don't need to come over till after Ammie's nap. That's when the women'll probably start getting ready for supper. You have the directions?"

Laurie wiped her mouth. "Yes. Should I take the wagon?"

"What for? The buggy's easier to handle." He paused at the door, looking at Laurie. "See you later."

Her eyes were bright, but she looked a little edgy. He hoped her going to the barn raising wouldn't be a mistake. He certainly didn't want her to feel embarrassed or hurt. All morning Laurie's smile kept him company while he worked.

By the afternoon the framework of the barn was up, and Gabe worked on top of the skeletal structure, nailing off roof rafters. From that vantage point he could see Stage Road. He only allowed himself one look per rafter, and he only had one more to nail down. Laurie had told him she'd come after Ammie's nap.

Gus had asked about her, but no one else had. Part of him

was relieved, but the waiting was wearing on him and soon the women would be laying out supper. He didn't go in much for socials, but he wanted to give Gus a hand.

"Hey, West. You ready to come down? Or do you want to start on the ceiling joists?" Gus stood at the foot of one ladder.

"Start passin 'm up."

He worked his way back across the top side of the barn, glancing at the road each time he raised a board. When he'd decided that Laurie had changed her mind, he saw a buggy in the distance. By the time she drew near, he had nailed off the last board.

He stepped off of the ladder and Gus approached. "I'll get started on the roof."

Gus motioned to the track leaning into the yard. "Wonder who that is?"

"I think it's Mrs. Preston. Ammie must have slept late."

Gus glanced sideways. "Didn't know you had a rig."

After depositing his tools on the ground, Gabe straightened up. "She needed a way to get around when I'm using the wagon."

"Glad she could make it. I'll go tell Nellie she's here."

Gabe wiped a sleeve over his brow and went to meet Laurie. She stopped the buggy several yards away from the nearest wagon. Her hair was pulled back as usual, but she wore a pretty green dress he hadn't seen her in before. She looked as straitlaced as a schoolteacher, not at all like the woman who'd hitched up her skirt to mount his horse.

Laurie stepped down from the rig and unfastened the belt securing Ammie to the seat. "Stay right by the wheel, sugar." She lowered the little girl to the ground. "I have to get the basket."

Ammie looked around and saw her father. "Daddy! C'mere."

"Hi, punkin." Gabe put his hand out and reached for the basket. "Let me take this."

"It really isn't heavy." She motioned to the other

package and glanced up at him. "Would you bring the ham?"

He picked it up and took Ammie's hand. "The ladies have some tables set up near the house." He measured his pace to Laurie's and noticed her looking at the new barn. "What do you think?"

She regarded the skeletal structure. "My goodness, it's almost finished. You must have been working hard." She heard her heart pounding and felt like everyone within a mile was staring their way. She took a deep breath and tried to appear at ease, as if she belonged.

Gabe led Laurie to the tables and set the ham down near Nellie Neilson. "Mrs. Neilson, I'd like you to meet Mrs. Preston. And this is my daughter, Ammie."

Mrs. Neilson held out her hand. "Pleased to meet you, Mrs. Preston." She smiled at Ammie. "My, you're big enough to play with the other tykes."

Laurie set the basket down and removed her glove before taking Mrs. Neilson's hand. "Thank you for including me, Mrs. Neilson."

"Everyone just calls me Nellie. It's easier."

"We might as well get back to work," Gus said good-naturedly, "and leave the women to theirs."

Gabe ruffled Ammie's hair. "You mind Mrs. Preston."

Ammie frowned. "Orie?"

As if shooing flies away, Nellie motioned with her hands. "Off with you men now. We'll be fine." When her husband and Mr. West were across the yard, she turned to her guest. "Come on in the house. I've got lemonade, and you can meet the other ladies."

Laurie took Ammie's hand and followed Nellie. She was a couple inches shorter and stockier than Laurie, her dusty blond hair pulled back in a braided knot. Laurie guessed her to be near her own age. At least Nellie seems pleasant, Laurie thought.

Nellie opened the door and entered the kitchen. "Ladies,

we have a latecomer, Mrs. Preston.'' She stopped at the table and poured a glass of lemonade.

The women stood unmoving and had quieted as soon as they saw Laurie. She smiled. A few of the women she had seen before at church or the general store. Nellie introduced everyone. Laurie was greeted with somber expressions, a couple of contemptuous looks, and one warm smile. The only names she recalled were Nellie, Hannah Tuttle, and Etta Kirk, who had light green eyes, ash-brown hair, and a generous smile. And her greeting was the friendliest Laurie had received in Ashly Mills.

Laurie accepted the glass and took a sip. The slightly tart flavor tasted good after the ride. She knelt down and gave Ammie a sample, too.

''Well, ladies, we'd better start spreading out the food or the men will be too tuckered out to dance later.'' Nellie lifted a large platter and went to the door.

The other women followed suit and filed out with their hands full. Taking their glass of lemonade, Laurie trailed after them with Ammie's small hand in her own. ''Hold on to Betsy and stay by me, sugar.''

Ammie hugged the doll to her chest with one arm and squeezed Laurie's hand with the other.

Nellie directed the women. ''Let's put the salads and vegetables here, near the plates and flatware, the meat dishes in the center, and the desserts at that end.''

The table was made up of planks resting on sawhorses. Laurie set the two lemon pound cakes down at the far end of the table. Others placed their dishes nearby. She attempted to help, but her efforts were thwarted, so she started unwrapping the ham she brought.

''Mm, that smells good.'' Etta set her serving dish down by the ham. ''I heard what happened in church, and I'm really sorry.'' She glanced around.

Laurie turned the dish. ''It'll take time to get acquainted.''

A young boy ran by her, chasing a little girl. Ammie

stepped closer to Laurie and hugged her doll. "It's okay, sugar. I'll be finished here in a few minutes."

After the children had gone, Laurie realized that Etta had also moved away. She took the knife from the basket and began slicing the ham. An older woman, who also brought a ham, placed it across from Laurie's. She finished and looked at the woman.

"You can use this knife."

The woman stared at Laurie. "Whose is it?"

"Mr. West's."

The woman shook her head and walked away.

Laurie laid the knife by the ham and began arranging the dishes. A tall, thin, dark-haired woman bumped her arm. When she glanced over, the woman sniffed, raised her nose skyward, and stomped away.

Deciding not to force the issue, Laurie stepped down to the end of the table and cut the lemon cakes. She fanned the slices in a small arc and moved a bowl of pudding closer. As she made room for more desserts Hannah Tuttle came up and set a large, sugar-dusted cake down, carelessly brushing aside Laurie's cake.

After straightening her pieces, Laurie took Ammie's hand and wandered over to the shade at one end of the house. Some children, all much older than Ammie, were playing nearby, and Laurie watched them, hoping Ammie would also. As Laurie watched the women she thought about Bernice and wished she had stayed over. She smiled. Bernice wasn't as narrow-minded and prudish as she first appeared to be. Soon Nellie called the men to supper.

As Gabe and the other men responded to Nellie's call, Laurie watched him talking and laughing with the other men. At least he doesn't seem to be contaminated by my presence, she thought. She didn't know of a solution to her dilemma. She was being effectively cut like a harlot at a church social.

Ammie tugged on Laurie's sleeve. "Want supper, Orie."

Ammie stood up and pulled on Laurie's hand. "Eat with Daddy."

"Did I hear my name mentioned?" Gabe squatted down by his daughter.

"Daddy!"

"Sit with me while Laurie gets your plate." He glanced at Laurie and didn't like the lackluster look in her eyes. "You feel all right?"

She smoothed back Ammie's tousled hair and forced a smile. "Fine," she said lightly. "Be right back, Ammie."

Gabe saluted Gus and took another swig of Gus's homemade beer. The men were milling about while three others were tuning up for the dance music. Each time he got a glimpse of Laurie, she was busy with Ammie. Only once did he see her talking with one of the other ladies.

"Well, Gabe, think the barn'll last the winter?"

Gabe chuckled at Franklin Tuttle's flat expression. "You just want more of Gus's beer."

Franklin nodded.

"And an excuse to dance with your missus." Gus winked and refilled their glasses. "Drink up. The ladies are waiting."

Laurie held Ammie in her arms, swaying to the music. When the second tune ended, she strolled over to the makeshift bed she'd laid out and put the little girl down. She was tempted to sit with the child. She hadn't seen much of Hannah Tuttle and was grateful.

With the younger children asleep, their mothers were free to enjoy the festivities. Several lanterns had been set around, casting a large portion of the yard in a soft yellow light. Laurie noticed three of the older girls standing across the grounds, whispering and watching everyone.

As Laurie busied herself with packing up the leftover food, she noticed some of the older boys trying to sneak drinks of beer and glanced away. She washed off a few plates she'd found near the steps and was surprised when Etta came up.

"I'll dry." Etta found a cloth and picked up a bowl. "Ammie asleep?"

"Finally. She had trouble settling down while the other children were still playing. She isn't used to being around a lot of people." The musicians called for a square dance. "You don't have to help. I just wanted something to do."

Etta glanced at the couples pairing up, then at Laurie. "You can't spend the evening cleaning." She finished drying the last plate. "We're done here. Let's get some punch."

Laurie dried her hands and stepped over to the table. She ladled punch into several glasses and set them out before taking one for herself. When Etta was claimed for a dance, Laurie shooed her off. Later Nellie came over, and Laurie handed her a glass of punch.

Nellie drank half of the fruit punch. "Dancing sure dries me out." As she fanned her heated face she glanced around. "You don't have to play hostess, Mrs. . . . Laurie."

"Really, I'd rather—"

Nellie cut her off. "Well . . . if you don't mind." She stared past Laurie. "My, it's getting late. Shouldn't last much longer."

Smiling at her friends and neighbors, Nellie called out, "Have more punch before the next set starts up."

Laurie filled more glasses and handed them out. The women sipped their drinks and visited until the music started. As Laurie gathered the glasses she saw Gabe walking toward her.

He set his glass down, gazing at her. "This hasn't been much fun for you."

Her focus stayed on him. The dim light added to the intensity of his stare. She had never seen his pewter eyes glow the way they were at that moment.

"The change has been nice."

Gabe held out his hand to her. "Dance with me?"

She glanced around nervously, her hands pleating her skirt.

"Just once."

He hadn't planned on dancing with her, fearing what it might do to her reputation. But Gus had encouraged him, saying Laurie had spent the evening like a servant rather than a guest. And Gabe had welcomed the excuse.

As if she were in a daze, she placed her trembling hand in his and stepped around the end of the table. The musicians played "Aura Lea." Gabe slid his arm around her waist, and her step faltered. Then his splayed hand on the small of her back steadied her. As they joined the other couples she stared at his shirt and attempted to slow her breathing.

He led her around the fringe of the other couples, at the perimeter of light. His movements were so fluid she felt like she was floating. The hard-packed earth might have been a polished dance floor for all she knew. She didn't notice anyone, only the warmth of his strong arm embracing her. As she moved in unison with him her heart beat double time to the music.

If asked, Gabe would have sworn the evening air was scented with spring blossoms. Laurie felt so small and fluttery in his arms he wanted to hold her close to his chest. But if he did, he wouldn't be able to see the sparkle now lighting her eyes.

The music ended and they stopped dancing. He stood there gazing at her wistful expression for a time before he became aware of the people milling around them and escorted her away from the dance area. "We can leave anytime you like."

She nodded, her hand still warm in his. "I'll get Ammie." When he released her hand, her gaze met his, and she stood there a moment longer. Too long, she realized when the voices penetrated her thoughts.

"It ain't seemly, I tell you," a woman's voice whispered loudly.

"A good Christian woman indeed!" another huffed.

"What did I tell you?" Laurie recognized that smug voice. "She's even flaunting their affair in our faces."

"Shush, Hannah. You can't mean it." That must be Etta, Laurie decided, her back still to the group.

Breathing became painful. Laurie felt the tremor start in her stomach and spread outward until her hands shook. She knew her face must be aflame also. She raised her chin and faced the gossips. Glancing around, she saw most of the women had gathered, murmuring among themselves. Staring at her.

When she started forward, a spindly little woman blocked her way. "Excuse me." Laurie moved to step around the smaller woman.

"I will not. We don't like hussies here, socializing with decent folks."

The woman glared at Laurie, her eyes glittering with a fanatical light. Laurie felt her temper rise. "How can a God-fearing Christian woman say such a low-minded thing about someone she doesn't even know? I thought God taught us compassion and love—not vindictiveness. I've done nothing more than care for a baby."

Laurie made eye contact with each of the three gossiping women. "It is God's place to condemn me—if He sees fit—not yours. And for your information, Mr. West's aunt employed me in his stead to care for his daughter. A position that would not have been available if anyone else would have offered to help him."

The woman continued scowling at Laurie. "What decent woman'd live *alone* with an unmarried man, a *wife killer*?"

❦14❧

Laurie gulped. All she had wanted to do was earn an income to support herself. Then she had seen Ammie, and the child became the focus of her life. She had been so wrapped up in the little girl, she hadn't considered the right or wrong of living with Gabe.

"With the well-being of a small child at stake, propriety is hardly the issue." Laurie felt a small measure of satisfaction when she heard a collective gasp and the women's mouths gaped.

She turned to Gabe, who remained just behind her. "I'll be with you as soon as I get Ammie."

Gabe watched her walk away, back straight as a beam, head high. He had to admire her gumption. He'd waited too long to stop the vicious talk. She had accomplished what few had ever done—namely, shock the gossips speechless.

When Laurie returned to his side, he took the basket from her arm and guided her to the buggy. Gus and Nellie bid them thanks, and Etta had carried the extra blanket for Laurie. Gabe thanked her and fastened the reins of his horse to the back of the buggy.

Laurie said good-bye to Etta and sat with Ammie in her arms on the way back to the ranch. Her mind was a mass of confusion. What she had said in Gabe's defense, she meant. Nevertheless she kept hearing the accusation against Gabe, that he killed his wife.

Yes, she thought, Gabe had a temper. Hadn't she seen it herself? She had also seen how tender and compassionate he could be with Ammie, and herself—the warmth of his hand when he touched her face, the respect he had shown her, especially in the general store, and he had even purchased a buggy for her use, something he hadn't even done for his wife. Oh, Lord, maybe that's what upset the women—his consideration.

Gabe couldn't have harmed his wife. It was impossible. Lose his temper—yes. Even now he sat silently, a somber expression on his handsome face. However, she could not, *would not* believe him guilty of murder.

Though he had witnessed it, Gabe found Laurie's support shocking. She hadn't even flinched after Mrs. Jessop's venomous question. She knows. She knows and defended me. Of all the people in town, she's on my side. He cleared his throat and leaned back on the seat.

I must tell him, she thought. "Gabe, I know you didn't kill Ruth. I'd never believe you would do anything like that." In the dark she could only make out his darker form. "I had to tell you so you wouldn't think I'd pay any mind to that woman's dreadful accusation."

I'm not alone, he realized, and smiled. "Thank you, Laurie. That means a lot." She had called him Gabe. He began humming. Who would've guessed that the proper Mrs. Preston would turn into his strongest ally?

Laurie stretched and cleared her mind of the remnants of her dreams. She had spent a good part of the night arguing with the spindly woman—all the while Gabe had stood by her, lending unspoken strength and support, and more.

Within the freedom of her mind, she spent hours in his embrace, dancing in a field sweet with honeysuckle.

In the three days following the barn raising, she hadn't said anything to Gabe about the woman's cruel assertions. If he'd wanted to explain, he would have, she rationalized. And it wasn't as if he hadn't had the chance to talk with her, because he had been working within sight of the house, in the barn or yard, all week.

Before she entered the kitchen, she heard him humming. It was a deep, rumbling sound, and one she had only first heard four nights before. She entered the room quietly and put on her apron.

"Good morning." His coal-black hair was still damp and glossy. A thrill passed down her back, and she hoped it wasn't apparent to him. Each day, it seemed, it was becoming more difficult to think of him as only her employer.

"Coffee's ready." He handed her a brimming cup and covered her cool, slender fingers with his. Though she was dressed for the day, her long auburn hair hung free. Unwilling to prevent the movement, he reached out and brushed a few clinging strands of hair from her cheek.

She stared at him, her breathing ragged. He'd hardly spoken a word and now he was touching her. An odd, fluttery sensation winged down through her chest into her stomach.

Why are you doing this to me? she thought. His rough fingers lingered on her cheek, and she felt like she was caught in a magical web, waiting for him to release her from his spell. It may have been only moments or several minutes, Laurie didn't know, but he at last lowered his hand and stepped back. She sank onto the nearby chair. Holding the cup with both hands, she sipped the much-needed coffee.

Gabe stirred the pot of oatmeal mush and turned the bacon slabs over. Her skin felt smooth and satiny, like fine suede, he decided. Only leather, no matter how soft, didn't quiver beneath his touch.

Laurie heard Mittens yowling outside and let the cat in. It ducked beneath her skirts and stayed there until she put a bowl of fresh milk down on the floor. Alert to an unmistakable sign that Ammie was awake, she went in to help her.

As soon as Ammie was dressed, she dashed from her room. "Mittens . . . Mittens?"

Gabe set his daughter's breakfast down at her place. "Food's ready. You have to eat now."

"Want to play," Ammie called, running for the door.

Laurie went after Ammie and held the front door closed while she tugged at the latch. "Not now, sugar. Your daddy has breakfast ready."

"No! Me go out!"

Laurie rested her hands on the little girl's shoulders. "Ammie, you may not go out until later—if you are good." Laurie took Ammie's hand. "Our food is getting cold."

Ammie planted her heels and refused to budge. "No. Me play with Mittens."

Gabe, having overheard this discussion, stood by his chair debating whether to step in or see how Laurie would handle it. The latter, he decided—for several reasons.

Laurie stared at Ammie, feeling the child's willfulness for the first time. "You will walk into the kitchen." She released the child's hand. "Go, or I will be forced to do something I'd rather not do." She pointed to the kitchen. *"Now."*

Ammie's gaze slid upward from the hem of Laurie's skirt, her lips puckered. Ammie glared until she saw Laurie raise her hand, then ran to her chair.

Without saying a word to his daughter, Gabe put her in her seat and fastened the belt. Standing behind his daughter's chair, he gave Laurie an encouraging smile before taking his seat. To his way of thinking, Ammie was lucky to be at the table, let alone sitting.

* * *

Laurie cut out two small nightgowns and saved the extra yard goods for the next time the little girl outgrew them. Since Ammie and Mittens were still resting, she set the gowns aside to be sewn later and took care of some household chores—filling the lamps, washing the chimneys, dusting. Mittens loved to swipe at the dust rag.

She would have enjoyed a short ride, but Gabe had taken more supplies up to the men. As she continued to clean she heard a buggy approach. A moment later she recognized Etta Kirk and waved.

Etta pulled up in front of the house. "Hello. I don't usually just drop in on people I don't know, but I wanted to see you."

"I'm glad you did."

Etta climbed down. "After the other evening I wasn't too sure you'd welcome a visit." She followed Laurie into the house.

Laurie closed the door and glanced at Etta. "I didn't hope to win any friends after what that woman said."

"Mrs. Jessop. She's got a lot of nerve saying those things to you." Etta untied her bonnet strings and removed the bonnet.

Laurie sat on the rocker after her guest was seated on the settee. "I didn't even know her name."

"I don't think you were introduced." She smoothed her bonnet ribbons and wrapped one around her finger. "I really didn't come here to talk about her." She looked at Laurie. "People can be so small-minded. I didn't want you judging all of us as one."

"I won't." Laurie grinned. "There is only one Mrs. Jessop in town, isn't there?"

Laughing, Etta managed to say, "Lord, I hope so."

Laurie heard the latch on Ammie's door. "Excuse me a moment."

She met Ammie in the kitchen. "Mrs. Kirk came to call.

Would you carry the cake out to the other room for me?''
She cut three slices and arranged them in a small tin pan.

"Me hep, Orie."

"Thank you, sugar." Laurie placed napkins on a small
tray, then poured lemonade into two glasses and Ammie's
cup before she handed the pan to the child. "Follow me."

Laurie stopped near the settee and nodded to Ammie.
"You can put the pan down on the table." Laurie set their
drinks down. "Ammie, please hand a napkin to Mrs. Kirk."

Ammie glanced at the lady. She shuffled around the table,
her eyes downcast until she held out the napkin. She stood
staring a moment. The lady smiled, and Ammie quickly hid
behind Laurie's skirt.

"Thank you, Ammie."

Laurie nodded at the child and passed out the slices of
cake. "Sit down here, sugar."

"I hope Mr. West won't mind my calling. I don't want to
cause any problems for you."

Laurie steadied Ammie's cup. "There shouldn't be. Mr.
West is a reasonable man." Well, usually, she thought,
swallowing a small bite of cake, and wondered how Etta
would answer her question. "Would you mind telling me
what was said the other night after we left the Neilsons'?"

Etta focused on her hands for an instant, then on Laurie.
"You might as well know." Her gaze darted around the
room, and she cleared her throat. "Mrs. Tuttle tried to get
Mrs. Jessop to quiet down, but she had worked herself into
a fine state and wasn't about to lose a chance to voice her
opinions."

"Or her audience."

Etta nodded. "She kept harping about you and Mr. West
living alone here, how he got you a buggy to drive, then she
reminded everyone that he danced with you, something
she'd never seen him do with his wife."

"Thank you." Etta's face was crimson, and Laurie
regretted having to press her. "I didn't know who else to
ask. Was Mrs. Jessop a close friend of Mrs. West's?"

"I don't believe so." Etta smoothed a wrinkle from her skirt. "It wasn't easy for me when we—my husband and I—moved here either." She reached for her cake.

Laurie sipped her lemonade and glanced at Ammie. "How long have you lived here?"

"Six years this fall. Owen and I were on our way up to Portland when our wagon lost a wheel. Several of the businessmen learned Owen wanted to open a bank, and they talked him into staying." Etta blinked rapidly when a tear pooled in her eye. "If we'd only moved on, maybe Owen would be alive today."

"I'm so sorry. I had no idea." Laurie wasn't sure how to console her.

"You couldn't have known. The talk finally died down." Etta cleared her throat and attempted a smile. "You might as well know the rest."

"No, please. There's no need."

Etta shrugged. "You'll hear about it sooner or later. Owen was shot one night when he went out to check on some noises coming from the barn."

"Oh, Etta." Laurie couldn't imagine what Etta had lived through, having never experienced anything of its kind.

Etta bit her lips, then continued: "I was carrying our second child. I lost him the next day." Her blank gaze rested on the cold fireplace. "At least I have Owen Jr. I would've been lost without him." She sniffed and her thoughts came out in a rush. "The house burned down a week later. The sheriff said I must've left a lamp burning." Her painful stare turned to Laurie. "I didn't. . . ." She started crying in earnest.

Laurie moved to Etta's side and clasped her icy hand, remembering comments made to herself after Sherman's death. He was more an occasional companion than husband to Laurie. And the meant-to-be kind words of reassurance hadn't really penetrated the numb shield she had erected to protect herself. Laurie couldn't bring herself to voice the usual words of condolence. She said nothing. Instead she reached out and hugged Etta until her tears slowed.

Ammie scrambled over to Laurie and threw herself on her lap.

Reaching down with one arm, Laurie rubbed Ammie's back while Etta gathered her composure. Once she calmed, Laurie released her. "Why don't we take a walk outside?"

Ammie stood up. "Mittens go out, too?"

"See if she's awake." Laurie looked at Etta. "Fresh air usually helps me."

"Oh, my goodness," Etta exclaimed, covering her mouth. "Whatever possessed me? You've lost a husband, too."

"No, it's all right." She had learned quite by accident that Sherman was with a prostitute when he died, and it still angered her. "It seems like a very long time ago." She heard a chair bump the kitchen table. "Let's go out before Ammie manages to catch the cat."

Mittens with Ammie close behind led the way out to the yard. Etta and Laurie wandered over to the corral. Carly trotted over and she petted the mare's velvety muzzle.

Etta watched Laurie. "Is she yours?"

"No. G—Mr. West allows me to ride her." Laurie scratched the mare's forelock. She looked around and made sure Ammie stayed within sight.

Etta quickly glanced away. "Sounds like he's very thoughtful. Most men aren't that generous with their wives." She blushed and gazed beyond Laurie at the hills.

Laurie toyed with the horse's mane and spoke softly. "More than some." Certainly more considerate than Sherman had been, she thought. He was more a friend than husband. Ammie's voice carried across the yard, and some birds squabbled in a tree near the stream—everyday sounds. Still, Laurie found herself listening for another daily occurrence—Gabe's return.

"It's getting late. I didn't mean to spend the afternoon." Etta grinned. "I'm glad I came. I live in town, across the bridge, first street on the left. I hope you'll come by when you have a chance.''

Gabe stood in the yard staring at the roof of the house. Sweat dripped from his brow and down his back. The gentle breeze felt good against his damp skin. Several shingles flapped in the breeze, and he was sure there would be more when he went up to inspect the roof. He gathered the materials he'd need and carried them up. Before starting work, he went in the house.

He found Laurie in the kitchen instructing his daughter in the art of making biscuits while his daughter attempted to dab flour on Laurie's nose. She was laughing, a soft throaty sound. His breathing quickened, as did the beat of his heart.

"I'm going to be working on the roof. Just call when dinner's ready."

Ammie turned around on the chair. "Orie teachin' me cook, Daddy."

Laurie stared at Gabe. She wiped the flour from her nose and steadied Ammie. Please don't do this. Can't you see how unfair it is? she thought. She glanced down at the bowl. I am only his daughter's nanny, nothing more. I'll never be anything more. I must remember that. She repeated the words over and over in her mind.

Gabe's scrutiny didn't waver from Laurie, willing her to look at him. "That's nice of her."

"Would you rather eat now?" she asked in a voice strange to her own ears.

The sultry sound of her words played havoc with his effort to think of her as only his employee. "No," he mumbled. "Whenever it's ready will be fine." He went back up to the roof, determined to relieve the tension knotting his groin with physical labor, though it was not the kind of release he desired.

Laurie watched his abrupt exit and sighed.

Ammie grabbed for the mixing spoon and knocked it onto the floor.

"Be careful!" As soon as Laurie snapped at the child, she reached for her. "I'm sorry, sugar. I'll rinse the spoon off."

Ammie watched Laurie. "You mad, Orie?"

"No, sugar." Laurie grinned and handed the clean spoon back to Ammie. "Stir very carefully while I add the shortening."

She was decidedly relieved to concentrate on her usual chores after dinner. Recently the meals had become increasingly strained, at least for her. It seemed as though he spent most of the time watching her—and she him, if she were completely honest.

That evening they sat in the main room. Laurie worked her needle on a scrap of cloth she was making into a beanbag. Ammie brought out a bowl and spoon.

Gabe glanced over at his daughter. "What're you doing?" His gaze went to Laurie. "Is she allowed to play with those things?"

"Making a surp-ise, Daddy."

Laurie glanced at him and returned her attention to her sewing. "It's all right. She can't hurt anything."

Gabe frowned.

Laurie tied off the thread. "Ammie, would you like to put the beans in the bag?" She set both on the floor.

Ammie eagerly obliged, dropping the beans in by twos and threes.

Gabe sat listening to the flat thunk of the beans dropping into the bag, each one seeming to pluck on his taut nerves. Was Laurie deliberately trying his patience? Oh, he'd seen that look on her face a few times, the one he felt sure meant that she was as aware of him as he was of her.

He hadn't felt this anxious, hot, since his youth. He watched Laurie with his daughter. They talked and laughed, and seemed so right together. When they'd gone to Jacksonville on the Fourth, they had been like a real family. But how much longer could he live in the same house with her and not touch her silky hair, her soft skin—make love to her?

* * *

Laurie dashed to the necessary, her skirts flying. She glimpsed huge thunderheads looming far to the west and realized they were the reason for the early twilight. The strong wind had an unsettling effect on her. She had been jumpy all day. On her return trip to the house, a gust nearly drove her into Gabe while he worked the water pump.

He grabbed her arms and hauled her up to his body. "Lose something?"

She gazed up into his eyes. "The wind." She gulped and leaned into his broad chest, seeking a shelter.

He slid his arm around her and placed his flat hand on her back. "We're in for a good one. You'd better stay in the house."

She shivered in his embrace, her heart beating like a drum. She savored his touch, the roughness of his shirt against her cheek, the smell of leather, horses, and the faint scent of soap. She felt safe and warm. She felt like a woman. She didn't feel like his employee. But she was.

Laurie stiffened her spine and stepped back. She glanced at the roiling clouds once more. "I'd better make sure the windows are latched tight."

She bolted to the house with the wind whipping her skirts about. Gabe watched her slim ankles and sighed. God, she'd felt good in his arms. He turned back to the barn.

Bracing the doors, he glared up at the darkening sky. Black clouds approached, and the temperature had dropped to near-winter levels. What was going on? The frosty wind whipped the barn doors from his grasp, straining the hinges. An empty barrel bounced around the yard like a tumbleweed.

Gabe worked quickly to secure the barn, outbuildings, and the agitated livestock. He couldn't recall such a storm, more like an approaching gale, in August.

Laurie heard the front door slam closed and went to make sure it was Gabe. "Are the animals all right?"

"They're jittery but okay." He slipped a thick plank in place, barring the front door.

"Is that necessary?" The board looked foreboding, as if they were under attack.

"The latch's strong, but it's old."

Ammie prowled around the main room, her room, and the kitchen before going to Laurie. "Where's Mittens? Can't find her, Orie."

The wind whistled through the loose window frame, startling Laurie. "You call her, sugar, and I'll look upstairs."

Laurie secured the gate at the bottom of the stairs behind her and went up to see if the cat had wandered into her room. There was no sign of her, so she opened the door to the other room. She checked the window again and searched the room, even though she knew the door always remained closed.

Ammie was still calling Mittens when Laurie returned. "She's not upstairs, sugar." She glanced at Gabe's door before finding him in the kitchen.

"Would you look in your room and see if the cat's hiding in there?" Ammie came up to Laurie and held on to her leg. She smoothed the child's hair back. "Ammie's worried about the cat, and I haven't seen it all afternoon."

Gabe nodded and left to search his room. He returned a few minutes later. "It's not there." He stooped down by Ammie. "It'll be fine, punkin. Cats are smart and good at hiding."

Ammie leaned into her daddy's arms. "Want Mittens, Daddy. Plllease find Mittens."

Gabe embraced his daughter, awkwardly at first. He kissed the top of her head and held her a moment longer. "I'll look outside."

Laurie watched Gabe and Ammie, and her eyes welled up with tears. Pressing her lips together, she stood staring at him. She wanted to join in, put her arms around him, but she couldn't bring herself to intrude on their moment. Dear

Lord, I love him, she thought, and turned away lest he notice her.

She started a fresh pot of coffee and heard Gabe go outside. The more she realized how much she had come to love him, the more she feared those wondrous feelings. After Sherman's death friends had reminded her that love could be painful. It hadn't been, not then. It was now.

Did she have the strength to remain at the ranch caring for Ammie *and* mask her feelings for Gabe? The pine trees outside bent with the force of the wind. As if lamenting with her, the house creaked and groaned. In her mind the wind murmured, "Widow Preston," and she shivered.

Laurie slid the beanbag along the floor to Ammie and tried to ignore the howling wind outside. "Here it comes."

Mittens darted after the skidding bag.

Ammie grabbed it from the cat's paws. "Mine."

"Good catch! Now slide it back to me."

Ammie sat with her legs out in front of her forming a *V* to help trap the bag. She shoved the beanbag across the floor in Laurie's direction and watched Mittens chase it.

Laurie continued passing the beanbag to Ammie, hoping to keep her amused and her mind off of the storm. The cat unwittingly helped. With each strange noise, the animal would arch its back, and its tail bristled, resembling an orange-striped feather duster. Gabe didn't want to risk a fire, so Laurie had dressed the little girl in several layers of clothing for warmth.

She rubbed her arms and looked at him. "Would you play with Ammie while I go upstairs?"

He glanced at his daughter. "Go on. We'll be fine." He got up from his chair and sat cross-legged where Laurie had knelt.

Laurie searched her wardrobe and groaned. She had packed with such prudence she never thought to bring a few woolens for winter. She quickly changed into her warmest nightgown and wrapper before putting a shawl around her shoulders. Warmth was more important than vanity, she decided.

Gabe watched her come down the stairs. She was bundled in nightclothes and had let her hair down. The thought of peeling those layers of cloth from her body caused a deep ache in his loins.

Laurie noticed an almost painful expression mar Gabe's strong features. "Are you feeling all right?" She went over to him and pressed her hand on his brow.

He took her cool hand in his. "It's nothing." He grinned at her. "Join us. We'll make it a three-way toss."

She stared at his large, suntanned hand and felt her legs grow weak. "How about some hot chocolate? It might warm us."

"Me too, Orie," Ammie chimed in. "An Mittens."

"I think she would prefer her milk plain and in her bowl."

The wind buffeted the front door, rattling the latch and plank. Laurie started, then moved to distract Ammie. "Ask your daddy to teach you how to throw the beanbag while I make our cocoa."

She poured the pitcher of milk into a pan and put it over the heat on the stove. As soon as Ammie's safely asleep, I'll go up to bed, Laurie assured herself. Though she wore more than enough clothing to cover her body, she felt quite uncomfortable as the object of Gabe's scrutiny.

She filled three cups with hot chocolate. The planks of the floor creaked as she carried them into the main room. The windows rattled; even interior doors swung with the draft blowing through chinks in the outer wall of the house. Then the air seemed to still, and Laurie sighed.

As soon as she had passed out the cups and sat down on the floor with Gabe and Ammie, another gust hit the house with a renewed vengeance. Moments later a thunderclap shook the log house. Rain lashed down. The cups clattered on their saucers, and Laurie could have sworn the whole house rocked from the force of the wind.

❧15❧

Laurie glanced at Ammie. "Want to sit on my lap, sugar?"
She held out her arms.

Ammie crawled over onto Laurie's lap, curled up, and
stuck her thumb in her mouth.

Ammie's warm little body acted like a tonic for Laurie.
She felt a protective calm spread through her. Holding the
child against her breast, she rocked slowly and hummed.
Mittens crept over and curled up on the hem of her wrapper
and covered her pumpkin nose with one white paw.

Gabe got up and looked outside before reaching for his
pipe. The darkness made it impossible to see anything, but
he could hear the ominous squeak of straining boards. He
filled the bowl of his pipe and lighted it.

He restlessly paced around the room, glancing at Laurie.
If he had one of those fancy cameras he'd seen, he'd take a
photograph of her now—sitting on the floor, her hair
flowing down her back and over her shoulders, holding his
daughter in her arms with the cat asleep on the edge of her
wrapper. Her image evoked sweet memories from his child-

hood, dreams he'd had of his future—hopes he'd long ago given up.

Laurie eased her legs around and tried to stand without disturbing Ammie, but the cat lay like a stone, and she couldn't gain leverage. Gabe appeared at her side and started to lift her up.

"Wait," she whispered. "The cat."

"She'll move."

"Just slide her away."

He cupped the small cat in his hands and set her down on the rug. Then he stood behind Laurie, placed his hands on her waist, and lifted her to her feet. He held her against him and bent to kiss Ammie.

Gabe turned his head, his lips near Laurie's ear, and whispered, "She's sound asleep."

His hot breath ruffled the hair over her ear and sent a delicious trickling sensation down her spine. "I'll put her to bed." That was obvious, but she had to break the spell.

After Ammie was settled for the night, Laurie turned down the lamp in the kitchen on her way through. She paused midway to the staircase, and her gaze met Gabe's. The air felt charged. She was uneasy but decided that the feeling was more within herself than a response to the gale outside.

Gabe stared at her. He wanted her to stay, but that would be dangerous. "Don't you want to take a light?"

She watched the way he held the bowl of the pipe and returned his gaze. "I won't need it."

The house was cold. She felt inordinately warm. She continued on up to her room but left her door open in case the cat wanted company during the night. She put the extra blankets and comforter back on the bed, draped her shawl, wrapper, and extra nightgowns over the end of the bed, then slid beneath the covers.

With her knees drawn up to her chest and the covers around her chin, Laurie lay listening as it rained. Tree branches scraped against the house like fingernails on a chalkboard. She fell asleep waiting for the sound of Gabe's bedroom door closing.

In what seemed like a few minutes, something crashed through her window. She screamed and jumped back against the headboard. She stared at the floor in bewilderment and finally realized that the object was just a piece of firewood. Icy wind and rain gushed into the room. Her teeth chattered, but before she could move, Gabe burst in.

"You all right?" He glanced past the window in his search for her. In two strides he was at her bedside. "Get downstairs. There's glass all over the floor."

"Will you bring my bedding?" She made her way to the door and went down to the main room.

Gabe scooped up the feather mattress, bedding and all, and followed her. "Where do you want this?"

More shattering glass, this time from the direction of the kitchen, stilled their words.

Ammie screamed.

Laurie raced to the child's room.

Gabe dropped the bedding and ran after Laurie. "Watch where you walk!"

Laurie reached Ammie first and snatched her up with the blanket. After motioning for Gabe to bring the rest of the bedding, she carried the frightened child into the main room to quiet her.

Gabe deposited the bedding on the floor. "I'll cover the window so we won't have to worry about that one."

After lighting a lamp and placing it away from drafts, he searched the room for something large enough to block the window. The marble-top table would have to do. He quickly cleared and upended it before bracing the settee against it.

He surveyed his handiwork. "That should hold, for a while, anyway."

Laurie sat on the rocker, keeping a gentle rhythm, trying to soothe Ammie's fears with low murmurings. She nodded at Gabe and continued calming his daughter. The gale blasted the log house. Debris smashed through the kitchen window and against the outer walls. She schooled herself not to jump, or flinch, or cringe.

When Gabe passed near the rocker, she reached out and touched his hand. "Would you lay out her bedding?" She motioned to where he'd left it. "She's almost asleep." She whispered so as not to awaken the child, but then she came close to laughing. Why was she trying to be so quiet? The storm made normal speech nearly impossible to hear.

Gabe straightened his daughter's bedding before closing the kitchen door. Again he paced around the room, wincing every time something struck the wall. He'd done all he could, but he hadn't had time to ride up to check on Ben, Danny, and Nate. He felt totally helpless.

Laurie eased out of the rocker and started to put Ammie down on her bed.

"Wait. Put her in my bed. The wind isn't battering that side of the house."

Laurie nodded and followed him. She tucked Ammie in and left the bedroom door ajar. In the main room she watched Gabe staring at the fireplace and went over to him.

Without a child in her arms she felt the cold and hugged herself. "It's not getting any worse."

"How could it?"

She shrugged and started for the stairs.

He reached out and caught her arm. "Where are you going?"

"I need my wrapper."

"I'll get it."

"It's over the end of the bed."

He took the stairs two at a time and returned to find she hadn't moved. He stepped up and slipped the wrapper around her shivering body. He intended to tie the sash. Instead he drew Laurie's slender body against his and fingered her silky hair. It was as soft as he'd imagined that first morning. She was, too, and she nestled so perfectly in his embrace. His breathing became labored.

She felt comforted by Gabe's strength and warmth. As

she melted into him the frigid wind and its danger was replaced with an excitement growing within her. She slipped her arms around his waist and closed her eyes, wanting to etch those feelings into her memory.

She heard a low rumble beneath her cheek, felt his chest muscles harden, and snuggled even closer to him. His fingers teased the nape of her neck, and her back arched in response. Waves of pleasure spread down her spine. She tightened her hold on him. As the storm raged outside, pounding against the side of the house, Laurie felt anticipation and desire building within her.

Gabe felt the heat rise. Dear God, he didn't want to stop. He played with the fine hair behind her ear, then tipped her head back and lowered his lips to hers. She was exciting, yielding, and passionate. He parted his lips, and she did also, allowing him entry.

Her breath mingled with his. She had never been kissed the way he kissed her. As his tongue met and teased hers the incredible weakness he had created became a hunger. She swayed against him. When she drew her fingers across his back, his powerful muscles bunched and rippled. A deep sigh of frustration escaped. She couldn't seem to get close enough to him.

Her throaty moan was the sweetest sound, a primitive mating call. "I've wanted to do that for so long."

"So have I." She couldn't believe her boldness, and she did not regret it.

Gabe released his hold with one arm. "You must be freezing." The wind rattled window casings, but he knew they were now in no danger, not from the storm, anyway.

She shook her head. "Not in the least."

He pressed his lips to her smooth forehead. "We have plenty of blankets." He went to where he'd made up the pallet. He quickly repositioned the blankets and added another comforter on top.

As Laurie watched his movements her hands trembled. She clasped them. Soon the icy air penetrated the heated excitement Gabe had woven around her. *What am I doing?* *He's my employer!* she thought. She paced a confined area, her fingers nervously twisting the ends of her sash.

Gabe watched her agitated stride a moment before he stopped in front of her. Her attention was fixed at some point behind him while he tried to warm her cold hands. He attempted to ease her down, but she stood like a bronze statue. "I'll get more blankets."

She nodded and gazed down at the bed. A cruel comment she had heard years earlier came to mind. *A desperate widow is ripe pickings for any man.* She wasn't desperate, was she? And he certainly wasn't just any man. *He's the man I love.*

Gabe encircled her trembling shoulders with the cover and held it close around her. She remained unyielding. He pulled her close and held her there. He rested his cheek on the top of her head and gently rocked her.

The heat of his breath tingled on her neck and began melting the frosty bearing she attempted to shield herself with. Her pulse raced, but she refused to give in to the urge to put her arms around him again. She wasn't a loose woman. Oh, but she wanted to know fulfillment in his arms, if only once. She had never felt this overwhelming desire she had heard whispered about. Not until now.

He brought the two ends of the comforter together over her breasts and stared at her. "Better?" he whispered.

"Much." She gazed up at him. The tenderness of his voice and earnest gaze of his silvery eyes began to weaken her resolve.

"Ah, Laurie . . ." He traced her cool jaw with his knuckle and twined his fingers through her silky hair, combing it back from her face. With her head resting on his hand, he tipped it back and trailed kisses along her cheeks, her slender throat, then he took her mouth. She submitted to his caress, but without her earlier fire.

"I want you, Laurie. God, how I want you. Have I moved too fast? Frightened you?"

She knew that if she didn't step away from him then, she wouldn't be able to later. His voice was deep, mesmerizing, and passionate. "I've never felt this way before." She stared at the smooth texture of his cheek.

"Never?"

She shook her head.

His chest expanded.

His lips touched hers. It was sweet torture beyond her imaginings. If she withdrew, she would surely regret it the rest of her life.

Moaning, she slanted her lips on his and found it made it easier for him to feed the fire burning inside of her. That heady, tantalizing feeling invaded her once again. The storm outside receded from her awareness. Only Gabe existed, and she welcomed him.

The blanket dropped to the floor.

"I want you, too."

"You're sure?"

"Yes."

He sank his fingers into her silky mane. "I don't want you to be sorry tomorrow."

"I won't be. I need you."

He guided her down onto the mattress. She gazed up at him with passion-glazed eyes and met his proffered lips with a fiery ardor that made his self-control almost painful. She was the first woman to return his love. He slid his hand down the lapel of her wrapper.

She never knew her body could be so sensitive, so alive. A strange, hollow hungriness grew and drove her on.

The rain drummed against the log house like a thundering heartbeat. He'd ignore anything short of the logs falling down around them. He pushed her wrapper aside and began unbuttoning the numerous tiny disks on her pristine gown, one . . . two . . . three . . . His finger slipped, plunged through, and ripped one of the buttonholes.

"Damn!" He yanked his finger free.

His swearing hit her like a pail of ice water, and she

shrank from him. She had made a fool of herself and worse. *Desperate widow* . . .

He stilled her movement. "It's not you, Laurie," he said gently. He bent to kiss her. "It's these infernal buttons on your gown. Why are there so many of them?"

"Oh." She sighed, her fears slowly subsiding. "To keep the gown together."

When she saw how much trouble his large fingers were having with the small buttons, she giggled nervously.

Gabe grinned, seized a handful of cloth with each hand, and pulled the sides apart. Tiny buttons flew off, from the hem up to the high neck of the gown, and clattered around the plank floor.

"There," he murmured. "That's much better."

"Oh! I could have . . ." She gazed up at him and forgot what she was about to say. His rapt expression was focused on her. She felt vulnerable and moved to pull the sides of her gown together.

"No."

His softly spoken word stopped her.

"I don't want anything between us."

He reached out and rested his trembling hand on her slim ankle and stared at the treasure he'd exposed. Her legs were willowy and tapered, her skin like rich cream.

"God, you're so soft."

He quickly unfastened his belt and trousers.

She watched as he shed his shirt and trousers. Muscles rippled beneath the tanned skin. The lamplight lent a golden cast to his large frame. She stared at him in wonder. "You're beautiful!"

He grinned at her, feeling inordinately satisfied with her praise, and lay down beside her.

Suddenly the house was pelted with hail. The noise became thunderous. She clung to him, awash in a myriad of sensations. The onslaught outside was like an echo of the turbulence she felt.

As she struggled to discover what she craved, Gabe took her to the brink and over. Wave after wave of delicious, wondrous sensations washed through her. Her heart pounded, and she simply *felt,* with every fiber of her being.

Heaven. He'd found paradise in one small woman. "Laurie . . ." He sank down on her, his breathing labored, and feeling completely satiated—totally contented.

She held him close as the pulsing lingered. She felt weightless, like a feather in a storm. She wanted to tell him how beautiful it had been, but she couldn't find words to describe her feelings. Instead she relished his weight pressing down on her.

Slowly his breathing returned to normal. He cradled her head in his hands and smiled at the dreamy expression on her face. Reluctantly he rolled to her side and pulled several covers over them.

"You're beautiful."

"I was shameless," she murmured into his damp skin.

He tipped her chin up. "Look at me, Laurie." Her gaze wavered, then met his. "You have nothing to be embarrassed about." He gently kissed her swollen lips.

Laurie rested her head on his chest. She felt replete, weak, and happier than she could ever remember being. The even beat of Gabe's heart steadied hers and lulled her to sleep.

Ammie woke up and bolted to the door. She looked around at the jumbled furniture and water on the floor in the main room. "Orie!" When she noticed the top of Laurie's head peaking out from the blankets, she ran over and knelt by her. "Orie, Orie, wake up." She saw a little button on the floor and picked it up. "Have to pee!"

Laurie snuggled closer to Gabe, enjoying those prewaking moments in his warmth. The cool air smelled of damp earth, wood, and the lingering scent of their lovemaking. She felt his arm tighten around her waist, then Ammie's urgent appeal penetrated her drowsy meanderings.

She peered over the edge of the covers. Ammie sat on her heels staring at a small button. Laurie wanted to die.

Gabe kissed Laurie's shoulder and raised his head above the blankets. "Mornin', punkin. You hungry?"

"Have t' go potty." She picked up another button, squirmed, and crawled around after more.

"Ammie," Gabe called. "Go sit on my bed. Be careful. There's glass on the floor."

He nuzzled Laurie's ear. "Time to rise and see what damage the storm left behind." He released her and grabbed his trousers. Once he'd pulled them on, he distracted his daughter, giving Laurie time to dress.

Grateful for his consideration, Laurie snatched up her discarded nightgown. She forced her thoughts to what needed her attention. After she secured the wrapper over her buttonless gown, she started to pick her way through the glass on the wet floor.

After attending to Ammie's needs, Laurie carried her to the rumpled bed in the main room. "You sit right here, sugar, and watch your daddy. I have to get our shoes."

Feeling like her feet were already frozen, Laurie raced across the icy floor and upstairs. When she returned, she heard Gabe cheerfully humming as he set split logs in the fireplace. She approached hesitantly, not sure what to say to him.

He was still shirtless, his back as bronze in the morning light as in the lamp's. He sat back on his heels. His coal-black hair was mussed, and he grinned up at her with an intimacy that warmed her cheeks.

"Did Ammie find all the buttons?" He grinned. Her cheeks and neck turned a deep shade of pink. He took her hand from the folds of her wrapper and held it. "Do you regret last night?"

Her gaze remained on him. She shook her head. "Not at all. Should I?"

He reassuringly squeezed her hand. "Never!"

Glancing at Ammie, Laurie sighed. The child sat playing

with a small figurine that had been among the clutter on the table. "I'd better get her shoes on and sweep up the glass."

He wanted to kiss Laurie, but she was watching Ammie. "I'm afraid today's going to be more hectic than I'd like."

She nodded and went about her chores. She had to keep busy, keep her mind on what needed to be done, keep her thoughts off Gabe and how wonderful it had felt to be in his embrace. Once she had buttoned Ammie's shoes, she swept up the glass from the main room, mopped up the water, then proceeded to do the same in the kitchen and Ammie's room.

She hesitated entering Gabe's room but knew she could not shrink from the task. The furniture in his room was similar to hers, only older, and held his scent. His bed was large, the wardrobe double-sized, and there was a heavy blanket chest in one corner. She turned around, stepped out of his room, and avoided noticing any of his personal items.

Gabe righted the settee and put it in place. The table was damp but the marble and oiled finish seemed to have protected it. The amethyst drapes caught his attention. Ruth had insisted they were fashionable. In fact he couldn't help laughing as he tossed the bedraggled, limp rags out through the vacant window.

His bedroom door closed, and he glanced over. Laurie was leaning back against it, looking miserable. He reached her side quickly.

He stood so close to her she could feel his breath on her cheek and her heart pounding. She fought the inclination, the desire to rest her head on his broad chest and be held in his arms again. They stood in the light of day. The storm had passed. Sanity must be restored.

He watched her brows knit as she seemed to struggle with her thoughts. "Something's wrong. Tell me."

She apprehensively gazed around the room. "There's . . . just so much to be done."

He slanted his hand on the small of her back and gazed down at her. "Yes. It was a bad storm."

~16~

Once they had finished a simple breakfast, Laurie began
restoring order to the house while Gabe went to work
outside. She even set Ammie to simple tasks. By noontime
the beds had been made and the knickknacks and the
daguerreotypes of Gabe's parents were back in place on the
table in the main room.

Gabe finished the last of the cold meat dinner and
watched Laurie as she tended his daughter. "Did you find
any more damage inside, besides the windows?"

"I didn't see anything. But the windows are enough."

"Tomorrow I'll see about new glass." He scraped his
chair back. "The windows will have to be boarded up. I'd
better do that before I go check on the herd."

"Do you have to do it now? Maybe just Ammie's
window." She reached for his plate and set it atop hers.
"It's so nice out today. The house needs a good airing, and
I've been leaving my window open at night, anyway." She
brushed the crumbs to her side of the table and onto the
plates. "You needn't worry about it now."

"Laurie . . ." He glanced at his daughter. "Isn't it time to put her down?"

"I will after you cover her window."

She continued clearing the table. She had watched him at every opportunity while he worked outside, but she couldn't look at him at that moment. Her feelings were too fresh, too apparent. She felt she had too much to lose if she didn't guard them well.

Sherman hadn't been a demanding husband, never making her feel the way Gabe had, and he had never pressed her to be intimate. But after the few occasions he had claimed his right, he was always more considerate of her the next day. Gabe was following suit. By tomorrow he would be himself again, and she herself. Anything more would be dangerous.

Gabe had never seen this pensive side of Laurie and didn't know how to deal with it. "Then I'll see you later."

He located three wide boards the right length. Nailing them in place over Ammie's window frame gave him an outlet for his frustration. Soon after, he saddled his horse, rode up to the rise, and paused to survey the ranch house and outbuildings. Several sections of fence were down, and even in the distance he could tell he'd have to replace more shingles. The creek had overflowed its bed earlier, though it was now back within its banks.

He reined the horse around and started off. Laurie didn't regret last night; anyway, that's what she said. Maybe she was just embarrassed this morning, unsure of herself. She seemed to trust him. Surely she knew he'd do right by her.

The sky was clear. Not a cloud could be seen from the previous night's storm. He made his way up to the pasture at a cautious pace. Several older pines had been felled by the wind, dried brush scattered about, and every ditch, furrow, and rut was brimming with rainwater.

As his mount made his way along the muddy track, Gabe remembered Laurie's satiny smooth skin and her surprisingly passionate response. Life with her at his side would be close to heaven. Of course, he couldn't take time off for a wedding and trip until after roundup, but he didn't think she'd mind too much. He whistled tunelessly and chuckled when a bird returned his call.

He reached the summer camp mud-splattered and relieved to see his herd grazing on the taller grasses. He tied his mount to a tree branch. Nearby, three shirts and pairs of trousers were draped over a bush to dry. At least the storm had rinsed off the men's clothes. Peering inside the cookshack, he saw Old Ben.

"Any hot coffee left?"

Ben jerked around and glared at him. "Ya shouldn't oughta scare a man like that." He shook his head. "It's in the pot, like always."

Gabe smiled and poured himself a cup. "Looks like the shack withstood the rain."

"Yep, right good." Ben scooped some flour into a chipped bowl and reached for the baking soda. "You gonna stay awhile? Or jest payin' a call?"

"I've got a lot of repairs to do at the house. I wanted to make sure you hadn't been blown or washed away last night." Gabe blew on the coffee and sipped it.

Ben grinned. "Well, you needed somethin' to keep you outta trouble."

Taking another drink from the cup, Gabe glared at Ben's back. "What do you mean?"

Shrugging, Ben started mixing the biscuit dough.

What the hell's the matter with me? Gabe wondered. One night with Laurie, and I act like everyone knows? "Sorry, Ben. Guess I need some rest. I'll see you next week."

A few minutes later Gabe located Danny. "Have you dried out yet?"

Danny slapped his hat on his thigh and rubbed his arm across his brow. "It didn't last that long up here. Nate's tracked down the last five head. Much damage at the ranch?"

"Enough. I have to replace at least four windows, some

fencing, and shingles." Gabe held his mount to a walk as they rode around the perimeter of the pasture.

Danny glanced sideways at Gabe. "How're Ammie and Mrs. Preston? They weren't hurt, were they?"

Gabe's grip on the reins tightened slightly. "They're fine." He gazed out at the herd and stifled a yawn.

"Am I keeping you up, boss? Must've had a rough night, what with all those windows breaking and all."

Gabe scowled at Danny. He'd always known how to get under Gabe's skin faster than any of his other friends. "It took a while to get Ammie quieted."

"I'd think that'd be Mrs. Preston's job." Danny smirked, staring at the ground.

"When I come up next week, I'll spell you for a couple days. Sounds like you need it." Gabe gazed across the pasture and waved to Nate. "Don't forget to check your laundry." With that, he rode over to speak with Nate before returning home.

Laurie momentarily considered resting, but she wanted to work upstairs while Ammie napped. She took the broom, bucket, mop, and dustpan up, since she hadn't swept her floor yet.

She checked Ruth's old room for the first time. Nothing had changed. The window was intact, so she closed the door and went to straighten up her own room.

Once all of the glass splinters had been disposed of and the water had been mopped up, Laurie set her nightclothes aside so she could tackle the bed. It was more difficult than she had thought it would be, but she managed to drag the cumbersome feather mattress up the stairs and put it on the rope supports.

She made the bed and placed her wrapper at the foot. When she held up her nightgown, the front panels parted. Even though she was alone in the room, she felt herself blushing. A fragrant reminder of their lovemaking clung to the gown. It was a tantalizing keepsake, proof that she had indeed spent an amorous night with Gabe.

Since she was finished in her room, she took the gown down to the kitchen. Using some of the water she'd kept heating on the stove, she washed it out and hung it at the far end of the line. Laurie stretched, arching her weary back and took pleasure in the sun's warmth.

She checked on Carly and meandered around the yard, wondering what she would make for supper. Something hearty, she decided, because Gabe mentioned having a lot of repairs to do. Pot roast sounded good. Simple, too, if she recalled correctly. She smiled. At the time she hadn't realized what a blessing Sherman's dislike of her cooking was.

Four hours later Laurie fretted over her decision to have roast for supper. Ammie was playing with her doll and Mittens in the main room. Laurie had nothing to do but pace the length of the kitchen worrying over the meal. It was silly, she knew, but she wanted it to be right.

She glanced at where the kitchen window had been. The air was cool, and the sun appeared to hesitate before sinking below the horizon. Where was he? She opened the oven door and checked the pot for the tenth time. Did the carrots and potatoes look dry? She added a cup of water, just to be safe, and closed the door.

Ten minutes later she checked the oven again. Well, she couldn't keep Ammie waiting forever. Laurie set the pot on top of the stove, put the biscuits in the oven, and went into the main room to check on the little girl.

"We'll eat in just a few minutes, sugar."

Ammie glanced up. "Betsy and Mittens eat, too."

"You can feed Mittens after we eat. I don't think your doll is really hungry."

Laurie had finally started to relax when the aroma of burning biscuits drifted into the main room. "Oh, Lord," she mumbled, running to the oven. She rescued the rolls but had to cut them off of the pan to save them. Suddenly Gabe was at her side, and she jumped.

"I'm starved." He rested his hands on her shoulders, sniffed, and said teasingly, "Hope you didn't burn supper."

Laurie groaned. "Just part of the biscuits."

Gabe leaned forward to see what she was doing. He cleared his throat. "The tops look good."

His stomach rumbled. He rubbed his hand down the soft cotton gown he'd taken from the clothesline on his way to the house. He showed her the gown, saying, "I thought you might need this tonight," and tossed it over the back of the nearest chair; his.

The cover on the iron pot bounced. Laurie thought it sounded like a death knell. "Thank you," she mumbled, adding in a lighter tone, "I'll serve supper now."

Feeling more than a little anxious and embarrassed, she yanked at the last biscuit. The golden top came off in her hand, leaving two thirds of the roll still firmly attached to the pan. "I was trying to keep the food warm. I guess I waited too long."

Gabe set the plate of half rolls on the table. "You shouldn't have held supper for me. I'm sure it'll be fine."

Laurie uncovered the pot roast. She had seen better, which would be no major accomplishment, she thought forlornly. The vegetables were easy to dish out, but when she stabbed the fork into the roast and lifted, the meat fell apart.

Gabe held up the plate. "Looks tender."

Laurie rolled her eyes. "Perfect, if you were a toothless old man." Using the skimmer and a large spoon, she managed to dish out large chunks of the meat.

While she tended Ammie and served her food, Gabe thickened the liquid in the pot and seasoned it. She'd told him she wasn't much of a cook that first day, but he'd forgotten since he hadn't found any fault with her skills in the kitchen. He tasted the sauce and took the pot to the table.

The rich brown gravy looked delicious. Laurie ladled

some over her meat, tasted it, and smiled at Gabe. "Thank you." She broke up a biscuit on Ammie's plate and spooned the sauce over it and the small bites of meat.

Ammie ate a piece of meat. She picked up another and dropped it over the side of her chair.

Gabe saw her toss the bite to the floor. "Ammie, you know better than to drop food on the floor." He bent to pick it up, but it wasn't there. Sitting under the table was the cat, licking its chops.

He straightened up and glared at his young daughter. "*Do not* feed that cat at the table."

Ammie glanced at Laurie. "I can too feed Mittens."

Laurie swallowed and wiped her mouth. "I said you could feed Mittens *after* supper, Ammie. You may not drop food down to her."

Gabe talked with Laurie about what needed repairing. He noticed his daughter sulking, but she didn't drop any more food to the cat. After supper, Ammie fed her cat and sat down to watch it eat. Gabe helped Laurie do the dishes. After all, he reasoned, he'd done them for months before she came, and he didn't mind giving her a hand with the chores, chores he had originally said she wouldn't have to do.

When she had finished the last of the dishes, Laurie glanced at the pan of dishwater, shrugged, and flung it out through the window frame. "Now I know why that bush is so healthy."

Gabe grinned. "That's what I always did." He went into his daughter's room to check the boards. They held fast, but it was awfully cold in the small room. Then he remembered that Laurie's hadn't been covered either.

Laurie brought a blanket in and met Gabe leaving Ammie's room. "Do you have any small nails?"

He nodded. "What's that old thing for? It's filthy."

"I plan to cover the inside of Ammie's window with it." She held it up. "I beat the dust out and aired it on the line all afternoon."

He took the blanket from her hands and pitched it out through the kitchen window. "I've been thinking about that. You and Ammie will sleep in my bed tonight."

He watched her expression closely, the way her gaze flitted to odd points in the room, the way she nibbled at her lips, and most telling of all, the way she kept flexing her fingers as if she needed to grasp something.

"Ammie can sleep with you. I prefer my own room." Her gaze fell on her nightgown. She grabbed it with one hand. "I'd better put this away."

He reached for her, but she stepped away too quickly. "Laurie . . ." He waited until she paused in the doorway. "She's so small. I'd probably roll over and smother her." He straightened up. "Besides, that's your job."

Clenching her teeth, she looked at him and silently implored, please don't do this. Why was he being so obstinate? They both knew there was another bedroom with the window intact, but Ammie seemed to fear that room, and Laurie couldn't bring herself to suggest it.

"If you insist. I'll be right back."

Laurie went up to her room and closed the door. Pacing back and forth, she tried to make sense of his last remark. The cool fresh air helped to clear her turbulent thoughts. He's making it easier for me, she realized.

With a woebegone smile she carefully folded the gown. It was still buttonless and would remain so. The idea of sewing the buttons back on seemed disrespectful, so she tucked all of the loose buttons within for safekeeping and placed the gown in the bottom drawer of the wardrobe.

Having dressed for bed, Laurie returned to the main room. "Come on, sugar. Let's get you changed." The cat brushed against her ankle and meowed. She bent to pick it up, but it trotted to the front door. "Good girl."

Gabe sat in his chair smoking his pipe. He'd calmed down, even regretted his remark about Laurie's duty. He watched her let the cat out and talk to his daughter. In a couple of months Ammie would be their daughter—as much Laurie's as his. He couldn't help smiling. Surely, after they were married, she would be more like the night before. She wouldn't have any reason to feel self-conscious.

Ammie ran to the front door, tugged on the latch, and opened it. "Mittens, c'mere."

"Don't go out, punkin. Cats sleep outside. It's about time that one learned." He set his pipe down and went over to close the door.

"No, Daddy. Want Mittens. Plllease . . ."

Gritting his teeth, he glanced outside. God, he hated the way she said "Plllease," just like Ruth used to whine when she wanted some doodad or other. He gripped the edge of the door and started closing it.

"The cat's playing." He took his daughter's hand and pulled her back. As the door neared the jamb the cat dashed back into the house.

Ammie ran after it. "Good Mittens."

Laurie turned out the lamp in the kitchen on her way to the main room. The last twenty-four hours had taken their toll on her, and she was drained. Feeling like her mind was working in slow motion, she realized that Gabe would need blankets and went in search of them. A few minutes later she placed the covers on the settee.

Ammie scooted the beanbag across the floor to the cat.

"Mittens must be getting sleepy. Sit with me awhile."

Laurie sat in the rocker, and Ammie climbed up in her lap. A few minutes of quiet should calm the child down. Anyway, Laurie hoped so. She rocked slowly and found herself watching Gabe. He occasionally drew on his pipe, his expression contented. She watched his lips clamp on the mouthpiece, lips that had felt so gentle and yet urgent. I'll drive myself crazy if I continue, she thought, glancing down at Ammie.

"She asleep?"

His deep, rumbling voice startled Laurie. "Close enough." She rocked forward and stood. "Good night."

"You don't have to stay with her now." He rose and walked ahead to open his bedroom door for her.

Laurie walked by him and tucked the little girl under the covers, then went back to the door. "I'm tired, too." She moved to close the door and stopped. "Sure you don't want to stay with her?"

He stepped back and nodded. "Sleep well."

Gabe listened for the click of the latch and crossed the main room, wondering if he'd find any peace in sleep that night. After spreading one of the blankets out over the settee, he pulled off his boots, shucked his trousers, and draped them over the rocker. He stretched out on the makeshift bed.

It didn't matter which way he lay—on his back, his side, or with his knees bent—he couldn't fit his large frame comfortably on the short makeshift bed. God, he was tired. Ammie's bed wasn't being used. Why not? He went in and sat on the side of his daughter's bed. It wasn't any longer than the settee. With four beds in the house you'd think . . .

Two minutes later he was stretched out on Laurie's bed—actually it was his old bed. He tossed the covers over himself and turned onto his side. At last he'd found a place to sleep. Inhaling deeply, he realized he'd pay a price after all. Laurie's floral scent clung to the pillow.

Gabe added the window measurements for the main room to his list. The first window to be repaired would be Ammie's, then Laurie's. A movement out in the yard caught his attention. Laurie. As she reached up to fasten the clothespin over the drape, her skirts swayed and allowed him a glimpse of her ankles.

She had found the drapes where he'd thrown them and couldn't be discouraged from laundering the damn things. As far as he was concerned, they were no better than rags. It was a pleasant scene. Not far from Laurie Ammie sat digging in the dirt. His family. He tucked the list in his pocket and went outside.

He held up the end of the drape for her. "Want to ride to town with me?"

He watched her hands. They were red from the hot water and puckered. But the sunlight seemed to accent their elegance and remind him of how exciting they felt when she touched him.

His voice felt like a rumble along her spine. With great effort she concentrated on her task, bent over, and picked up the window curtain from Ammie's room. She raised her hands and shook the cloth. It made a crisp, snapping sound. She pinned one end of the material to the line, then secured the other end and smoothed out more creases with her hand. "When do you want to leave?"

"Whenever you're ready."

"I'll hurry." She picked up the laundry basket and glanced around for Ammie. "Come on, sugar."

Gabe hitched the horses to the wagon. By the time he had finished, Ammie and Laurie joined him. She took her seat and he handed his daughter to her. He sat at her side and started the horses up the drive.

Turning on the bench, Laurie stared back at the house. It was a sturdy building, she knew, and seemed to beckon to her. All it needed was a flower bed or two across the front. She turned back around. Peonies and lilacs would be nice, maybe sweet peas.

She felt better, even optimistic. "I feared there would be more damage from the storm."

"We were lucky. Pa was right when he built with logs rather than clapboards, like so many used then."

"What about the buildings in town? Etta Kirk said she lives across the river from the general store."

Gabe reached over and patted Laurie's knee. "I'll take you by Mrs. Kirk's so you can see her."

❦17❧

As they rode along the muddy Stage Road Gabe noticed several older trees down among the younger more supple ones. He also became apprehensive. He slowed the team when they came to Ashly Mills. Sam stood on a ladder in front of a boarded-up window, hammering a nail into one of the posts that supported the overhang of the store roof.

"Maybe you can visit with Mrs. Kirk while I see to the glass and shingles." Every building he saw had boarded up windows. He didn't voice his doubts to Laurie. She was already anxious about Etta.

Laurie scooted over closer to Gabe, hoping to avoid being splattered with the thick muddy clods flung up by the wagon wheels. "I've heard stories about tornadoes. It looks like one moved through here."

She looked around in dismay. Bushes, splintered boards, and even material that resembled tattered old clothes had been shoved to the side of the street. Among the rubble, fragments of glass sparkled in the sunlight. Then her gaze met that of Hannah Tuttle. The woman stared with disdain.

Laurie clung to Ammie as they crossed the small bridge.

The horse's hooves sounded dull, hollow to Laurie, the way her mind felt. The river was fast flowing and high on the bank, but it seemed unimportant. Gabe stopped in front of a neat house a couple blocks from the center of town.

He set the brake and handed Laurie down. "I'll be back in a while." He waited until Mrs. Kirk had shown Laurie in before heading for the store.

When he entered, his expectations were met. There wasn't a tool left in sight. Sam hadn't even replaced the broken pane of glass in his own window.

Gus Neilson stood at the counter and waved to Gabe. "How're you doing, West? Everything okay at your place?"

"Mostly a few windows. Yours?"

Neilson nodded. "And a lot of cleanup. God, I never saw anything like that here."

"Me either." Gabe glanced over at Sam. "Looks like everyone's been stocking up."

"Heard it was even worse over in Jacksonville." Neilson removed his hat and wiped his brow. "Had a tornado, and a wall of water two feet high flooded the streets."

Gabe shook his head. "Strange summer weather."

Sam walked down the counter. "What do ya need t'day?"

"I need glass. I've—" Neilson stopped midsentence when Sam shook his head.

"All out. Won't have any till next week, the soonest."

"Do you have any shingles left?" Gabe glanced toward the back of the store.

"Best I can hope for is next week. Had to send to Portland for supplies." Sam wandered off.

Neilson fell into step with Gabe. "Want to see what's happening at Bella's?"

"Sure." Gabe knew Laurie wouldn't be ready to leave so soon. Besides, he hadn't had an opportunity to sit and swap stories with his friends since before last Christmas.

He and Neilson walked around the corner from the store

and entered Bella's Saloon. It wasn't a fancy saloon like one might find in San Francisco, but it was a place where a man could talk, gamble, and ease his loneliness if he so desired. He ordered two beers and took them over to where Neilson had taken a seat.

"Thanks. I'll get the next round." Gus gulped a generous portion of the brew.

Gabe sat down on one of the wooden chairs at the table facing the bar and took a swig of his beer. "I'm surprised this place isn't full, considering Sam's out of supplies."

Neilson glanced at the door and waved. "Hey, Franklin, over here." He glanced down at his beer and spoke softly to Gabe. "Surprised Tuttle's old lady let him off his lead."

Gabe chuckled and raised his glass in a mock salute.

Franklin Tuttle stopped by the table. "I'll get a pitcher."

Gabe watched Tuttle's narrow chest puff up, thinking it was hardly noticeable considering the man's spindly build. He was tempted to leave. He'd seen Mrs. Tuttle glaring at him and Laurie, and wondered what the woman would make of them riding in the wagon together.

"Here we are." Tuttle filled his glass and put the pitcher down in the middle of the table.

Neilson refilled his glass. "How'd your place fare in the storm?"

Tuttle shrugged. "Wind blew like the devil, didn't it?" He sipped his beer. "Always knew those shutters would come in handy." He sniggered. "Even quieted Hannah for a spell."

Gus drained his glass further. "Never thought I'd see a blow as bad as that here."

Lifting his glass again, Gabe just listened to the two men. He heard someone enter the saloon and waited to see who else might join them. He glanced over at the man. Lester. His mouth usually ran about as fast as Mrs. Merkle's.

Gabe nursed his beer. He couldn't very well pick up Laurie reeking of drink. He heard two more men wander in. Another swig or two wouldn't hurt. It wasn't long before he was able to distinguish one particular conversation from the drone of the others, mostly because it concerned him.

"Surprised to see West here." The man jerked his head in Gabe's direction. "Thought he'd be layin' low." The man gloated over his drink.

"Why now?" the shorter man sitting across from the first one asked.

The first man shuffled his feet. "Just heard rumblin's about Jenkins not doin' his duty."

"Shit, it's been months since his old lady died. Jenkins said he wasn't sure who'd done it."

Gabe's knuckles turned white against the glass of beer.

"I dunno. Miz Tuttle saw him leavin' an' there weren't nobody there 'sides her," another chimed in.

Neilson downed the last of his beer and belched. "I'd better get on back to the house." He shoved his chair back. "You coming, Gabe?"

Gabe rose to his full height and settled his worn felt hat on his head. He left the saloon ahead of Neilson, his mind working so rapidly he held a single thought for no more than an instant.

Neilson broke the silence. "They must've been drunk. Or trying to rile you." He glanced back as they rounded the corner. "Field hands can be like a bunch of old hens. Pay 'em no mind."

"I won't." Gabe stepped off of the boardwalk to the wagon.

The nightmare was starting once again.

Laurie responded to Etta while wiping cake crumbs off Ammie's chin. "Mr. West hasn't said anything. Is the gossip getting worse?"

"Vicious, that's what they are." Etta smoothed loose strands of hair back from her face. "When I went to the general store yesterday, everyone seemed to be talking about Mr. West."

"What were they saying?"

Avoiding Laurie's gaze, Etta reached over and straightened a doily. "Laurie, I hate to repeat it. Who knows how many times the story's changed with the telling."

Laurie stilled Etta's hands. "I'd really like to know."

Tears filled Etta's eyes, and she took her hankie from her skirt pocket. "I am so sorry." She started crying in earnest.

Laurie moved over on the settee and put her arm around Etta's trembling shoulders. "It's not your fault."

Etta nodded and composed herself. "Someone pointed out that Owen's murderer was never caught." She paused, pressing her lips together for a minute before she continued. "And they want Ruth's killer jailed."

Laurie patted Etta's shoulder. "We all want justice."

"You don't understand," Etta sobbed, shaking her head. "Hannah found Ruth and said she saw Mr. West riding away from the house when she arrived. She said he must have killed Ruth."

"Oh, Lord." Laurie sighed.

Etta slowly moved her head up and down.

"I wonder who started it? I can't believe *everyone* thinks he murdered his wife." Laurie cleaned Ammie's hands with her handkerchief and gave the child her doll.

"I think the women were just repeating what they'd heard. Some of the men nearly dragged their wives out of the store." Etta watched Ammie.

"Mr. and Mrs. West must have had friends." Laurie thought back to the barn raising. He appeared to get along with the men. "Was Hannah Tuttle one of Ruth's close friends?"

Etta covered her mouth discreetly. "Not that I know."

Laurie watched the amusement light Etta's lovely soft brown eyes and wondered about the cause. "Did Ruth have many friends?"

"I didn't really know her that well."

She inhaled and tried again. "Would you say Ruth was friendly?"

Etta shrugged. "Not with me, but that doesn't mean she wasn't with others."

"I rather expected people to tell me what a nice woman Ruth had been, such a devoted mother." Laurie watched Ammie try to feed her doll a piece of cake and smiled at her.

She could still hear Mrs. Jessop's shrill voice and venomous accusations. The hardest part, Laurie conceded to herself, was that she and Gabe had made love, and she didn't know if she could defend herself so quickly against another vocal attack. But no one knows that, she thought, playing devil's advocate with herself, and you needn't tell them. She was just reaching for the tray when she heard a wagon approaching.

Etta went over and looked out the front window. "Oh, it's Mr. West."

Laurie gathered up Ammie and her doll. "Thank you, Etta."

"Nonsense. I'm glad you came by."

Laurie walked out with Ammie and met Gabe on his way to the door. His expression was glum.

He waved to Mrs. Kirk and held out his hand to Laurie. God, what had started the talk this time? Gabe knew if Jenkins had had enough evidence to arrest him last winter, he would have.

Laurie felt the tension in him all during the ride back to the ranch. Since he seemed preoccupied, she didn't ask any of the questions that came to mind. Instead she distracted Ammie. While the child watched for birds, Laurie reflected on how much she had changed during her time in Ashly Mills.

In Sacramento, it had never occurred to her to question Sherman about anything. And when she tried to recall if she had ever heard her mother ask her father about his affairs, she knew she hadn't. Well, she thought, I drifted through my marriage in ignorance, but I'm not going through the rest of my life in that naive state.

* * *

Laurie dried the last supper plate, put it in the cupboard, and hung the towel over the back of Gabe's chair. She pushed it in, turned down the lamp, and went into the main room. Gabe was swinging a piece of string with a small twig tied to the dangling end. Mittens stood up on her back legs grabbing for it.

Ammie was laughing. She went over to her daddy and reached for his hand. "Me do it."

He held out his arm. "Okay. Come here." He steadied her on his lap and showed her how to hold the string up just beyond the cat's reach.

Laurie stood watching father and daughter a moment. Ammie giggled at the cat's antics, and Gabe appeared to be enjoying himself. Laurie sat and slowly rocked, waiting for the little girl to get sleepy. The movement had a soothing effect, and her gaze became distant.

Ammie teetered on Gabe's knees, and he tightened his hold. His attention was drawn to Laurie. The bun at the back of her head had worked its way loose. It softened her looks, making her appear rather drowsy, vulnerable. He liked the effect.

Laurie glanced over and smiled. Ammie was trying to stay awake, but she was losing the battle. "Kiss your daddy good night, Ammie." Laurie picked up the cat and put it outside.

While Laurie put his daughter down for the night Gabe lit his pipe and settled back in his chair. Finally they'd be alone. He needed her, wanted her in his bed every night. Should we marry now? he wondered, and knew it wouldn't be fair to Laurie. She deserved a wedding trip, even if it was only to Portland.

He listened for her soft steps and smiled when she approached. "Ammie settled for the night?"

"I think so." Lord, his smile made her feel tingly and want to be in his arms. For a moment she was tempted to curl up at his side. Memories of their night together started playing in her mind, but she pushed them aside and took her seat on the rocker.

Gabe drew on his pipe before he spoke. "Did you enjoy your visit with Etta?" He'd noticed a fleeting look of desire light her eyes, but she'd evidently resisted it.

"Mm-hm." She idly ran her finger up and down over a small blemish on the arm of the chair. "Did you hear the latest gossip?"

His gaze met hers. "A few comments. What have you heard?"

"Some people remembered that Etta's first husband's murderer was never found. They want Ruth's killer arrested." A cricket rhythmically chirped outside of the window while Laurie's heart pounded in her ears. "And you?"

Did she understand the implications? "Comments about Jenkins not doing his duty."

"That's all?"

"Don't you think that's enough?" He shook his head. This wasn't what he'd planned for tonight, he thought irritably.

She nodded and waited for him to continue.

"I was hoping it was over. God, how I've prayed that this nightmare would end." He drew on the pipe. "No matter how many times I go over what happened, I still can't believe anyone killed Ruth."

"What did the sheriff do?"

"Not much. I saw him the other day, and he still hadn't learned anything new."

Laurie blinked back the tears as she hastened over and put her arms around his shoulders. "Oh, Gabe. I'm so sorry." So many things made sense to her then. "You've lived with this so long. Ammie's very fortunate you claimed her as your own."

He stared up into Laurie's tear-filled eyes. "What else was I to do? Let everyone know what my wife was?"

She kissed his brow. "That wasn't your only reason."

He held her close. "The blame wasn't the babe's. She hadn't chosen her parents."

"She couldn't have a better father than you."

"You've given her the love she needs, what I wasn't able to bring myself to do."

She rested her cheek on his soft hair. "You did your best. No one could ask more." She felt his arms encircle her waist.

He held on to her for several minutes. "You realize you might be in need of another job if the sheriff arrests me, don't you?"

She snapped upright and glared at him. "Why? Ammie will need me." She frowned. "Do you think I'll just walk off and leave you?"

"You won't have a choice."

"You're wrong, Gabe." She let go of him and stood up. "Thank you for trusting me with the truth." There had to be a way to help him, and she would find it.

He rose and pulled her to him. "Don't leave me now. Not tonight." He held her close, savoring her sweet scent. "God, I need you," he rasped near her ear. He kissed her hair and felt the silken strands catch on the stubble of his chin.

She gazed up at him. It may be wrong, she thought. Or was it?

I love him.

I want him.

He needs me.

"Then come with me."

They went upstairs hand in hand, he to his old room, she to the comfortable surroundings of hers. Their lips met, and Laurie felt that delicious weakness sap her strength. Hands fumbled with buttons and fasteners, then they were touching flesh to flesh from shoulder to knee. As if he might try to escape, she wrapped her arms around his smooth, muscled back and held him close.

It felt right to him, sharing his old bed with Laurie. They

were good together, as if meant for each other. He wanted to satisfy needs she wasn't aware of, give her as much pleasure as she gave him. In a leisurely way he aroused and teased her—and himself.

The craving he caused so easily overtook her again. His skin was smooth and hot. She had never believed a man's touch could be so exciting, but he wasn't just any man. How can I feel so weak, yet exhilarated all at once? she wondered. Then she was beyond thought. She felt complete, as if they had become one.

He lay spent, feeling wonderfully drained of all energy. Her auburn hair was spread across the pillowcase and threaded between his fingers. He kissed her damp forehead and fell asleep with her snuggled against his chest.

Laurie waited until Ammie was asleep, then went up to Ruth's room. Since Gabe had told her he would be away for two days, there was no hurry. However, she felt an urgency. All morning she had thought about what he had said the night before. She wanted to search the empty bedroom and had asked his permission.

Climbing the stairs, she smiled. He had told her to dispose of anything she didn't find useful. He wanted the room cleared out.

She opened the door to Ruth's room. Next she tied back the drapes and opened the window. The room felt oppressive, even with fresh air flowing through. Bernice had stayed in this room, she mused, but had not left any sign that she'd been there. She could still feel Ruth's presence.

Laurie checked the inside and outside of the drawers, inside the frame and the back of the chest. She found nothing. She sat on the edge of the bed, her elbow resting on her knee, her chin on her palm. Lord, she didn't even know what she was looking for, but she knew she hadn't discovered anything that would help solve the mystery of Ruth's death.

In one last desperate attempt Laurie felt the hem of the

drapes. The only thing untouched in the room was the dusty basket of dried, bedraggled flowers. As she reached for several stems a moth flew out and startled her. She instinctively pulled her hand back. Instead of taking the flowers out, she upended the basket.

Dry petals, stems, crumbling moss, and lumps of soil fell to the floor. So did two envelopes. They were covered with dirt. Laurie dusted them off and stared at them. She could hardly believe her eyes. As she lifted the flap of the envelope Ammie's shrill voice echoed through the house.

"Orie, where're you?"

"I'll be right down." Laurie tucked the envelopes in the pocket of her skirt and left the room. She patted her pocket and went to dress the little girl. Once the child was busy playing with the cat, she sat down and took out one of the envelopes.

She scanned the page. It took her less than a moment to realize that the letter confirmed what Gabe had said about Ruth. Laurie returned it to her pocket. Ruth and her lover had obviously known one another for a while. She didn't want Gabe to see the letters, at least not yet.

Gabe rode to Jacksonville early to make a purchase. It was probably a waste of money and would never be used, but Laurie had faith in him. He wanted to show he believed in her also, though she wouldn't see it until the time was right.

He entered the small jewelry store next door to the dry-goods shop on California Street. He ambled by two glass cases, noting the intricate pieces, and feared he couldn't afford more than a plain band. There was one ring with a little diamond chip. But if he was going to buy a diamond, he'd want it large enough to be able to see it without spectacles in a few years.

"May I help you, sir?"

Unaware of the clerk's approach, Gabe jerked upright at the sound of the little man's voice. "I . . . that is, ah, I was just looking." Damn. How did other men manage to buy all those fancy bangles and gewgaws? Ruth had wanted a ring she'd seen at a fancy-goods store.

The clerk cleared his throat. "What did you have in mind? A brooch? Or maybe a necklace?"

"A wedding ring," he blurted out.

"That can be a difficult choice. I have a nice selection of rings right over here, sir." The clerk walked across the aisle. "If you don't see anything you like, I can design something more to your taste."

One ring resembled a rainbow with different-colored stones. Most had stones of some sort. There were also four plain bands, three gold and one silver. Gabe shrugged.

"If you would tell me what kind of jewelry she usually wears, it may help."

Gabe frowned. "I don't know. She doesn't wear much." He glanced at a nearby display. There was one gold ring with two clasped hands forming the band.

"Those are friendship rings, but would do very nicely."

"That one with the hands, is it real gold?"

"Yes, sir." The clerk placed the band on a small satin pillow. "I could add a small, discreet diamond, if you like. Or possibly engrave your names inside."

Gabe slipped the ring just over the fingernail of his pinky. Friendship. They had been friends before they became lovers, the way it should be. "Could you put our names on it now?"

An hour later Gabe was heading up to the summer pasture. His insides felt like someone had jumbled everything up. If his life wasn't such a damn mess, he'd be racing home to ask her to marry him today. Disjointed thoughts kept running through his mind, harsh images of Ruth; softer ones of Laurie began and ended like in a nightmare. By the time he became aware of his bearings, he had reached the meadow.

The sight of his tranquil grazing herd brought a smile to his face. Their lowing had a soothing effect, just what he needed. He met Danny riding along the edge of the pasture.

Danny watched Gabe and glanced back at the cows. "How're the repairs going?"

Gabe tipped his hat back. "They're not. No supplies. Jacksonville was hit harder than Ashly Mills. The glass won't be in till next week. But you'd better get going."

"Where?" Danny frowned, then raised his brows. "You mean I've got a couple days off?"

Gabe nodded. "It's quiet. When you return, Nate can take off, then Ben."

"Ah, a real bath with hot water."

Gabe smiled. He wouldn't have minded one either. In a month to six weeks, after he and Laurie married . . . No, he had to concentrate on now, no farther ahead than next week. "Enjoy."

As Danny dismounted he watched Gabe and shook his head. "You don't need to spell me. Everything's quiet."

"Just what I want," Gabe muttered, untying his bedroll from the back of the saddle.

Gabe deposited his bedroll near the others and went to see Ben. Two days of peace. Two days without Laurie. Well, he'd take a late watch and hope he'd be too tired to think.

He slipped into the familiar routine with ease. He was sure Sheriff Jenkins hadn't discovered anything new about Ruth's death. That meant if he was going to arrest anyone, it would be Gabe.

His affairs were in order, except for writing a new will. When he returned home, he'd have to ask Laurie if she would be willing to raise Ammie if he weren't around. He'd deed the ranch to both of them, providing an income. He was sure Danny would continue running things for her, but he reminded himself to discuss it with Danny when he came back.

All was quiet that night and the next day. The second morning Gabe was up at sunrise, anxious to see Danny. He rode in just before suppertime.

Danny tipped his hat back and grinned at Gabe before dismounting. "Who's bitin' your tail?"

Gabe grimaced and shook his head. "I've got to talk to you and get back to the house."

Danny sobered immediately and followed Gabe away from the camp. "What's gnawin' on you? I haven't seen you like this since—" He stopped short and stared at his friend.

Gabe halted on a low rise just east of camp and gazed out over the pasture. "There's talk that the sheriff's getting pressured and will charge someone with Ruth's murder."

"Not you?" Danny stared mutely at Gabe. "Who'd believe it? Christ A'mighty! That's the most insane thing I ever heard of."

"Evidently not, from what some are saying." Gabe idly pulled a clump of dead needles from the pine tree at his side. "Did you get to town?"

"I rode over to Linkville." Danny shrugged. "Ashly Mills's too genteel for me."

Gabe smirked, understanding Danny's meaning, then he turned serious again. "If anything happens, Danny, I'd like you to keep on running things for Laurie Preston."

"Sure, but you're not going to make this easy for them, are you? Jesus, I just don't understand how anybody could believe you killed Ruth."

Gabe made a disgusted snort. "Mrs. Tuttle seems to."

She also had reason to want to believe it. Gabe had never mentioned Ruth's affair to Danny, nor Ammie's true parentage. Even though Danny was his closest friend, that was more than he was willing to share.

Hell, what man'd want anyone to know he'd been cuckolded?

❧18❧

Laurie sat in the bed with a lamp turned up high and opened the first of the letters she had found in Ruth's room. She scanned the first note. The handwriting was not just neat but elegant. She glanced at the bottom of the page. It was signed with a flourish that resembled an intricate letter *V*. It meant nothing to her.

The missive began, "My Dearest Ruth." The man wrote about his great love for Ruth and how he would demonstrate his love with various parts of his anatomy when next they were together. Laurie skimmed over the last half of the page and returned it to the dirt-stained envelope.

When she looked at the second one, she realized it had been wadded up and later flattened out. Her curiosity piqued, she carefully removed the single page. The penmanship was neat but more formal. As she read she understood why. "V" sent his congratulations on the coming addition to Ruth's family. He also denied any possible relationship to her offspring.

That would be enough to make an expectant mother either enraged or totally despondent. Which way had Ruth reacted? Laurie refolded the letter and put it into the envelope. The information wouldn't help Gabe. If he didn't already know, she couldn't add to his grief—unless there was good reason.

If "V" was Ammie's father, then the letters must be about two years old. And if Ruth was carrying again, who was the father of that child? He, whoever *he* was, was the one they needed to find—the one who might have wanted to silence Ruth.

Laurie placed the letters in the drawer beneath her underclothes. She turned the lamp out, slid down on the bed, and pulled the covers up to her chin. She had spent her whole life sleeping alone—Sherman had insisted on separate rooms—except for the two nights with Gabe. Now the bed had never felt so empty.

Curling up on her side, her knees drawn up to her chest, she tried to clear the letters and the painful anger she had heard in Gabe's voice from her mind. The harder she tried to forget, the more she remembered. Words and phrases tumbled through her thoughts while Gabe's handsome but tense face was as clear as if he were there in her bedroom.

If she had this much trouble putting the letters out of her thoughts, what would they do to him? He was bitter and hurt, she thought, and he hid behind that cool, impersonal exterior to avoid being wounded again. The least she could do for him was to leave the letters where they were.

Gabe returned home anxious to see Laurie. Wanting to surprise her, he had walked his mount into the yard and gone directly to the house. He found her just serving supper to Ammie, and there was a place set for him.

"Smells good," he called, closing the front door.

"Daddy!" Ammie twisted around in her chair. "Orie, Daddy's home!"

Laurie stood by Ammie's chair, watching him. She smiled the moment his gaze met hers. He looked tired and worried, but the corners of his mouth curved upward. "You're just in time."

"Good." As he passed by his daughter's chair he ruffled her soft blond hair. He rested his hand on Laurie's waist as he stepped around her. "It's good to be home." He stared down into her eyes, then kissed her forehead.

Laurie leaned against him, and sighed, her hands still holding the pot of soup.

Ammie stared at her daddy and Laurie, then tugged at Laurie's skirt. "Orie, me want supper."

Laurie glanced up at Gabe and smiled. "You must be hungry, too."

"Starving," he mouthed, staring at her.

Laurie felt his hand lightly massaging her back and the familiar liquid warmth coursed through her body. She almost dropped the pot.

"I'd better serve the soup while it's hot."

Her voice was breathless, and to eat supper was hardly a close second to what he really wanted to do. However, he'd have to bide his time. The sooner the meal was over, the sooner Laurie could put Ammie to bed.

Laurie set a bowl down and smiled at Ammie. "Here, sweetie." She ladled soup into the child's bowl. "Use the spoon like I showed you."

Ammie looked from her daddy to Laurie and picked up her spoon. With brows knit the child dipped the spoon into the soup and slowly raised it as she bent forward.

While serving Gabe, Laurie observed Ammie's effort. "Good girl." She beamed at Gabe and moved to fill her own bowl.

Gabe ate half of the hearty beef soup and paused. "What did you two do while I was away?"

Laurie glanced at Ammie before meeting Gabe's gaze. "I aired out the other room."

He looked up. "What did you do with her dresses?"

"I bundled them up and stored them in the barn after

Bernice came." She glanced at Ammie, who was sitting quietly.

"I'll have to get rid of them. Once the room has been painted, it would make a nice bedroom for Ammie when she's a little older." He'd always liked having his room upstairs.

The meal passed quickly with Gabe talking about his herd. He had such plans, though Laurie was surprised he had thought about Ammie moving upstairs. His voice had a hard edge at times, and she wondered why he sounded as if he were instructing her on the management of the ranch. As she began clearing the table Gabe stood up with the dishes.

"I'll clean up in here while you tend Ammie."

Laurie stared at him and placed her dishes in his outstretched hands. His gaze felt like a caress, and she had to look away.

"We need to talk after you put her down."

He had spoken softly, but she had a feeling that she might not want to listen to what he had to say. After she unbuckled Ammie's belt, the little girl held up her arms to be held.

Gabe reached for his daughter's plate and noticed her clinging to Laurie. "She's tired early." He took the dish and scraped the food into the bucket, frowning as he noticed how little Ammie had eaten.

Laurie looked down at Ammie and felt her forehead. Not hot, but she clung to Laurie as if she were sick. She hugged the little girl and carried her into her room. After prying the child's small hands from behind her neck, she got her ready for bed.

"I see one tiny toe," Laurie teased, but Ammie just sat quietly.

"Wonder where the others are?" Laurie reached for the small foot, but Ammie didn't move, or look at her.

"Does something hurt, sugar?"

Ammie stuck her thumb into her mouth, shook her head, and reached for Laurie.

Without hesitating, Laurie took her into her arms and held

her close. "Oh, little one, if you could only tell me what's wrong."

Laurie sat on the side of the small bed, rocking Ammie, and felt her pitiful sigh. After a few minutes Laurie's back began to tire. She stood and carried Ammie to the old rocker.

She was more comfortable and the child didn't seem to mind as long as she continued holding her. Hoping to lull her to sleep, she recited Ammie's favorite nursery rhyme, "Hey, Diddle Diddle" and followed with a very soft, lulling rendition of "Hush-a-Bye, Baby."

As Gabe rubbed the towel over a clean plate he ambled out and watched Laurie. By the time he finished drying the dishes, his daughter should be sound asleep. He needed Laurie tonight. Maybe he should tell her about his plans for their marriage. But the next minute he thought better of that. He probably should prepare her for the worst, then after things worked out, he would tell her.

When he joined her in the main room, she was still gently rocking his daughter. Before taking his seat, he wandered around the rocking chair. "She's asleep. Want me to put her down?"

Waiting until she could see him, Laurie moved her head just enough for him to understand. Very slowly she eased the chair forward so she could stand in one smooth movement.

As she stood Ammie clenched her hands around Laurie's neck and mumbled, "No, no, no. Don't want to."

Ammie started thrashing, so Laurie wandered around the room rubbing her back. After meandering across, up and down, and in large figure eights around the room for nearly forty minutes, she felt the little girl sag over her breast. She continued walking until her back ached, her toes cramped, and Ammie felt like a hundred-pound bag of flour.

Gabe sat watching Laurie for a while and had to get up. He felt too restless to sit still. The room was clean. The floor didn't even need sweeping. As he glanced around he noticed

Ruth's knickknacks. Perfect, he thought, and went out to the barn. He returned with an old gunnysack. Dropping the odds and ends in the sack served as a great relief, and when he was finished, only the two wooden framed daguerreotypes of his parents remained.

He left the house again and tossed the sack in the deepest corner of the barn. When he returned, he saw Laurie trying to rub her back as she paced with his daughter. She was exhausted, and his daughter appeared to be asleep. Enough, he decided, and blocked her path as she crossed in front of the fireplace.

Ignoring her silent protest, he reached for Ammie. The muscles of her little body seemed to resist his touch. He mouthed to Laurie, "Is she sick?"

"I don't think so, but she won't let go," Laurie mouthed, and stepped around him.

Gabe sighed and joined her, his hand on her back lightly massaging. Soon he realized the only way he was going to get her to put his daughter down was if she lay down with the child. With the flat of his hand on the small of Laurie's back he urged her to his room. When she paused at the door, he whispered in her ear, "You can sleep with her. My bed'll be more comfortable."

Laurie nodded and allowed him to guide her to the bed. She didn't understand why Ammie wouldn't let go of her, but she was not about to upset the child any more than she was already. After Gabe had pulled back the covers, she lay down in the middle of the bed with Ammie fast against her breast. Ah, she thought, relaxing for the first time in the last hour, this is infinitely better.

Gabe turned the wick down on the lamp and Laurie closed her eyes. A moment later the side of the bed behind her sank down. She lay as rigid as the child. Surely he wouldn't . . . not with his daughter in bed. . . . Then she felt his arm slide around her waist before he snuggled up to her.

He rested his head on the pillow near Laurie's, his chin

near her shoulder. "Happy dreams." He knew his daughter was much better off with Laurie than she had been under Ruth's care. Ruth used to let her child cry, saying, "It'll give her strong lungs."

Gabe bent his knees and fit her bottom into the curve. She felt warm and soft. And he could have sworn she murmured in contentment. Keeping his hand at her waist was torture, but he was near her.

Laurie couldn't resist the heat of Gabe's body when he wrapped himself around her. Lord, he felt good. Each time he breathed in, she felt his heart beat against her back, and she leaned into him.

Their sleeping arrangement would have been called scandalous, but they were three people who needed one another. And Lord, she needed Gabe's nearness.

Gabe stretched his stiff legs. Laurie was still in his embrace, and he was aroused. Taking it slowly, he moved away from her and out of his bed. It was light outside. The cow had to be milked and fed, the horses tended, and he wanted to watch the sunrise. He'd just keep at the chores until his daughter went down for her nap. Then he and Laurie would talk, but first he had to write out his will.

Laurie woke up scooting backward, searching for Gabe. She glanced over and saw Ammie sleeping peacefully, then slid to the edge of the bed and stepped out onto the cold floor. Her dress was a wrinkled mess, and she was sure her hair looked no better. Hoping Ammie would rest awhile longer, she left the bedroom door open and hurried up to her room.

She nearly had breakfast ready to serve when Ammie started screaming as if her life were in danger. Laurie ran to Gabe's room and found the little girl huddled in the middle of the bed with all of the covers pulled up around her.

"Orie, c'mere. Hep me!"

Laurie dashed over to the bed and pulled Ammie up into her arms. "Did you have a bad dream, sugar?"

Ammie quivered. Her gaze darted frantically around the room.

Laurie carried her across the entry to her room. "You go potty, and we'll look for Mittens."

Ammie sucked her thumb into her mouth and nodded.

After attending to Ammie's needs, Laurie encouraged her to look around the house for the cat while she served their meal. The little girl's behavior was puzzling, and she had no idea what might have frightened her. The child was used to her father's gruff voice when he was angry. Surely his tone at supper the night before hadn't caused Ammie's fear of being alone.

Ammie kept her thumb in her mouth and looked for Mittens. She heard her daddy come in. She ran to him and held up her arms. "Daddy, me up."

Gabe closed the door and was surprised by his daughter's demand to be picked up. "Morning, punkin." He lifted her high over his head before lowering her to his chest. "Feel better today?" He strode into the kitchen and stifled a chuckle when Laurie blew a strand of hair from over one eye. "Mornin'."

She glanced over her shoulder and grinned. "Mornin'." She turned back to the stove and finished dishing out the food. "Sit down. It's ready."

Gabe settled Ammie in her chair before taking his own. He winked at her and said to Laurie, "'Bout time. Ammie and I are starved!" He beamed at his daughter. His effort was rewarded with the beginnings of a smile.

"Well, I don't know," Laurie countered, playing along with him. "That young'un eats an awful lot."

She served father and daughter. When she took her seat, Ammie was picking at her food. Better than last night, Laurie thought. She and Gabe bantered throughout the meal, and Ammie seemed to enjoy their lightheartedness.

Striving to entertain his daughter, Gabe held up the last three bites of ham one at a time for the cat to grab. They were laughing so hard, the pounding on the front door startled them.

Gabe shoved his chair back. "I'll get it." He hoped he sounded easygoing. But in fact, he was worried. He hadn't heard anyone ride up to the house, and that didn't happen often.

By the time his hand touched the door latch, Laurie was coming out of the kitchen with Ammie in her arms. He glanced at her. For two heartbeats he wanted to bar the door and take her in his arms. Instead he opened the door.

Sheriff Jenkins stepped across the threshold, forcing Gabe back into the room. "I suppose you know why I'm here?" Then he noticed Laurie. "Morning, ma'am." His attention returned to Gabe.

Gabe stared at the sheriff. "Why don't you tell me."

"I'm arresting you for the"—he glanced at Laurie—"murder of Ruth West."

❧19❧

Laurie stood rooted by the open front door with Ammie in her arms, watching Gabe. She felt Sheriff Jenkins's cold stare and shivered. He appeared to be serious.

Gabe took his hat from the peg near the door while watching Laurie. Dear God, he thought, he was out of time. He didn't dare take her in his arms, not in front of Jenkins. He ruffled his daughter's hair.

Sheriff Jenkins reached for Gabe's arm. "Come on, West. They can visit you in jail."

"Daddy!" Ammie shrieked, struggling to reach him.

Gabe cupped his hand around his daughter's little head and kissed her. "Bye, punkin. You mind Laurie." He leaned forward again and kissed Ammie's cheek. Then he nodded. "If you need anything, Mrs. Preston, you know where to find me."

Laurie blinked, automatically adjusting Ammie's position when she began to slip. As the sheriff turned to lead Gabe outside she grabbed his arm and jerked hard.

"You can't do this! He didn't kill his wife!" She heard herself scream and didn't care how she sounded.

Ammie held on to Laurie with one hand and held the other out to her daddy. "Daddy, Daddy c'mere! Don't go, Daddy!"

Laurie's outraged voice and his daughter's screeching nearly broke Gabe's restraint. Turning back to them, he hugged his daughter and whispered to Laurie, "I'll be okay."

She clamped her lips together and stared at him. Lord, she wanted to put her arms around him, but that would probably make him look even more guilty. As he walked away she blinked her tears back. "I'll see you soon."

Gabe paused by the hitching post and looked up at her. "Don't count on it." He wanted to see her, but not in jail. "Don't visit me, Mrs. Preston." He glared at Jenkins and headed for the second horse tied to the rail.

Ammie snuggled into Laurie's chest and peered at the strange man. "Where Daddy goin'?"

"Your daddy's going to town, sweetie."

Laurie stepped out onto the porch and waited to see Gabe off. Last night he'd wanted to talk to her; instead he had held her close. She had slept peacefully in his embrace. Feeling bereft, she hugged his daughter to her. She wouldn't cry, not now.

Mounted and ready to leave, Gabe stared at Laurie one last time. She was poised on the porch. He noticed how she clutched Ammie to her. I love her, he realized, I do! He abruptly wheeled the horse around and rode out.

"Bye, Daddy!" Ammie called.

Laurie watched until he was out of sight before she allowed the tears to spill onto her cheeks and bent her head down to Ammie's. Dear God, there must be a way to help him. When she glanced up, she couldn't even see any dust rising from the roadway.

Ammie looked at Laurie. As if in slow motion, the child reached up with her finger and touched one of Laurie's tears. "What's matter, Orie?"

Laurie managed a weak smile. "Oh, sweetie, I love you. We'll be fine."

Gabe rode into Ashly Mills at a gallop. He dropped the reins over the rail and strode into the jailhouse. He'd be damned if Jenkins was going to lead him in like some common criminal.

"Do I get to pick which cell I want, or is one reserved for me?"

Sheriff Jenkins motioned toward the two cells, mumbled, "Whichever," and slapped his dusty hat on his desk.

Gabe stood near the window in the first cell and gazed out to the adjacent lot. "What's the bail going to cost me?"

"Not sure yet."

Turning from the window, he fixed the sheriff with a hard stare. "Jenkins, who put you up to this? You told me months ago that you didn't know who murdered my wife."

The sheriff glanced in Gabe's general direction and back down at his desk to a small book. "You'll find out soon enough." He shrugged. "Seems Mrs. Tuttle accidentally picked up Mrs. West's diary."

"*Accidentally?* Just when did this *accident* happen?"

"Said when she found Mrs. West." Jenkins sat at his desk, shuffling papers around. "Don't know why she waited. Must've had a reason."

As if locked in his cell, Gabe went over and gripped the bars. "Well? What the hell could Ruth's diary have to do with my arrest?"

Surely Ruth didn't think he hated her enough to kill her? He shook his head. Hell, he hadn't known what went through her mind most of the time. Then a horrifying thought occurred to him. Could she have made it look like he was responsible for her death?

Gabe watched Jenkins and noticed how the man had looked at the small volume now beneath several papers on his desk. He hadn't locked the cell door. Gabe wandered around the small area and paused just outside the opening.

"You must have a lot of paperwork to do after arresting someone. Surprised you don't have help." He ambled over near the desk to where several wanted posters hung from nails and added up the rewards. "You ever catch any of these desperadoes?"

Jenkins tipped his chair back and sighed. "I don't like this any more than you. But everyone's fussin' about your missus dying and all, and Mrs. Tuttle has a point." He tapped the diary.

Gabe stared at the book. "What's that?"

Jenkins handed the diary over. "Now get back in there." He followed Gabe and locked the door.

With the small volume in hand Gabe sat in his cell. He didn't want to read his late wife's words. He'd heard enough of them to last forever. However, there was nothing else to occupy his time. He stretched out on the sagging cot and opened to the first page.

"Mr. West and I were married today. He is very attractive and assured me I will be happy. Oh, I do pray that is so. Daddy says that God wants us to work here for our reward in heaven, but I do not see why I have to work my whole life to be rewarded in the hereafter."

Gabe covered his eyes and rubbed them. Ruth had been such an innocent when they married. He'd never understood why she'd changed so much. Even though it was too late to help her, he might finally get some answers.

Laurie played with Ammie all morning, nearly running the child ragged so she would take an early nap. After she had fallen asleep, Laurie went to the creek to bathe and think. She recalled how relieved she had been to get this position. Everything was rather straightforward; all she had to do was care for one small child. Now here she was trying to figure out how to prove that her employer—no, not just her employer, the man she loved—was innocent of his wife's murder.

By the time Ammie woke from her nap, Laurie was

dressed and anxious to get to town. She wasn't sure if Etta could or would watch Ammie, or how the child would react to being left with her, but Laurie knew she must see Gabe—alone.

She greeted Etta and visited for a few minutes before explaining the reason for her call. "Sheriff Jenkins arrested Mr. West this morning."

Etta pursed her lips and nodded. "I was afraid of that. The sheriff kept saying there wasn't anybody else there that morning." She rubbed at a spot on the arm of the wooden chair. "He does look guilty, unless you think Hannah might have been the one."

Laurie stood and wandered around the room. "I don't honestly think she did it, anyway, not the Hannah I met. But I can't believe that he did it either." She glanced out through the window. It was a lovely summer day, but she felt neither warm nor hopeful.

"I wish I could help, but I don't know how." Etta's shoulders sagged. "I used to lie awake nights wondering who killed Owen and why. It didn't make any sense. Everybody seemed to like him."

"I am sorry, Etta." Laurie resumed her seat near Etta. "I should have known how much this would upset you. I just wasn't thinking clearly."

"It's all connected." When she saw Laurie's shocked expression, Etta quickly added, "I don't mean the same person murdered both of them. Because of Owen, the town doesn't want Ruth's killer to escape punishment, too. Don't you see?"

Laurie silently admitted that this situation was probably making it more difficult for Gabe. "Someone else must have been in the house, but who? It was so long ago."

Etta lowered her voice. "Have you gone by the jail to see him?"

"I didn't want to take her," Laurie whispered, motioning to Ammie. "And I don't know where it is."

"Go past the general store and turn left. You can't miss it. Or the saloon across the way."

"Would you watch her while I'm gone?"

Etta reached over and patted Laurie's hand. "Of course. You go on. We'll be fine." She smiled at Ammie.

"Thank you." Laurie dropped to her knees beside Ammie. "You are going to stay here with Mrs. Kirk and play while I go see a friend. I'll be back soon." She watched the child's brows crease and her mouth take on a pinched look. She held out her arms to the little girl.

Ammie clung to her. "Want go, too."

After smoothing back Ammie's soft blond curls, Laurie kissed her cheek. "I shouldn't be long. I want you to be a good girl for Mrs. Kirk. Will you do that for me?"

Ammie buried her face in Laurie's chest.

Etta sat down on the floor near them. "Ammie, I'm hungry. Do you like pudding?"

Ammie peered around at Etta and nodded slowly.

Laurie loosened her embrace. She knew the little girl would be fine, but she hesitated all the same. She wasn't abandoning Ammie, but she almost felt like she was.

"Come on, Ammie. You can help me dish out the pudding." Etta motioned Laurie to leave.

Taking Etta's suggestion, Laurie picked up her reticule, stiffened her back, and walked out of the house. She paused near the buggy and listened. The only sounds she heard were the normal sounds, birds chirping, a dog barking, and a wagon in the distance. Needing to work off some of her anxiety, she set off on foot.

She retraced her way back to the bridge crossing Mill Creek, beyond the store, and turned onto Oak Street. Ahead on the left was Bella's Saloon; some distance behind it was the livery stable. Opposite the saloon was the jail. She came to a standstill at the door to the jailhouse.

She didn't want to give Gabe cause to worry about her, or Ammie, so she forced herself to remember how he had looked playing with his daughter and smiled. Without giving herself time to think, she opened the door and stepped inside. Sheriff Jenkins was sitting behind a scarred desk scratching his paunch.

"Good day, Sheriff. I'm here to see Mr. West."

As she glanced around she tugged at her gloves. There he was! He stretched out his long legs and came to his feet with the grace she so admired. She felt like she hadn't seen him in days, when it had been only hours.

"He's right there." The sheriff pulled a pocketknife from his trousers and glanced down at his fingernails.

Gabe set the diary facedown on the cot and took two steps to the bars that separated him from Laurie. Her bonnet hid her beautiful auburn hair but not her smile. Those bright eyes stared at him unblinking as if she thought she'd never see him again.

"I told you not to come here. This is no place for a lady, unless . . . What's wrong?"

"Nothing. Ammie's fine. And you?"

"Mrs. Preston." God, he hated doing this. "I told you not to come here. If you defy me again, I'll dismiss you." He glared at her to drive home his seriousness and mask his love for her. She didn't say a word, but her eyes filled with tears and her lips quivered. He felt like a bastard. He just hoped she thought he was.

She took a deep breath and folded her hands at her waist. "You did not tell me not to visit you."

The sheriff coughed and stood up. "I'll be outside if you need me, ma'am." He removed the keys from the desk drawer, picked up his rifle, and went outside.

Gabe watched him leave. "You've never been simple before. Now leave. If I can post bail, I'll be home. If not . . . well, I'll have to make arrangements for Ammie."

"Are you all right?"

He shrugged. "I've been reading." He held up the book.

She reached for it, but he tossed it onto the bed. "What's that?"

"Ruth's diary." He rubbed the back of his neck. "That's what condemned me. Now please leave."

Laurie glanced down at the journal. "What could Ruth have said to make anyone believe you would've harmed her?"

"Oh, she didn't accuse me of anything." He clenched his jaw. "The sheriff never believed I hadn't seen Ruth that morning. He wanted to arrest me then. Just didn't have an excuse beyond the fact that there wasn't anyone else to blame." He went over and gazed out through the barred window, one foot on the edge of the cot as if it were a fence rail. "Hannah gave him the diary and the ammunition he wanted."

Laurie clasped her hands in her lap and felt her heart twist with pain. "What can I do?"

"Go back home." He heard the anguish in her voice and wanted to hit someone. Anyone would do, most particularly the sheriff. Or Hannah Tuttle. "Take care of Ammie and yourself. If anything happens to me, the ranch is deeded to you and Ammie. Danny can run things for you. I told him if I didn't get up to the pasture next week, he was to come down to the house. He'll take care of you in my stead. Now get going."

She couldn't stand the icy, distant tone in his voice. "I hadn't thought you would give up so easily." She kept her voice light, hoping to tease him out of his dark mood.

He spun around on his heel. "Why, you—" She was grinning, and it stopped him cold. God, he wanted to take her in his arms. "Get out." He spun on his heel, turning his back on her.

Hell, most of what Ruth had said to him was foolishness. If she'd told him how she felt, or if he'd found and read her words before she died, would it have made a difference? She was miserable and seemed to want him to be also.

As Laurie's footsteps faded, he opened the diary.

"The nights are so very long. I pray each evening that I

will sleep and wake to find it all a terrible dream, but I lie awake. Soon I will escape from this hell. I must.

"I feel yet another child growing in me, though it does not show. Father was right. God demands punishment for our sins."

He saw the pattern of Ruth's thoughts—sin, guilt, retribution. Her handwriting became shaky.

"I've paid the price. Soon this will be behind me.

"I know what I must do."

He turned the page to the last entry. The writing was uneven and wispy, difficult to read.

"Tonight I . . . sleep. So tired my eyes hurt . . . hard to think. Tomorrow, I'll be free."

As she walked back to Etta's house at a brisk pace, Laurie could still see Gabe's strong-featured face as if he were walking with her. When she passed the general store, Hannah Tuttle marched out across her path. Laurie's step faltered, but she managed to sidestep the larger woman without getting her toes trampled. There were questions she would have liked to ask her, but at the moment she was too hurt and angry with Gabe.

Laurie returned to Etta's house and found Ammie helping Etta set the table for supper. "I hope she wasn't too much trouble."

"No bother at all."

"Orie!" Ammie cried, and ran over. "Me hepin'."

Laurie squatted down and hugged the little girl. "I'm sure Etta appreciated your help." She stood up, still holding Ammie's hand. "Come on, sugar, we'd better be getting home."

Etta wiped her hands on the towel. "Why not stay for supper? There's plenty." She heard the kitchen door open and glanced over. "Owen, how nice. I'd like you to meet Mrs. Preston and Ammie West." She grinned at Laurie. "This is Owen Jr."

Owen snatched the old hat from his head. "Ma'am."

"How nice to meet you, Owen." Laurie judged the boy to be about ten. He had his mother's clear green eyes, a smattering of freckles across his cheeks, and wavy reddish-blond hair. He was adorable.

"Mama, can I go fishin' before supper? Jimmy's waitin' out back."

"You'll come when I call?"

"Yes'm." Owen ran back outside and caught the door just before it slammed shut.

Etta shook her head. "That boy, he's always running one way or the other."

"He's a handsome lad." Laurie felt embarrassed. "Thank you again. I seem to be saying that every time I see you."

"You needn't. What're friends for?" Etta shrugged. "Will you come by tomorrow?"

"I'm not sure. If not, I'll see you soon."

During the ride home Ammie chatted about things she had seen and done at Etta's. That's what she needs, Laurie thought, to spend more time around other people, especially children.

That evening after she had let the cat in and put Ammie down for the night, Laurie dressed for bed before rereading the letters she had found in Ruth's room. She left her bedroom door open. A light breeze cooled her room. She sat Indian fashion on the bed with the pages spread out in front of her.

They were signed "V," but she hadn't heard anyone mention a Vernon or Victor, or any other name beginning with the letter. Of course, the man didn't necessarily have to live in town. Gabe had said that Ruth went to town in the wagon, but which town? If she had gone farther than Ashly Mills, it would have taken her the better part of a day.

Laurie wished she'd been allowed to read Ruth's diary. She put the letters back in the drawer. Ruth's preference for other men didn't make sense to Laurie. Gabe's honest, kind, a hard worker, she thought, and handsome. What more would a woman want in a man? Excitement? Gabe was exciting. Wealth? He was a good provider. Or did Ruth know what she wanted?

As Laurie drifted off to sleep Gabe's unrelenting features stared at her. She had managed to block him from her mind, until she closed her eyes. She pulled the covers up over her lips. Lord, he was angry. Was he embarrassed? Or had she inadvertently done something to offend him? She spent a restless night.

She woke feeling exhausted the following morning. She rolled onto her side and saw the cat curled up near her. "Did you get lonely?"

Petting the feline's soft coat, Laurie couldn't remember dreaming, but she knew she had thought of something she wanted to ask Gabe about, only it was gone. Mittens purred in her gravelly way, and Laurie's eyes closed.

"Orie? *Orie?*" Ammie screamed from the bottom of the stairs. She pulled on the gate barring her way and called again.

Laurie jerked upright and startled the cat. "Coming, sweetie." Mittens sprang up and yowled at her. "It's okay." She scratched the cat's neck and got out of bed.

Since they were alone in the house, Laurie didn't bother with her wrapper before she went down to Ammie. "Morning, sugar."

Ammie wrapped her arms around Laurie's legs and held on.

Laurie smoothed the hair back from the little girl's face. "What's wrong? Did something scare you?"

Ammie nodded and squeezed tighter.

Loosening Ammie's grip, Laurie spoke softly. "I won't *ever* leave you alone." She lifted Ammie up and carried her over to the front door, where she set her down.

"Will you help me move this board? Mittens will have to go outside."

Ammie pushed up on one end and smiled when Laurie moved the board away from the door. Ammie pulled the door open and looked around for her pet. "Mittens, come on. Go out."

Watching the cat trot to Ammie made Laurie grin. She didn't think it was wise to let the cat into Ammie's room, especially at night, but Mittens was good company for her. "Why don't we go out, too?"

Ammie followed Laurie to the necessary and later on while she tended to the chores. She finished gathering the eggs by midmorning and set some aside for Etta.

"Ammie, would you like to visit your daddy?"

"Me go see Daddy." Ammie took Laurie's hand and started for the door.

"Wait a minute, sweetie. We should change clothes."

Ammie was dressed first, then helped Laurie. After she fastened the little girl in the buggy, she hitched up the horse. Soon they rode along Stage Road. Laurie was anxious to see Gabe. She searched her mind for a momentary diversion and started humming "Molly Malone." "Too complicated," she murmured to herself. "Want to help me tell a nursery rhyme?"

Ammie's eyes lit up and she grinned. "Mm-hm. 'Hey, Diddo Diddo.'"

"Okay. 'Hey, Diddle Diddle, the cat—'"

Ammie interrupted with, "Mittens!"

Laurie nodded. "'Mittens and the fiddle . . .'" With Ammie asking questions all through the rhyme, they arrived at the jail as they finished the last line.

❧20❧

After making sure their bonnets were straight and their skirts brushed free of wrinkles, Laurie took Ammie's hand and opened the door of the jail.

"Good morning, Sheriff. We came to visit Mr. West." She didn't care if Gabe got angry, though she prayed he wouldn't frighten his daughter. She wanted him to know they believed in his innocence.

Sheriff Jenkins glanced up and waved to the cell. "You know where he is."

Laurie bent down and whispered to Ammie, "Say hello to your daddy and give him a kiss." When Ammie stared at her, Laurie gave her an encouraging grin punctuated with a nod.

Gabe stiffened at the sight of Laurie. Damn it to hell, couldn't that woman do what she was told? He relented. As he crouched down he smiled at Ammie and held out his arms. She was all fancied up in the new dress and bonnet Laurie had made and looked like a little porcelain doll. "Hi, punkin."

"Daddy?" She tipped her head back and stared up where the bars joined the ceiling, then down to the floor.

"They're bars, punkin. You look pretty, just like Laurie."

Ammie beamed and glanced over at Laurie.

Laurie nodded and faced the sheriff. "Would you open the door? Mr. West's daughter isn't old enough to understand."

Sheriff Jenkins shifted his weight and stood up. After rotating his shoulders, he went over and unlocked the cell door. "I'm going across the street. I'll be right back, so don't get any ideas."

Gabe picked up Ammie and held her against his chest. "You think I'd run off and leave my daughter?"

Jenkins glanced to the side, where Laurie was standing, and back to Gabe. "Guess not."

Ammie put her head down on her daddy's shoulder.

Laurie stepped over to the cell door. "Has the sheriff heard from the judge about your bail yet?"

Gabe shook his head and gazed at her. "Why won't you do as I asked? This is no place for either of you."

"Ammie wanted to see you. So did I." Laurie tugged at her glove.

He said softly, "Laurie, I'm sorry about yesterday." He shifted Ammie to his other shoulder. "Can you forgive me?"

She nodded, trying valiantly to keep from crying.

Gabe ached to comfort her, but he couldn't, not there. He quickly changed the subject but kept his voice soft. "I don't like you being alone at the house. I didn't even get the windows replaced." He grumbled more for his benefit than hers. Reading Ruth's diary reminded him how unhappy she was with him, but he didn't find any suggestions about how he could have made life better for her—except by leaving his home and moving to a big city.

Following Gabe's lead, Laurie whispered. "We're fine,

aren't we, Ammie? And I think Mittens likes jumping between the boards covering the windows.''

Laurie had been watching him closely and thought she could see a slight change in him, that he seemed less energetic. He clung to his daughter in a way he never had before. Was he thinking about giving up? she wondered. Well, *she* was not about to acquiesce and wouldn't allow him to either!

"Did you order the glass?"

He nodded. "For all the good it'll do me." Oh, God, he mentally ranted, I can't even repair my own home! "You'd better have Danny do it. Anyone could—" No, he wouldn't say that aloud. "My rifle's by the door. Have you ever used a gun?"

Laurie shook her head. "Why would I need to?"

"You're alone at the house. I should've sent word to Danny!" He took Laurie's hand and squeezed it. "You can't stay there."

"We'll be fine. I may not have made many friends in town, but I don't think I made any mortal enemies." She had to do something. Now he was becoming suspicious, and she didn't think that was his nature. "Did you finish reading the diary?"

"Her mind rambled. She never said anything to me about not sleeping." He shook his head. "She didn't look right the last week. I asked her if she needed the doctor, but she just started screaming. I figured it must have had something to do with her woman's time."

Didn't anyone tell him Ruth was carrying another child? Or did anyone else know? Why did she of all people, Laurie wondered, have to be the one? She straightened one glove finger and snugged the others, one by one.

Gabe went over and took her hands in his. "Laurie, please. What is it?"

She stared into his soft gray eyes and wondered how Ruth could have hurt him so. "She was . . ." She swallowed hard. It would be easier to say it straight out. "She was carrying another child, Gabe. That's probably why she wouldn't see the doctor. She didn't want you to know.'' She slipped one hand from his and smoothed his black hair away from his face with trembling fingers.

"How do you know that?"

"I found a couple of her letters."

"We'll talk about them later." He turned his face to her hand and kissed her palm. A noise outside reminded him they had no privacy. He gazed at her. "You shouldn't stay here any longer."

Ignoring his suggestion, she continued: "She died in December. Do you have any idea who she was seeing that fall?"

"By then I spent as much time away from the house and her as possible."

She untangled the strings on her reticule. "You said Ruth's diary is what condemned you. What part of it?"

"I'm not sure, but I think Hannah Tuttle convinced the sheriff that I found the diary, discovered that Ammie wasn't really mine, or the one Ruth was carrying, and killed her." He shook his head. "Hell, I knew Ammie wasn't mine from the time of her birth."

"But you didn't know about this child?"

"No, not until I read the diary. Ruth knew how I'd feel about a second child I hadn't fathered." Hell, he would've *wanted* to kill her—but he couldn't have.

She had to ask, be prepared for questions should they arise. "Would you've accepted the child the way you did Ammie?"

"I wouldn't have given it away. It was Ruth's doing. How could I blame a babe?" He had looked forward to having his own children, and Ruth seemed to have been bent on providing him with other men's. "I might have sent her away. In the diary she mentioned a woman who might help her."

"With what?"

He shrugged.

Laurie heard approaching boot steps and stood up. "Do you know when you'll be released?"

Gabe took her arm and walked her to the door. "Jenkins hasn't heard from the judge." He rubbed his thumb on the back of her arm. "Remember what I said about the ranch." Her scent created images of her laughing, smiling—naked in his embrace.

"This's been a dreadful mistake. I have to believe it will be corrected. Surely no jury would convict you." His touch was warm, exciting. Lord, she hated leaving him. He belonged at home with his daughter—with her.

"We'll have to wait for the trial; pray for a miracle." Just when he thought he had everything—Laurie, a happy little girl, and a potential profit from his ranch—it was all snatched away by a woman who'd made his life a living hell. Even from the grave, Ruth hadn't relented.

"You mustn't give up." Laurie stepped ahead of him. She hesitated at the threshold and faced Gabe. "How did the sheriff get Ruth's diary?"

"From Hannah Tuttle." Laurie's eyes narrowed, and he wanted to laugh. "He said she picked it up when she found Ruth and must've put it in her reticule."

"I see. Does Hannah do that very often?" That woman again!

He lifted one shoulder. "It doesn't matter now. She can't hurt us any more than she already has."

Us. What a wonderful word. "No, she can't." Laurie stepped outside and gave him a radiant smile. "I'll see you tomorrow."

"Don't come here again." He saw Jenkins's sleeve outside the door and released Laurie's hand. "Mrs. Preston." He emphasized the words for the sheriff's benefit; Gabe didn't want Jenkins gossiping about Laurie's visit. "Must I remind you that you work for me? And since I'm paying your wages, you'll do as I say."

She couldn't believe what he said, then he motioned toward the door and she understood. "How will you pay my wages while you're in jail? I believe I'm due a month's salary. Unless you can pay me today, I'll do what I feel is in Ammie's best interest.'' She stared at him and tried not to laugh.

Gabe gritted his teeth to keep his amusement to himself. God, she was beautiful. He loved to see her eyes sparkle with devilment.

''Jenkins! I need to get to the bank.''

The sheriff peered around the edge of the doorway. ''You know better than to ask that.''

Gabe kissed his daughter's head and addressed Laurie. ''You're responsible for my daughter. I'll have to trust you to keep her safe. Both of you.'' He mouthed the last three words.

''You may depend on me, Mr. West.'' She reached for Ammie. ''Come on, sugar. We have to go now. Say good-bye.'' Laurie didn't gaze at him, but hoped he could see her love for him in her eyes.

Laurie went to the general store to see if the plate glass had come in and was told it should be available in two days. From there she rode over to Etta's house. When Etta answered the door, Laurie handed her the basket of eggs. ''Can you use them? The hens keep laying, and I haven't been baking.''

''How nice of you. Come on in.'' Closing the front door, Etta continued: ''I was going to call on you this afternoon. I'll be watching two little ones in the morning and thought Ammie might enjoy playing with the other children.'' She clasped her hands and smiled at Ammie.

''We really can't stay.'' Ammie yawned, and Laurie chuckled. ''It's almost her nap time.'' She glanced around Etta's orderly parlor. ''Are you sure you want another child playing in there?''

''I think I'll let them run loose outside. We can have a picnic. Please come. It'll be fun.''

Laurie had wondered how long it would be before Ammie would get to play with other children, when the women didn't feel particularly friendly with herself. "What time? And what can I bring?"

"Ten, and you've already brought eggs."

Ammie stood in Etta's backyard and watched a girl chasing a boy around a big tree. They were giggling. She took a few shaky steps toward them and glanced back at Laurie.

Laurie smiled and motioned for Ammie to join in. "Oh, Etta, she doesn't know how to play with the children. Maybe I should help her." She started to rise, but Etta's words stopped her.

"Ammie'll learn. She plays at home, doesn't she?"

"Yes. With me and her cat. But that isn't the same."

Ammie only has her father and me, Laurie thought, adults. She had been an only child, too, and had prayed for a big brother. Of course when she told her mother, she was informed that it was too late to ask for an older brother. But she had grown up in town, where it was easier to meet playmates.

"She's doing fine. Look, Bethy's talking to Ammie. It won't take Jake long before he joins them."

Following Etta's gaze, Laurie felt like any nervous mother and sighed. "Think we should give them the cookies and milk now?" Beth and Jake were redheaded twins, and adorable.

"Let's wait until they get bored or start bickering. Can I get you some coffee? Lemonade?"

"I'm fine, thank you." Laurie picked a clover from the grass and twirled it between her fingers. "I got rid of some of Ruth's things this morning."

"Did you donate them to the church?"

"No. Some weren't really suitable for that."

Etta glanced sideways but said nothing.

"I left the bundle behind the saloon before I came here."

Etta grinned. "You didn't!"

Laurie smiled and nodded. "It was that or burn the dresses."

"Oh, my." Etta's gaze went from the children to Laurie. "How is Mr. West?"

"I fear he's getting discouraged." Laurie idly kept watch over the youngsters as she talked. "Ruth mentioned a woman in her diary. Someone she thought would help her."

Etta shaded her eyes. "With what?"

"She didn't say, but *I* think it may have had to do with . . . a personal matter." Did she have the right to tell Etta about Ruth's secret? Laurie wondered. Would Gabe object? But if Etta could help them find this woman . . .

Etta moved to Laurie's side, the sun now at her back. "Something a doctor wouldn't help her with?"

Laurie nodded. "Ruth didn't mention a name. I thought maybe, if I could find her, I could ask if she had given Ruth any advice . . . or tonic." She shrugged. "I'm probably stirring an empty pot."

"Not necessarily."

Laurie looked at Etta. "Do you know of someone, maybe a midwife, who could have helped Ruth?"

"I can't say I do. I'll have to think."

Laurie heard a buggy and glanced to the front of the house. A few minutes later a mature version of Beth came around the house.

Beth and Jake squealed and ran to the woman, calling, "Mama, Mama, Mama."

Ammie followed them only as far as where Laurie was sitting and watched the other children.

Jenkins had gone after Gabe's dinner. He paced back and forth in his cell. His seventh meal in this damn jail. Just then, a bone-thin boy scrambled through the door.

The youth frantically searched the small room. "Where's the sheriff?"

"At Bella's, I suppose. What's wrong?"

"Got a telegraph for 'im." The boy waved a paper in the air and ran out.

Gabe went to the corner of his cell and tried to peer out through the open door, but he couldn't see the saloon. Damn! Hope he hadn't realized he possessed began to grow. He stood there listening for the sheriff's heavy footsteps. Long minutes later he heard Jenkins returning.

Sheriff Jenkins held up the telegraphed message. "You're mighty lucky. Judge Underwood's approved bail. Fifty'll get you out till the thirteenth of September."

"Fifty for two weeks!" Gabe shouted. "Hell, maybe I'll just stay here. The meals are free." He sprawled out on the cot, his fingers interlocked behind his head.

The sheriff frowned. "Thought you were worried about the widow and your young'un."

"She won't run off without her wages." Fifty dollars. It was highway robbery. He kept enough money in the local bank to cover his needs. This definitely qualified.

"Well?" Jenkins started out and paused at the door. "You going to be an idiot? Or get back to your ranch?"

Gabe stared down the length of his body at the chubby sheriff. "Your charm's almost irresistible, but I might as well get back home. I suppose you'll walk me to the bank?"

The sheriff nodded and went to his desk.

Gabe was off the cot, jacket in hand, hat on his head, and waiting at his cell door before the sheriff got the key into the lock. Gabe withdrew the money from the bank as quickly as possible.

Sheriff Jenkins started to leave, then turned back. "You have to be in court on the thirteenth of September, in Jacksonville. That's a Monday."

Jenkins left Gabe standing on the boardwalk. As he started off for the livery the same boy skidded to a stop in front of him and held out another message. Gabe flipped the youth a nickel and unfolded the paper. He only glanced at the bottom of the page to see who it was from. Judge Underwood. Probably advising him to hire an attorney,

Gabe decided, and stuffed the message into his trouser pocket.

A half hour later he was riding to the ranch on a rented nag. The midday sun beat down on his shoulders, and the fresh air swept away the dusty stale odor of the jail. He was finally on his way home to Laurie.

He urged the old horse to a gallop. He wanted to see the look on her face when she came out to see who had ridden into the yard. He wanted to hold her in his arms and never let go of her.

Bringing the nag to a halt on the rise, he gazed down at his ranch, the barn, the log house he and his father had built. He felt a renewed sense of pride. This was his, and his legacy to his family.

That reminded him, he and Laurie had to talk about their future—get things settled between them, though it didn't seem right to tie her down to marriage with a man who might be hanged for murder. He'd witnessed a hanging once and hoped never to again. He reached up and touched his fingers to his neck.

He approached the house and waited for Laurie to open the door. She didn't come out. He dismounted and entered the house, hoping to catch her unawares. The house was quiet. He checked each room and found no one. It felt hollow, lonely without her, and he was more than a little disappointed in finding her gone.

After making a pot of coffee and pouring a cup, he wandered into the main room to read the judge's message.

"Mr. and Mrs. Franklin Tuttle have filed suit for the custody of their granddaughter, known as Ammie West. The hearing will be on September 20. Judge Underwood, Jacksonville."

The paper crumpled easily in Gabe's fist. Who the hell did those goddamn bastards think they were? Never! No way in hell would he hand over his daughter. Ammie was *his*. He stormed outside. What would happen to her if he was convicted of Ruth's murder? At that moment Gabe would have loved nothing as much as smashing Tuttle into fodder.

He would never give up Ammie, *his daughter*. Never!

He stormed outside in search of some chore that would relieve his anger. At the side of the barn he grabbed the ax and attacked one of the logs he'd left to dry for firewood. He was so enraged, the muscles in his arms quivered and his jaw locked. Ruth! He swung the ax and buried it deep into the timber. She was dead, yet she still haunted him and their daughter from the grave.

He swung the heavy ax, again—damn her selfishness. And again—damn her lover and his parents. And again, each time trying to rid himself of her image, her lover's image, and that of his parents. Ammie was *his*.

He'd cut nearly a cord of firewood by the time he heard the rig. He stood by the side of the barn, watching, and began to calm down. He saw her expression the moment she noticed him. At first she looked puzzled, as if she wasn't sure who was there. She glanced at the old nag, then back at him, and a beam lighted her lovely face.

Laurie grinned at Ammie. "Your daddy's home! Wave to him, sugar." He was standing in front of a large stack of freshly cut wood and looked like he'd never left home. Lord, he was a handsome man! Excitement spread through her, and she had to make an effort to slow the horse to a walk as they approached him.

Ammie bounced up and down, waving and calling her daddy.

Laurie pulled up near the barn door and set the brake. "Welcome home."

Gabe lifted Ammie up in the air and spun her around. He lowered her and helped Laurie down. "Where were you?"

"Ammie was invited to play with two other children at Etta's this morning. We stopped by the jail on the way back." She glanced at the old horse. "Whose is that?"

"A rental." He set Ammie down and took Laurie's arm.

"Is there anything to eat? I posted bail as soon as Jenkins got word from the judge—just before supper."

Ammie ran ahead. She scampered up the step and tugged at the door latch. Then she turned to Laurie and called out. "Mama, c'mere. Can't open."

❧21❧

Laurie stumbled to a halt. Surely she couldn't have heard the child right.

"Ma-ma . . ." Ammie wailed again.

Tears brimmed in Laurie's eyes and blurred her vision. She opened her mouth to answer, but no sound came out. She gazed up at Gabe.

He stared down at Laurie in awe and knew Ammie had used the word for the first time. For all his plans, his daughter had just said what he'd wanted to for days. He smiled. "Not yet, punkin, but soon." While staring at Laurie, he said in a husky voice, "Very soon."

Tears ran down Laurie's cheeks. She dashed them away with the back of her hand and hurried to open the door. Ammie's voice calling her "Mama" sang in her mind.

Gabe reached out, slowly loosened Laurie's bonnet strings, and slid it off of her head. He buried his fingers in her hair and lowered his mouth to hers.

She slipped her arms around his waist and held him close. They were together. She prayed they would stay that way.

Ammie came back to the door and tried to peer around Laurie's skirt. "Mama, can't find Mittens."

Laurie dropped her forehead to Gabe's chest and grinned. She couldn't resist the laughter that bubbled forth.

Once she was sure Ammie had gone to sleep, Laurie went outside to meet Gabe. "Finally." She had expected him, wanted him to take her into his embrace, but he didn't.

Gabe saw the desire in her eyes, and it almost sidetracked him. Instead he took her hand and started walking slowly. "Mind if we sit by the creek? We need to talk."

As they strolled the short distance she noticed his resolute gait, a tautness in his jaw, and worried about the cause. This was the first time they had been alone in almost a week. Maybe he's just anxious, or worried about her reaction to his arrest, she decided. She would assure him that she hadn't lost faith in him.

He chose a patch of soft grass near the water. With her smaller hand still in his, he sprawled out on the ground and drew her beside him. She melted down at his side like butter in the noonday sun. Just one kiss, he thought, one to bolster his courage, to reassure him she was really there.

Laurie lay at his side on the sweet-smelling grass beneath the canopy of an old pine tree. Gabe's gaze told her what she wanted to know. She leaned forward and pressed him backward. It was a heady feeling knowing she affected him the way he did her. His intimate caress was bold, branding, and started spreading that delicious weakness through her veins.

He reluctantly ended their heated kiss. He should have known one kiss would only ignite their need. "Laurie." Her auburn brows drew together as she stared at him. God, her confusion hurt. "It's about Ammie."

Laurie sat back. "Ammie?" It took a moment to understand the subtle change in him. "Oh. Are you upset because she called me Mama?"

"Never that." He reached for the crumpled telegram in

his pocket. "Maybe you'd better read this. It came after I'd posted bail."

She smoothed out the wrinkled paper on her leg. After she had read it the second time, she met his gaze. "How can they do it? Why? They're nothing to her."

"If their son had been married to Ruth, they'd have a right."

Laurie's mouth dropped open. "Then they are her grandparents. . . ."

"Don't they know what it would do to her? My God!" Laurie drew her knees up and hugged them to her chest. "You'll fight them, won't you?"

He fingered a wisp of her hair. "I thought *we* would. Together." Her hair was so soft it caught on his callused fingers.

We. Laurie closed her eyes and smiled to herself. She knew he loved his daughter. "Of course I'll help you." She glanced at him, weighing her words. "Do you know someone whose initial is *V*?"

Gabe leaned back on the grass. "Virgil Tuttle. Why?"

"Oh. I found two letters from him to Ruth. Does he live here?"

"Not anymore. Heard his gun misfired—last winter. More likely he was shot. The Tuttles were pretty close-mouthed about it."

"That doesn't sound like Hannah."

Laurie imagined how very hurt Ruth must have been after reading Virgil's last letter. But that still didn't point a finger at her killer, unless there was more to Hannah than Laurie suspected.

"Ruth could have threatened him." She shrugged. "And he might have poisoned her." She watched the dappled sunlight on the surface of the creek a moment. "I guess I was hoping for an easy answer."

"I spent months doing that."

"I didn't find anything in Ruth's room, except for the letters. One may help your case." Laurie thought about Etta and wondered if she could find the woman who used herbs and made curatives, without tarnishing her own reputation. "When is your trial?"

"Two weeks."

Ammie held a bit of string up over her cat's head and jiggled it. When the cat sprang up, she jerked the string out of reach. "Mama, see Mittens." She repeated the trick and giggled.

Laurie scraped off the plate and glanced over. She watched Ammie and smiled. "Be careful, sweetie. She might scratch your arm."

The cat looked at Laurie and trotted over to investigate. "You want supper?" The cat meowed and stood up, batting at the plate in her hand. "Ammie, would you feed Mittens?" Laurie held out a small bowl.

Ammie took the dish and set it down on the floor near the iron stove. She watched for a minute, then went over to the slop bucket and grabbed a bit of potato.

Laurie gently took hold of the child's wrist. "No, Ammie. You can't eat that."

"Mittens eat it?"

"Cats don't eat potatoes. Here's a little meat left on your plate. Give her that." Laurie scraped the gravy and meat into the cat's bowl and handed it to Ammie.

Ammie picked up her glass and handed it to Laurie. "Me hep you."

"Thank you." Laurie washed the flatware and gave it to Ammie to dry, then set the dishes aside to dry herself. She actually enjoyed sharing the mundane chore with the child.

After putting the last dish away, she hung the towel over Gabe's chair. "Ready to go out and play?"

Ammie nodded. "Come on," she called, dashing to the door.

The apron landed over the back of Laurie's chair as she followed Ammie. The sun had dipped below the tops of the trees, but it was still light and the air was refreshing after the heat of the kitchen. While Ammie and the cat chased crickets Laurie wandered over to the corral to visit Carly.

The mare pranced over to the fence and nuzzled her hand for a treat. "Sorry, girl." She rubbed the mare's soft muzzle and scratched around her ear. "We'll take a real ride soon. I promise." She stepped up on the bottom rail of the fence and put her arms around Carly's neck.

Gabe came around the side of the barn and saw Laurie's skirts swaying above her ankles as she hugged the mare. That was a sight to warm any man's heart. The mare had always been a horse with spirit, but he suspected she was completely devoted to Laurie. He ambled over to Laurie and put his hand on her waist.

"What are you two plotting?"

Laurie gulped and stepped back down to the ground. Of course, he was teasing, she thought. He couldn't possibly know she had been planning a visit he wouldn't approve. She shrugged and patted Carly's neck. "I haven't had a chance to ride her for over a week. I just promised her some exercise. I'm sure the cow's glad you're back. She didn't seem too happy with my efforts, and I don't blame her."

"Sorry you had so many extra chores." He leaned against the fence and glanced around the grounds. "Maybe it was for the best. You should learn how to tend all the livestock. Tomorrow I'll show you what has to be done."

He had to prepare Laurie, he reminded himself. There were so many things she needed to know. Tomorrow he'd work with her. The next day he'd bring Danny down to the ranch. He leaned over and lightly rested his chin on her shoulder. "Isn't it almost Ammie's bedtime?"

Laurie felt the flutter down her spine and sighed. "Yes, I do believe it is." When she turned around, her lips brushed his. She started to raise her arms, but she remembered where they were and lowered them.

"Hurry," he whispered, his lips brushing hers. "You don't want me to go crazy, do you?" He smiled.

She grinned and shook her head before calling Ammie.

As she crossed the yard she glanced heavenward and murmured, "Thank you, Lord." She cleaned the little girl up and dressed her for bed, all the while making up a fairy story. After Ammie kissed Gabe good night, Laurie tucked her into bed.

Ammie smiled up at her. "Night, Mama."

Laurie bent down and kissed Ammie. "Good night, sweetheart." *She really shouldn't call me that,* Laurie thought on her way out to the main room. *It's not fair for her to believe I'm her mother. Oh, but it sounds so very nice.*

Gabe heard Laurie close his daughter's bedroom door and tamped out his pipe. At last they'd be alone. He ran his fingers through his hair and rose to meet her.

When she neared the settee, Laurie found herself being hugged and swung around. She braced her hands on his shoulders. "What are you doing? Have you been drinking?"

"Thinking . . . about you . . . us, and this." He traced the outline of her lips with his tongue before probing the warm interior of her mouth.

She encircled his neck with her arms, her breasts pressed into his chest. She felt his heart pounding in time with hers and a rush of anticipation spread through her. She wanted to snuggle closer, but her feet were above the floor, and she couldn't gain any leverage.

If only he could shout to the world, "This is my wife! She loves me as much as I love her!" She was soft and passionate. He wanted more, much more.

When she started to unbutton her dress, Gabe brushed her hands aside and took pleasure in doing it himself. Once the first buttons were free, he kissed the creamy skin above her chemise and quickly released the remaining buttons. He cast off her dress and proceeded with the camisole, then the tie at her waist.

Her soft petticoat slid down and landed on the floor in a soft whish around her ankles. She grinned up at him. "It's my turn now."

* * *

Early the next morning Gabe was roused from sleep when Laurie eased her thigh between his and snuggled up to him. A perfect way to begin the day. He rolled onto his back, taking her with him. "Mornin'."

She grinned and stretched out along the length of him. "You weren't thinking of going back to sleep, were you?"

"Uh-uh." With a hand under each of her arms, he slid her up to eye level and kissed her lips.

Their lovemaking was impassioned, urgent, and they lay spent a short time later. She woke again and felt Gabe playing with her hair.

"Are you hungry yet?" God, she's beautiful. He watched the light sparkle on the strand of reddish-gold-brown hair.

"Starving." She stretched her legs out, reluctant to jump up and start cooking.

He outlined the curve of her waist down to her hip with his hand and gazed at her. "Laurie." Her skin reminded him of a pearl. She met his gaze. She must know what he was about to ask. It was just a formality, but women expected such, and he didn't want to insult her by not declaring himself in the proper way. It seemed so much easier the times he'd thought about it. But now. . . .

"Will you be my wife?" he asked in a rush. His heart pounded, and he felt like he'd just run a footrace. He expected her to smile and say yes. Instead her eyes grew large and though she opened her mouth, she said nothing. "We can be married as soon as you want, or"—he glanced at his tanned hand resting on her pale hip—"after the trial. It's up to you."

She stared at him. She was lying on top of him, face-to-face, both of them as naked as newborns. What a time to ask for my hand, she thought. Besides, he had never mentioned love, not even hinted at it. Of course, she had never told him she loved him, but a woman simply didn't tell a man that until he had declared himself—which he just had.

She focused on the dark curly hair on his chest and tried to twine a longer strand around her finger. He grasped her hand and grinned.

"That tickles."

She sobered, not looking at him. "You don't *have* to marry me. I've been a willing partner. You aren't obligated to marry me."

He grabbed her shoulder. "You believe I feel *obligated* to you? Well, I don't! What made you think that?"

Laurie rolled off of him. "Will you answer a question, honestly, and not spare my feelings?"

"Of course. Ask me anything. You know the worst."

She gazed at him. "Why did you ask me to be your wife?" *Oh, God, please don't let it be pity.*

"*Why?*" He frowned. "Because I want you for my wife. You love Ammie. And, well, you must've known I wouldn't have slept with you and not done the right thing. Surely you didn't think I was just . . . easing myself with you!" He abruptly swung his legs over the side of the bed and stared at the wall. Hell, how can something so simple get so muddled?

Laurie scooted back against the head of the bed and drew her knees up. "I do love Ammie, but that's not reason enough to marry. After all, I can go on as before, taking care of her."

"Is that what you want?"

"No. Do you?" He had been married. Doesn't he know a woman wants to hear how a man feels about her?

He shook his head. "The decision is yours."

She leaned over and rested her open hand on his back. "Gabe, do you like me?"

"Like?"

His laughter sounded harsh, humorless, and she shivered.

He spun around and hauled her up to him. "I like my friends, a sunny day, a hot fire on a cold winter night. A man should more than *like* his wife. Don't you know that?"

"I would hope so." She pressed her lips to his, her

breasts to his chest. When she sat back, she almost giggled at the consternation apparent on his handsome face. "I love you, too."

His gaze narrowed. "Then what is all this about?"

She reached for the sheet and pulled it up, mechanically pleating it. She had not said it aloud, but it was time. "After my first marriage, I didn't see any reason to consider entering into another marriage of convenience. Then I fell in love with you. If we married and you didn't love me, I would be miserable."

"Oh, Laurie." He took her into his arms and held her against his chest, smoothing her hair. "I've tried to show you how I feel in every way I know." He gently rocked her.

She pulled back. "I'd better get dressed. Ammie must be awake."

As she moved away from him he cupped her breast in his hand until it slid from his grasp. "You didn't answer me?"

Her smile came straight from her heart. "Yes." With a fleet, wicked glance at his loins, she kissed him and reached for her discarded clothes. "I would be proud to be your wife."

"You minx. Maybe I should ask why you want to marry me." He grabbed his trousers.

She paused, her chemise gaping open, and looked over at him. "Because I love you." She quickly fastened the buttons and added, "And because I like the way you show me how you love me." She snatched her petticoat and skirt up, feeling decidedly embarrassed by her boldness.

Gabe tucked his shirt into his trousers and pulled on one boot. "When?" He shoved his foot into the second boot. "Or do you want to wait until after the trial?" Damn it, he shouldn't have asked her until afterward. But he needed her. Needed to know she was his. Needed to know she would always be there for Ammie, too.

Laurie sat down, facing him. "People might misunderstand if we marry beforehand. They already believe the worst. I think we need to prove your innocence first. I don't want anyone to spoil our wedding day.''

''Neither do I.'' He kissed her cheek and went to the bedroom door.

Laurie checked in on Ammie and found her just waking up. ''Good morning, sugar.''

She mixed the biscuit dough and set the table. When she turned to put the rolls into the oven, she walked right into Gabe's waiting arms. She nervously glanced around for Ammie.

''She's playing with the cat, in the other room.''

He lowered his lips to hers. This was what love should be like. Then he just held her, his thoughts roaming to the obstacles to their happiness—his trial and the custody hearing. If he and Laurie were married before the hearing, she would be Ammie's mother, which might help.

''I don't know what I'd do without you, Laurie. Together, we'll be a family and we'll keep Ammie safe from the Tuttles.''

Something in his voice alarmed her. She listened to his heart beat. She did love Ammie, but Laurie had that feeling again that maybe he needed her to be a mother to his daughter more than he needed her as his wife. She went cold inside.

''Is that the real reason you asked me to marry you? Did you think our marriage would keep the Tuttles from taking Ammie away from you?''

❧22❧

Laurie felt numb with fear. For a few golden minutes she had thought he returned her love. How could she have been so wrong. Well, she wouldn't tolerate another loveless marriage—not after having spent five years in that kind of limbo. Living alone was preferable.

Gabe dropped his arms to his side. Her complexion turned an unhealthy ashen color, her mouth pinched, and a drawn look changed her warm eyes to cold, distant orbs. He pulled her to him. She stood rigid in his embrace, as if a lifeless statue. He tightened his arms around her, willing her to respond.

"God, Laurie." He sighed near her ear. "I never wanted to love again. I thought I loved Ruth, but she shattered that possibility. Then you came along."

He kissed her hair and rested his cheek there. "You took to Ammie as if she were your own. You said what you thought."

She interrupted him. "No, not all the time."

He chuckled and continued. "And you made me care again. God, how you made me care." He tipped her chin up with his knuckle. Tears streamed down her cheeks. He wiped them away and lightly touched his lips to hers. "I love you, Laurie Preston. I tried my damnedest not to, but I do."

Ammie called from the main room. "Daddy, c'mere!"

"Hold on a minute, punkin." He took a deep breath. "Believe me, Laurie. I refused to remarry in order to give Ammie a mother when Aunt Penelope suggested it, and I haven't changed my mind. I wouldn't consider marriage unless I loved the woman and knew she returned my feelings."

She felt the trembling start in her chest and sweep outward, becoming apparent in her fingers. She pressed her lips together and waited for him to continue.

Gabe ran his callused thumb along her smooth jaw. "Will you be my wife?"

Laurie nodded, spilling fresh tears down her cheeks. "I will be proud to be Mrs. Gabe West."

All morning, Laurie was eager, and yet nervous, about seeing Etta. She and Gabe had agreed not to announce their intentions to wed. But she felt so utterly overjoyed, how could Etta not suspect something?

After instructing her to feed and care for the various animals, Gabe suggested having a picnic dinner by the creek and swung Ammie up to sit astride his shoulders. "Hold on, punkin." He galloped around the house and up to the creek.

When they reached the stream, Ammie tightened her grip around her daddy's neck. "Mo, Daddy. Go mo."

"More?" He worked her small hands loose. "Maybe later. Right now we should help Laurie."

She handed the old blanket to him, and he spread it on the ground. She set the food out and noticed that Ammie was nearing the water. "Come back, sugar. You can wash off in the water after you eat."

Ammie squatted at the edge of the creek and watched

the way the sunlight reflected on the water. She made a splash.

"Ammie. You get over here like your mama said." Gabe fixed her with a frown and pointed to the blanket. It was hard for him to look angry when he'd rather laugh, but she had to learn to mind.

Laurie dished out the cold meal, all finger foods. When she leaned over to set Gabe's dish down in front of him, he kissed her. She grinned and saw Ammie watching them, so she kissed the little girl on her cheek.

Ammie giggled and crawled over to her daddy. "Me too." She put her cheek up for her daddy to kiss.

He kissed her with a loud smacking noise. "We'd better eat before the ants get hungry."

Ammie glanced around and grabbed a piece of meat.

Laurie struggled to keep a straight face. "He's teasing you, sugar."

She hadn't seen him so carefree since the Fourth of July. He joked, laughed, and played with Ammie. Every time she started to think about his trial, she watched him until the gray mood that threatened to spoil the day had passed. She and Gabe splashed and waded in the creek right along with Ammie.

Gabe stretched out on the blanket and watched Laurie teach Ammie how to play patty cake. God, Laurie was pretty. He wished they could go on like this, just the three of them, but that wasn't possible. Every time he thought about his upcoming trial, he felt an impotent rage boiling within.

Gabe stared at the undamaged window in Ruth's old room. Cursing himself for not thinking of it before, he measured his daughter's sill. When he opened the door to his former wife's room, he smelled Ruth's scent. He found himself looking around as if she might jump out from a hiding place. The carved flowers and scrolls decorating the heavy bureau and headboard of the bed made the room uncomfortable. It certainly felt different from the other rooms in the house—which was probably why Ruth had spent most of her time there.

The first thing he did was open the window before yanking the ugly drapes from the rod. The effect was immediate—fresh air and sunlight flooded in. He measured the window.

He set to work and took out the moveable sash. By the time he'd worked the fixed sash free, Ruth's scent was not noticeable. Before leaving the room, he threw the drapes out into the yard.

He carried the window sashes down to the kitchen. He'd install them in Ammie's room after she got up. Taking a box of sulfur matches, he went outside to get rid of the drapes. He put a lighted match to some dry brush and the material in a clearing far away from the house. He was watching the fire when he heard a rider approach.

Danny slowed his horse when he neared Gabe. "What the hell are you burning? It sure smells awful."

Gabe chuckled. "Just some old drapes. Why are you down here? The herd okay?"

"Fine. I couldn't wait two more days to see if you were still a free man." Danny tipped his dusty hat back and wiped his arm across his brow. "So, was it a false alarm?"

Gabe shook his head. "I spent three days in jail before Judge Underwood set my bail."

"Holy Christ! Why didn't you send word?"

"Wasn't time." Gabe kicked dirt over the dying embers. "Come back to the house. Ammie should be waking anytime."

Danny dismounted and led his horse to walk with Gabe. "Mrs. Preston's day off?"

"She's riding."

Gabe glanced at the corral as he passed on the way back to the house. Laurie hadn't returned. He also paused at the corner of the house and gazed to the west. He'd give

her another thirty minutes before he started looking for
her.

He stirred the fire in the stove, put a pot of coffee on, and
checked on his daughter. He motioned Danny to take a seat
and glanced out the kitchen window.

Danny pulled out the chair opposite Ammie's and sat
down. "Lose someone?"

"Laurie's a good rider, but she's not used to the trail."
When he saw the smug grin on Danny's face, Gabe realized
what he'd said. "I've asked her to be my wife. We're not
telling *anyone*." "My wife" had such a nice sound.

Danny lunged forward and slapped Gabe on the shoulder.
"Congratulations! That's great. When?"

Gabe shrugged. "After I'm acquitted. If I'm not, I don't
know. I won't make her a widow a second time. The
ranch'll be hers and Ammie's, so she'll have a home and
security."

Danny tipped his chair back. "You think she'll want
to remain here if you're . . . hanged?" The chair came
down on its front legs with a loud thud. "Good God, I
can't believe it! Will that woman never leave you in
peace?"

"I buried Ruth's body last December, but it seems
she's not finished with me yet." Gabe got up and poured
two cups of coffee. Before resuming his seat, he looked
out the window. He spotted rising dust not far off and
sighed.

Ammie wandered out of her room, yawning, and went
over to Gabe. "Where's Mittens, Daddy."

He lifted her up and held her against his chest. "She's
probably taking a nap outside." He tucked her hair behind
her ear. "Say hello to Danny."

Ammie rubbed her eyes and peeked at him before doing
as her father asked.

Gabe gave her a dipperful of water and sat down with her
on his knee. She felt so small and warm. He kissed her

cheek and hoped he'd be around to see her wed. He eyed Danny. "Don't forget, you're Ammie's godfather."

Danny frowned. "You're not going to tie the noose for them, are you? You have to do *something*! It must have been one of Ruth's . . . friends. Maybe she threatened him."

"How am I to find some man—any man—who she was seeing ten months ago? I've no idea who she kept company with." Gabe heard the front door open and watched the kitchen doorway.

"Mama!" Ammie scrambled down from her daddy's lap and ran to meet Laurie.

"Hi, sugar." Laurie caught the little girl up in her arms and entered the kitchen. She was more than a little surprised to see Danny and Gabe sitting at the table. "Hello. I hoped to get back before she woke up."

Gabe grinned. "No problem. How was your ride?" Her cheeks were rosy, her eyes were sparkling, and he felt his pride surge. She'd agreed to be his wife. A blessing when his world seemed to be filled with menace and doom.

"Wonderful. I'll have to start taking Ammie on excursions around the yard." Laurie's gaze went to Danny. "The herd is all right, isn't it?"

He chuckled. "Fine, Mrs. Preston. I just came to see how Gabe's doing."

"Good." She set Ammie down. "You'll stay for supper?"

Danny bowed his head. "It'd be my pleasure." He glanced sideways at Gabe, who was watching Laurie.

"Don't get your hopes too high. My husband hired a cook rather than subject himself to my concoctions."

As Laurie swept the main room she glanced at the new window. Danny and Gabe had ridden into town and waited at the general store for the shipment of glass. She had been sure they were wasting their time, but it had come in and Gabe was first in line for the precious panes. They were replacing that last window; hers.

As soon as Gabe finished, she would put Ammie down for her nap. Then she planned to ride into town. She had taken some of her savings and put it in her reticule. While looking through her own small wardrobe, she had decided to make a woolen shawl for Etta, a thank-you gift. Laurie worked the dirt and dust into a pile near the door. When she started brushing the mound toward the doorway, Mittens suddenly ran out from the kitchen and swiped at the bristles of the broom.

She pushed the cat back with the object of its interest. "Shoo, go on."

The cat stood up on its hind legs, batting at the broom. After two more tries to finish her task, Laurie dragged the broom along the floor, out the door, and swung it over the edge of the porch. The cat pursued and leaped after the broom. Working quickly, Laurie swept the dirt out onto the porch and from there to the yard.

Ammie came running out and saw her pet. "Oh, Mittens!" The cat jumped a foot straight up, its back arched, tail bristling, and scampered around the corner of the house. "No. Come back!"

Laurie put her hand on Ammie's shoulder. "She's just playing. I'm thirsty. Let's get a drink of water."

After two dippers of water and an abbreviated story, Ammie finally lay down and closed her eyes. Laurie changed into her riding skirt and shirtwaist. A hat would be nice to shade her eyes, but her bonnet would look ridiculous. She grabbed her leather gloves, hurried downstairs, checked on Ammie, and went out to the barn.

Danny and Gabe were looking at a harness. Gabe glanced over at her, and she grinned. "Do you mind if I ride to town while Ammie sleeps?"

His shirt had worked loose from his trousers, and a dark wave curved across his forehead. If Danny hadn't been there, she would have combed his beautiful black hair back with her fingers. Instead she put her gloves on.

"You sure you don't want to take the rig?" She was

properly dressed for riding. Gabe decided he preferred her with her skirt hiked up between her legs—but only when they were alone.

"I won't be long. Besides, Carly and I need the exercise." She hooked the strings of her reticule over a post and took down the mare's bridle.

Gabe caught himself before he reached out to relieve Laurie of the harness. She needed to saddle the horse herself. She'd done it before and would have to if he weren't around. Damn it all, how was he to live like this? He spoke to Danny while watching Laurie out in the corral.

"After she leaves, I'd like you to witness my will."

"What?" Danny stared at his friend. "Think a half-breed's signature is legal?"

Gabe glared at him.

Danny grimaced. "I'll sign."

Laurie looped the reins around the post in front of the barn, then went in for the blanket and saddle. She noticed Gabe watching her. His mood seemed to have changed. As she tightened the cinch she decided he must be concerned about her riding so far from the ranch.

Once Carly stood ready, Laurie returned to the barn. "Ammie usually sleeps a couple hours, and I just put her down about fifteen minutes ago." She started for the door when she remembered her reticule.

Gabe walked her outside. "No need to rush. What's so important in town?" He handed her the reins, and their fingers touched.

She gazed at him. It would be so easy to lean forward and kiss him. She glanced at the barn. "I want to make something for Etta and need the yard goods."

He stepped back and held the cheek strap while she mounted. "Enjoy your ride."

She wound the strings of her reticule around the saddle horn, then reached down and patted Carly's head. "We will."

Carly didn't need any more encouragement than a slight nudge from Laurie's heels to start trotting up the road. She held the mare at a lope, though she longed to give the horse her head and take off at a run. The little mare kept pace easily, and Laurie was disappointed to see Ashly Mills drawing near so soon.

At the edge of town she slowed Carly to a sedate walk. A man, one that she had never seen before, stared at her when she passed. Laurie nodded and proceeded on to the general store. As she dismounted she caught sight of two women watching her from inside the store.

Don't any of these women ride? she wondered, but really wasn't concerned. She entered the store and saw the two women who had observed her arrival suddenly turn their interest to a hoe leaning against the wall. She smiled and went over to the table where the yard goods were stacked.

She recalled seeing a wool paisley in shades of green and Chinese red on a bronze background. She searched through the folded lengths of material before weeding through the heavy bolts. She found a lovely green wool, the shade of new ash-tree leaves, close to the color of Etta's eyes. But Laurie had her heart set on the paisley.

Two thirds of the way to the bottom of the stack, she felt a cashmere-soft wool. She tugged on the bolt and managed to pull it out far enough to see the pattern she remembered. It was perfect—emerald green, vivid Chinese red, fine black designs, and muted shades of green.

After a few minutes Laurie caught Sam's attention, and he ambled over. "I would like two yards of this wool."

Sam pulled the bolt out. "This here's one dollar and twenty-five cents a yard. You still want it?" He stared at her with an almost challenging expression.

A woman standing nearby interrupted. "Now, Sam, you know that ain't right." A tall, reed-thin woman with few dark strands still showing in her gray hair marched right up to Sam's face. "Those wool goods are made right here in the valley. Shouldn't be more'n four bits an' you know it."

The woman smiled at Laurie and held out her hand. "Miranda Grubb."

Laurie took the woman's hand. "Laurie Preston. Thank you for your help. It's for a gift." Miranda was a breath of fresh air, and she wished she had met her months before. Now she knew two—no, three friendly women, if she counted Bernice.

Sam stomped over to the counter and measured out the yard goods.

Miranda stood at the counter by Laurie and ran her hand over the material. "It's cassimere. I don't think they're making this pattern anymore." Miranda glared at Sam. "Now I know why it didn't sell."

"I just made a mistake, Mrs. Grubb. Can't recall the price of everythin' in here," Sam grumbled.

Miranda harrumphed and winked at Laurie. "Preston . . . Aren't you the lady Gabe West hired?"

"I am." Laurie watched Sam carefully fold the wool. "I'll need a spool of thread to match the bronze color, if you have it."

"I've heard about you, of course. I just got back from Portland. Stayed with my daughter while she had her first young'un. A squalling, healthy girl." Miranda glanced around. "Well, I'd better get that piece of plain goods I came in for."

Sam returned with a spool of thread near the color Laurie needed. "What else will ya be needin'"—he glanced around—"Mrs. Preston?"

"I would also like one pie tin." Laurie loosened the ties of her reticule.

Sam got the pan, tore a piece of brown paper from the roll, and wrapped Laurie's purchases. "A dollar fifteen cents." He secured the package with a length of string.

She handed him the money. "Thank you." Before she had a chance to bid Miranda Grubb good-bye, the woman spoke.

"If you can wait till he cuts my piece, I'll walk out with you." Miranda told Sam to cut a dress length for her.

Laurie browsed along one table of kitchen tools—apple corers, parers, eggbeaters, and vegetable choppers. She was turning the crank on a large, wooden flour sifter when Miranda stopped at the table. "I don't even know what some of these tools are for.

"Most of 'em are probably some man's hare-brained idea and are more trouble than they're worth." Miranda picked up a single-blade chopper. "Look at this. Who cares if the handle's got little flowers carved on it as long as the blade's good?"

Laurie nodded and they silently agreed to leave. She paused at the edge of the boardwalk near the mare. "Thanks for helping with Sam. I had no idea this wool was made near here." She stepped down and went over to secure her parcel behind the saddle.

"Glad to help. You take care and don't let the gossips get to you." Miranda watched Laurie. "That's a handsome horse."

Laurie walked to the hitching rail and loosened the reins. "Carly's a dear." She started to turn and hesitated. "I wanted to call on Mrs. Tuttle, but I'm not sure where she lives. Would you mind giving me directions?"

Miranda stepped down near Laurie. "Follow this road west. Their farm's the first big place on the left. Yellow. Can't miss it. Sure nice meetin' you."

"I appreciate your help."

Laurie mounted and wheeled Carly around. She waved at Miranda Grubb and rode out of town. It's amazing, she thought, what a smile and a few kind words can do for your outlook. She felt there was hope. If only Hannah were as pleasant as Miranda.

* * *

During the next four days Laurie worked on the shawl. Gabe kept busy, though she felt he pushed himself to avoid thinking about the upcoming trial. When he didn't think she was around, tension showed in the tightening of his jaw, his stilted movements, and she would have sworn she heard him grinding his teeth more than once. She had attempted to distract him, but his gloom prevailed.

Only seven days from the trial she knew she had to speak to Hannah Tuttle. Wearing her beige muslin dress with little adornment, her hat and gloves, Laurie felt ready to face her main adversary. As she drove the buggy through town she noticed a few people watching her. She smiled or waved to the ones she had met, and felt surprisingly good.

Miranda Grubb's directions were very simple and took Laurie to a yellow, two-story house trimmed in green, with a porch the width of the building. Miranda was right. Laurie couldn't have missed it, and she wondered if that's what the Tuttles had in mind. She pulled up in front, fervently hoping Hannah would be home.

After a quick brush at her clothes and making sure her bonnet was straight, Laurie picked up the lemon pie she had made to smooth the way with Hannah and walked up to the door. Her knock was soon answered.

Hannah opened the door and stared in total surprise. It didn't take long for her expression to turn into a tight-lipped frown. "Yes . . ." She held the door halfway open.

"Hello, Mrs. Tuttle. I hope you will accept this." Laurie handed her the pie. Hannah eyed it suspiciously, but Laurie continued as if nothing were amiss. "I do hope you can spare me a few minutes of your time."

Hannah gave her a stiff nod and showed her into the parlor. She took a seat on a chair in a room filled with daguerreotypes, paintings and whatnots all jumbled together among potted plants. "I'm here on Ammie's behalf. Mr. West was notified about your custody suit. Since

I am responsible for her, I am concerned about her welfare.''

Hannah glanced at the pie she had placed on top of a book on the marble-topped table. "I think it's plain enough. Ammie's my granddaughter. She should live with her kin, not Gabe West. Besides, he'll be hanged for murder, and she'll have nowhere else to go. I just want to make it legal." She sank back on the settee, looking smug.

Laurie's face felt like a mask. She dared not show how much she loathed this woman. "You sound as if Mr. West's conviction were a foregone conclusion. Do you really believe he killed his wife?"

"I saw him leave that morning. No one else was there, except the child, of course, and everyone knows she couldn't have done such a thing. He's guilty."

Hannah lowered her jaw, which made her jowls even more pronounced. Laurie smoothed the gloves over the backs of her hands. "Couldn't someone else have been hiding there? Possibly in the barn?"

Hannah vigorously shook her head. "Who would have wanted to harm Mrs. West? No. It was him. I guess he had reason, her being a hussy and all. But he broke the law and will pay with his life." She sat up with her hands braced on the seat.

"Mrs. Tuttle, what about Ammie? She doesn't know you, and she loves her father. If you were worried about her welfare, why have you waited so long to gain custody of her?" Laurie watched as Hannah's face became mottled, and her jowls quivered.

"It's my Christian duty and none of your business, young woman. You're nothing but hired help." Hannah rose ponderously and glared at her. "Get out of my house."

Laurie stood up, the strings of her reticule tangled around her gloved fingers. "Mr. West has lived here for many years. He seems to be respected and well liked. Do you think he really could have murdered his wife?"

"Huh!" Hannah marched to the door and flung it open.

Laurie departed the Tuttle house with her chin up. Damn the woman! She couldn't take the chance of irritating Hannah any more than she already was, but Lord, she was tempted to slap her—just once.

Pausing on the top step before Hannah closed the door, Laurie faced her. "If you had *any* love for Ammie, you wouldn't do this."

All the way back to the ranch she fumed and muttered to herself. The woman knew nothing about Christian duty, and Laurie doubted her ability to really love a child. Suddenly she remembered the second letter from "V." He had denied fathering Ruth's child, but the note was not dated. Laurie knew she must take the letter to the custody hearing and pray the judge wouldn't require proof that "V" was denying any relationship to Ammie.

The return ride seemed to pass much more quickly. She came to the rise leading to the ranch and slowed the horse to a walk. As she descended to the yard she noticed Etta's buggy parked in front of the house. She left her rig near Etta's and hurried inside.

"Mama," Ammie called, and ran to her.

Laurie scooped the little girl up in her arms and kissed her before her gaze met Gabe's. "Sorry it took me so long." She smiled at Etta. "I'm glad you waited." She put Ammie down and removed her bonnet and gloves.

"I just arrived. Mr. West insisted you'd be back soon." Etta watched Laurie and noticed Gabe doing the same.

"I'll get refreshments." Laurie started for the kitchen, but Gabe's voice stopped her.

"Don't bother getting anything for us. Danny and I'd better get back to work." He nodded to Etta. "Nice seeing you again."

Etta followed Laurie into the kitchen. "Don't fuss, Laurie. A glass of water would do fine."

"How have you been?" Laurie filled three glasses and stooped down to help Ammie with hers.

Etta pulled out a chair at the table and sat down. "I've been asking around. I have the name of an old woman. Some say she knows more about cures and herbs than doctors do."

❧23❧

Laurie grinned. "What's her name? Do you know where she lives? I've got to talk to her. Will you go with me?" She stood up and promptly dropped back down to her chair. Dear Lord, there was hope. She picked up the glass of water and stared, her mind whirling.

Etta had begun shaking her head after Laurie's first question. "Dacia is all anyone called her. She left without saying anything to anyone."

It took Laurie a full minute to understand. "Left? She moved away?"

Etta nodded. "It seems she doesn't stay any one place very long. Sort of like a gypsy. I'm sorry."

"Oh, God!" Laurie felt the sudden burst of tears and covered her face. It wasn't fair! The old woman was her last chance to prove Gabe innocent.

Ammie pulled on Laurie's arm. "Mama? You cryin'?"

"What, sugar?"

Ammie reached up and patted Laurie's face. "You hurt?"

Laurie lifted the little girl onto her lap and rocked her.

She would never hand this child over to Hannah Tuttle. "I'm fine, now." Glancing over Ammie's head to Etta, she pressed her lips together and closed her eyes to regain her composure. "The Tuttles are suing for custody."

"What? That's insane!"

"I went to speak to Hannah this afternoon." She absently rubbed Ammie's back. "It was a waste of time."

"I don't understand. Why would Hannah . . ." Etta stared at Laurie, awareness slowly apparent. "You mean her son and . . . Ruth . . . were . . ."

Laurie nodded.

"But the whole town will find out then. What about her reputation? Surely she can't win." Etta sipped her water. "Poor Mr. West. As if he didn't have enough problems."

"Hannah's convinced Gabe will be convicted, and they'll be granted custody. I had planned on finding the old woman."

Ammie sucked on her thumb and clung to Laurie with her other hand.

"What will you do? If I'd known Ruth better, I'd testify she had talked about killing herself."

"Thank you, Etta, but neither Gabe nor I would want you to lie. Somehow the truth must come out."

Gabe woke early and slipped out of bed without disturbing Laurie. He'd spent the night holding her close, savoring her nearness. That was all he had been able to do. Bitterness over his inability to do more had kept him awake most of the night. Not only was he going to be tried in two days for a crime he didn't commit, he'd been stripped of his manhood.

He'd managed to get the house repaired and now would go up to the summer pasture. He dressed quickly, left a note for Laurie telling her where he'd be, and rode out as the sun was rising. The air was cool, the sky clear, and he felt his spirits revive. He arrived at the camp and smelled the fresh-brewed coffee. Ben glanced at him as if he expected him.

"Mighta knowed you be early." He handed Gabe a battered tin cup.

"Everything quiet?" Gabe warmed his hands around the cup before setting it down to cool.

Danny walked up and poured himself a cup of coffee. "Any more news?"

Gabe shook his head.

"Did'ya find out what upset Mrs. Preston?" Danny blew on his cup.

"She and Etta had this crazy idea about Ruth getting some tonic from an old woman that poisoned her. When Etta told Laurie the old woman had left town, she took it pretty hard." Gabe took a sip of his coffee.

"Doesn't sound crazy to me. What was the old crone's name?"

"Dacia. And don't tell me you've heard of her." He couldn't fault Laurie for trying to help him, but who'd believe an old Gypsy poisoned Ruth? It was too much to hope for, but a small part of him did hope.

"No. But I might ask around." Danny gulped down the rest of his coffee and wandered off.

Gabe refilled his cup and roamed closer to the herd. The grass smelled good; so did the wood smoke. Unless someone came forward in his defense, he would be hanged—never hold Laurie in his arms again, or make love to her, grow old with her, or watch Ammie grow up. He went back to the shack and waited for Danny. Nate came in from his watch. When everyone was together, he spoke.

"You can start moving the herd down gradually so they'll be just above the house come November. Danny, the culling will be up to you. You know what I want from this herd, so do what you have to. It's asking a lot, but our futures depend on successful breeding. If . . . if anything comes up, Danny's in charge."

He swallowed down the remainder of his coffee and

tossed the dregs on the ground. "I know I can count on you."

As he mounted up and rode off he heard Nate and Ben and Danny's voices. He felt anxious to get home to Laurie. However, he paused above the ranch house and gazed at the grounds. Laurie was at the pump, her skirts billowing. Then he kicked his mount and rode down the low hill.

That day and the next Gabe felt like he was grasping at smoke. He wanted to laugh, play, and make love to Laurie, but the harder he tried, the more he failed. Ammie clung to Laurie constantly. And Laurie worked to keep life normal, only it wasn't.

The morning of the thirteenth, he got out of bed after spending a sleepless night alone. He pulled on his pants and found Laurie dozing in the rocking chair, his daughter asleep on her lap. He removed the bar from the door and eased it open as quietly as possible and went outside. He'd have to wake her soon. They had to be in Jacksonville by nine o'clock.

The aroma of fresh coffee woke Laurie. The little girl's weight brought back the long night spent rocking and walking her. Before she stirred in Laurie's embrace, Gabe held a steaming cup beneath her nose.

"Mornin'. Let me take her."

He set the cup down and lifted his sleeping daughter. She felt soft, warm as she curled into his chest. He kissed her brow, thankful she had at last found peace.

Laurie stretched and groaned. She felt ninety years old and arthritic. She sipped the hot brew and let it warm her. She finally stood up and peeked at Ammie.

Gabe watched her hungrily. "Go on. Get dressed. She's fine."

Laurie put on her fawn traveling dress and went down to start breakfast. Today of all days time seemed to speed by. They were in the buggy and on the road to Jacksonville when Gabe would normally have been milking the cow. It was a dismal journey, fraught with tension.

As they approached Phoenix Gabe heard a rider and slowed the horse. Danny came alongside.

"Pull up."

Gabe brought the horse to a stop, his heart pounding. "What's wrong?"

Danny shook his head. "The herd's fine. I left for Linkville right after you the other day. She'd been there until last week. No one knows where she went." He wiped his brow and sat back. "I just thought you'd want to know. Should I keep looking for her?"

Laurie glanced at Gabe. "Who?"

"Dacia."

"Maybe she stops at each town along the way. Don't you want Danny to try to find her?" It was a chance, only that, but it was something for Laurie to grasp onto.

"North of there's Indian territory. If you went south, you'd be riding for days. No. That'd take too much time. I've run out of that." He glanced at Danny. "Thanks. I owe you, but you'd better get back. Check at the house in a couple days." He snapped the reins and continued on to Jacksonville.

When he arrived at the narrow brick building that served as the city hall, Gabe had to search for a place to leave the buggy. "Ghouls. That's what they are. I guess I'm to be their entertainment."

Laurie said nothing. She felt numb. It was hard to believe strangers would actually want to attend Gabe's trial. She passed through the crowd and entered the building with him. She didn't focus on any one face or on any voice that rumbled around them.

"Gabe West?" The man dabbed at his face with a wrinkled handkerchief.

Gabe nodded, and his hand tightened on Laurie's arm.

"Ah, good, good. Judge Underwood said I should speak with you. Have you retained counsel, sir?"

"All I have is my reputation and word to defend myself. I don't see what an attorney could do for me." He started to move on, but the man blocked his way.

"Please, we need to talk." The man glanced around. "This way. It should be less hectic." He motioned to a dim hallway.

As soon as they had moved away from the noise, Gabe stopped. "Who are you?"

"Delbert Mullen, at your service." He seemed to notice Laurie for the first time. "Ma'am."

"This is Mrs. Preston. She takes care of my daughter."

Mullen nodded to her, and his attention returned to Gabe. "You will find my fee most reasonable. I'm not out to become a wealthy man at the expense of my clients. That would be near impossible in this town, anyway. But that's not the issue. You are charged with murder and must have an attorney." He ran his finger around the inside of his tight collar.

Gabe looked at Laurie before he answered. Her cheeks were pale, and there were blue-gray circles beneath her eyes. If he weren't so damned selfish, he'd send her back to Sacramento with Ammie. That was an idea he hadn't thought of before and suddenly realized it had merit.

"Do you really think you can defend me, Mr. Mullen?"

"At least as well as you would yourself. I'm familiar with the charges and believe the most damning evidence is the implication the diary makes; then there's Mrs. Tuttle. We haven't much time, Mr. West. Tell me your side of it."

Laurie was holding Ammie in her arms, which were growing tired. "We'll be right back. If you're not here, I'll go inside." As she went out back to the necessary, she silently prayed that Mr. Mullen was the miracle Gabe needed.

Gabe told his new counsel what had happened the morning of Ruth's death, what he'd learned from her diary, and lastly: "If I'd have wanted to kill her, I'd have done it long before then. I didn't even know about the damn diary

until Jenkins told me. Rather convenient of Hannah Tuttle to
have mistakenly pocketed it, don't you think?''

Talking rekindled his anger, anger he'd thought was long
gone. But it wasn't. He thought of the hell he and Laurie had
gone through, and blamed Ruth and Hannah for it.

''There does seem to be coincidence on their side. Well,
let's go in now. I'll do my best for you, Mr. West.'' Mullen
continued questioning Gabe as they walked. ''No one else
was at the house that morning? A hired hand? House-
keeper?''

Gabe shook his head. ''I hired Mrs. Preston late last
spring.''

He entered the main hall where the trial was to be held.
Most of the spectators were already seated. He saw Laurie
come in and take a chair in the back of the room. His
acknowledgment of her was barely perceptible. After all, he
didn't want to draw any more attention to her than he had
already.

Seated in the rear of the room, Laurie had the advantage
of being able to observe the crowd and listen to their
comments. She fussed with Ammie's bonnet and skirt.
When the judge entered, it was a relief. The whispers
quieted.

The trial began.

Almost immediately the attorney for the state regaled the
jury, which Laurie hadn't even noticed up until that moment, with a horrid description of Gabe's crime. The man
only spoke for a few minutes, but he had completely
damned Gabe in that short time. Mullen gave a sketchy but
glowing account of Gabe's character.

Hannah Tuttle was the first witness called for the state,
and Laurie steeled herself to hear the worst. Hannah
advanced to the front of the room with her skirts swaying
and paused near the chair the attorney indicated. She swore
to tell the truth and lowered her ample form onto the seat.

Ammie stayed nestled against Laurie, peering around
occasionally with narrowed eyes.

Laurie tugged at her gloves, torn between leaving them on and taking them off. She soon realized her arms were squashing Ammie and stopped. As Hannah's voice blared through the room Laurie rubbed Ammie's back and sent up a silent prayer for Gabe's exoneration.

The prosecuting attorney stood in front of the jury. "Mrs. Tuttle, did you discover the body of Ruth West?"

"I certainly did, just days before Christmas."

"Please tell us how you came to find Mrs. West."

Hannah patted her graying hair and looked at the jury. "I called on Ruth West early that morning. I saw him"—she pointed at Gabe—"riding away from the house. I knocked on the door. No one answered, so I went in. I knew she had to be there. I thought the child might be sick." She yanked at her jacket and lifted her chin.

The attorney cleared his throat. "Where did you find Mrs. West?"

"The house seemed empty. Then I thought I heard a voice upstairs. I knocked on the first door, but she didn't answer, so I peeked in—just to make sure she was all right, mind you. And there she was, layin' on the bed. She didn't look right," she stated, shivering. "Thought she might've had a fever, so I went over and touched her brow." Hannah shuddered and glared at Gabe. "She was dead cold, facedown on the pillow."

ie kissed Ammie and started rocking ever so slightly. Hannah would be done soon, she assured herself. But what would come next? She accidentally bumped the man seated next to her and apologized. She spied Gabe for a moment. He appeared so composed, but she knew better. He was terrified, and she was, too.

"Tell us what you did after you realized Mrs. West had passed on."

Hannah fumbled with her reticule and finally pulled out her hankie. "Well"—she sniffed and dabbed at her nose— "I covered her up and . . . and straightened the blankets and ran downstairs to find the child." She blew her nose and wiped her eyes. "I couldn't leave that young'un there alone while I went for help."

"No, no, you couldn't. Now . . ." The attorney moved over to his table. He picked up a small book and held it out. "Have you seen this before?"

"Yes, sir. I found it on the bed, right by poor Mrs. West."

"Do you know what kind of book this is? Poetry? A novel?"

"A diary," Hannah said clearly, without hesitation.

The attorney stared at the jury. "Yes. Ruth West's diary." He skimmed his thumb across the side of the pages. "Did you hand this over to Sheriff Jenkins?"

"It was the right thing to do. I know my duty."

The prosecuting attorney smiled at her and nodded. "Did you give it over when you notified the sheriff of Mrs. West's death?"

"Well, no. I didn't think about it then. I . . . I must have tucked it in my reticule when I was righting the bed." She suddenly stiffened her back. "He did it!" She shook her fist at Gabe. "I know he did."

Mullen bounced to his feet. "I object, Your Honor."

"Sustained!" Judge Underwood pounded his fist on the desk. "That'll be enough of that, Mrs. Tuttle."

The prosecuting attorney raised one brow at Mullen. "Mrs. Tuttle, why do you think Mr. West murdered his wife? Did he admit it to you?"

Hannah pointed to the diary. "Ruth says her daughter wasn't his. And . . . and she was carryin' another one. He must have read it!"

The prosecuting attorney nodded and resumed his seat.

Gabe rubbed the spot between his brows. Hannah sure put on a show, as he knew she would. God Almighty, how was he to convince those twelve men that he hadn't known of his wife's death until the sheriff told him? He flexed his cramped fingers. He wanted to look at Laurie but that would only confirm Hannah's suspicions. Instead he shifted on the hard wooden seat and kept his attention on his lawyer.

Mullen approached Hannah Tuttle. "You said you saw Mr. West riding away from the house that morning. How far away was he?"

"On a rise the other side of the house. Not that far."

"How can you be sure it was him? Did he wave at you?"

"He's tall and has black hair. Nobody else around there like him." She relaxed with a look of smug contentment on her face.

Gabe motioned to Mullen and whispered, "My foreman, Danny Whitefeather, is almost my height with black hair."

Mullen fixed Hannah with a curious stare. "Surely there must be other men in Ashly Mills with black hair."

"But he's taller than most. I tell you, it was him!"

"You said he was on a horse, at some distance. A few inches would be near impossible to distinguish. What was the man wearing?"

Hannah frowned. "Hat, shirt, and trousers." She shrugged.

"If he was wearing a hat, how could you see the color of his hair?"

"I just knew." A few spectators laughed, others murmured among themselves, and Hannah glared at them. "But I recognized his horse. Black as his own hair."

"Yes, well, I'm sure there must also be other black horses." The lawyer rubbed his forehead. "If I heard you correctly, you said that before you found Mrs. West, you thought you heard a noise upstairs." He took a few steps and paused. "That's why you went up. Is that right?"

Hannah nodded.

"What did it sound like? A voice? A shutter banging? Maybe something landing on the floor?"

Hannah frowned and clasped her hands on her lap. "I don't recall."

"Did you ever find out what made that noise?"

"No. I forgot all about it when I saw Mrs. West."

Mullen nodded. He picked up the book the prosecuting attorney had introduced. "When did you discover you had this in your possession, Mrs. Tuttle?"

Hannah glanced at her husband. "Well . . . that is . . . it must have been a few weeks later. It was in a reticule I don't use every day."

"I see. Why didn't you return it to Mr. West then?" Mullen faced the jury and lifted one brow.

She twisted her hankie with both hands. "I set it aside to do just that, but it got mixed up with some other books on the table. I just found it a month ago and didn't think it would make any difference. After all, Mrs. West was gone."

Mullen tapped the book. "Since you knew this was her diary, you must have been curious about what she had written in here."

Hannah glared at the man and shrugged.

"When did you discover this volume was a diary, Mrs. Tuttle?"

"When?" She crinkled one side of her mouth. "Guess when I saw it. Looks like one."

"How long did you have this before you read it?"

She braced her hands on the arms of the chair. "I didn't read it until last month."

Mullen stood in front of the jury. "Were you and Mrs. West close friends?"

"I wouldn't say real close. Actually . . . I didn't actually get to know her until last fall."

"Was it your habit to call on her so early in the day?"

"I never . . . she said she wanted to clean out her closet and had some clothes she'd donate to the church, and I said I'd come by for them. *She* didn't have her own buggy." Hannah glared at Gabe, then around the room, until she spotted Laurie.

"Mrs. Tuttle, before you read this diary, did you know that your son, Virgil, had been seeing Mrs. West?"

Hannah emphatically shook her head.

"Ashly Mills is a small town. You must have heard something."

"No! I tell you I didn't."

"Mr. and Mrs. West had a child. After reading this diary, did you decide you wanted custody of that child?"

She nodded.

"Please tell us why."

"The child isn't his! She's *my* granddaughter. She looks like my Virgil did at her age. Her mother's dead. I have a right to raise her. She's mine!"

❧24❧

"That will be decided by the court. But if Mr. West is found guilty of killing his wife, it would help your custody case, wouldn't it, Mrs. Tuttle?'' Mullen gazed at the jury and raised his brows before resuming his seat.

The judge nodded to Hannah. "That's all, Mrs. Tuttle."

Laurie watched Hannah leave the witness chair and hugged Ammie. Virgil's second letter to Ruth was in her reticule, but she didn't think it would help Gabe—yet. She noticed the sheriff walking forward. Her gaze moved to the left and rested on Gabe. His expression was grim, as if he had given up hope. She kissed Ammie, wanting to do the same to him. I believe in you, she thought, willing him to know her thoughts.

Sheriff Jenkins was sworn in and the prosecuting attorney began his questioning. "Sheriff, who notified you of Mrs. West's death?"

"Mrs. Tuttle raced up to the office shrieking about finding Mrs. West's body."

Gabe watched the jury. If they believed Hannah saw him riding from the house that morning, he'd be hanged. His only hope rested with Mullen getting the jury to think Hannah was lying in order to get Ammie. He shifted on the chair and managed to catch a glimpse of Laurie.

She sat stock-still, her lips pressed into a thin line. Her slender fingers patted his daughter, and he doubted she was even aware of the gesture. If he made a move to console her, Hannah might very well make a scene, so he continued to stare straight ahead while his life fell apart, bit by bit.

Laurie listened to Sheriff Jenkins's statements. His testimony didn't reveal anything Gabe hadn't told her, nor did it hurt his defense. The third and last witness for the state was Dr. Satterlee, who had been called to examine Ruth West's body. The people in front of Laurie moved restlessly in their seats and blocked her view. She stretched her neck and peered between several balding heads to see better.

The prosecuting attorney stood up. "Did you see Ruth West the day she died?"

"Late that day. I was out at the Anderson farm delivering twins and didn't get back until near suppertime."

"Did you examine Ruth West? Determine if her death was natural or otherwise?"

Dr. Satterlee nodded. "I'd say it was poison, though there's no telling—"

The attorney interrupted. "Dr. Satterlee, are you sure she didn't take too much of . . . say laudanum?"

The doctor shook his head. "That would have put her into a deep sleep and her heart would have stopped. It was poison and not an easy death."

"Thank you." The prosecuting attorney nodded to the jury and sat down.

Mullen rose. "I believe one of your answers was cut short. You were about to say something regarding the poison. Would you like to finish your statement, Dr. Satterlee?"

"I was just going to add that I can't tell who gave her the poison. I do know she miscarried."

"Terrible thing to happen." Mullen shook his head. "Do you know what kind of poison was used?"

"I'm not too sure." Dr. Satterlee shifted on the chair. "Her face appeared paralyzed, and her pupils were dilated. She'd emptied her stomach, of course." He shook his head. "Any one of several plants would be my guess."

"Plants? Which kind?"

"Larkspur, monkshood, and oleander are toxic. Impossible to tell which in this case."

"Which part of the plant would be dangerous?"

"All. Sometimes the root of monkshood's mistaken for a radish."

"Are those plants common in this area?"

"If you know what to look for, it wouldn't be hard to find at least one of them in the hills."

"How much would be lethal?"

"I'd say a tablespoon would be enough to kill an average-size man. Maybe less."

"If Ruth West had dosed herself with the poison, could she have suffered the effects without anyone knowing?"

"If she were very determined."

"Thank you." Mr. Mullen started back to his seat and paused. "One more question, doctor. If any of those plant leaves or roots were added to food, would you be able to taste it?"

"Alone, there'd be a bitter taste. Of course, if it were mixed with food, you probably would not taste it."

The prosecuting attorney sprang to his feet. "One more question, Your Honor."

Judge Underwood frowned. "Go on."

"Doctor, do you believe a woman would voluntarily ingest such a violent poison?"

"I would think falling asleep and never waking would be more appealing to someone contemplating suicide."

The prosecuting attorney smiled and gave the jury a confident nod.

Judge Underwood sat back. "Call your first witness, Mr. Mullen."

Laurie clamped her teeth down on her lips to keep quiet. The jurors glanced at one another, and her apprehension grew. Not one of the twelve men was familiar to her. She could only pray some would be good judges of character.

"There's only one, Your Honor. Gabe West."

Gabe rose to his full height, stepped forward, and swore to tell the truth. His voice was deep, his throat dry as a desert wind; his stomach felt like a quagmire, and his thoughts spun around and around.

His word was his only defense.

Laurie sent up a silent plea on Gabe's behalf. Her palms were damp, and she kept fussing with Ammie's skirt. It was only ten o'clock. She felt like she had been sitting in the room for days, but she had to be strong for him.

Delbert Mullen walked around the table. "Mr. West, when was the last time you saw your wife alive?"

"Sunday night."

"That was the evening before she died?"

"Yes."

"How did she seem? Normal? Overwrought? Tired?"

Oh, God, how could he make them understand in a few words? "Happier than usual at supper. Later, before I retired, she got upset and demanded a new wardrobe."

"Did you argue?"

"She did. I just told her I couldn't afford more new clothes right then." Ruth always harped on more dresses and on moving away from Ashly Mills, he recalled. She wanted to be where she could live a fancy life and go to the theater.

"I see. Did she tell you why she wanted new clothing?"

"No."

"Mr. West, did you and your wife have many arguments?"

"A fair amount."

"What were these disagreements about?"

"Ruth never liked living at the ranch." Gabe shook his head disparagingly. "There wasn't much I could've done to make her happy, except sell out and move. She wanted to move to San Francisco."

Mullen glanced at the jury. "Could you have gained employment in the city?"

"I'm a cattle rancher. That's all I know."

The men of the jury nodded and mumbled comments to one another. Judge Underwood banged the gavel once. "No talking."

"Now, back to the morning your wife died. Did you see her?"

"No." He remembered Laurie pushing for more information. "She wasn't downstairs when I got up. Ammie was still asleep, so I didn't see any reason to wake Ruth."

"Was that unusual?"

"No." Just answer each question. Don't think.

Mullen picked up the diary. "Have you ever seen this before today?"

Gabe nodded.

"When?"

"While I was in jail. Sheriff Jenkins showed it to me."

"Did you know your wife kept a diary?"

"No."

"Have you read this?"

"Yes. While I was in jail."

"Were you surprised by any of the entries?"

"Many."

"Did they anger you?"

"No."

"How about her admission that Virgil Tuttle was Ammie's real father? Surely that had to have made you angry."

"I'm the only father Ammie has or knows. She bears my name. Besides, Ruth had already admitted who the father was."

"You're saying that nothing in this book could have angered you to the point of wanting your wife dead?"

"Nothing."

"What would have provoked you to violence?"

"If she'd tried to harm Ammie, I would've stopped her."

"Mr. West, did you kill your wife?"

"No! I did not."

"No more questions." Mullen resumed his seat as his adversary rose.

Laurie smiled at Gabe, hoping to lend him courage. His voice was strong, and the jury appeared to be swayed. She watched him as if he might disappear any moment, and prayed.

The prosecutor approached Gabe. "Mr. West, you said that your wife hadn't come downstairs the morning of her death. Were your rooms upstairs?"

"Hers was."

"I see. Did you hear any unusual noises during the night? Your wife crying out? Calling for help?"

"She kept her door closed. So did I. If she'd screamed, I probably would've heard her." He shrugged. "Maybe not."

"Didn't she usually make your breakfast?"

"No. I did. She wasn't an early riser."

"What did you eat that morning?"

"I didn't. I was late."

The prosecutor rubbed his jaw and glanced down at his notes. "Who cooked that supper Sunday?"

"Ruth."

"He's lucky his old lady didn't poison *him*," a man called out from the rear side of the room.

The prosecuting attorney glared at the crowd before continuing. "What time did you leave the house that Monday morning?"

"Later than usual. I don't know the exact time."

"Did you see Mrs. Tuttle that morning?"

"No. I rode straight to the pasture."

"What color is your horse, Mr. West?"

"Black."

"Last December, did you employ anyone to work around the house? Or the yard?"

"No one."

"Had anyone been at the house the night before your wife died?"

Gabe shook his head.

The prosecuting attorney picked up Ruth's diary and searched for a specific page. "'I've paid the price. My way is clear. I know what I must do, and soon this will be behind me.'" He stared at Gabe. "What does that mean to you, Mr. West?"

"Sounds like she'd come to a decision about something."

"Surely you have an idea of what she was referring to."

"It could be nothing. Ruth talked in circles a lot."

"Was she planning to leave you, Mr. West?"

Gabe leaned forward and frowned. "She never mentioned it, but I wouldn't have been surprised."

"Would you have allowed her to leave?"

"She wasn't a prisoner. She was my wife."

"Same thing." A female spectator cackled.

"No more questions, Your Honor."

Judge Underwood folded his hands on the desk. "Keep your conclusions short, gentleman. We're close to the dinner recess."

Laurie strained to get Gabe's attention as he returned to his seat, but he didn't look her way. His expression appeared to be all angles, hard lines, and shadows. The prosecuting attorney was speaking, and she had never felt so helpless in her life.

"Gabe West was the only adult at the house, besides Ruth West, that night and the next morning. Just imagine how you would feel if you found out your wife had been unfaithful at least twice and had presented you with a child that was not yours. She may have feared him and tried to run away. It is clear—Gabe West was at the house with his wife that night. He's alive, and she isn't!"

Mullen stepped around the prosecuting attorney and faced the jury. "Gentlemen, Gabe West has a reputation as an honest, law-abiding man. He's as good as his word. He took his wedding vows seriously. That's why he didn't forsake his wife.

"That's also why he did not kill Ruth West. Who knows what went through her mind that night. He retired to his own room believing she was upset about not being able to buy new clothes. Like any of us"—he cocked his head to one side and shrugged—"he left the next morning hoping to avoid continuing the same argument.

"As far as we know, someone else may have visited Ruth that night and poisoned her. That we'll never know." Mullen stood in front of the jury, feet apart, hands in his pockets. "Gabe West is innocent, and I think after considering everything that's been said, you'll agree."

Judge Underwood banged the gavel once. "The jury will have dinner right here. Send me word when you've reached a decision." He rose to his feet. "Clear the courtroom."

Delbert Mullen gathered his papers and turned to Gabe. "Would you and Mrs. Preston join me for dinner?"

"If you don't mind, I'd like to spend some time with my family."

"Surely. Don't go too far. We'll have to come back when the jury's reached a decision. Why don't you leave by the rear door, down the hall. Less crowded."

Gabe nodded. "I'll be back."

Laurie didn't move until she heard the footsteps fade out the front door. When she did make her way to the aisle, she glanced outside. Sure enough, there were men and women crowded around the front door. No doubt waiting to see Gabe. She walked up to him and smiled. "Hungry?"

God, she was being brave. He guessed they had at least an hour, and he wanted to spend it alone with her. "Not very. But you must be. Let's get out of here."

Laurie braved going into a restaurant and ordered fried chicken, biscuits, and apple pie. Gabe waited outside with

Ammie. Laurie joined him with the food, and they wandered down near Daisy Creek to eat.

As she served their meal her heart pounded in her ears. Every move was normal, extremely so. She handed Ammie a leg and Gabe a breast. She poured cold milk into the glasses for each of them—she'd have to remember to take the basket, plates, and glasses back to the waitress and thank her. She tucked the end of a napkin in the neck of Ammie's dress, spread another out over Gabe's leg. What was she forgetting?

"Laurie?" Gabe grasped her hand. "It's okay. You should have something to eat, too." It was tearing him apart seeing her like that. He'd never seen her so disconcerted, like a windup toy.

She gazed into his lovely gray eyes and wanted to weep. "It's so unfair! And I feel so useless. I don't know what to do."

"Sit next to me and eat."

"Daddy, see . . . buggerfly!" Ammie announced, pointing with the chicken leg.

Judge Underwood silenced the crowded courtroom and motioned to the jury. "What have you decided?"

Laurie held her breath and scooted forward on the wooden chair. A stocky man stood with his arms at his side. His voice carried around the deathly silent room.

"Guilty, Judge."

❧25❧

Gabe's heart beat like a water pump in his chest. He had to remember to inhale, but his throat felt like he was being strangled. The air stuck in his throat. Was this how his life was to end?

Laurie sprang to her feet and shrieked, "Nooo!", mindless with panic. "You can't do that, you can't! He didn't do it!"

Ammie had been dozing and woke up screaming.

Laurie dropped to the seat, sobbing, and tried to quiet Ammie. How could this be happening? She hadn't really believed he would be convicted. She bent her head to Ammie and prayed it was a nightmare. She would wake soon. However, the voices around her proved it was all too real.

Even standing up, all Gabe could see of Laurie was her bonnet. It shielded her face and his daughter from the many inquisitive stares. She shouldn't have come, but she had, and it was his fault. He hadn't wanted to leave her, so he'd brought her. Damn his selfishness.

Judge Underwood banged his gavel. "Everyone sit down

and be quiet!'' Slowly the spectators returned their attention to the front of the room. "Gabe West, you've been found guilty of murder. You will be hanged three days from now." The judge rose. "Everyone go home." His scowl swept the room before he left through a side door.

Laurie whispered to Ammie and finally managed to calm her while men and women filed past them out of the room. She didn't want to see their expressions, whether of pity or scorn. She simply did not feel up to confronting anyone.

The room was finally quiet except for Mullen and Gabe's low voices. She put Ammie down and righted the little girl's clothes. After Laurie dried her own tear-stained cheeks and straightened her attire, she took Ammie's hand, pausing a few steps from Gabe.

He was thanking Mullen. Determined not to embarrass Gabe any more than she already had, she raised her chin and with great willpower, gazed at him as if they were meeting on the street. The sheriff of Jacksonville stood several feet away. She and Gabe would be allowed no privacy.

Mullen took his leave, and Gabe gazed at Laurie. He saw the tension around her reddened eyes and drawn lips, even though she was trying to appear hopeful. He cleared his throat and stepped up to her.

"You'd better start back. I don't want you on the road tonight." *God, she's beautiful. Why hadn't he met her a few years earlier?*

"It's only two-forty. We have plenty of time." She wet her lips, feeling self-conscious. "I'm sorry about my outburst. I didn't mean to do that. I—"

"It's all right," he cut in. "I felt like shouting myself."

The sheriff put his hand on Gabe's shoulder. "Let's go. She can visit you in jail."

"One more minute, please."

The sheriff moved back one pace.

"Laurie, remember what I told you. Danny'll help you with anything. We grew up together. He won't fail you."

He reached out and took her hand in his. Then he knelt down and hugged his daughter, so scared and small.

"Daddy, what's matter?" Ammie squirmed free of his grasp and put her hand on his cheek. "You sick?"

"No, punkin." He struggled to speak in a normal voice. "You be a good girl for Laurie." He held her close, kissed her, and turned to face Laurie.

She fidgeted with her skirt and stared into his eyes. "We'll visit tomorrow."

"No. Don't come back. There's no need."

"I won't say good-bye like this."

"Then I will." He squeezed her hand. "Take care of my little girl and yourself, Laurie Preston." He stepped back and mouthed, "I love you," and turned to join the sheriff.

Laurie bit her lips and blinked back the threatening tears. She breathed deeply, until her roiling emotions were under control once more. "Don't give up."

Gabe stopped at the door and pivoted around. "Don't forget to buy new drapes for the main room. Something cheerful, nice." She gasped, covered her mouth, and he continued out of the room with the sheriff.

Although Laurie wasn't anxious to return to an empty house, she kept a steady pace and arrived home by early evening. She changed Ammie's clothes and her own. Restless energy coursed through her. Ammie tagged along behind as she checked on the animals, collected the eggs, and found herself marking a flower bed on each side of the front steps.

Ammie sat on the dirt and dug with her hands. "Me help you, Mama."

Laurie knelt on the ground and gouged the earth like a madwoman. She would go out and gather wildflowers. When Gabe came home, he'd be surprised. Yes, she had to hurry because he would be home Wednesday, after the custody hearing. Drapes, he had told her to buy them, but she wouldn't be able to get them before he returned home.

She had enough money to pay for them. She'd have to see to that tomorrow.

Supper. She had to fix Ammie's supper and feed the livestock and milk the cow and . . . what else? There must be other chores she was forgetting. The ground was ready for planting. "Come on, sugar. We need water."

Laurie went to the pump and filled a bucket. Together she and Ammie dribbled it over the dirt. Next she went to the springhouse for meat. When she came out, she saw Danny walking out of the barn.

He stopped in his tracks and watched her frantic movements. "Mrs. Preston, let me take that." He lifted the ham shank from her arms and fell into step at her side. "Hi, Ammie."

Ammie stayed at Laurie's side and wouldn't look at him. "You must be hungry, Danny. I'll have supper on the table shortly." Laurie smiled down at Ammie. "Aren't you happy to see Danny?" She came to a halt. "Mittens . . . I haven't seen her since we got back." Her gaze darted around the yard. "Mittens, Mitt—"

"Mrs. Preston," Danny interrupted her hysterical outburst, "why don't you rest for a while. You look tired. I'm here to help you."

As if she just realized he was there, Laurie smiled. "Hello. Gabe isn't here, but he'll be back in a couple days." Suddenly she felt like a marionette after the puppeteer had dropped the strings, and she slowly sank down into a blessed void.

Danny dropped the ham and lifted her up in his arms.

"Mama!"

"She got sleepy, Ammie. Let's take her inside. Show me where to put her."

Ammie nodded and ran to the house.

Danny carried Laurie into Gabe's room. He covered her with the blanket and returned with a wet cloth to bathe her face. Before he roused her, Ammie came running into the room with the cat.

"Mama?" Ammie climbed up onto the bed and pulled at Laurie's shirtwaist. "Wake up, Mama. Pleease . . . I got Mittens."

Laurie heard Ammie's high-pitched voice and felt her bouncing on the mattress. She was being pulled from a peaceful nothingness back to reality and part of her resisted. However, another part of her wanted to respond. Slowly her eyes opened.

"Sugar." She hugged Ammie to her, then noticed Danny standing on the far side of the bed. "What happened?" She struggled to rise.

"You passed out. Take it easy. There's no need to rush. Have you eaten today?"

Laurie nodded and sat up. "You know?"

"I guessed. I'll go see him tomorrow." Danny left them alone.

Laurie tended to Ammie's needs and found Danny preparing supper. "Gabe told me not to come back, but of course I will. Besides, there's the custody hearing day after tomorrow. He'll be there, won't he?"

"I would think so."

With Danny to distract and help her, Laurie made it through the evening without losing control. She slept in Gabe's bed so she would be nearby if Ammie woke during the night. She had offered Danny the use of Ruth's room, but he had declined, saying the bunkhouse would do fine.

Laurie awoke the next morning, feeling drugged. Her mouth was dry, her eyes gritty, her mind numb, and her stomach threatened to empty itself. She moved about slowly until the nausea subsided. While she dressed she knew she must keep busy or go crazy. The shawl was wrapped and ready to be given to Etta. That would get her out of the house, she thought distractedly. And she needed to collect wildflowers—Ammie would like that—and see about drapes. Yes, there was enough work to keep her occupied.

* * *

Pacing back and forth across the cell allowed little outlet for the restless energy that coursed through Gabe. Why didn't they just hang him today? Get it over with. He rubbed his neck and gulped. The only consolation was that in two days this torturous waiting would be ended. If there'd only been time to track down that Dacia, but only God knew where the woman had gone or if she had even seen Ruth.

Instead of continuing on in that state, he envisioned Laurie—the very proper Laurie Preston the first time he'd seen her, hat, gloves, and so sure of herself. Laurie with her long hair hanging down her back as she waited for her wrapper in front of the cold fireplace the night of the storm, Laurie lying bare to his touch after he'd ripped the buttons off of her nightgown.

What was she doing now? By midmorning she should have milked the cow, collected the eggs, and fed the stock. Life would be a hell of a lot harder than she'd bargained for, but she'd have a home. Maybe in time she would even grow to like the stock. Damn, he should have taken her up to the pasture more, explained his plans. But there was Danny, and he would take care of the herd.

The outer door scraped open, and Gabe spun around to see who was coming. Danny approached the cell ahead of the deputy. "Didn't she get home?"

"She's just fine and keeping busy. You?" After the deputy opened the cell door, Danny entered. The door was closed and locked again.

Gabe shrugged and gazed around the rough walls of the cell. "They don't provide much entertainment here."

Danny glanced to the outer office. "If you want girls, I'll ask around for you." He lowered his voice. "Or I could get you out of here."

Gabe spun around and stared. For one fleeting, wonderful moment he was sorely tempted, but he shook his head. "I couldn't run out on Laurie and Ammie. It'll be over with soon." He wouldn't drag Laurie and his daughter all over the country while he hid from the law, and he wouldn't be able to leave her. He was damned either way.

Danny watched his closest friend, his features not betraying his feelings. "It's up to you."

Since Danny had taken care of the chores before he left, and Laurie had already cleaned house, she and Ammie went for a walk. They gathered wild flag and buttercup plants that would yield blue and yellow blossoms next spring. Laurie added Scotch broom to the full basket.

Ammie pulled two stems from a plant firmly rooted in the ground. "What're these?"

Laurie looked at the leaves and smiled. "Buttercup. They have pretty yellow flowers."

Ammie added her stems to Laurie's basket. "I get more."

"Okay. You point to the plant, and I'll dig it up for you."

Ammie picked out a milkweed and another buttercup.

"Will you help me plant these, sugar?"

"I help you, Mama."

They returned to the house and each drank a full glass of water before Laurie arranged the plants and started digging holes to accommodate the roots. She held the stalks in place, and Ammie pushed the dirt over the roots.

After all the plants were firmly set, Laurie showed Ammie how to water the flower bed. She stood back to appreciate their labor. She was proud of their effort. The little orange poppies that grew wild in California would be a perfect addition. Maybe she would ask Penelope West to bring a few plants when she came to visit. Laurie noted she would have to write and ask her.

It was midmorning by the time they had finished. Needing to keep busy, she cleaned up Ammie, changed her own clothes, and drove the buggy to town. There was no need to check for drapery material at the general store. She had seen the selection. She'd have to remember to look while they were in Jacksonville.

Etta answered the knock at the front door and grinned. "Come in. I'm so glad you came by." As she noticed Laurie's somber mood her delight faded. "Ammie, I made a fruit punch. Would you like a drink?"

Ammie cast a pleading look at Laurie.

Laurie nodded. "Don't forget to say thank you." Etta returned shortly with glasses and a pitcher. She served Ammie first.

Taking the glass with both hands, Ammie stared up at Etta and whispered, "Thank you."

Etta smiled. "You're welcome, Ammie."

By the time Etta and Laurie had their drinks, Ammie was playing with her doll. Laurie took a sip of the juice and handed Etta the package. "I want to thank you for all you've done for me."

Etta untied the string. "I can't imagine why you'd think . . ." She folded the paper back. "Oh!" She lifted the shawl up. "My goodness . . . it's beautiful."

"I hope the colors are right. That shade of green reminded me of your eyes."

Blushing, Etta stood up and swirled the shawl around her shoulders. "It's so soft. Thank you. You shouldn't have. This is too grand for Ashly Mills."

"Nonsense." Seeing Etta's pleasure cheered Laurie a bit, and she felt at ease for a few minutes.

Etta removed the shawl and carefully folded it. "This is the nicest present I ever received." She tilted her head. "How are you doing?"

"Gabe's trial was yesterday." Laurie twisted the strings of her reticule around her fingers.

"Oh, Lord, what happened?" Etta sat down on the settee near her friend.

Laurie inhaled before she forced herself to say the words. "They found him . . . guilty." She covered her mouth and stared straight ahead, determined not to cry.

"What can I do? Did you find Dacia?"

"There wasn't time to locate her. I don't know what else

I can do. She could be anywhere. Danny said she was in Linkville for a while. I just don't know.''

"You and Ammie stay here with me. You don't want to be out there by yourself.''

"Thanks, but I can't. There are chores, and Ammie has Mittens. I have to get new drapes for the main room. Gabe wants something cheerful. I'll have to look for yard goods in Jacksonville tomorrow.''

Etta frowned. "Would you like company? I'll take Ammie while you visit with Mr. West.''

Laurie heard a wagon and automatically looked up. "The custody hearing's tomorrow. I'm still hoping he'll be able to come back with us.''

Etta nodded and looked away.

They visited awhile longer before Laurie took her leave. Ammie yawned during the ride home and was put down for her nap after dinner. Laurie dusted already clean furniture throughout the house, made sure Gabe's room was ready for his return, and started a pot of stew. As an afterthought she went up to Ruth's room.

She was surprised and happy to see that the ugly drapes were gone. The room was bright. Glancing around at the heavy furniture, she thought it a shame to get rid of it. But she didn't want it. Ammie was afraid of it or the memories it inspired, and she had heard Gabe's opinion of it.

She needed to make a change, a start on clearing the room. She pulled the mattress off the bed frame. She wanted to take the bed apart, but she was unable to, so she unpended it in one corner of the room. Next she pulled the drawers from the chest and shoved them near the bed. Better, she thought, the room looked empty except for the dismantled furniture in one corner. Those items she would sell.

The sound of a horse entering the yard drew her to the window. Below, she saw Danny walk his mount into the barn. She left the door open and went down to greet him.

* * *

Long after Danny had retired to the bunkhouse and Ammie had gone to sleep, Laurie paced the main room. Every muscle and joint in her body ached, as did her head. She longed for sleep, for peace, but she found no solace in knowing she had done everything within her power to help Gabe.

When she was a little girl, her mother used to recite Bible verses to her. Feeling a desperate desire to read passages from that book now, she began searching the room. There were few places to look, and they yielded nothing. The only room she was not completely familiar with was Gabe's. Surely he had a family Bible.

She looked through the chest of drawers, the trunk, and the wardrobe. Lastly she pulled out the bottom drawer of the wardrobe. At one end was a large, old Bible.

Laurie curled up on Gabe's big bed and reverently opened the volume. She glanced at the list of family members and read the entries. Births and deaths were recorded, the stillbirths of a brother and sister of Gabe's, and the deaths of his parents. Gabe's marriage to Ruth had been entered but not her death.

Laurie didn't know what psalm or verse she was looking for, she just thumbed through the pages. As she turned to the book of Job the large volume slid over one leg, and she grabbed for it. A single sheet of paper floated over the edge of the bed and down to the floor.

Laurie slid the Bible aside. As she reached for the page her attention darted to the signature. *Ruth.*

❧26❧

Laurie was ready to scream her frustrations for all Jacksonville to hear. First, she had gone by the jail for directions to Judge Underwood's house. She finally located it but was told he had left a few minutes earlier. When she returned to the jail, she learned that the sheriff had taken Gabe to the courthouse.

She entered the courtroom just as the custody hearing was about to begin. She had hoped to show the letter of Ruth's she'd found in the Bible to the judge in private, but she had no choice now. Holding Ammie's hand, she marched to the front of the room and stopped in front of Judge Underwood's desk.

The judge frowned. "Madam, please take your seat."

"Your Honor, I have a note written by Ruth West. Please read it." Laurie worked her reticule open and pulled out the two letters.

"Madam, who are you?"

"Mrs. Preston. I take care of Ammie West." She smiled down at Ammie, then watched the judge.

The attorney representing Franklin and Hannah Tuttle

jumped to his feet. "I protest, Your Honor. This woman isn't involved with this case."

The judge looked at Laurie. "Are you aware this is a custody hearing to determine the child's fate?"

"I certainly am."

Judge Underwood held out his hand, and Laurie placed the two pages in it. She hadn't even glanced at Gabe, but she desperately yearned to do so. At the moment, though, she needed to observe the judge's reaction.

The judge read each of the letters and handed them back to Laurie. "I think Mr. West's attorney should have these."

As she gave the pages to Delbert Mullen her gaze went to Gabe. He didn't smile with his mouth, only with his brilliant gray eyes. Laurie moved Ammie to stand in front of her and gave him an encouraging close-lipped grin. Then she spoke to Mullen.

"The diary and these two letters should prove Gabe's innocence."

"Please sit by Mr. West." The lawyer brought two chairs forward before he read the two sheets of paper.

When Laurie burst into the room, Gabe had just stared. Her cheeks were flushed, her eyes bright, and her skirts were flying as she charged forward. He felt like he'd been jolted from a nightmare.

"Your Honor," the Tuttles' attorney pleaded, "can't we get on with the custody issue?"

"Yes, yes, by all means. Present your case."

"You have the diary, Your Honor, which states in Ruth West's own hand that her child, Ammie, was fathered by Franklin Tuttle's son, Virgil Tuttle."

The judge nodded.

Mullen rose quickly. "Excuse me, Your Honor. My esteemed colleague has presented Ruth West's diary as evidence of her daughter's parentage. May I see that volume?"

The judge handed it to him and motioned the Tuttles' attorney to continue.

"Last November the Tuttles lost their beloved son in an accident. Their only wish is to raise this child as their own. And since Mr. West will be hanged tomorrow for the murder of Ruth West, I see no reason for the child to go to an orphanage when she has grandparents willing to adopt her."

Gabe glanced at Laurie. She was seated beside him, and he inhaled her flowery scent. Even though she'd tried to restrain Ammie, his daughter wriggled free and climbed up on his knees. God, was there a chance for him? At least Laurie appeared to believe their was one.

She drank in Gabe's handsome features. He appeared tired, but now there was a spark of hope. She straightened Ammie's skirt while she stared at him.

Mullen caught Laurie's attention. "Would you show me the passage in the diary you were referring to? I don't have time to look for it."

"It must be near the end from what Mr. West said." Laurie opened the small book to the back and quickly found the page. "Here. Ruth sounds like she's planning a trip. And here. She says she's going to see someone who will help her. She realized she was carrying another child and wasn't happy about it. She may not have wanted to give birth to it."

The letters were on the table between Mullen and Gabe. Although he didn't want to look away from Laurie, he had to see what she'd found. The note signed "V" didn't surprise him. Virgil never did own up to his responsibilities. However, the second page made him pause.

"Gabe, I implore you, take care of Ammie. I will never bother you again," it read.

He whispered to Laurie. "Where did you find these?"

His voice was deep and seemed to vibrate through to her heart. "The one from Ruth fell out of your family Bible when the book slipped. Do you think it will help?"

"Mr. Mullen," Judge Underwood's voice thundered,

"do you have testimony for this hearing?" He raised his brows and stared at the attorney.

"I beg your indulgence in this most unusual case. Mrs. Preston just found this note last night, and I feel it will greatly influence the verdict rendered in Mr. West's murder trial."

Mullen handed the judge the letters and diary with the entries marked that Laurie had found. "Pieced together, it is obvious that Ruth West died by her own hand, whether accidentally or intentionally. It is also plain that she was planning on leaving her husband. I ask the court to reconsider the judgment against my client before considering the matter of custody."

The Tuttles' attorney approached the bench. "Your Honor, I have seen no such letter. Who's to say Ruth West wrote it?"

The judge glanced over the top of the page. "Sir, you'll see them in good time." Before looking back down, his gaze went to Gabe and Laurie.

Murmurs rose behind her, and Laurie listened to the tone of the crowd. She watched Ammie cling to her father and was able to see Gabe's expression without staring directly at him. He was grinning, a heart-throbbing, ear-to-ear grin.

Judge Underwood cleared his throat. "After seeing this new evidence, I hereby reverse the decision against Gabe West. Ruth West died due to an accidental overdose of an unknown drug."

Gabe met Laurie's gaze. It was as if they had touched. He was free! He raised Ammie up over his head, lowered her, and kissed her. The spectators applauded, shouted, and one whistled.

Judge Underwood banged his gavel to quiet the crowd. "Now, for the custody of Ammie West." He scrutinized Franklin and Hannah Tuttle for one full minute, then his gaze moved to Gabe, Laurie, and Ammie.

"Your Honor," the Tuttles' attorney called out. "I

remind the court that Mr. and Mrs. Tuttle are blood relatives of the child. Mr. West has no legal claim to the child.''

Hannah bounded to her feet. ''That's right, Judge. I'm the child's grandmother. She's mine!''

Judge Underwood cleared his throat again and motioned for Hannah to be seated. He leaned forward with his arms on the bench.

''Gabe and Ruth West were married more than a year before Ammie West was born. And I have a letter from Virgil Tuttle denying any relationship to Ruth's daughter.

''It is the decision of this court that Gabe West is the legal father of Ammie West.'' The gavel hit the bench one resounding time. ''Case closed!''

Whoops and cheers made it nearly impossible to hear any one person, but Laurie didn't need words. She touched Gabe's arm and smiled. Then she cried.

Still hugging his daughter, Gabe took Laurie's hand and raised it to his lips. A slap on his back shoved him forward, and he came close to bumping heads with her.

''Oh, sorry, Gabe. You're a damned lucky fellow. Congratulations.'' Mullen gathered up his notes and left his client staring besottedly at Laurie.

Laurie simply stared at Gabe. She watched the way the corners of his eyes crinkled when he grinned, which he couldn't stop doing. She enjoyed the deep timbre of his laughter, and the pure pleasure of knowing they would walk out of the courthouse together.

Gabe finally managed to get to his feet, but he had no room to move. It seemed everyone present wanted to clap him on the back or shake his hand. At long last the men and women slowly filed out of the room. Laurie was smiling and crying at the same time.

''You hussy!'' Hannah screeched. ''Her mother,'' she continued, pointing straight at Ammie, ''took my son away from me!''

Ammie grabbed for Laurie, shrieked, ''Mama,'' and dived for Laurie's chest.

Franklin Tuttle rose by his wife's side. "You drove Virgil away. Now shut up and walk out of here with me."

Hannah clamped her mouth closed, yanked her full skirt aside, and stomped out of the room.

Franklin Tuttle tipped his hat to Gabe and followed his wife out of the room.

Judge Underwood shoved back his chair. The scraping sound echoed in the now almost empty room. "Mr. West, I strongly urge you to make your relationship with Mrs. Preston legal." Then he winked and started for the side door.

"Judge Underwood." Gabe eyed Laurie, and she nodded. "Would you do the honors tomorrow afternoon?" He patted his trouser pocket. The ring he'd gotten for her was there.

"One o'clock. Don't be late."

Ammie patted her daddy's arm. "I'm hung'y, Daddy."

Laurie thought she heard the judge humming. She looked at Gabe, and they both laughed. After their nervous release of laughter faded, she took his arm. Tomorrow Etta and Danny would stand up with them.

Laurie grinned at Gabe. "I'm starving, too, Mr. West."

"Oh, so am I. My appetite may not be sated for many years, madam. I love you."

She knew which nightgown she would wear tomorrow night.

If you enjoyed this book, take advantage of this special offer. Subscribe now and...

Get a Historical

No Obligation

If you enjoy reading the very best in historical romantic fiction...romances that set back the hands of time to those bygone days with strong virile heros and passionate heroines ...then you'll want to subscribe to the True Value Historical Romance Home Subscription Service. Now that you have read one of the best historical romances around today, we're sure you'll want more of the same fiery passion, intimate romance and historical settings that set these books apart from all others.

Each month the editors of True Value select the four *very best* novels from America's leading publishers of romantic fiction. We have made arrangements for you to preview them in your home *Free* for 10 days. And with the first four books you

receive, we'll send you a FREE book as our introductory gift. No Obligation!

FREE HOME DELIVERY

We will send you the four best and newest historical romances as soon as they are published to preview FREE for 10 days (in many cases you may even get them before they arrive in the book stores). If for any reason you decide not to keep them, just return them and owe nothing. But if you like them as much as we think you will, you'll pay just $4.00 each and save at *least* $.50 each off the cover price. (Your savings are *guaranteed* to be at least $2.00 each month.) There is NO postage and handling—or other hidden charges. There are no minimum number of books to buy and you may cancel at any time.